CHASING
SYMMETRY

Tempeste
Blake

Pocket Acorn
Press

Printed in the United States of America

First Printing, 2016

Cover Design by Nancy Smith
Interior Design by Catherine Trizzino

ISBN-13: 978-1533356864
ISBN-10: 1533356866

Pocket Acorn Press, LLC
11392 East Indian Lake Drive
Vicksburg, MI 49097

www.tempesteblake.com

I would take a bullet for you;
you know who you are.

*In our life there is a single color, as on an artist's palette,
which provides the meaning of life and art. It is the color of love.*

—Marc Chagall

✥ ONE ✥

SOMEONE had been trying for the perfect shade of red—a blend of crimson and cadmium speckled the floor in a careless array.

Bianca envisioned one of her students rushing into the supply room, oblivious to the paint dripping from a hastily sealed container. Understandable that cleaning up wasn't a first priority. A college student's life is led by a higher power—hormones.

She moved into the storage room to fish through a bin of rags, squinting in the dim light. All she wanted was a little more light, not a studio renovation. It was an ongoing battle with Chet, the custodian. He'd flicked her a requisition form, his standard rebuttal, and she'd filled it out, twice. If he didn't change the burned-out bulb tomorrow, there was always Miller's Hardware.

Back to the mess at hand, she squatted, rag suspended. But upon closer examination, this wasn't paint. The odor was cloying. Familiar. She followed a trail snaking from under the supply cart, nudged the cart aside, and gasped.

A woman sat slumped against a stack of canvasses, head lolled back, legs extended like a large doll, arms reaching out in an unsettling symmetry.

Lifeless eyes frozen in horror.

Bianca's gaze slid over the woman's gray uniform, the splattered blood. Terror built, a scream that wouldn't come. She scrambled to her feet, lost her footing, and toppled against the shelves. A basket of yarn slammed down, and she clawed through the unraveling skeins, tangling them in her hair.

Her voice returned in the form of a low keening.

She had one foot out the door, but a sound, a muted gurgle, drew her back. Moving closer, she placed shaky fingers along the woman's neck. A pulse—thready, but there. Or was that her own pulse vibrating through her fingertips? Bianca held her breath, checked again. Her heart climbed up her throat and lodged there as she positioned the body for CPR. *Please, oh please, help me remember how.*

She tilted the woman's head back and saw the source of all that blood, her right temple. Pressure. Apply pressure. She clamped the rag over the wound, pinched the nostrils to start mouth to mouth, stopped. Hadn't they changed the rules? What were they now? Compression only? Placing her palms on the woman's chest, she pushed. Twenty? Thirty? With each compression, her voice cracked in a whispered demand, "Breathe. Breathe. *Breathe!*"

In an instant of suspended time, Bianca realized the futility of her efforts, but she couldn't pull herself away. Again, her fingers reached for the neck. Nothing. Damn it. *Nothing!*

Her cell. She bolted to her feet, slapped her pockets. Where . . . ? A tendril of ice seized her spine. Something rooted her in place as a thunderclap of self-preservation boomed.

Whoever did this has a gun.

A new crop of chills surfaced. *Go!* The thought propelled her forward, but she had a sense of being dragged backward.

She spun around. Her cell was on her desk. Across the room, yet miles away. Bianca willed her legs to comply, to move in tandem with her thoughts, but a noise froze her in place. A door opening? Closing? She raced for her phone and dove under the desk.

"911. What's your emergency?"

"I need help." Bianca's voice was reedy, high-pitched.

"I can't hear you, hon. You need to speak up."

Calm down. Steady. She struggled to match the operator's tone. "I need help."

"Is this an emergency?"

"Yes."

"Okay, honey. Tell me where you are."

"Room 108, the Weaver Fine Arts Building at Brookefield College." Tears welled, spilled down her cheeks. "A woman's been . . . she's dead."

The last word loomed above her in three dimensions, heavy and defined, the way she instructed students to sketch tree trunks and bowls of fruit.

"You're sure she's not breathing?"

"Yes."

"Are you alone?"

"I . . . I don't know." Bianca opened a drawer, grabbed scissors, and curled back underneath the desk.

"I'm going to stay with you, okay? I won't hang up until the police get there."

Bianca's eyes fell to her hands, now covered in blood. She scrubbed them over her pants in desperate swipes. A roil of nausea festered through her as she huddled deeper, tried to escape into herself. Her skin crawled. If only she could shed these clothes. And shoes. She toed them off and dropped them into the waste basket with a thud.

A flurry of activity transformed the once quiet studio. Men and women in uniform measured and scraped, photographed and bagged. One man personified composure and self-assurance— Chief Carmichael, lime-scented cologne clinging to him like an efficient assistant, still pristine at 8:00 p.m. in suit and tie.

"Did you know Ms. Divac?" His tone, his body language delivered a clear message: he was still furious with her about what had happened two years ago.

Bianca stared past him at a Dali print on the wall. Butterflies. Lizards. Fluttering wings and flicking tongues intertwined. A print she loved for its systematic confusion and ability to transport her to another plane.

But now the tongues were daggers.

"Lisette Divac." Carmichael's voice yanked her back. "The cleaning woman?"

Lisette. Knowing her name somehow made it worse. "She must have been filling in."

The commotion, people spinning through the studio, along with Carmichael's imposing form, and the unspoken history between them, made her dizzy. She searched for a stabilizing focal point and spotted Tucker Baranski. He dipped his chin, throwing her a visual lifeline. She'd known him for years. A gentle giant in police-issue blues, a sharp contrast to Carmichael's bristly dictator in wingtips.

"Chief, Channel 8 and a bunch of gawkers are sniffing around outside," Tucker said.

"Don't let them cross that tape."

"Trying, but we don't have the manpower. Want me to call over to Whistler for reinforcements?"

"Absolutely not."

"Roger that." Tucker turned and collided with a man who kept hiking his pants as if they might otherwise fall down. The reporter fumbled with his notepad and craned his neck around Tucker. "Chief Carmichael, can I have a moment?"

"I'd think you'd have a better command of the English language," Carmichael barked. "It's *may* I have a moment, and the answer is, no, you may not."

"Come on, Chief. A shooting in the Peak and you're shutting us out?"

"You'll get your story when I call a press conference. Not before. And tell your clones if anyone else crosses that tape, they'll be writing about what it's like to spend a night in my jail." Carmichael jerked his head toward the door. "Sergeant, get him out of here."

Tucker moved for the door with a look that said he wouldn't hesitate to bulldoze anything in his path, including the pants-hiking reporter.

"Why were you in the storage room?" Carmichael asked Bianca as if they hadn't been interrupted.

"I usually check things," she said. "Before I leave."

Bianca eyed the half-eaten sandwich on her desk. She started to sweep it into a trash can, but Carmichael slammed his hand down, blocking her. "This is a crime scene, Ms. James." He edged onto a drawing table, balancing a Montblanc pen between his fingers like a cigarette. "Where were you before you went into the storage room?"

"I've been here since my last class."

"Which was what time?"

"It ended at 4:30."

He squinted in disbelief. "So, you're saying you've been in this room the entire time?"

"In the building."

He unbuttoned his suit coat, rolled his head from side to side. "Tell me again the state of Ms. Divac when you found her."

Bianca did a slow pivot to the storage room. "I thought I felt a pulse. I started CPR, but—"

"When did you call 911?"

"After. When I realized—"

"You have medical training, do you?"

She crossed her arms.

"Well, obviously you think you're skilled enough to determine time of death."

"Chief Carmichael, I used my best judgment. Nothing I was doing was helping, so I called 911. Is there another question?"

"How much time passed between finding her and making the call?"

"It all happened so fast."

Carmichael turned his pen end over end, brought it down hard, and scratched something on his notepad. "Ms. James, I need you to be very specific regarding your whereabouts tonight."

Bianca squared her shoulders and forced herself to rise above the current of tension in the room. "I was across the hall in the lounge for a bit, had some tea, and then brought my sandwich back here." She winced as "Hollywood's Best & Worst Dressed" paraded across her mind from the time-suck posing as a magazine.

"How long is *a bit*, Ms. James?" Carmichael's gaze riveted on the seductively posed, life-sized skeleton adorned with satin push-up bra, thong, and red sandals that laced up the tibias.

Is everything here on trial? "I didn't check my watch." When he continued to gawk at the scantily clad skeleton, Bianca added, "It's for a bypassing technique, a light approach to drawing the human figure."

Carmichael flexed his jaw, projecting judgment before he crossed the room to walk along the row of windows. "Anyone else here tonight?"

"Ralph from Campus Security usually makes rounds. But I haven't seen him."

"Ralph's last name?"

"Monroe." If Carmichael asked for more, she'd give the abridged version, editing out Ralph's penchant for napping in Weaver's basement.

Carmichael lifted a blind with his pen and peered out. "Why is this one closed?" Without turning he snapped, "Baranski, will this room get measured sometime before I retire?"

Tucker rose from where he was squirreling along the baseboards and moved to the storage room, thumping a corner cabinet along the way.

"I close them when the sun goes down," Bianca said. "I didn't get to all—"

"And you're the only one here?" Carmichael interrupted yet again. "At night? Alone?"

If you'd let me finish. "I like the quiet."

He ran a finger over his precisely groomed, pewter-colored mustache. "You're not with Dylan Tierny anymore, are you?"

So she'd been right. His animosity, treating her like a suspect, was about Dylan.

"I don't have to tell you you're better off," Carmichael continued past her silence. For a moment his face shifted in a tiny, subtle way, and she saw what she thought was a hint of mercy. "So, no other teachers here tonight? Students? You're the only one in the building?"

The reality grabbed and twisted as his questions, the equivalent of an index finger, pointed to the solitary state of her life.

"As you know, Chief Carmichael, this is a small college. It's not uncommon for the campus to be dead on a Friday night." *Oh, God.* "I mean deserted."

"Any idea why Ms. Divac was in the storage room?"

"I suppose she wandered in by mistake." *Or was chased in by a gun-wielding psycho.* "I told you, she's a fill-in . . . was a fill-in." Bianca pondered the tense shift. A life whisked from present to past in a blink. She looked beyond the window into the soupy gray. *Why are you grilling me? Whoever did this is out there!*

Carmichael pulled something from his pocket. "You don't know this woman?"

Lisette Divac smiled from the plastic ID badge. Young, blond, gap-toothed grin, shimmering with anticipation, eager to unwrap each day to see what it held, and—

The classroom door swung wide. A woman in a strapless gown, hair braided in an elaborate updo, rushed in clutching a black medical bag. A man shuffled behind her, bald head reflecting the studio lights. Bianca didn't know what she expected the medical examiner to look like, but it wasn't Queen Latifah—a modern Botticelli with walnut skin.

"Fundraising event." The ME glanced at Bianca and pointed to her own outfit with a look that said she'd prefer a power suit. "What do we have, Chief?"

As if pulled from a trance, he sidled close, updated her, then shifted to Bianca. "Ms. James, that's all for now. I'll be in touch. Bear in mind, we'll need to cordon off the area. No classes until I say so. And if you remember anything else, call me." He handed her a card with a dismissive wave.

Bianca pressed a fresh line of teeth marks into her tongue to block the comeback crawling up her throat.

The ME studied her with the sympathy Carmichael lacked. "You found her?"

"I tried to revive her, but . . ."

"This must be difficult," the ME said. "Do you need someone to drive you home?"

Carmichael straightened, rebuttoned his suit coat. "Of course. I'll have an officer—"

"That won't be necessary," Bianca said.

"Necessary or not, I'd prefer it." He spoke into his radio. "Need you inside. Now." And to Bianca, "Have a seat."

Ignoring his directive, she instead turned her attention to the buckle digging into her ankle and propped her foot on the rung of a stool to adjust it. The shoes were strappy and high-heeled, a pair she kept in her desk drawer for . . . well, she didn't wear them often. She glanced at the trash can where she'd tossed her clogs, started to remind herself to buy another pair, but swatted the thought away. Worrying about shoes made her feel small.

The noise in the studio faded to white, stained intermittently by somber metallic riffs coming from the storage room.

Click click. Click click.

While the bald one snapped pictures from every angle, the ME swept her gown aside and crouched near the body. She pulled tweezers from her case, lifted something off Lisette's sneaker, dropped it into an evidence bag, and handed it to Carmichael. "You missed something." She rose, a glimpse of leg peeking from cascading folds of chiffon, camera flashing, adoring fan soaking it in.

Like a photo shoot. A macabre photo shoot.

The scene blurred until Bianca could no longer make out the contours, only movements. She closed her eyes and replayed the last few hours. Was she across the hall eating her sandwich as Lisette lay in the storage room dying? Did her music drown out cries for help? If she'd been there a minute sooner, could she have saved her?

Or would her lifeless body be laid out next to Lisette's?

The chaos in the room continued to churn while Bianca took long swallows of air, desperate slurps of oxygen. She hazarded a step, and when her legs didn't betray her, she grabbed her purse and headed for the door. "I don't need an escort."

Before the chief could object, she left without a backward glance.

She raced from Weaver, only aware she'd left her coat when the cold air hit like a slap. Going back wasn't an option, so head down, cupping an elbow in each palm, she forged ahead. As she whipped around a corner, she slammed into someone with such force it nearly knocked her down.

"Sorry, I . . ." A puddle of light from a street lamp fell across his face. So much like his brother, firm jaw, the same lacerating charisma. "Finn Tierny!" She rested her hands against his chest for the space of a heartbeat, then snatched them away.

He splayed his arms in a ta-da gesture. "I'm back."

She took him in, tried to parse out what had changed. Maybe it was the exaggerated breadth of his shoulders. Time on the force had certainly bulked him up, added a layer of maturity. Was it four years now or five since he'd left? And the uniform—such a contrast to the faded T-shirts and ripped jeans he'd worn to class as her student.

Finn touched her shoulder. "Chief Carmichael radioed, a couple of times actually. He wants me to see you home."

"I'll be fine."

"I've got orders."

"I have my car." She pointed to the parking lot. The area always seemed well lit, but now . . .

"You can get it tomorrow."

"I'm capable of driving," she snapped. Carmichael's inquisition had illuminated all the mistakes she'd made tonight. A strobe light flashing: Fail. Fail. Fail. Now Finn had her tied to railroad tracks in a black and white movie with a train barreling toward her.

She started for her car, ignoring his objections, ignoring him behind her. When they reached her Pathfinder, he opened the door.

"I'll follow you then," Finn said.

Bianca allowed her eyes to trail him to his cruiser. Something moved in her periphery, streaking through her field of vision. She slammed the door, ducked, but when she ventured another look, it was gone.

She chided herself. Her mind was playing tricks. Like the Dali painting, butterflies and lizards intertwined, creating tension and confusion between the real and unreal.

She looked down at her shirt, and her eyes ran from one bloodied badge to the next.

This was real.

❧ TWO ❧

FINN thumped the steering wheel before clenching his fingers around it. There hadn't been a murder in Riley's Peak in thirty years, but instead of diving into the investigation, he was babysitting his brother's ex-girlfriend. Since Finn had transferred from Pittsburgh last month, Chief Carmichael had done nothing but yank his chain. *Wash the squad car, Tierny. You missed a spot, Tierny. Some drunk puked in the holding cell; don't forget to spray air freshener after you clean it up. Pine, not that lavender crap, Tierny.* The name alone was enough to bring out the ass in Carmichael.

"Thirty-three here," Finn said into his shoulder radio.

"Thirty-three," acknowledged dispatch. "Helluva night."

"You know it, Ford. Conveying . . . well following . . . one female to three, four, seven Waterton. Beginning mileage fifty-seven, one, one, three."

Reporting mileage seemed over the top. This was the Peak, not Pittsburgh. Carmichael practiced CYA like he'd invented it; as if working in a little misconduct would be on anyone's agenda tonight.

"Ten-four," Ford said. "May the road rise to meet ya and all dat."

"Ten-four. Wind's at my back," Finn countered. A good Irish

boy knows the Gaelic blessing by heart. Old school, but oddly comforting. He heaved an exaggerated sigh, and stuck close as Bianca zipped from the parking lot. Why wouldn't she just let him drive her home?

He uncurled his hands from the wheel and gave each a shake but couldn't escape the gnawing frustration of being jerked away from the murder scene. A pang of guilt replaced the adrenaline rush. It seemed both twisted and morbid to be pumped about working a homicide.

On the short drive to her house, Bianca wove in and out of her lane, slowed down and sped up. If Finn hadn't known better, he would have pegged her for a drunk driver. He thrust his hand out the open window, let the air sieve through his fingers. Thoughts careened in a thousand directions as a November chill slid across his face, the night breeze a tongue of defeat, licking fresh wounds from the 'Burgh. What made him think things would be better here? More spokes jutted from his hub of worries. The tumor eating at his dad's brain for one—savoring each bite. Then there was his brother. Watching Dylan's life unravel sucked, plain and simple. Add a boss who probably accepted Finn's transfer to even an old score, and it all made for a wheel that might as well be square.

Bianca pulled into the driveway of a single-story, sage-green bungalow. He'd heard she'd bought a new place awhile back, but for some weird reason he'd always pictured her in a turn-of-the-century Victorian with fancy spindles and curlicues.

Finn parked along the curb and watched as she left her car, didn't turn, didn't wave him away, but charged the front door like she'd left a faucet running inside.

"Thirty-three, twenty-three." He let dispatch know he'd reached his destination, exited the cruiser, and followed her up the sidewalk, between two rows of balding shrubs. The wind bullied a fern hanging from the porch eaves, and Finn side-stepped it.

Under the porch light's amber glow, Bianca aimed a shaky key for the lock. Finn took her hand. His arms circled her awkwardly, stabilizing her, holding her a beat too long. It surprised him when she pressed her forehead into his shoulder. He waited for tears, but there weren't any.

11

"Let's get you inside," he whispered.

Bianca met his eyes, then looked away.

"Give me your keys."

She opened her tightly balled fist, and the keys rolled into his hand. The way her fingers opened made him think of flowers blooming in time-lapse photography, and he registered each subtle movement. Before he could close his grip, she snatched the keys back, rammed one into the lock, and threw the door open.

Independent. And shocky. Carmichael had instructed him to stay until someone else came. Concern from Chief Hardass? More like a move to keep Finn far away from real police work. But he agreed, she shouldn't be alone. "Mind if I come in?"

Emotions played over her face, misty-edged and cobbled, that finally angled toward yes. He followed her inside.

Piles of books lay stacked on the floor, towers of varying heights. Jackets and scarves covered what he guessed was a wingback chair. On the couch, nestled in a mountain of unfolded towels, a monstrous, orange cat lifted his head and yawned.

"Picasso." Bianca picked him up and cradled him under her chin. He answered with a harsh yowl, and she lowered him to the floor. "I know, I know. You're hungry," then to Finn, "You don't need to stay."

"You should call someone."

A beat of silence. Bianca pulled her phone from her pocket, jabbed at the screen and waited. Disappointment tugged at her lips. She ended the call and pressed the phone onto the pile of towels. "I'll try Maris again in a bit."

Finn had first met Maris Romero five years ago when he was a student in Bianca's class. The two struck him as an odd pair from the start. Maris with the "I Heart Differential Equations" pin on her briefcase and Bianca whose eyes glazed over when she calculated lines and angles in perspective class.

Finn shrugged off his jacket, looked around for a place to hang it, and ultimately added it to the heap on the chair. "I can wait a little longer."

Bianca unwound the scarf from her neck, and it drifted to the floor. She picked it up, folded it, and then, almost as an afterthought, shook it out and draped it over a hanger in the closet. Next, she stripped off her shoes and tucked them under a bench. She unclasped her hair clip and tossed it into a ceramic bowl on the cluttered coffee table, where it landed with a clank. Her long, blond hair unraveled, and she finger-combed through the tangles. This whole process seemed to play out in slow motion, and Finn felt his mouth go a little slack as he stood there, mesmerized. There was a certain sensuality to the casual dismantling of Bianca James.

The blood stain on her shirt drew his attention, and she followed his gaze. Horror clouded her expression. "When I found her I . . . I'll be right back."

While he waited, Finn checked the front and back doors and returned to the living room. He took in the space. Plants in every corner, threatening to take over. Books—some flat, some vertical, spines pushed in and pulled out, anything but flush, a couple about to topple off—covered shelves along the back wall. Disarray at first glance, but as he looked closer, he noticed little statues and trinkets had been carefully placed amidst the fray. He envisioned Bianca, finding knick-knacks at flea markets, bringing them home to add to already crowded, buckling shelves and stepping back with a triumphant smile.

She returned wearing a robe, cinched at the waist, that made him think of an old bedspread. Finn wasn't sure how she could make something so unsexy look sexy, but she did, and it took all his willpower to drag his focus away from the V of creamy skin framed in dark pink. Picasso twined around her legs, and he was thankful for the whining fur-ball's interruption.

"All right, all right." Bianca started for the kitchen.

Finn hesitated, then followed. While the cat paced, Bianca spooned something fishy into a bowl on the counter. Before she could finish, he leaped up and started picking at the food.

"About what happened tonight . . ." Finn began, but Bianca was someplace else. Someplace he hadn't been invited. He wasn't sure how long they stood there like that, void of any kind of connection, listening to the eager, wet frenzy of Picasso's chewing. When the cat finished, he batted his food and water bowls off the counter in rapid succession.

Bianca swished past Finn, grabbed a bucket from under the sink, filled it with water, and gave it a squirt of soap. Kneeling to the floor with a sponge, she started scrubbing in a slow, circular motion, a knee-jerk, robotic reaction to the almost non-existent mess.

"It's just a little water," Finn said.

This place wasn't exactly a contender for the Good Housekeeping Seal of Approval. Unopened mail, magazines, and enough cans of tuna fish to feed an army littered the counter; chaos reigned in the living room. Now an OCD cleaning spurt? He wished she'd look at him, but her eyes stayed trained on the floor.

Definitely shocky.

"It's late." He bent down and reached for the sponge. Would he have to keep taking things away from her? He held her wet hands in his for a long moment.

Her eyes spoke first. Annoyance flashed in Catalina blue. She moved to a sitting position, long legs folded to the side, hands fidgeting in her lap. "When I'm nervous, I clean."

Finn looked around the kitchen from one mess to another. *Doesn't happen much, huh?*

She traced a finger around the rim of the bucket. "I know what you're thinking. The truth is . . ." A laugh, unconvincing.

"Want to talk about what happened tonight? If not now, maybe Jewel Glasser at the college can help." Finn instantly wanted to retrieve the suggestion. It was a dumbass idea for her to confide in Jewel, his brother's on-again, off-again girlfriend.

Bianca shook her head, almost a shudder. There was a hint of something horrible playing in her mind, but he doubted it had anything to do with Jewel.

A loud clatter shook the front door.

Finn scrambled to his feet, pulling Bianca with him. He reached for his gun and motioned to the corner pantry. If someone was at the front door, someone could be coming around the back. Or busting through the windows. "In there."

"No!"

Despite her protest, he nudged her in and pressed a finger to his mouth. A second after he closed the door, it sprang open and Bianca emerged, anger bending the corners of her mouth.

Another commotion from outside, a tirade of obscenities.

"Damn it, Bianca." Finn crept across the kitchen floor, gun at low ready, as the clamoring continued. Sweat soaked into his collar and ringed each vertebra on his back.

The front door creaked open and hit the wall with a thud. Heavy footfalls sounded before a familiar bellow, "Biaaaancaaaa!"

Finn holstered his piece.

And now for the bonus round of the evening. A visit from my drunkass brother.

Dylan stumbled toward the doorway dividing the living room and kitchen, stopped, and dragged his bloodshot eyes between the two of them, settling on Bianca, specifically what she was wearing. Finn read his brother's unspoken question loud and clear.

Dylan's face hadn't seen a razor for days, and a small apron of fat cushioned the six-pack abs he'd spent hours in the gym to achieve.

But that was before. Before life taught Dylan the lesson they both knew well: the road doesn't always rise to meet a Tierny, and the wind is rarely considerate enough to stay at their backs.

Bianca stretched out a hand. "You were supposed to return that."

"Oh." Desperation flickered at the edges of Dylan's steely exterior before he dropped the key into her palm.

Finn pitied him for a moment. "What're you doing here?"

"Funny you askin' me that." Dylan rested his fists high on each side of the doorjamb. "What the hell're you doin' here?" Without waiting for an answer, he cast bleary eyes on Bianca. "You okay? Said down at Lost there was a murder at Brookefield." Strung together in a long, slurred strand.

"I'm fine." She cinched her robe tighter and infused her reply with a convincing calm.

"C'mon. I'll drive you home," Finn said. A little side trip that would give Carmichael yet another reason to rip him a new one.

"I got this," Dylan said. "You go. I'll . . . take care of Bee."

Finn planted himself in front of her, clasped arms across his chest. "You're too wasted to take care of yourself, much less anyone else."

Dylan's eyes went wide with rage as he lunged and took an

exaggerated swing. Finn ducked the slow punch. His brother came at him again, and they toppled onto the bucket of water. Picasso shrieked, and flew from the room.

"Stop!" Bianca tried to pry them apart, and Finn could tell that she'd love nothing better than to knock their heads together. He couldn't blame her. As he turned to apologize, Dylan's fist connected with his jaw, flooding his mouth with the coppery taste of blood. His brother straddled him at the waist, pinning him with hands calloused from hours of wielding the haft of a sledgehammer.

At least he didn't have it with him.

"Only an asshole tries to hook up with his brother's girlfriend." Dylan's anger rushed out in a furious, wet spittle.

Finn scrambled out from under him, turned the tables, and held Dylan in place. "Is that what you think? I'm doing my *job*."

And it's *ex*-girlfriend.

"Big cop, just like the old man wanted. It don't matter, he's gonna die soon anyway." Completely out of breath, gasps for air punctuated his gin-laced tirade. Finn let him up.

Scooting himself to sit against a cabinet, Dylan propped folded arms on his knees and hung his head as if their dad's diagnosis had just crash-landed on him. "I screwed everything up, baby bro."

It hurt worse than a kidney punch; the brother he'd always admired, now diminished, retreating.

Bianca moved to Dylan, placed a hand on his shoulder.

"I love you both," he said, three long blinks away from sleep.

They didn't get a chance to return the sentiment before he slumped onto his side and passed out.

"When he drinks," Finn started, "hell, I don't have to tell you."

"He'll sleep it off."

An unspoken moment passed between them. They'd both witnessed this behavior too many times before.

She took a towel from a stack on the counter and handed it to Finn. "You're bleeding."

He pressed it to his mouth and attempted a smile, but pain throbbed at the stretch of his lips.

Bianca kneeled. Back to cleaning.

Finn grabbed another towel from the counter and dropped down beside her.

"Guess I'm washing the floor after all." Her eyes crinkled in mild amusement as they narrowed on him. "You're soaking wet. At least let me get you something dry." She disappeared and soon returned with a shirt, blanket, and pillow. She threw the blanket over Dylan, smoothed it into place, and lifted his head to push the pillow underneath, her every movement purposeful yet tender.

Finn unrolled the shirt and read the white letters, stark against a scribbled rainbow. "Fear no color?"

Bianca shrugged. "A freebie. One size fits all."

After debating which would piss Carmichael off more, showing up in a wet uniform or this shirt, he tossed a mental coin and voted for comfort.

Bianca stalled on his bare chest before she turned to fiddle with a teapot on the stove. "I need tea."

He draped his uniform shirt over a chair, and wriggled into the borrowed one, pulling at the sleeves. One size fits all if *all* means all ten-year-old boys. "I really should get back."

"Of course."

No one could have missed the note of apprehension.

"Maybe a quick cup of tea." Had she even asked if he wanted one? Or was he making up excuses to stay? There was the matter of his uniform—maybe he should give it time to dry. But tea conjured thoughts of being wrapped in a blanket with a thermometer clamped between his teeth. Why else would anyone drink it? And having tea with his brother's ex while he was passed out on the floor? Where was the camera? This was starting to feel like reality TV at its best.

Surely Maris would hear what happened and call soon.

While Bianca was busy at the stove, Finn, hands stuffed in pockets, scanned the framed art on the wall. "You do all these?"

"No. My students did."

Rubbing a hand across his jaw, he zeroed in on a pen and ink sketch of a medieval castle. "There's something familiar about this one."

"That's because it's yours. Remember Perspective 101?"

She offered him a tall, thick glass. He'd never seen hot tea served in something that seemed better suited for beer or ice water. His hands instantly warmed. Cocking his head, he examined the drawing again.

"You fed it to the recycling bin." Her mouth quirked to the side. "But the recycling bin spit it back out."

"Why'd you keep it?"

"Because it has value." A you-should-know-this tone attached.

"The turrets look like they were done by a three-year-old."

"They do need a little work." She touched his forearm with a light hand. "But when I look at this, I'm there . . . safe in that castle."

Finn's heart rammed against his ribs. For a tender moment, they studied the details of that faraway place, the contours of a fortress rendered in shades of chivalry.

Dylan broke the spell as he rolled to his stomach, arm thrust behind him at an unnatural angle, and settled into cartoonish snort-whistle breathing.

Their attention traveled back to the castle.

"You're very talented," she said.

An odd time for this discussion. Maybe she'd talk about anything at this point. He took a gulp of tea and winced. Hot. Bitter. The hint of a sick-chill. But fresh mint washed over his tongue.

"Don't judge it on the first sip. I got hooked on this stuff in Morocco." She sampled her tea as if to prove her point. "Let me see if I can remember how they put it. 'The first glass is as bitter as life. The second as strong as love. The third as gentle as death.'"

Finn took a minute to absorb her words. "I don't think I'll get to the second glass."

All of a sudden, she seemed flushed and guarded, nervous, displaced. She dumped water from the kettle into the sink, tea bags into the trash. Had he said something wrong or did the Moroccan maxim send her into another cleaning tailspin? All the talk about life. Love. The inaccurate definition of death.

Death is anything but gentle.

Finn shuffled through the Rolodex of events that had brought him to this point. He'd strayed so far from where he thought he wanted to be. It was a gargantuan leap from aspiring artist to cop.

Being here felt wrong. A murder in Riley's Peak and Bianca was shocky one minute and hosting a tea party the next. It was surreal, like he'd been sucked down the rabbit hole with Alice.

But wasn't her erratic behavior even more reason to stay?

She reached for her cell. "I'll try Maris again." After a moment, her expectant expression creased. Grabbing her jacket, she started for the door.

"What're you doing?"

"I need to go find her," Bianca said, threading one arm into a sleeve.

Finn wrapped his hand around the other sleeve, blocking it, and eased off her jacket.

The radio beeped. "Thirty-three?"

"Thirty-three," Finn answered.

"Are you still at three, four, seven Waterton?"

"Affirmative."

"Ten-four, thirty-three. Chief wants you back at the scene."

"On my way."

Finn grabbed his uniform shirt from the chair. "I need to go. Stay put. I'm sure Maris is fine, but if you don't hear from her—" He rifled through his wallet and handed her a card. "It's from Pittsburgh, I scratched out the old number—"

"I see that."

"Anyway, if you need anything . . ."

"I'll call."

Finn glanced at his brother.

"Don't worry about him," she said.

"He hibernates. Could be a long winter for you." A stupid joke, delivered at a bad time. Open mouth, insert size-twelve steel-toed boot.

A handful of emotions coalesced at the sight of his brother passed out on the floor, at the thought of Bianca, who'd already been through so much tonight, acting as his nursemaid. Anger, pity, and resentment swirled, searching for a place to land. He jerked the door open, smacking it against the wall. Bianca startled, blinked hard.

Adding embarrassment to the heap he slipped out the door.

❧

Carmichael stood in the middle of Bianca's classroom like a conductor who had just led an orchestra through a crashing finale. The concert was over. They'd dusted for prints, scraped for blood, gathered, tagged, and bagged evidence. Time to pack up their instruments.

"I asked you to get her settled, not make an evening of it. A family member can do the hand-holding. Priorities, Tierny. They should have schooled you better in Pittsburgh."

Of course Chief would ask for one thing and expect another. "Yes, sir."

If Carmichael noticed Finn's split lip, he didn't mention it. "Load up this stuff. It all goes to the lab."

So Carmichael had saved part of the investigation for him after all: hauling away the trash. Finn should have skipped police academy and gone straight for a job with the sanitation department. On the way to the storage room, he ventured a glimpse at the black body bag.

Tucker clapped his shoulder. "How ya doin' there, little bud?" His brother's longtime friend had always called him that, even after Finn surpassed both of them in height. But what Tucker lacked in height, he definitely made up for in girth.

"How do you think I'm doing?" Finn brushed at his shoulders. "Could've sworn I'd find puppet strings there."

"Whoa. What's with the lip?"

"Bumped into my brother."

"What the hell?"

"He didn't like finding me at Bianca's."

"Not much he does like lately." Tucker lowered his voice and notched his chin to Carmichael. "Speaking of pissy. It's been neons since this kind of action in the Peak. The old man's got us walking on eggshells."

Eons. Finn suppressed a chuckle. He and Dylan had given up correcting Tucker's malapropisms years ago. A glance at the chief confirmed Tucker's observation.

"Here, I'll help ya," Tucker said.

As he scooped up one bag, Finn rewound to Bianca stowing her shoes under a bench at her house. "There's a pair of bloody shoes in here."

"This is no time to talk like a Brit," Tucker said. Then more seriously, "Chief saw 'em."

Carmichael stopped scribbling in his notebook and crossed the room. "Baranski, Tierny doesn't need your help." He scrutinized Finn. "Chief Almeida gave you free rein in Pittsburgh, didn't he, son?"

"Things were different there."

"Well, here you're expected to follow protocol."

Finn took a step toward the evidence bags and could have sworn he heard those eggshells Tucker was talking about crack underfoot.

Alice in Wonderland all right. And he was working for the Mad Hatter.

❧ THREE ❧

BIANCA locked the door behind Finn and watched through the sidelight as he returned to his cruiser. After a long while, the headlights flipped on and he pulled away from the curb. As the engine's roar faded into the night, a chill feathered across her neck. She rubbed her arms and headed for the kitchen.

Dylan had rolled out of the blanket, still sound asleep. Her eyes skimmed over him, followed the rise and fall of his chest. Should she wake him, tell him she was sorry for the way things had fallen apart, beg him to change for his brother, his father—himself? But she'd already tried. Nothing could steer him from his self-destructive course.

Her phone rang, and she raced to find it, flinging pillows and a sweater off the couch.

"Lo siento. I fell asleep watching TV. My cell was on silent and—"

"Maris!" Bianca interrupted her friend's breathless spiel. "A woman . . . in my studio . . . someone shot her." She skipped over the CPR, not able to form one syllable about how she'd tried to revive Lisette . . . and failed.

"I'll be right there."

"We can talk on the phone. I don't think you should be out alone."

"Don't worry. I'm not."

The line went dead before Bianca could object. While she waited, she wended her way through the living room, transferred a stack of art books from one shelf to another then back again, twisted a candle on its holder, and snapped off the blackened wick. Her heart skipped a beat as her eyes landed on a small wooden box wedged between a pair of overgrown spider plants. She opened it, and her fingers tripped over the smooth white gemstones as an apparition materialized, a row of pearls resting against her mother's porcelain neck. Pearls she wore that night—

Rap a rap rap, Morse code-style. Her friend's signature knock. She must have doubled her speed to get there. Or had more time passed than Bianca realized?

Maris. Dark eyes and enviable cheekbones, gifts from her Peruvian mother. Hair knotted and tucked behind her ears, she held her puffy, down coat closed with one fist. Bianca's eyes fell to the tennis racquet in her other hand.

"It was on the back seat, so I grabbed it." Maris twirled the racquet before opening her purse to reveal a small pistol. "I don't want to break out this bad boy unless it's absolutely necessary."

Bianca pulled her inside and locked the door, trying to ignore the clutching in her stomach at the sight of the .22.

Maris wiggled from her coat, propped the racquet against the coffee table, and sat down. "Thank God you're okay." Her arms encircled Bianca, crushing with abandon. "What happened?"

"I was cleaning up my studio and found her in the storage room. I can't believe a woman was killed, and I was just down the hall."

"I'm afraid to ask . . . who was it?"

"She worked for the cleaning agency." Bianca called up the image, filtered through the blood and horrified expression. "Pretty girl. Early twenties I'd guess. Her name was Lisette Divac."

Maris drew back, made a practiced sign of the cross. "Lisette was in my Precalc class, one of my hardest working students. She had a little girl. ¡Pobre niña!" She choked back tears. "Lisette brought her to class once, and she sat quietly coloring while her mom took a make-up test."

Bianca's eyes filmed as she pulled a pillow into her lap and toyed with the fringe. "Who would do this?"

"I can't even imagine."

Bianca didn't need to imagine; she could still see the body, posed, as if . . .

"So quiet and polite, people like that don't have enemies."

Bianca chewed her lip while Maris continued. Teen pregnancy, baby's father ran off, Lisette desperate to give her child a normal life.

"Maris, I . . ."

"What is it? You look like you've seen a ghost."

In many ways, she had. "When I saw her like that, and all the blood, I knew it was too late, but then I thought I heard something." She swallowed hard, dug her fingers deep into the pillow. "So I felt her neck, and—"

"She was alive?"

Prickles surfaced on Bianca's skin; nausea sawed through her. If she'd done something different would that little girl still have a mother? She jumped up from the couch. "I need . . . give me a minute."

She hurried to the bathroom where she circled, etching a path in the tile floor. The ceiling collapsed, trapping her. Unlatching the small window, she shoved up the sash with the heel of her hand. *Climb out. Run. Far away from here.* She did a clumsy pirouette to the sink, slammed on the faucet, and splashed cold water on her face, pressed a towel to her eyes, then stared at her reflection in the mirror. "Get a grip," she whispered to the crazed woman staring back.

Sucking in desperate gulps of air, she felt a sliver of sanity come slinking back. She closed the window and returned to find Maris standing over Dylan, tennis racquet raised for an overhead smash.

Bianca couldn't believe she'd completely forgotten Dylan was on her kitchen floor. "Maris!" she demanded in a furious whisper.

"It's just so damn tempting," Maris said, lowering the racquet. "What's he doing here, anyway?"

Barely able to suppress a smile at the bulldog determination on

Maris' face, Bianca pulled her from the room. "He came to check on me when he heard what happened. He and Finn got into it, and he passed out."

"A Tierny brawl. Like you needed *that* tonight," Maris said. "So Finn returned from Pittsburgh in a big way. I haven't seen him yet. Of course, if I had a brother like Dylan, I'd lay low too."

Dylan's phone sounded, and Bianca raced back into the kitchen to snatch it from his pocket before it woke him. When she saw the screen, her first inclination was to pass it off to Maris like a hot potato, but she answered. "It's Bianca, Dylan's fine, but he . . . Jewel? Hello?"

"Seriously, I'll never get what either of you see in him," Maris said with an exaggerated eye roll.

"I should have turned the ringer down and let it go to voice mail."

"You amaze me."

"What?"

"After what he did to you—the drinking, the lies, and that night—"

"Stop." Bianca rubbed at the tension teeming in the pleated skin between her eyebrows.

"I still say too bad Finn's Dylan's brother, because that boy is hot."

Bianca ignored the remark. They'd agreed years ago, even the subject was off limits. When Finn was her student she couldn't even see him in that light, but once he was older, she started noticing, taking one look, then another. Off limits, taboo but unquestionably hot.

"So why's he back?" Maris asked.

"I'm guessing because of his dad. It must be so hard."

Bianca thought about the Mack Tierny she'd known before he was diagnosed with an inoperable brain tumor, a man whose eyes absorbed every action, every reaction.

She'd met the Tiernys her first week in Riley's Peak, six years ago, on Miner's Day, the town's biggest celebration. At the grocery store, she'd literally collided with Dylan as she barreled through the aisles—something about food shopping always made her crank it into high gear. But if she hadn't bumped into him, she was certain an announcement would have echoed over the loud speaker: "Bianca James, a contender for Mr. Right is waiting in frozen foods." Mr. Right and then some. Tanned face and a body chiseled by hours in the gym. A knowing smile, an inside-joke kind of smile.

He invited her to the event, and it didn't take much convincing. Bianca returned a bottle of tarragon vinegar and a bag salad and accompanied him to the town square where Mack and Finn were sitting at a picnic table in the shade of a large oak. They welcomed her with beer toasts and hearty grins, and when Bianca told them she'd be teaching art at Brookefield, Finn's eyes lit up. He was starting his junior year in the fall and had declared art as his major. Seizing the public moment he informed his dad, which earned a burst of unexpected laughter from Mack. "Still? Thought you'd outgrown that," he said, reaching into a large bucket of ice for another beer. "It's a hobby or a time killer, but an art degree ain't worth the paper it's printed on." He twisted the top off the bottle and tilted it to Bianca. "No offense."

Finn's face hardened, and it was then she noticed his eyes, hazel, with a splotch of brown, almost star-shaped, swimming in the left. He pushed back, telling his father he had plans of his own. "Tiernys are cops. Your grandfather was a cop. I'm a cop. Your brother's a cop." Mack slammed his bottle on the picnic table. Beer spewed. "You'll be a cop."

From what Bianca could see, Mack always got his way.

"I heard he had a breakdown at the grocery store," Maris said. "Didn't know where he was and started throwing bags of rice at a stock boy who was trying to help."

A sensation of futility swept over Bianca. One day, life is charging forward on the tracks you've put down, and then without warning, you're derailed. "It's very sad. Apparently, he has only six to eight months." She turned to find Dylan leaning against the doorjamb, his face pale and eyes red-rimmed.

"Dylan." Bianca crossed the room. "Are you all right?"

He tried and failed to tame spikes of black hair running haywire across his head. "Yup." He bobbed his chin toward Maris, a hello.

"I'd ask how you're doing," Maris said, "but that would mean I give a damn."

"Guess I'm still at the top of your shit list."

Maris whipped around to face him. "Numero uno, ever since—"

"Seriously?" Bianca's hands shot up to referee.

Dylan kissed her cheek. "Glad you're okay," he whispered and moved toward the door.

"Jewel called while you were gin-napping," Maris said.

Bianca wedged herself between them. "Your phone rang and—"

"S'okay." Dylan shoved his hands in his pockets, chuffed a laugh. "I was supposed to have the night off."

"She must have found a gap in her busy schedule." Maris continued to stalk Dylan with a predatory smirk. "Guess she doesn't trust you either."

Dylan ignored the jab and ran his hand along Bianca's arm. "Goodnight, Bee. I'm glad you're okay."

"You said that already." Maris pressed the sentence into a firm line.

"Let me drive you home," Bianca offered.

"Durwood's on his way. I already called him."

When the door closed behind him, Maris was taking a stance, hands on hips. "He'll keep coming back like the dog he is if you keep leaving a pile of Milk Bones on your porch."

"You know what? Your timing sucks." Bianca powered into the kitchen, grabbed the blanket and pillow, and stormed down the hall to her bedroom. Before she could slam the door, Maris appeared.

"You're right, I'm sorry." Maris pulled her into a hug, blanket and pillow crushed between them. "But I'm worried about you."

Bianca softened. "You don't need to be."

"I'm wired for worry. Nine younger brothers and sisters, remember?" Maris stifled a yawn.

"We could both use some sleep," Bianca said through a matched yawn.

"Give me that stuff, and I'll be snoring before you even get into bed."

"You don't have to stay." Bianca guided Maris to the front door. "The last time you slept on my couch your chiropractor sent me flowers."

"That couch *has* seen better days. You know, you're not twenty anymore, Bianca. It's time to buy some big girl furniture."

Bianca never tired of the way her friend said her name, with a flourish, condensing it to two syllables instead of three. Byan-ka. "Thanks for the reminder about my rapid slide toward middle age, Mare. Go home."

"If you insist, but make sure everything's locked. Sleep with your phone in hand," Maris said. "Promise?"

"Promise. You need to be careful, too. Call me the second you're deadbolted in. And keep your phone charged."

Maris pointed to her purse. "You don't have to worry about me. Remember, I'm not alone."

The gun. Lisette's face, the dark hole marring unblemished skin, surfaced again. She rerouted her focus, picked up Maris' racquet. "Don't forget this."

"The Williams sisters have nothing on me." Maris swung a deliberate forehand before her face turned serious. "They'll find whoever did this."

After Maris left, Bianca headed for the shower, eager to scrub off the day.

As the hot water pelted her skin, she replayed the events. Finding Lisette. Trying to help her. Failing miserably. Did she do more harm than good? Carmichael's relentless questions. The chaotic atmosphere in her studio.

She imagined Lisette's family, getting the news, breaking down.

Maris said the little girl's father had disappeared. Did the police know? Surely they'd cover every angle, but what if they didn't, giving the killer more time to get away?

She cranked off the water, reached for a towel.

A clatter in the bedroom. Bianca crept toward the sound, pulse racing. Her vision telescoped around the room, sweeping over her familiar surroundings, but everything had fallen out of alignment, taken on a different edge. An icy thumb caressed her spine as a fluttery unease spread through her.

Then she saw him.

Picasso, stretched across her dresser, oblivious to the frame knocked over beside him. She stopped short of scolding him with his namesake's crazy-ass full name as she sometimes did: Pablo Diego José Francisco de Paula Juan Nepomuceno María de los

Remedios Cipriano de la Santísima Trinidad Ruiz y Picasso. A name she loved to put on the occasional pop quiz for extra credit.

Bianca lifted the picture of her and her grandma, Gemma, in front of the elephant enclosure at the Milwaukee zoo. Gemma, eyes hooded by a floppy sunhat, hand gripping Bianca's, a matching grin ringed with chocolate ice cream. Bianca ran her thumb across the faded photograph, diluted to shades of amber and sand.

They'd read all about elephants the day before, about how you can tell where they're from by the size and shape of their ears. Asian elephants' ears are smaller and shaped like India. African elephants' ears are larger and shaped like Africa.

The past filled her throat like a balloon. "I remember, Gemma," she said. "And about their trunks too, how they drape them over their tusks once in a while when they get too heavy."

It was amazing the little things she remembered about Gemma now. The way she wrapped her wet hair in a lime green turban twice a week after shampooing and rolled it in sponge rollers when it was nearly dry. She only wore make-up to funerals, insisting it was a celebration of the person's life. A strange, but beautiful juxtaposition. But the thing Bianca remembered most was her advice. "When life gets too heavy, and it will, remember the elephants. You're strong like they are. You can handle anything. Just remember to look for another way to manage your burdens, and all will be fine."

Bianca returned the picture to her dresser. Tightening the towel around her, she went into the living room to find the card Chief Carmichael had given her. She picked through her purse: wallet, keys, lip balm, receipts, gum wrappers. No card. She spotted Finn's on the table, picked it up, and tapped it against her leg before she dialed his number. When he didn't answer, she left a message about Lisette's boyfriend, complete with long pauses and fumbled words.

Her head grew heavy. Cocooning between the sheets, she curled next to Picasso, and tried to relax to his rumbling purr.

Exhaustion claimed every part of her, but closed eyes only conjured more visions of Lisette. She'd read somewhere that life leaves the lungs first and the eyes last. In the final seconds of that poor girl's life, she didn't have the breath to scream. And Bianca was the last person she saw. The person who held her very life in her hands.

The person who had let her down.

Bianca kicked off the covers, grabbed her robe from the end of the bed, and went into the kitchen.

She was pawing through her stash of tea bags when something hit the back door. Had she remembered to lock it? She seldom did when she was home, but surely tonight . . .

The kettle screamed, unraveling her last nerve. She flicked off the burner and checked the door. Finn must have locked it. Her hand moved to the deadbolt and eased it to the left. The blue-black night crawled in like an unwelcome guest. She flipped the light switch and the cypress trees circling her lawn swayed in response. Cold slashed her ankles. The temperature outside had plummeted, and she was about to hurry inside when she noticed several terracotta planters, shattered.

She hustled inside, slammed the door, and turned the lock. Metal thudded against the strike plate, a harsh sound she'd have to get used to, the sound of being locked in. Backing against the wall, she plastered her hands there, as if the wall could steady her wildly beating heart. She stumbled to the couch where she'd dropped her phone. Her hand closed around it, and she punched redial.

This time he answered.

"Finn." Her hand fluttered to her chest. She paused to get her breathing under control and all at once felt foolish. Last week a raccoon family had rummaged through her trash can—the likely pot-smashing culprits.

"Bianca? You okay?"

She scrambled to salvage what little was left of her dignity. "I wanted to make sure you got my message about Lisette's ex-boyfriend."

"I told the chief." He sounded worn-down, frustrated. "Sorry I didn't call you back. I should have. Called you back."

Ridiculous didn't come close to how she was feeling right now, calling him at the slightest noise. "Right. Just thought it might be important."

Bianca ended the call and walked through the bungalow, checking the doors and windows, Gemma's wisdom bolstering each step. "Be strong, little Bee."

◈ FOUR ◈

AFTER they'd finished in the studio, Carmichael and Tucker left to break the news to the victim's family. Finn was relieved to stay behind. Back in the 'Burgh, not long after he'd started, he and Walters shared the grim task of telling a young mother that her husband flipped his car on the interstate. He'd expected her to cry, or collapse into him, but the shock froze her to the porch steps. He could hear the panic ripping through her as clearly as if she'd asked the question out loud, "What now?"

No. He didn't need to see another person crushed under the weight of life-altering news.

He'd made plans to meet Tucker afterwards at Half Way There, the all-night diner on Highway 51, a second home to truckers, cops, and the occasional insomniac. Finn was already on his third cup of coffee when Tucker arrived, stress twisting his broad face. Finn filled a mug from the carafe, pushed it toward him.

Tucker tore into four sugar packets and poured them into his coffee. "Carmichael's delivery sucked. Lisette's mother kept clawing fingernails into my arm, actually drew blood." He smoothed a hand over his sleeve. "Talked mostly in some other language. About her five-year-old granddaughter, I think. Sad."

Envisioning the now motherless girl, Finn raked hands through his hair, threw his head back, and let the urge to scream pass.

"Carmichael left," Tucker continued, "but I stayed until some neighbors came."

"Let's hope we dig up something soon that leads us to this bastard."

"Two bullets." Tucker held up two fingers. "In a small space, at close range like that, you'd think it'd take only one."

Finn rubbed at a water spot on his mug. "I got a chance to take a look, the half-a-second Carmichael wasn't riding my ass, and it might've been a .22. Recoil's almost non-existent and not as loud as other guns. Odd choice though. I mean, it's only a few steps up from a pellet gun."

Tucker considered this briefly. "A lady gun usually, but could be a guy who grabbed whatever was handy. Still too much we don't know."

As usual, they were on slippery terrain with more questions than answers.

"And Bianca finding the body," Tucker said, "then trying like that—"

"Like what?"

"You know, CPR."

"I thought the vic was already dead when she found her?" He rewound to Bianca's blood-splattered clothing. She'd done more than find the body.

"She felt a pulse, or thought she did, and tried to revive her."

What's that Aunt Sara liked to say? Gobsmacked. The word knuckled Finn now, the utter astonishment hitting him like a rap to the head. No wonder Bianca had been so shocky. The only thing worse than finding a dead body was finding someone damn near death and being unable to do shit about it. And why hadn't it occurred to him to ask more questions? The bloody clothes would have triggered a little curiosity in a good cop.

The door swung open, startling the waitress lounging in the adjacent booth, feet up, eyes closed. A man rushed in and flew straight to the can, fingers already fumbling for his fly. Finn stood, headed over to refill the carafe. Back at the table, he topped off their mugs, then raised the pot in her direction.

"No thanks," she said. "Got a hot date with my pillow in about an hour."

Finn nodded, but sleep was the furthest thing from his mind.

Tucker added more sugar, took a long draw of coffee. He

chewed at the inside of his mouth while they skirted the issue that might have surfaced if someone other than Dylan's ex-girlfriend had found the body. The shooting happened in Bianca's studio while she was in the break room across the hall, yet she didn't hear or see a thing.

Tucker wagged his head from side to side. "Must have been awkward, huh?"

"Meaning?"

"Dylan showing up while you were at her place. You haven't seen her since they broke up, right?"

"Right."

"It was strange for me at first too, but my gut says they'll get back together." Tucker patted his belly, indicating plenty of room to store some intuition alongside the daily special. "They're made for each other, don't ya think?"

"What do I know about who is made for each other?"

The waitress pried herself from her booth and skated over, slipper-clad feet buffing the floor. She closed her hand over the empty sugar packets and stuffed them into her pocket. "You need to bring your sister in again," she said to Tucker.

A grin split his face. "I will. I need to."

"I'll tell the boss to stock up on relish."

"Dill, not sweet."

"I remember." She patted his shoulder, yawned, and skated away.

"Melanie puts it on her ice cream, and the last time we were here they didn't have any. It wasn't pretty."

Finn marveled at Tucker's devotion to his older sister, who had Down's syndrome and thought her brother single-handedly plopped the moon in the sky, ordering it when to rise, when to set. Tucker tried to move out of his parent's house once, but Melanie pitched such a fit he decided to stay on, conceding he would have missed her too much anyway.

"Guess what she's begging for now?" Tucker asked.

"No telling."

"She saw a stapler in a catalog that can staple through 200 pages at once."

"Sounds industrial."

"I'll probably get it for her." Tucker lifted a shoulder. "If it makes her happy."

"What about the shredder?"

"She still shreds, but wants to staple packets of paper, too. I've got Alden Press saving overrun stock for me."

The notion momentarily restored Finn's waning faith in humanity. He suppressed the thought of a murderer on the loose and chose instead to focus on his friend who gathered paper and spent hard-earned money on office equipment to please his sister.

After Finn left Half Way There, he headed to the station to finish his shift, which amounted to paperwork and water cooler chatter about the murder. When he finally started for home at 6:45, the sun was just beginning to crest the horizon. A beautiful deception. Approaching daylight usually meant a fresh start, made it seem like events could be relegated to the past.

They couldn't.

Finn opened the front door of the small brick ranch he and his brother had grown up in. "Dad?"

"In here," Mack called from his usual corner of the living room. His voice was gravelly and weak.

"Why don't you open these shades? This place is like a cave."

"Heard about what happened on the scanner. And I like it dark."

Since returning from Pittsburgh, each time Finn stepped into this house, he had to adjust his thinking. Half of him wanted to settle in; the other half wanted to bolt. There were good memories here, but the truth of the matter was, things really hadn't been the same since his parents' split sixteen years ago.

Now his dad's diagnosis. Surgery wasn't an option. The brain tumor was too large and still growing at an alarming rate. Years earlier he'd suffered a heart attack; they'd almost lost him then. Life sucked sometimes. Plain and simple.

Finn was glad Mack wasn't up tottering around. He often seemed on the verge of falling, but other times his steps were in the confident stride of a young cop strutting his beat. And his moods were nearly impossible to predict, volleying from dizzy with rage to downright affectionate. His dad had never been touchy-feely. All Finn could do was negotiate each emotional hotbed as it appeared.

Despite his illness, Mack was still a fortress of a man, imposing and barrel-chested, but each day it seemed like he lost a little more physical ground. His erratic diet didn't help. Finn noticed an empty bologna wrapper on the TV tray and felt a rush of guilt. "I see you ate."

Mack grunted. His gaunt face glowed in the flickering light of the television.

Finn settled on the couch. "What's on?"

"Nothing but crap." Mack flipped through the channels, no doubt searching for his favorite new diversion—game shows.

"Was the nurse here last night?"

Mack waved a hand. "The one with the raspy voice, that Jewel."

"Jewel's out of town, and she's not a nurse, Dad. She's Dylan's girlfriend."

"I know who the hell she is, and she was here."

"You must have your days mixed up. You're thinking of Tammy, the one who brings pictures of her kids. Jewel doesn't have kids."

"Jewel was here," Mack said. "She's always coming over, bringing something. Cookies, those little cupcakes, a pie. What's she tryin' to do, give me the sugars?"

Jewel. Not the gem her name suggested. Beautiful, sure, but she was abrupt and meddling, and no doubt these visits, her oohing and aahing over Mack, were meant to win his approval. She knew the power he wielded over his sons, and she wanted Dylan's ring on her finger; she'd made that clear enough.

Mack stared off for a moment, before his face turned red. "She was here. Last night. I never forget a voice. What is that? The way she talks. Sounds like she just stepped off a surfboard."

"I still say you're thinking of Tammy, and she just stepped off a bus from Ohio a couple weeks ago."

Mack slammed his hand on the TV tray. "Don't tell me what I'm thinking!"

"Okay, Dad, okay."

Dylan had said Jewel was away at a conference in Pittsburgh, but Finn saw no value in continuing to dispute his dad. And maybe Dylan was too blind drunk to remember if Jewel was away this weekend or if that was four months ago.

Mack shifted, and the chair's spine stretched and groaned in protest.

"So you know all about the murder," Finn said.

"A silent fart doesn't go unnoticed in this town."

That about summed up the Peak. Mayberry with a touch of Pleasantville. A great place to grow up, but no place to keep secrets. "I'm glad Tucker got to the vic's family before someone else did."

"Definitely better that way." Mack regarded Finn with a mixture of concern and doubt, and an expression that said he'd seen it all. "You up for this?"

"Guess I have to be." Finn was tired, pushed to the brink of exhaustion, but not sleepy. "Want some coffee?"

"That sounds good right about now." Mack folded himself forward and kicked his feet into the footrest. "But you've been up all night. Shouldn't you go to bed?"

"A lecture on astrophysics couldn't put me to sleep now."

Mack made his way to the kitchen, holding on to furniture, running his hand along the wall, in a manner that added decades to his sixty-five years. He lowered himself into a chair while Finn made coffee. Poking at the pie in the middle of the table he said, "See what I mean? Cherry. I hate cherries."

Finn wanted to ask if Jewel brought it yesterday or the day before, but he let it go. Mack would say he should stick around more if he was so damned concerned about who was coming and going. Truth. He poured coffee into Mack's favorite mug, the one boasting "Riley's Peak's Finest" and planted it in front of him before he poured himself a cup. Like he needed more caffeine sprinting through his veins.

Mack took a sip, made a face. "No cream?"

"Since when do you take cream?"

"Since now."

Finn peered in the refrigerator, moved some things around, then closed the door. "Powder okay?"

Mack growled in the back of his throat. He'd been doing it more and more when he was upset, like finding the right word had become too much of an effort.

"I'll pick some up later," Finn said.

"I'll do it myself."

Finn placed the powdered cream and a spoon next to Mack's coffee mug. "I wish you wouldn't."

"I can drive."

It had been an ongoing battle, but Finn didn't feel up to arguing about Mack's driving, or anything else right now. "Any advice for me—on this murder?"

"Keep your eyes peeled." Mack sliced the air with his hand. "Trust your gut. Follow instincts and hunches, no matter how far-fetched. Comb the scene. They always leave something behind."

The creases on his dad's face fell into pleasant lines. Every once in a while that old part of him would surface—complete with smiling eyes and a good story—this was one of those times.

"Years back, in Whistler, drunks at a party start brawling and somebody gets beat to death. When we hit the scene, there's only a dead guy *and* one of those disposable cameras. Pictures of the fight that left no reasonable doubt. Open and shut. Those guys were careless. Your killer might not be, but I'll bet dollars to dumbbells there's probably something there you can use."

Finn thought about the shoes he saw in the garbage. They were those generic clogs—could have belonged to a man or a woman. He dragged his index finger over his lips. For all he knew, he could have been having tea with the murderer tonight. But that seemed about as likely as the Pirates trading McCutcheon.

"Who was first on the scene?"

Finn drew a breath, scratched at his cheek. He knew how Mack felt about Bianca. She had two bold strikes in his book. As Finn's teacher, she'd encouraged him to pursue an art career over public service. And Mack was convinced she'd single-handedly driven Dylan to drink, even though he'd been drinking long before their break-up.

"Bianca James." Finn steeled himself for his dad's reaction.

Mack's mouth shifted. He seemed to be considering something.

"She's a looker."

Finn felt relief, a loosening in his tense shoulders.

"But a wicked bitch," Mack added. "She'll be the death of your brother."

Bianca. He couldn't get her out of his head. Couldn't stop seeing the way her golden hair caught even the smallest parcel of light. So damn gorgeous, yet she had no clue. The few times he'd been out with her and Dylan, he'd seen men look at her, then look again. And again.

Wicked?

"Don't rule her out, son. Wouldn't be the first time a perp claimed that as their alibi, finding the body and showing how broken up they are about it."

The old man knew police work like no other, but fake CPR on a woman you just murdered?

"What does your brother think of all this?" Mack asked.

"I haven't talked to him." A lie.

Mack's eyebrows shot up. "You think he'd call. It's been days."

"He's busy, Dad. Working."

"Hittin' the bottle more like. Drinks his life away. We'll see how long he lasts on this job."

Dylan had bounced between gigs since he lost his police badge—janitor, freight handler, even short-order cook. This time he'd landed at a construction site where the once rising star on the police force now wielded a nail gun instead of a .45.

"He always shows up when we need him," Finn said.

At least he used to.

Mack batted the air. His chair scraped the floor as he scooted from the table. On his way back to his recliner, he stopped, jabbed a finger at Finn. "You think about what I've said."

Finn put their mugs in the sink. A rusty streak from the dripping faucet glared at him. So many things around here needed fixing, and he made a silent vow to get to it. One less thing for Mack to obsess about. Finn returned to the living room, resuming his place on the couch next to the easy chair. He hadn't been back from the 'Burgh long, but watching Mack, day after day in the same spot, doing the same thing, was eating away at him.

Something caught Finn's attention, a large open book on the coffee table he hadn't noticed before. His parents' wedding album. Hadn't it been in the hall closet for years? Why bring it out now? Was the tumor pushing on a nerve that made Mack nostalgic? A bedlam of questions competed for answers. He turned on the lamp next to him, and held the album under the light. "Michael and Rosemary Tierny Forever" embossed in fancy gold script on the cover. Miles from the truth.

Mack stared at the television, transfixed, as Vanna White—doesn't that woman ever age?—turned a letter and the audience applauded.

Finn flipped through the pages, stalling on one in particular. The bride and groom shoving cake into each other's mouths. He ran his fingers over the image. Mack, impressive in a dark double-breasted suit, protective arm wrapped around his new bride. Rose's blond hair was swept up and back, emphasizing her fair skin and delicate features. Her dress was lacy and pale peach. Finn imagined the conversation around that non-traditional choice. A dislocated feeling took up residence deep inside. It always did when he thought about his mother. Hardly his mother anymore. Rose had been out of his life more years than she had been in it.

He closed the album and felt his dad's gaze on him. They exchanged a long look.

Mack swiped at his eyes and nose in one circular motion, and his face crumpled in embarrassment. "Remember, be careful about the art teacher." He snorted. "Still say she's your prime suspect."

Tears or no, the warning irritated Finn. "No, Dad. Someone else is responsible for that woman's murder."

But if he was being honest, the events of the night were colored in many shades of wrong.

"Suit yourself," Mack said, shifting away.

Finn flopped back on the couch and laced his fingers behind his head. He stretched his legs and stared at the ceiling fan, spinning and humming above him. The tinny and mechanical game show music receded, and a dull ache surfaced from the commotion treading water in his head.

❧

Two hours before his 7:00 p.m. tour, Finn drove through landscape that opened like the palm of a hand at the east end of Riley's Peak. Gradually, the fields rolled into wooded hills, rock formations rising between them, and the scenery clenched to a tight fist—Pittsburgh. He waited for a double-stack train chugging over the Vanport Bridge as conflicting information gnawed at him with each clanking coupling. Mack had said Jewel was at the house. Dylan said she was away at a conference in Pittsburgh. Neither of them rated high in the credibility department right now.

Everyone's a suspect. Damn if Carmichael's pep talk at the scene didn't echo a line from *Scream*. Finn had only been eleven when he snuck into the slasher with Dylan and Tucker. The gore and cheesy dialogue had long since faded, but that one line stuck.

Everyone's a suspect. Even Jewel Glasser, PhD. Finn shook his head. He'd find someone at the hotel who had seen her and put his crazy suspicions to rest. Off the reservation sure, but doing this by the book would only delay the investigation. And probably reveal nothing. Easier to apologize later than get permission now.

People remembered Jewel. And it wasn't just her looks. It was more about how she took situations by the throat and shook them. He'd heard about the students she'd helped at Brookefield. A good psychiatrist. But even a good psychiatrist couldn't be in two places at once. He was heading for a dead end and suspected this side-investigation had more to do with assessing how far his dad had slipped than Jewel's connection to a murder. Worst case, he was out a quarter tank of gas.

An apple core on the passenger floor rolling backward as he accelerated, forward when he slowed, and Finn found himself grinding his teeth about it. Whenever his brother borrowed his car, he always left something behind. As careless about his garbage as everything else. But that hadn't always been the case. An indelible line now divided him in two distinct sections, Dylan before the accident and Dylan after.

At the check-in desk, Finn flashed his badge. Carmichael would have his hide. No one was allowed to take a piss without his say-so.

Carmichael be damned. If the chief didn't give him hell about this, it would be something else. The manager tapped on his computer keyboard, ran his finger down the screen. "Yes, Ms. Glasser checked in at 3:00 p.m. yesterday." He continued to look past Finn, eyeing a noisy group of hockey players. "I really can't help more than that." He returned to his papers.

Poor guy's in over his head. He was young, maybe twenty, but he looked twelve, thirteen tops, probably wishing for those carefree high school days of slogging through classes and choking down cafeteria lunches.

So Jewel had checked in, but did she actually attend the sessions? Finn decided to do a little more snooping. On his way through the lobby, a young woman stopped him. "I couldn't help but overhear. I'm the concierge here, Donna Davenport. The one you're talking about, is she a stunning redhead?"

It was hard to think of Jewel as anything but a hot mess. "Do you remember her?"

"We get so many people through here on a daily basis, I'm lucky to recognize the hotel staff." Her laugh sailed above the noisy lobby. "She certainly stood out though. That one could model. I moonlight as a photographer, and those cheekbones—they're what we call moneymakers. She really caught our bartender's attention in the Cameo Bar."

"And you're sure this was last night?"

"Oh, yes. And I remembered seeing her nametag and thinking, 'Isn't it interesting, a shrink with the same last name as a psychologist I studied in school.' I was a psych undergrad, but the courses were so intense I switched to hotel management, which gave me more time for my photography."

Finn nearly bit off his tongue. *Get to the point.*

"I wondered if she chose psychology because of William Glasser or if psychology chose her." She beamed as if she'd shared a witty anecdote.

"This bartender. Is he here?"

"Yes." She pointed across the lobby. "Adam."

"Thanks." Finn was already moving toward the bar.

He introduced himself and again pulled out his badge. Unfazed,

Adam favored him with the liquid smile bartenders seem to be born with. "Too bad you're on duty. I make a mean Long Island. Just can't tell you my secret ingredient."

"Hate to miss out. Water would be great though."

Finn knew bartenders were protective of their customers. *Approach him like you would a guard dog; offer a nice, juicy steak.* And there it was in Adam's right eye.

Finn pointed to the splotch of brown in his own. "Fight with a coffee table, age three."

Adam squinted at him for a moment. "Got me beat. I was born with it. Guessing you're not here to talk about my eye though."

"I'm following up on some attendees from yesterday's conference. May be a long shot but—"

"That still gets me. Bringing all the nutjobs who treat nutjobs here on Friday the 13th. I get a little wacked with those big groups anyway but especially with them. They must have a theory that tipping is bad for the psyche. I do a helluva lot better during the plumber's convention."

Finn described Jewel. "Any chance you remember her?"

Adam propped his elbows on the bar top and lowered his head on stacked fists. "That one's hard to forget." After a long moment, he stood tall again, looked over both shoulders, and lowered his voice a notch while hiking an eyebrow. "Musta been on the gymnastics team in high school."

Had Finn heard correctly? Maybe bragging rights trumped a bartender's "what happens in the bar, stays in the bar" mentality.

"So, yeah, she was right there on that stool for a while, hung on my every word like I was Confucius or something. Gave me her room number and said she wanted to hook up later. Women like her don't usually put it out there like that, but like I said, this one was different." He leaned back, smiled. "Glad I wasn't scheduled to close that night."

"Any chance you remember the time?"

"Sorry, dude. Time was the furthest thing from my mind."

Finn rapped on the bar top. "Thanks, man. I'll be back to take you up on that Long Island."

⊸ FIVE ⊱

BIANCA crossed the lawn from the parking lot to Weaver and smiled as she neared Prince Caspian. He was perched in a catcher's squat on a bench, the same purple beret he wore year-round low on his forehead. She'd only missed a day, but the routine was important to him, to them both. She wouldn't let him down again.

College administration had reprimanded Bianca for feeding the homeless man instead of directing him to a shelter, but she couldn't bear to think of him as another cog in a broken wheel. She handed him a brown paper bag, which he opened and sniffed as he'd done nearly every day for a year now. The contents were always the same—tuna on wheat with a slice of tomato, juice box, and a quartered apple, held in place with a rubber band. Gemma's trick to keep the apple from turning brown. She'd once tried to give him ham on rye, thinking he might want some variety, but he'd clapped the sandwich hard between his hands like he was closing an infuriating book and slammed it in the garbage before he turned into a human tornado.

He peered into the bag, grunted something she claimed as a thank-you, and scurried off, leaving a sour odor behind. If only she could do more for him. Still, it wasn't pity she felt, but the contagion of his loneliness spreading through her like a virus.

Inside her studio, seconds twisted to minutes as she tiptoed through a minefield of thoughts and feelings and singled out guilt.

But her guilt was all out of proportion. She hadn't murdered anyone. The yellow tape from the crime scene was gone, but a stifling imaginary line still cordoned off the area, still created a line of blame she couldn't break through.

Bianca stared at her lesson plan for tomorrow's art history class. Sunday evenings had always been her favorite time at Brookefield. She could work uninterrupted, acoustic guitar streaming in the background. Tonight she struggled as the words melted to inkblots on the page.

Forty-eight hours since the murder, and it was eerily quiet, as if nothing had even happened. The police went about their investigation as school administrators rallied to return things to normal. She needed to fall into step.

She pulled a tube of lotion from her drawer and massaged it into the dry spots on her knuckles as she studied the images in her plan book. Her eyes stalled on an aquamanile, a jug-like vessel traditionally used for washing hands over a basin. This one depicted a bearded Samson perched on a lion's back, hands in the beast's mouth, pulling its jaws apart.

A seemingly impossible task.

Her cell rang, and she shuffled through papers to find it. A glance at the screen told her it was an unknown caller. The third that day. Phone to her ear, she listened. A garble of noise then a whoosh of air as she felt her own drain from her lungs. "Who is this?" she demanded. Another sound, unrecognizable. She ended the call, slapped her phone on the desk.

Back to her notes, she spent some time tweaking the section about animals in medieval art, trying to enliven the lecture. Most of her students were willing participants, but several grew antsy if they couldn't relate.

From the corner of her eye, she saw a vapor wisp through the hallway. She eased from the room and checked in both directions as strobes of fluorescent light flickered above.

Nothing.

Her mind was playing tricks again.

She put her lecture notes aside and spent the next hour ambling from task to task, project to project, incapable of completing anything, hands shaking every time she reached for a paintbrush or needed something from the storage room. How could she create with hands as quivery as Jell-O? How could she do the job she loved when images marched around her in a morbid parade? Bloody footprints, Lisette's ashen face splattered with red, her body limp, despite Bianca's efforts.

A murderer lurking in the shadows.

Annoyed, she gathered her messenger bag. She'd let fear win, and felt exposed as if she'd left her queen unprotected on the chessboard.

As she grabbed for her coat, the students' leaf tessellations scattered across the floor. Several slid under a tall cabinet. When she reached for them, her hand grazed something. She curled her fingers around it and pulled out a necklace, a loopy L speckled with black stones on a thin gold chain. She traced the L with her finger, admiring the unique trio of stones. Someone would be happy to get it back. Laura in Drawing 101? Lendra in Mixed Media? She'd shoot her students an email.

As she slipped the necklace into her pocket, a thought rendered her immobile.

Chet moved that shelf across the room the day before the murder. If the necklace had been there before that, she would have spotted it. They'd argued because she wanted him to use his two-wheel dolly, but he insisted on hoisting it himself. Sure enough, he strained his back and called off work the next day. The agency had sent a replacement.

Lisette.

The only other people in the room last Friday were the students in the three classes she taught that day and the police officers that night. She pulled the necklace from her pocket, studied it, noted the broken clasp. It had to be Lisette's. She'd take it to the station in the morning. Maybe having it would bring the family a sliver of peace.

Bianca's attention riveted to a sudden intrusion of noise in the hallway. A startling sneeze, followed by a trumpet-like nose blowing. She stepped from the room and saw the reporter from the other night, alternately wiping at his nose with a blue handkerchief and hiking up his pants. The last thing she needed. Where was

Ralph? Shouldn't he be patrolling the building instead of snoozing in the basement?

"Professor James," the man said, juggling a pad and his phone and looking every bit as harried as the other night. "May I ask you a few questions?"

Apparently, Carmichael's grammar lesson had stuck.

"I'm on my way out," she said.

"It'll only take a minute."

Bianca hated the idea of the murder plastered all over the news. Lisette's family would see and hear about it relentlessly, knife jabs to an open wound.

"You found the body, correct?" he pressed. "People will want to know your story. It's a pretty heroic thing you did, trying CPR."

Trying was the operative word, wasn't it?

"Please," Bianca said. "I need to get home."

As she took a step to bypass the reporter, Ralph's telltale whistle rounded the corner. When she heard it, it was nearly impossible to be angry with him for occasionally nodding off on the job. It was only the arthritis taking its toll. Ralph had been a steadfast sentry at Brookefield for decades, as much a part of the college as the entryway's stone arch wreathed with sprawling ivy.

"Everything okay, Miss James?" Ralph asked when he'd made his way to her.

"Fine, I'm just *trying* to leave for the night."

Ralph flicked his wrists at the reporter, *shoo*. "Well, sir, that means you best skedaddle."

"If I could—"

"Go ahead, off with ya. You'll have to get your story somewheres else."

The reporter held firm. "Talking about it may give other people the courage to help in an emergency." He ran the folded handkerchief under his nose. "Unless of course you've got something to hide?"

Ralph stepped in front of Bianca, creating a buffer. "Let me see if I can make this clearer than the mud you're slinging. Move it, or I'll move it for you."

The reporter grumbled, clamped his pad under his arm.

Bianca blew out a breath as he walked away. "Thanks, Ralph. Guess I'm still a little rattled."

"You've got every reason to be all shook up." He peered over his bifocals, moving his torso in a cranked sway. "Like Mr. Swivel Hips himself." Despite his gyrations, unease held tight to Bianca. "I'd be skittish too," Ralph went on, "spendin' so much time around those striped-haired, metal-faced artsy types like you do. Kids are mighty different anymore."

She sighed.

"There I go again. Wife always says my timing is off as a battered Timex. Might as well laugh at funerals and cry reading the funny paper. Don't mind me none."

It wasn't the first jab she'd heard about artists. They could be temperamental, sometimes on the fringe of "normal," but she was protective of her students. A sharp-clawed den mother.

"It's okay. They're good kids—expressing themselves. And who knows, there may be a new Monet among them."

Ralph sawed at his ear with a shaky finger. "That guy who lopped off his own ear?"

"That was van Gogh." A moment of silence ticked by. "Did you know the woman who was murdered? Lisette?"

He shook his head in a measured cadence. "Can't say that I did. Sad thing for sure. If only I'd been—"

Bianca placed a hand on his arm. "You couldn't have known."

"Well, just because you let me off the hook doesn't mean I do." He pointed an arthritic finger at "security" embroidered on his shirt. "It's my job to know what goes on around here. I put my notice in yesterday. Once they find a replacement, I'll only be a distant memory."

"Ralph, no, you shouldn't—"

He patted her shoulder. "Comes a time in everyone's life, Miss James, that they accept what's what."

"Well, you'll be missed."

"Thank the good Lord you were there to at least try to give that poor girl a chance."

A chance. For a moment they stood stock-still, each wrapped in their own brand of regret.

Ralph's eyes flew wide, and he slapped a palm to his forehead. "I plumb forgot." He reached into his pocket and handed her a pink vial of pepper spray. "They were all out of the one on a key chain. You can put it in your handbag though, right?"

"I will, Ralph. Thank you."

He flicked his chin. That's that.

"You haven't seen anyone unusual in the building lately, have you?" Bianca asked.

"Other than that barnacle of a reporter?" Ralph tapped his cheek. "No . . . can't say that I have. But the police already questioned me up one steep hill and down the other. Why?"

"Curious, I guess."

"You know what they say 'bout curious cats. Don't mean to frighten you none, but you best leave this to the authorities. You're too delicate to get wrapped up in this ugly murder business."

Delicate. She let it slide. "Speaking of cats, I better get home to feed Picasso."

"Can't your husband do it?" The right side of his mouth hitched.

His perpetual hounding about her imaginary husband. Never around when she needed him. A figment. A dream. Mr. Non-existent.

"No, Ralph. I'm single. Remember?"

He sized her up. "Woman your age—pretty as you—ought to have a mister. Forgive me for sayin' so, but you should be havin' babies."

She forced a smile and shifted away, longing to be home, family or no.

Ralph pointed at his ring finger. "Me and the Mrs. married at seventeen."

"Things are different now."

"Different ain't necessarily better. You need a man to look after you."

"Like I said, I need to go. Picasso will be chewing the leg off the table when I get home."

"Let me walk you."

"Ralph—"

"Miss James." His voice slid to a lower register. "It's not a good idea for you to be out there alone. Not until they find this animal."

"How about you watch me from the doorway?"

"Well ... I suppose." He rubbed his lower back. "Arthritis don't trouble the eyes and ears."

As she made her way to her car, she thought about Ralph's incessant need to marry her off. She'd spent the better part of her Sunday in her studio as she often did. She was content alone, but . . . A clank made her nerves jump. Her knees locked. She clutched the portfolio to her chest, scanned the parking lot.

"Is someone there?" She rifled through her pockets for her keys. She should have had them in hand before she left the building. But the reporter, his insinuations, and Ralph's lecture had knocked her off course.

A figure stepped into the faint light of a nearby lamppost, and her anxiety meter, already bobbing in the red zone, spiked.

When he stepped closer, anger supplanted her fear. "You scared me to death."

"Sorry, I didn't mean to."

She composed herself while her stress gauge dialed back to orange and then yellow.

"We combed every inch of this place," Finn said. "But I can't help but think there's something we missed."

"No progress?"

He shook his head. "You okay? Working in there?"

"Why wouldn't I be?"

"Until we wrap this up, I think you should—"

"Ralph was there."

Finn rolled his lips inward before they eased into a grin. "Ralph?"

"Under that wrinkled, shuffling exterior he's a ninja warrior."

"If you say so." He watched as she settled into the driver's seat, door ajar, one foot out. "I do have a question for you." His hesitation burned a hole in her last ounce of patience. "We found some shoes in the garbage. Clogs. With blood on them."

"They were mine."

"Why'd you throw them out?"

She stared at him, dumbfounded.

"Listen, Bianca, I get that it was traumatic, the way she died on you. But it's also a crime scene, and if we're going to solve this thing, we need every bit of physical evidence we can get our hands on. Even the clothes and shoes you were wearing that night."

"First of all, you *don't* get it. Come back when it's happened to you, and we'll talk. Second of all, nobody ever asked for my clothes."

"I'm asking now."

"You'll need to chase down the garbage truck then."

"You shouldn't throw away anything from a crime scene."

"I'll remember that the next time I find someone bleeding to death," she snapped. "Am I under arrest?"

"Of course not."

"Then this discussion is over." She tucked herself in and yanked the car door shut, barely missing his leg.

As she pulled away, she glanced at him in the rearview mirror. So much of this reminded her of the night she'd found Lisette. Repeating like Escher's birds that morphed into fish, or better yet, his staircases that conjured an endless bewildered wandering. Bianca massaged her forehead while she flipped through radio stations in search of a distraction.

How dare Finn treat her like a common criminal? She was an innocent bystander, caught in a murderer's web. She knew all about the callous treatment of victims and families. Suddenly she was nine again, stunned by an officer's impassive face and flat tone as he practically tossed her mother's mud-encrusted pearls to her father. "From the scene." Bianca's world had careened from its axis as she watched her father hurl the necklace against the wall and the pearls clatter onto the floor.

Enter Gemma. Bianca's waif of a maternal grandma with a spine of steel. Before Bianca could cry, her face was in Gemma's hands, and Gemma planted a kiss on each cheek. They crawled across the floor together and collected each pearl, placing them in a cranberry-colored candy dish. Gemma went straight to work, restringing them, tying the clasp back into place. She put them around Bianca's neck, gave them a pat, and held her until she fell asleep. The string of pearls wasn't the only thing Gemma fixed that night. As Bianca rested in Gemma's lap, she absorbed her strength, banking it for future use.

She drew on that strength now as she fingered the L necklace in her pocket. Maybe there was something in all of this she could put right. Lisette must have bent over while dusting the base of the cabinet, and the chain fell off without her realizing it. Did the necklace have a special meaning?

She'd do better by Lisette. She'd return this necklace with compassion.

And Finn. He should have stayed in Pittsburgh if he was going to become a carbon copy of Carmichael. That's exactly why she hadn't told him about the necklace. They'd barge in like robots, not giving a damn about what Lisette's belongings meant to her family.

Satisfied she'd made the right decision, she focused on the dips and sways of a saxophone solo.

As her galloping heart calmed to a trot, her mind wandered to Dylan. They'd been happy until the accident two years ago, the accident that unraveled his life along with her hopes. After that, no matter what she said or did, he couldn't tie the fragments together again. While they were together, she'd learned his two basic modes, relaxed and intense. Lately he was the latter, a flame working its way along a wick toward a bundle of dynamite.

She hadn't seen that dichotomy in Finn ... He seemed less complicated somehow. And he'd come back to take care of his dying father, hadn't he?

Thoughts of Mack brought on a twinge of grief. His sons had no choice but to watch his slow demise. Would they take the opportunity to soak up every second with him, appreciate the chance to say goodbye? A chance she never had. Neither option seemed fair.

She cranked up the music and wound through the maze of streets until she turned onto Waterton.

Light filtered through her neighbor's slatted blinds, making Bianca wonder what Helen was up to tonight. No doubt she was busy aligning someone's auras. Or do you align chakras? The thought teased a smile. Helen was unlike any seventy-nine-year-old

Bianca had ever met, clad in skinny jeans and nails painted to match the seasons—burgundy in winter, tangerine in summer.

Weariness claimed Bianca as she pulled into her own carport. Her nightly routine was calling, and once inside, she beelined for the kitchen. Frozen grapes, two or three savored. Gemma's specialty. Her grandma would plop the grapes into a fluted champagne glass of white grape juice for Bianca—a whole new level of kiddy cocktail—as she sipped her own Chablis. Tonight Bianca would chase the grapes with a glass of wine, Chantal Chamberland's toasty ballads on her iPod, and then bed.

She popped open the freezer door and felt a germ of confusion, which quickly grew to dread.

A paintbrush?

The handle was frosty to the touch. She ran a thumb over it to reveal something written with a Sharpie. She tried to cast it across the room, but her fingers froze around it.

One by one, she pried them away, and the paintbrush toppled to her feet. She kicked it, watched it skitter and scrape along the kitchen tile as she swung her purse off her shoulder and ransacked it. Items rained to the floor. She plucked Finn's card with his number from the mélange.

Before he could speak she blurted, "He came to my house."

∽ SIX ∾

FINN flipped a U-turn, headed for Bianca's. "Where are you?"

An excruciating moment passed before she answered. "Helen's. Next door. The yellow house."

"Stay put. I'll meet you there." He radioed for back-up. Pressing the accelerator, he settled his hand on his gun. He'd only used it for target practice and would be happy to keep it that way.

He whipped into Bianca's driveway, and before he could bolt from the car, a Crown Vic pulled up behind him.

Tucker jumped out, drew his gun. "I'll take the back. You take the front."

Easing his service weapon from its holster, Finn sucked in a breath as a cloud of doubt settled around him. He nudged the front door open with his boot. Gun at low ready, he slipped inside and moved toward the kitchen, looking left, then right. The refrigerator hummed. Floorboards creaked.

After disengaging the deadbolt, he swung open the back door. Tucker flashed the "all clear" sign and stepped into the kitchen. Finn motioned for him to follow. In the bedroom, he flicked on the light and the bedside lamp cast an eerie glow on the back wall. The antique clock on the nightstand droned. *Tick tick tick.*

On to the bathroom. He stepped over a green razor, blade side up on the bathmat, and flung back the shower curtain. Empty. He opened a linen closet. Towels, sheets, toilet paper rolls, crammed into every possible nook.

A thud drew him back to the bedroom. The curtain rustled.

54

Finn motioned to the window, locked his stance, and drew down. Tucker yanked back the curtain.

A ball of orange fur flew from the sill and tunneled under the bed with a hiss.

"Shit!" Finn dropped his gun to his side.

"So much for being quiet," Tucker said.

"Should have known it would be the damn cat." Finn ran his hand along the window frame. Unlocked, but no sign of forced entry. After securing the window, he checked the walk-in closet. Was he still in the same house? Shoes lined up in cubbies, handbags hung from a pegboard, clothing actually on hangers. A curious sign posted above Bianca's purse collection proclaimed, "Fool me once shame on you. Fool me twice shame on me." The phrase, "Never again" scrawled across the bottom of the quote in red marker.

A clamor redirected them to the kitchen where they found the feline terror mincing through the soil from a knocked-over planter. Dirt wasn't good for cats, was it? Finn righted the plant, pushed it into a corner.

He moved to a tall, pantry-style cupboard, the one he'd wanted Bianca to hide in the night of the murder, and recalled her obstinate refusal. Now he noticed spices and canned goods lining the shelves, organized. The rest of the kitchen was a virtual disaster area with stacked dishes waiting for transport to cabinets above. Cereal boxes. A jar of brush cleaner sitting perilously close to a bowl of fruit. Yet the insides of this pantry spoke of an alternate world.

Tucker peered over Finn's shoulder, took off his hat, scratched his head.

"What do you make of it?" Finn asked.

Tucker looked around the kitchen then back to the tribute to Martha Stewart. "Damnedest thing I ever did see."

So much about Bianca was a mystery.

"Let's do a quick run outside before we head next door," Finn suggested.

Tucker forged ahead, still on high alert as he moved across the back lawn, and it struck Finn how graceful he looked in motion, lighter and leaner than his bulky frame. "You take the carport. I'll take the shed." Finn indicated one direction and then the other.

The door of the small shed was ajar. He eased it open, imagining the place lousy with spiders. He hated spiders. As he inched forward, a branch snapped behind him. He spun around, gun raised, to find Tucker.

"Man!" Finn shoved his piece back in its holster.

"Nothing suspicious. Is she sure someone was here?"

The panic in Bianca's voice came back to Finn. "Sure as hell sounded like it. Mind locking up while I head to the neighbor's?"

"Have at it, little bud. Be there in a sec."

Bianca met him on the porch. A tinsel-haired woman sporting cheetah-print reading glasses stood beside her.

"You okay?" Finn asked.

Bianca nodded, and he followed them inside. Her neighbor thrust out her hand. "I'm Helen."

The firm grip surprised him. "Officer Tierny."

Bianca presented a thick-handled paintbrush. He examined it, tested the weight of it. *This* was the evidence? "Helen, do you have a plastic bag? One that seals?"

She left for the kitchen.

Finn forced his attention back to the paintbrush. Two letters were written on the wooden handle—V R? He turned it over. N E X T.

V R NEXT?

Finn cast a questioning look at Bianca before he realized it wasn't a V but a U.

U R NEXT.

Bianca squared her shoulders, but the distress on her face was unmistakable.

Helen returned with a Ziploc bag. "There might still be a few crumbs. I took my Shredded Wheat out and put it in a Tupperware container, but if you ask me, it stays fresher in the baggie."

"Thank you, Helen." Finn hesitated. He'd have to transfer the evidence to an official bag before bringing it in. He could hear Carmichael now. *Sloppy police work, Tierny.*

He wrapped the bag around the brush. "Where'd you find this?" he asked Bianca.

"In my freezer."

Freezer? Lipstick scrawled across her mirror, a note patched together with letters cut from magazines, or wall graffiti. Those would make sense. But a message on a paintbrush?

"I got home from school and was getting some grapes," Bianca continued, "and there it was."

"Frozen grapes?"

"Maybe I shouldn't have touched the paintbrush but—"

"I'm still on frozen grapes."

She sighed. "Call it a guilty pleasure."

Finn's imagination exploded from the starting block like Usain Bolt. *Focus, Tierny.*

"We both touched that brush," Helen broke in. "And why the freezer? Makes no sense."

"Makes sense to whoever did this. We won't get prints anyway, they likely wore gloves. Is it yours?"

"See the purple stripe?" Bianca said. "I always mark my brushes."

A sturdy knock and a friendly face peeking in the small rectangular side window prompted Helen to open the door. Tucker tipped his head in greeting.

Finn handed him the brush. "She found this in her freezer."

Tucker's mouth pulled to the side as he read the letters.

"Turn it over," Finn said.

"Whoa. Any idea who would have done this?"

"Someone who has a Sharpie?" Bianca said.

She had to be scared out of her mind, yet here she was, trying to make light of the situation. A desire to pull her close overwhelmed Finn, threatening to suck him into that dangerous current and sweep him downstream.

Tucker put the brush in his shirt pocket.

"I can take it in," Finn offered.

Clamping his hand over the evidence, Tucker said, "I've got this," superiority creeping into his tone.

Tucker pulling rank? That was a first. A virtual ping-pong ball, Finn bounced back to Helen. "Did you see anyone strange in the neighborhood this evening?"

At first she dipped her head from side to side, equivocating, but then she raised her chin. "I usually keep an eye out, but I had company."

"Company?" Tucker asked.

Her chin rose a notch. "If you must know, I had a hook-up."

Finn and Tucker exchanged a look. *Go Helen.*

Finn took in the space. There was so much going on that he almost missed a sickeningly sweet smell that seemed to be masking something else. A hook-up . . . and a hookah? It was hard not to crack a smile at the atypical elderly lady décor. A large lamp featuring a naked woman in a seductive pose. Tarot cards fanned across the coffee table next to an oversized book entitled, *Kama Sutra for Life*. An enormous rug, woven with sparkling threads and gold fringe, hung above the couch and screamed for attention.

Helen followed his gaze. "You like my magic carpet?"

"It's . . . interesting," Finn said.

"It's a kilim," Helen said. "Derived from the Persian word gelim, which means to spread roughly. But look, it's actually quite soft. Go ahead, touch it."

"That won't be necessary."

Tucker jammed a knee into the couch, ran a hand over the rug. "Sweet."

Helen clapped her hands together and held them tight against her chest, pleased.

"We're getting off track here." Finn turned to Tucker. "Mind if I get Bianca secured at her house?"

Tucker arched an eyebrow. "Yeah . . . okay."

There was no objection from Bianca. A rare compliant moment.

"How 'bout you give Carmichael a heads-up," Tucker said, "then let's meet at the station later."

After thanking Helen, Finn escorted Bianca to her porch. "Any idea where the paintbrush was before the freezer?"

"I was painting patio furniture, in the back."

"Show me." They slipped around the house and walked the yard's perimeter. Under different circumstances, this could have been a pleasant stroll under a cloud-mottled sky, stubborn stars pushing through. It felt so right, and yet . . .

"I used it here." Bianca pointed to a paisley-painted Adirondack. "Before I brought it in to clean it."

Finn secured the shed and surveyed the patio. A planting table scattered with terracotta pots pressed against the house. A few lay smashed on the ground near the door. "What happened here?"

"I suspect the raccoons living in that tree."

"When?"

"When what?"

Finn let out an exasperated sigh. "When did this happen?"

"Friday. The night of the murder. I heard something and found them smashed."

"Why didn't you tell me?"

"I'm supposed to report raccoons?"

Finn scanned the array of empty pots. "Why do you have so many?"

"I use them to collect rainwater."

A stash of frozen grapes and pots of rainwater. Something about the determined set of her jaw made Finn want to smile, and he worked to keep the corners of his mouth under control.

She threw him an irritated look. "It's important."

"No, no. I can see that."

As if on cue, the sky opened and rain began to fall hard and heavy. A flash of lightning illuminated Bianca's face so that the rain spilling down her cheeks resembled tears. Finn reached for her, but she hurried inside.

And what if she hadn't?

In the kitchen, she swiped droplets from her face with a towel. Picasso wound around her with his motor idling until she picked him up.

"Did you leave your bedroom window open?" Finn asked.

"That's how he goes in and out." She stroked the culprit and buried her face in his fur.

A burst of frustration. "Ever hear of a doggie door?"

"I close and lock the window when I go to bed."

"Bianca, that's not good enough. Someone is probably watching you, learning your habits. They know about the open window. Know about your trips to the freezer. What if you'd walked in on them?"

"I—"

"You'd have more than an embellished paintbrush."

She glared at him.

"And leaving your window wide—"

"I get it!"

Finally. "I hope so."

Finn dialed Carmichael, who answered on the second ring. "Chief, it's Finn."

"I have caller ID. You may have heard of it."

Carmichael's sarcasm pounded like a gong. "I'm with Bianca James. She found a suspicious item in her house."

"And what would this *suspicious* item be?"

Translation: get to the point.

"A paintbrush with U R NEXT written on the handle. Tucker's bringing it to the station."

A long expelled breath that felt like a rebuke. "I'll check it tomorrow." *Click.*

Tomorrow. The swift hand of justice at its best.

This case was an inconvenience to Carmichael. A murderer in the Peak, and he acted like they were looking for a jaywalker. He'd barely moved to check out Lisette Divac's old boyfriend, Rusty Gallagher. Turned out the guy had an alibi. He'd been holed up in County on drug charges since September.

Bianca was on the couch, one hand clasping the back of her neck. She had cleared the place next to her, and Finn eased into it.

"Who wants to scare me like this? Who wants to *kill* me?" She searched Finn's face. His gut ached, unable to give her an answer. "It's possible whoever did this came in the window, but who has keys to your house? Besides Dylan?"

"Helen, but no one else."

An unmistakable reconsidering on her part.

"A student used them once, the beginning of the semester," she said after a moment. "I forgot my portfolio at home, and he offered to run and get it for me—"

"Who?"

"Only the nicest kid on the planet."

"The nicest kid on the planet's name?"

Her lips pursed in exasperation. "Connor Branson, but I promise you, he had nothing to do with this."

"Could he have made a copy?" Finn asked.

She sighed. "Anything's possible, but again, he's a good kid."

She was probably right; the kid was surely harmless, just a willing student eager to please his beautiful teacher. "Doesn't hurt to check him out."

She winced and reached for her neck again.

Finn scooted to the edge of the couch, keenly aware that he was rocking the boat of some unwritten code that keeps men's hands off brothers' ex-girlfriends. "I used to know . . . well, there's this thing my mom did when I got a cramp in my neck."

"Really?"

"Would you like me to . . ." He motioned with his finger for her to turn.

Bianca posed her back to him and flopped her head forward. Finn swept her hair to the side until it streamed down the front of one shoulder. He rested the fingertips of both hands gingerly at the base of her neck as if locating middle C on a piano keyboard. At the center of her neck, he rubbed in small, circular motions all the way to her shoulders, increased pressure, kneading, making wider circles, and then worked back to his starting place.

"You're very tight," he whispered, but in his mind, he was thinking of a million better ways to describe Bianca James.

She relaxed under his touch, and Finn paced his breathing, bridled and held it steady, as he massaged her neck. Then he stopped. Sinking back into the couch, he clamped his arms against his chest.

Bianca threw a confused look over her shoulder. Swiveling, she gathered her hair and let it tumble down her back again. She curled up on the end of the couch, her eyes at half-mast. She looked completely spent. "Don't you have to get back?"

"I can stay for a while. Ford will bang me soon."

Bianca's eyebrows furrowed.

"Cop talk for 'dispatch will radio me.'"

"Oh."

"Why don't you go to bed?" Finn suggested, rising to his feet.

He crossed the room to pull the drapes and lock the front door. A lot of good that would do if extra keys were floating around. He'd install new locksets. The sooner the better.

An exaggerated yawn from Bianca and a losing battle with heavy eyelids.

Finn settled back onto the couch, and Bianca stretched her legs, her feet landing in his lap. He slowly wrapped his fingers around her toes and shook her foot. "It's late. Go to bed."

She didn't respond, but her breathing, the steady rhythms of her body, told him she was already asleep. Finn studied her face in peaceful repose, her hair decorating the couch pillow. His eyes roamed the length of her body, noting her tiny waist, her perfect hips. He tightened his grip on her foot to keep his hand from wandering the length of her leg and over those luscious curves.

You're supposed to protect her, not fall for her.

He let himself fantasize, if only for a second, a glimmer of that forbidden free-fall lighting his mind.

He'd do anything to protect her.

Gently moving her feet from his lap, he fought the temptation to lift her up and carry her into the bedroom. Instead, he checked every door and window, scribbled on a sticky note, and grabbed her keys. After one last look, one last visual stroll across her gorgeous face, he forced himself to leave, locking the door behind him.

In the squad car, he booted up his laptop and searched Rusty Gallagher, Lisette's ex. Three-time loser. Three stints at County. Finn scrolled through a list of Rusty's crew and settled on one that made his rap sheet look like a priest's resume. Taz Blazek. A badass name for a badass wannabe. He sat back, searched his memory. Taz Blazek. Legit badass. Taz Blazek, aka Tasmanian Blaze, walked on a murder charge when some prosecutor, who didn't know legal briefs from boxer briefs, botched the case. Blazek was known to toy with his victims. And anyone was fair game.

Finn glanced back at the bungalow.

Anyone.

⚹ SEVEN ⚹

SOMETHING grazed Bianca's cheek. She bolted upright. "Picasso," she whispered as if someone other than the cat could hear her at 5:00 a.m. "It's too early for breakfast."

He kneaded the pillow for a moment, curled into a ball, and stared at her with one sleepy eye. While she ran her hand over his silky coat, she battled oncoming thoughts: a scene she couldn't unsee, one that came back with crisp definition every time she tried to discard it.

She threw her legs over the side of the bed and stretched, wiggling her toes, nearly knocking over the statue sitting on her bedside table. A girl perched on a toadstool, legs tucked protectively under her. After finding Finn's note last night, she'd looked around for something, anything. Silly to assume the statue would keep her safe. Squat and unwieldy, certainly not Maris' .22. But she'd finally been able to relax with it close by.

Yawning, she moved to the window, started to open it for Picasso, but checked the lock instead, consumed by the feeling that the painting that was once her life had been redone by Dali himself. All that was missing was the melting clocks.

She padded into the kitchen, the tile floor pricking her feet. Despite the chill, she loved the sensation against her bare skin. But every muscle in her body was woven into a tight Celtic knot. She put the kettle on the stove and massaged the back of her neck. Finn's hands had been there, his transforming touch, his stroke both tender and firm. It was impossible to extinguish the memory of his skilled fingers.

Maris. When things had gone wrong with Dylan, it was Maris' voice in her ear, reminding her that she needed to strip away emotion and see the situation for what it was—unfixable.

But it was still too early, even for her early-bird friend, so she looked around for something to do. A stack of mail, thick as a dictionary, cluttered the kitchen counter. She flipped through it, keeping two bills and recycling the rest. After adjusting the sugar bowl lid and returning a jar of honey to the pantry, she scrolled through emails on her phone. Mostly junk, but several from her students, answering the one she had sent about the necklace. She'd kept her message vague. "See me if you've lost something of value." Responses ranged from "Not me" to "I lost a winning lottery ticket."

She opened the refrigerator and sorted through condiments, checking expiration dates, tossing old containers into the recycling bin. A jagged smell drifted out when she opened the crisper. She slammed it shut and closed the refrigerator with a *pop*.

Only one thing brought her peace when she was this out of sorts.

She needed to create. She needed to reclaim her life. A life where she wasn't constantly looking over her shoulder.

Art had always been her escape, a ticket to another world where she was in control. Even as a child, when things seemed arbitrary and distorted, she'd stuffed crayons into her pockets, retreated to her bedroom, and scribbled her way through her problems.

This morning, she'd work on her Wildlife Conservatory entry. The contest generated money for the Wildlife Refuge System, one of her mom's greatest passions. It had been Bianca's father's dream—to paint something for the competition and win. Not for the recognition, but for the love of his life. He'd started a painting the year her mom died. Bianca and Gemma kept encouraging him to finish, but he never did.

There were many species to choose from, but her dad always had a soft spot for ducks. He'd painted mallards, wood ducks, gadwalls, cinnamon teals, and blue-winged teals. Her dad's cinnamon teal had been one of her favorites. The duck, deftly painted, sat on the shore under an umbrella of switchgrass. She'd chosen a similar scene, but included a second duck, a male nestled close to the female. But like her dad, she hadn't finished one yet. A bin under her bed was an overflowing reminder of attempts that fell short, that never made it to the judging.

Teacup in one hand, box of granola under her arm, she went into the narrow room off the kitchen. Dylan had installed picture windows on both exterior walls along with two skylights their first Christmas together. She loved the way bright glints of sunshine usually danced through the space, highlighting the paint-splattered floor, emphasizing the endless pigments that had escaped becoming part of her work.

But now the room was masked in shadow, as if the sun had been relegated to a far corner of the universe.

Bianca selected a paintbrush, squirted warm red oxide and naples yellow on her palette, and played with the color until she achieved the desired hue. She worked on the male duck's wing, dabbing here and there, trying to show a slight wind ruffling the feathers.

This wasn't going to work.

She jammed the paintbrush into a jar filled with brush cleaner.

On her way to the bedroom, she plucked Finn's sticky note off the hall table along with a couple of brassy keys. "You have new locks. Talk later—F." There was something intimate about the way he'd signed with only an initial and the way he'd changed the locks while she slept. She pictured him now, the determined set of his jaw, the caring in his eyes. His mismatched eyes. But obsessing like this was crazy. There wasn't anything between them. There *couldn't* be anything between them.

After sticking the note on the door frame, she sifted through clothes piled on a chair. She pulled on jeans and a white turtleneck, added a down vest and scarf, and flew out the door.

The sky loomed a dolphin-gray, dipping toward gun-metal. The season's first snow was imminent, threatening to snuff out the last colors of fall.

She wanted to freeze-frame the calendar, capture the rusts and auburns before they vanished. A car at the curb snagged her attention. Finn. Lounging against the headrest. She studied him for a moment. His strong, straight nose. Full lips. The early morning prelude to a beard stippling his jaw.

He was a work of art.

But she didn't dare test Tierny waters again; she'd nearly drowned in the undertow the last time. Bianca bit her lower lip. Besides, she didn't know Finn at all. What she did know was that he and Dylan were braided together by history and their father's intractable love.

The internal tug of war continued as she moved toward the car and rapped on the window.

Finn startled. He shook his head, and forced his eyes wide, rolled down the window, yawned and spoke at the same time. "You okay?"

"Why are you here?"

He stared at her as if she'd spoken gibberish.

"I don't need a babysitter." *Too snarky*, Bianca self-edited. He was only trying to help. "Thanks for changing the locks. Do you always carry around new locksets?"

"My buddy's the night manager down at Miller's. So anytime you have a middle-of-the-night hardware need . . ."

That damn smile again.

"Well, I appreciate it. I really do, but aren't you working today?"

"It's my day off. All I have to do today is shower and shave. And actually, I don't even have to do that."

Finn, water beading on burnished skin. *Come on in, the water's fine.* She sighed the vision away. "Go home and get some rest. Don't you ever sleep?"

His face twisted. Was he angry? Frustrated? He leaned out the open window as if he intended to yank her into the car. "Bianca, I—"

"I'm all right," she said. "I can't let this . . . this thing take over, and you shouldn't either."

Bianca pulled up to a white antebellum on a manicured corner lot. On the heels of Maris' divorce, she moved in with the elderly owner who'd been diagnosed with congestive heart failure, caring for her as a daughter would—shuttling her to appointments, helping her in and out of bed, and putting pillows under her legs to keep them elevated. Ida Hampton balked at her assistance, threatened to evict her if she didn't "stop this nonsense," but Maris kept on.

When Ida willed her the old place, Maris had been shocked but also relieved, since her ex had left her languishing in a pile of credit card debt.

Now, Bianca used the keypad—punching in Ida's birthday— and slipped in the back door. The décor always brought a smile. Her friend preferred clean lines, silver fixtures, and black leather to heavy velvet drapes and elaborate scrollwork, but hadn't changed a thing since Ida passed away.

Soon Maris entered the kitchen with her hair sectioned off and tied up in rows of rags. "Don't say it," she said, her voice lacquered with sleep. "I've no intention of going out like this and scaring small children."

"You haven't worn your hair curly in ages. Angling for a promotion?"

"I'd take one, but no, Charity and I have a breakfast meeting."

Charity. The name put Bianca in a dental chair, sans Novocain, drill bearing down.

"So the extra effort is for Charity or her lawyer brother?"

"You know there have only been a handful of guys I've *really* liked since Fernando and I split, and I *really* like Brett, so if Charity wants to talk me up, I won't stop her. Last time I wore my hair super curly she fawned over me like I was a Redken model."

"At least you're honest."

"To a fault. And I can honestly tell you that even for me this is wicked early." Maris popped a pod in the coffee maker. "I'm all out of tea. Would be so much easier if you drank coffee like the rest of the human race."

Bianca fell into a chair at the kitchen table and toyed with a vine-covered placemat while she thought about where to begin. So much had happened, and she didn't want her account to spew out in a jumbled mess. Maris would want to know every single detail, but Bianca couldn't disclose everything. She'd hold back one thing.

Logical Maris would try to talk her out of taking the necklace to Lisette's family. Bianca wanted—needed—to return it. "Still don't get why you keep these placemats."

Maris grabbed her mug and sat across from her. "You didn't come here to talk about my table décor. Spill it, girl."

A drumbeat pulsed from deep inside as Bianca shared the events of last night—the paintbrush, Finn and Tucker searching the house, the unnamed presence lingering as she tried to sleep.

Anger and fear mingled in Maris' dark eyes. "Someone was actually in your house?"

"It's surreal. I've been getting these strange calls, too." Bianca hesitated. Maris was a math professor at Brookefield and didn't believe in anything she couldn't see, touch, hear, or calculate. "I just have this overall bad feeling."

Maris arched her eyebrows.

"I know," Bianca said. "But there is such a thing as a sixth sense."

"And Haley Joel Osment still sees dead people."

How could she respond? Her friend no doubt had a list of comebacks as long as her brocaded floor-to-ceiling drapes.

Maris lifted her coffee, stopped short of drinking it. "What about Dylan—"

"What about him?"

"Maybe he's trying to scare you so he can come swooping in, you know, to rescue you? Or maybe he's just trying to get back at you. He's not the most stable—"

Bianca raised her hand. "Stop. You don't like Dylan, and maybe he earned that, but what you're suggesting is too much."

Maris left the table and put her mug in the sink with a clatter. "I don't like what he did to you. Please don't forget the long nights wondering if he was okay, the distracted days when you couldn't focus on teaching or your art—the things you love more than anything—because you were worried about him."

"It can't be Dylan." She refused to believe, even in the state he'd been in, he'd stoop so low.

Maris clamped a hand on Bianca's forearm. "I'll keep the tennis racquet handy just in case." It was so like her to use humor to temper her anger. "Let's shift from the who to the why. A woman was murdered at Brookefield, and you get a message saying you're next. What's the connection?"

The doorbell rang before Bianca could respond. It wasn't like she had a good response anyway.

Maris looked at the clock. "Damn. I need to hustle. I'm supposed to meet Charity at nine, and I have to swing by the office to pick up some files. Mind grabbing that while I run to get dressed?" She shot halfway up the steps, raced back down, and hugged Bianca. "I'm not brushing this off. We'll figure it out."

"You're right. Now go." Bianca gave her a gentle shove. "Get yourself gorgeous for your meeting."

"You'd be going with me if you hadn't refused the invitation."

Refused. More like got pushed out by . . .

Charity Beacham.

Bianca opened the door to a life-sized, red-headed Barbie doll clutching a briefcase to her chest as if guarding it from a purse-snatcher. She rolled her permanently lined eyes over Bianca and turned up her already upturned nose. "You're here?" The question as icy as the air wafting in.

"Good morning, Charity."

"Where's Maris?" she asked, brushing past Bianca and filling the house with the thick scent of gardenia.

"Getting dressed. For your meeting. At nine."

Despite the almost fifteen-year age difference, the three had been friends once. Charity, the self-appointed queen of Riley's Peak, made it a habit to snatch up unsuspecting young women as they moved into her kingdom, befriending them, and making a show of helping them "acclimate." But it didn't take long for Bianca to see Charity for who she was, a mink-cloaked vampire bent on feeding off their youth.

When Bianca distanced herself, Charity tried to reel her back in with the Cassatt she'd bought at auction and the Renoir that had been in her family for generations. Paintings Bianca would never in her wildest dreams be able to afford. Though curious, Bianca had a low threshold for arrogance and avoided Charity's invitations to drool over her acquisitions.

But Charity's self-importance was, well, important to her, so she found a way to bring the art to Bianca. Last April she'd made the magnanimous gesture of donating her latest purchase to the Weaver Fine Arts Center. A gaudy display case was constructed for the Miró sculpture. Alleged Miró sculpture. Because Bianca knew after one glance, it wasn't a Miró. Charity insisted that a million dollars said otherwise, but Bianca encouraged her to have it evaluated. An appraisal revealed the truth. Bianca suggested they could still keep the sculpture on display in Weaver as long as they put "after Miró" on the plaque instead of "by Miró." Charity had whisked it away, leaving a bare display case behind. Their relationship took a final plunge when the school board president commissioned Bianca, right in front of Charity, to create "one of her stunning pieces" to fill it.

Now Charity lowered herself into a chair.

"Can I get you some coffee?" Bianca asked, taking the high road.

"I really don't have time for a social call." Each word clipped off like dead flowers. "I just need to speak to her privately before we meet with the rest of the team."

Charity's phone vibrated. "Yes, I know," she said after a quick exchange of greetings. "We were all set before this happened. The board is very distracted right now over this cleaning girl." She drummed her French tips on the arm of the chair impatiently. "It's not like the president of the university was murdered."

Fury heated Bianca's skin. As soon as the call ended, she blurted, "You're talking about a person with a family."

"Oh, Bianca. Don't get all tethered. I was merely making a point. Life moves on. Why should the students suffer?"

Bianca held her tongue. Nothing she could say would get through to a woman who clearly had no soul.

Charity checked her watch, rose, and clicked across the floor. Only Charity would wear stilettos before 9:00 a.m. "Almost ready, Maris?" she called up the stairway, her voice all sweetness and light.

"I'll go check." Bianca pushed past Charity, hurrying up the stairs, hatred trailing her like a shadow.

✤ EIGHT ✤

THE only thing that made working long hours bearable was time alone in his two-door sanctuary, his metallic-blue '69 GTO. Finn guided a key into the ignition, lounged against the headrest as the supercharged engine purred.

Four days since the murder and the Divac case hung in limbo. One bullet pulled from the victim and a second pried from the wall didn't reveal a thing. Lab rats' tinkering confirmed what they'd already suspected: the shooter used a .22. They might as well be searching for a specific stone in the Allegheny River ... blindfolded.

Forensics followed through in record time regarding the suspicious fiber from Lisette's sneaker. Part of a feather duster. The only other person in Weaver that night was a student, a music major, who had been closed off from the rest of the world in one of the sound-proof practice rooms upstairs. When he exited his studio of oblivion, he dropped his cello and nearly passed out at the swarm of activity. He'd been summarily questioned and dismissed.

Finn had spent yesterday learning about Lisette's baby daddy, Rusty Gallagher, digging into his known associates, a list of KAs longer than a stretch limo. Sources at his old precinct shared that Taz had been under tight surveillance for the past month. They had someone on the inside, an undercover who'd worked her way into

71

Taz's crew on her beauty-pageant looks and hard-ass demeanor. She'd verified his whereabouts the night of the murder. Finn rolled that over in his mind for a minute.

It was a relief to check a guy like Taz off the list, but that put them back at square one without a single lead.

They had a victim without a culprit, bullets with no murder weapon, and the mysterious paintbrush. An innocent woman gunned down, and there was nothing to tell her family.

At times, Finn doubted he was cut out for this. In the long line of Tierny cops, he felt like a dead end. If only his dad, or even his grandfather, had aspired to something else. Why couldn't they be bakers or truck drivers? But Tierny fingers weren't meant to knead dough or maneuver shift knobs on big rigs. Tierny fingers were meant to curl around grip frames and trigger guards.

And Bianca . . . He kept seeing her long hair unravel from its clip and tumble down her back in slow motion. Her scent lingered, one day flowery, citrusy the next. Lemon? Orange? As long as he'd known her, he'd fought feelings, didn't allow himself to stroll down that path, to even think about her. But now, if he was honest with himself, he realized he'd never wanted anything, or anyone, more. He needed to see her, to protect her. His college professor. His brother's ex-girlfriend. His crush. He told himself it was nothing more than infatuation.

A lie.

Yesterday, when she'd found him parked outside her house, she was obviously annoyed. But she never looked better. Bianca James smoldered.

Of course there was that one little detail—Dylan was still in love with her.

Finn swiped some dust from the corner of the instrument panel with a rag. Months and months of searching and waiting for mint condition parts had paid off. In a moment, he'd check under the hood, maybe re-gap the spark plugs, and change the air filter. He'd push thoughts of Bianca and the murder away and float on the gentle sounds of his most prized possession.

As a boy, he'd first glimpsed a GTO at a swap meet they'd happened upon while driving to the cabin. Tracing the cold steel letters on the front grill, he'd announced, "I'm going to have my own Geeto someday." His parents and Dylan laughed. Mack told him it was called a GTO, but Geeto stuck.

When he was a junior in high school, he'd bought the classic convertible, a heap of junk, but he only saw potential, her underlying beauty. Art in need of a gallery.

He and Mack had spent hours in the garage, cutting out and sanding down the rusted frame, welding new sheet metal into place, polishing and painting until the GTO dazzled. As good as the day it rolled off the production line, maybe better. Dylan even pitched in, and it seemed to help mend their fractured family, fill a void.

He wished he could backtrack, if only for a day, to experience the same connection to his dad and brother.

A subtle misfire in the engine.

"You need an adjustment, Geeto." He popped the hood and fiddled with the six-pack carburetor. What would it take to understand Bianca the way he understood this car?

Once he had the engine humming again, he checked the sky. A thick dampness hung in the air, but he couldn't resist taking one last spin before throwing on the cover and retiring her for the winter.

He eased out of the garage and wended his way through the neighborhood. As tires met a decent stretch of asphalt, he punched the gas and opened her up. His heart thrummed with the engine's low growl. The smell of another time, a different era, seeped from the upholstery and mingled with the crisp morning air.

As much as he wanted to joyride through his day off, all roads funneled to the same place. He pulled into his usual spot at the station, and stuffed his keys into his jeans.

Carmichael stood just outside the station door cradling something furry and black. At first glance, the dog looked like a large stuffed animal against his double-breasted suit. A woman stood beside the chief, her face shiny with tears. Finn slowed his pace and kept a respectful distance.

"Such an old fool," the woman said, "I thought this was the vet's office."

"It was, many years ago," Carmichael replied. He smoothed a

hand over the dog's head and down his back. "When Doc Fisher retired, we bought this building."

The woman swiped at her tears with the backs of her wrists. "Is it the right thing to do?"

Carmichael cupped her shoulder.

She raised a shaky, age-spotted hand in slow motion and stroked the dog's graying muzzle. "He can't hardly walk, and when he does, he's so blind he bumps into the furniture. I can't stand to see him in pain." She broke down.

"It's the humane thing. Let me help you get him settled back in your car." Carmichael cast a glance at Finn. "Tierny, get the door."

Finn opened it, and Carmichael tenderly laid the dog across the backseat. "Just take a left at Chalmers, and Doc Lawton's office is right there on the corner."

"Thank you, Chief Carmichael. You've been a world of help to me today."

When she was out of sight, the chief turned to Finn and motioned to the GTO. "I'll never understand what you Tiernys find so fascinating about those old heaps."

Carmichael slipped inside before Finn could respond and breezed past the reception area.

"Hey, Ford," Finn said. "Is Baranski here?"

"Isn't it your day off?" Ford said, barely glancing up. "Tiernys are sure gluttons in the punishment department, huh?" He hurled a playing card in the direction of the recycling bin. It bounced off the rim and joined a smattering of others on the floor. He slowly collected his lanky frame and bent to pick up one card, and then another. "No offense, man. I mean it like a compliment. Tiernys give two hundred percent, nose to the grindstone and all that."

Finn's gut clenched. The dead end thing, the fact that he might be the first Tierny who wasn't a natural-born cop, nagged again. The last thing he needed was a reminder about the shoes he was trying to fill right now. The shoes he'd been trying to fill his whole life. Dylan had screwed it all up, but he certainly had the instincts, and everyone knew it. "Not a problem, I get it."

"Baranski's back there somewhere." Ford sent another card flying with the same result.

Finn motioned to the deck of cards.

Ford handed one over, and Finn flicked it, landing it squarely in the bin.

"Pays to be Irish. All that luck."

If you only knew.

Tucker and Dylan had been best friends since high school. On rare occasions, they let Finn tag along, just to have someone to jerk around. To the swimming hole, the movies, and Lesher's Field where they shot rusted-out pop cans off a tree stump with BB guns. Finn was eleven and Dylan sixteen. He worshipped his brother, and Dylan tolerated it, but once Dylan started driving, Finn's shadowing days were over.

"Working hard, I see," Finn said, leaning over Tucker's desk.

He startled, and sauce from his meatball hoagie dripped onto his shirt. "There goes my shot at officer of the year." He took a wadded napkin and mopped up the mess.

Something about the way he was put together today, crumpled uniform shirt half tucked in, reminded Finn of an unmade bed.

"Why is it every time I see you, you're eating?" Finn reached for the tie Tucker had flung across his shoulder, and pressed it over the stain. "There. You're still in the running."

"Fun-nee. What the hell you doin' here?"

"Missed your smilin' face."

Tucker stopped mid-chew and forced a saucy grin.

"I could have waited until you were done."

Tucker shrugged, took another bite.

"Hey, I just witnessed something strange in the parking lot."

"The lady and her dog?"

"Yeah, and Carmichael, was . . . almost human."

"He's different with animals. A regular dog whisperer. Like with old Shep."

"Shep?"

"You know, his dog."

Finn shook his head.

Tucker looked around to make sure no one was listening. "Carmichael gets his manties all twisted when we talk about it, but when we first moved into this building, a stray was hangin' around

75

out back. A mutt, with some German shepherd in the mix. Carmichael said he'd make a fine police dog. Named him Shep."

"What's the big secret?"

"Let me finish?"

Finn made a be-my-guest gesture.

"Everybody loved the dog, then some meth-lab junkie waiting to be booked teased him, and Shep bit the guy's hand. Pretty good judge of character if you ask me. Anyway, Chief Jones, chief at the time, said the dog would have to be put down. Carmichael volunteered to take him to the vet, but took him home instead. He's had him ever since."

"Doesn't sound like the Carmichael I know."

"See, that's the thing, nobody *really* knows him. He's like one of them reptiles that keeps changing colors."

"A chameleon?"

"Yeah, that."

"Anyway, I didn't come to talk about hoagies or reptiles." Finn pointed to a folder on the corner of Tucker's desk. "Let me see those again."

Carmichael had shared the crime scene photos briefly with the team, but now Finn needed another look.

Tucker passed him the file.

The close-up of Lisette Divac's swollen face twisted Finn's stomach. The same clutching he'd felt in police training. Each dead body, a new adventure in nausea. He braced himself and spread out the rest of the crime scene and autopsy photos.

Tucker returned to his sandwich and continued to eat despite the grisly display. A dollop of sauce splattered onto his desk, and Finn slammed a hand on the pictures. "Careful, man, an inch more and Carmichael has something else to rag about."

Tucker sprawled across his desk, reached for a ruler, and measured the space between the sauce and the folder. "Yep, a freakin' inch, Rain Man."

Finn ground an elbow into Tucker's back—a rough-housing move that felt all wrong for how he was actually feeling—but he didn't want to let on how consumed he was by the case.

Another look at the autopsy photos that made him wince.

"Shoulda had a front row seat like I did," Tucker said.

An officer had to be present at the autopsy, and they didn't exactly fight over the assignment. Finn was surprised, and relieved, Carmichael hadn't drafted his favorite puppet for the show. "Please tell me you refrained from eating when you were with the ME."

As if in response, Tucker made a great show of taking the last bite of his sandwich, crumpled the tin foil, and lobbed it into the waste basket.

Back to the photos. Lisette wore her hair pinned up loosely. Despite her swollen features, she was an attractive woman. And the pictures confirmed what he'd been trying to repress since the night of the murder.

"What are the stats on the vic again? Specifically height and weight," Finn asked, rifling through the preliminary report.

Tucker maneuvered his chair forward, scanned a page, and planted a finger. "Five seven. Buck twenty. Why?"

"Just wondering." Finn studied Lisette as Tucker happily worked his way through a pile of greasy fries. "Might want to get those arteries checked out one of these days."

Finn marched to Carmichael's office and entered without knocking. The chief whirled around and leveled him with an icy glare. Shit! Finn stepped back and rapped his knuckles on the door.

Carmichael adjusted his demeanor. "Come in, Tierny. Have a seat. What's on your mind, son?"

The hairs on the back of Finn's neck stood on end every time Carmichael called him "son." Condescension dripped from the word. "I've been looking into the vic's boyfriend's KAs, finding squat."

The icy glare reared its ugly head again. "And who authorized this investigation?"

This wasn't the time to share his hunch about Lisette. Finn silently counted to three before he responded. "I think we need to move on this. Knock on a few more doors. Ask questions of some people who live off campus."

"Let me remind you, this isn't Pittsburgh, and I sure as hell don't intend to pull guys from Whistler and pay them overtime when the town budget is tighter than a hooker's leather skirt. I'll decide what measures need to be taken here." He zoned into a foggy open-eyed nap, before he went on. "I was about to call Baranski in, but since you're here, and so gung-ho . . . You know Ms. James personally, don't you?"

Carmichael was ambitious and unpredictable—a volcanic combination. Walk on eggshells—Tucker's warning. But this was more like walking barefoot on shattered glass in a window factory after an earthquake. And Finn was stomping hard. "I do."

"I've been thinking." Carmichael rocked back in his chair. "Let's bring her in. I have more questions."

"We already questioned her."

"Homicide 101, Tierny. Means, motive, opportunity. She had opportunity."

"But what about means? What's her motive?"

"Let. Me. Finish." The chief's venom-filled tone froze Finn in place. "She doesn't have an alibi. She had access. She was *there*. We need to do our job, uncover that motive and find that weapon."

"But she tried to save—"

"So she says. Which only made things worse for us. And ultimately worse for her."

"Meaning?"

"It's simple, Tierny: only two people know what went on in that room that night. One of them is dead; the other has blood on her hands."

"What about the paintbrush, the threat?"

Carmichael turned and selected a framed picture from the collection on his credenza; he pulled a handkerchief from his pocket and began shining the glass. The photo featured a sunburned Carmichael with his wife and two sons on the deck of a fishing boat. "I was walking a beat while you were still crawling around in your shitty diaper." He looked at Finn. "I've seen criminals try every trick in the book to divert attention. You'll learn, son."

The word probed Finn's sore spot again, a firecracker in his ear, an M-80 that prompted him to explore the elastic possibilities before him. Slam his badge on the desk. Tell this prick to go to hell and take his condescension with him. Walk away. But as he sat there, his blood seemed to thicken and slow with dread, maybe conviction. He was excruciatingly aware that he needed this job. Mack needed him here. Bianca. Who would keep Carmichael from lumping her in with criminals if Finn threw in the towel?

"Give her a call." The chief returned to the photograph. He placed it back on his credenza, and Finn's eyes stalled on the picture next to it, Carmichael with his dog, Shep.

For a nanosecond Finn considered arguing his point, but he knew Carmichael's finger was too close to the eject button, the one that would catapult him back to Pittsburgh, back to the shitstorm he'd barely escaped.

❧ NINE ❧

BIANCA walked with a determined gait to the squad car, leaves crunching underfoot, Finn trailing close behind. It had surprised her when he'd called to say Carmichael wanted her to come in. Surprised her even more when she heard herself accept a ride. She'd made arrangements to have her first two classes of the day covered, but hoped she'd be back in time to teach the second class herself.

In the distance, a plume of black smoke belched into the pale gray sky. Someone burning leaves, maybe garbage. She was tempted to suggest that the police department deal with the ones bent on burning a hole in the ozone instead of harassing law-abiding citizens, but she held her tongue. What good would it do?

Finn opened the passenger door. She slipped inside and yanked it shut, leaving him dumbfounded on the curb.

Why did she need to be questioned again about the murder? She was the one who found Lisette. She was the one who still tried to save her every night until she woke up in a cold sweat. Shouldn't they put their energy into looking for the real culprit?

Finn climbed behind the wheel and threw her a glance before starting the engine. And there it was, that lopsided smile, the turn of his lips that made her put her frustration on hold. She felt a shift when he was around, a sense of comfort, a heightened awareness.

The short ride to the station was quiet, and a part of her wished for conversation. She stole another look at him. A cop doing his duty. Nothing more. How was it so easy for him to ignore the chemistry that had been bubbling between them like a high school science experiment gone wrong?

Bianca began sorting through the contents in her purse, rolling items destined for the trash into her fist—an envelope covered in doodles, a phone bill she paid six months ago, expired coupons.

Finn glanced at her quizzically. "What're you doing?"

"Cleaning out my purse."

"Now?"

"Yes, now."

He made that face again, a twitch away from a smirk, which only made her buckle her lips together in firm resolve.

At the station house, Bianca jumped out and nearly sprinted to the front door. She slammed the wad of trash into the garbage before she entered, ignoring Finn's request for her to slow down. He caught up as she barreled toward Chief Carmichael's office. Questioning stares from the handful of people in the station were enough to brand a single word across her chest: Guilty.

A chair wheeled from a cubicle and Tucker landed in front of them. "Hey. This stuff is routine. That's all."

His genuine affability, akin to a perpetually grinning teddy-bear. "Thanks, Tucker."

He sailed back to his desk, and Finn said to Bianca, "He's right," but the lines crosshatching his brow spoke otherwise.

Outside Carmichael's office, Finn stood tall, demonstrating the full effect of his height. He knocked, waited for an invitation before opening the door. "Ms. James is here."

Carmichael glanced up from his papers and eyed her over reading glasses. "Good morning, Ms. James. I'll be right with you. Tierny, take her downstairs."

Finn's hand cupped her elbow as he guided her away. "I thought we'd just talk in his office."

"What's going on?"

He didn't answer but led her down a metal staircase, cinderblock walls closing in on her with each step. The damp, musty smell of a place forgotten made her sneeze. She wiped her nose and shoved the tissue back in her purse.

Pausing at the end of the stairway, he turned and propped one foot on the bottom step. Her stomach clenched. "Wait, am I a suspect?"

"You're not—"

"I'm not budging until you tell me what's going on." She clamped her hand on the iron railing.

"You're a person of interest, but that doesn't mean—"

"And that's supposed to make me feel better? That I'm a *person of interest* instead of a suspect?"

Time stretched while Finn studied his boots. His gaze shot up. "What should make you feel better is that you have nothing to hide."

Bianca detected the hint of a question in his statement and wondered if he believed her.

Finn opened the door and waved her in. A long table and three chairs were the only pieces of furniture in the room. He pulled out a chair, motioned for her to sit. "This shouldn't take long."

Bianca sat down, clutching her purse on her lap, and Finn settled across from her.

"It's freezing. Isn't there any heat down here?" She undid the clip from her hair, twisted a new coil, and clasped it back into the same spot. "This place could make Mother Teresa feel guilty."

Finn rose from his seat, removed his jacket, and draped it over her shoulders.

An overhead light buzzed, a single bright bulb floating at the end of a cord like a prop in a low-budget gangster movie.

"Is this part of his tactic? Make me wait in this room so I'll blurt out a confession as soon as he walks through the door?"

"Carmichael thinks his time is more important than anyone else's." Finn glanced from wall to wall as a staccato note of laughter burst and then died. "We call this place the box. Original, huh?"

Did he think the detail was helpful? The door opened, and Chief Carmichael breezed in carrying a cup of coffee, a leather-bound notepad, and a canvas bag. He wore a crisp pinstriped suit, an expensive-looking white shirt with French cuffs, and a grin that troubled Bianca.

Dropping into the rolling chair he scooted himself forward and made a show of arranging his cup and notebook on the table, tucking the bag underneath. "Thank you for coming down." Now a long sip of coffee. "Where are my manners? Finn can get you something. Coffee? Tea?"

"No thank you." Actually, her throat was dry, but not dry enough to accept a beverage like this was some kind of social call.

A clipped nod from Carmichael. "This won't take long."

Carmichael and Finn were teamed up on one side of the table with Bianca opposite them, and it struck her—even her vivid artist's imagination couldn't have created this scene.

"Did you know Lisette Divac?" The chief began.

"No," Bianca answered flatly, composed and in control. "I told you this before."

Carmichael rubbed his index finger down the corner of his mustache. "Are you certain?"

"Yes, I'm *certain*. I can't prove it. You'll have to take my word."

"Then there's a possibility you knew her."

"No. My answer is still the same. I did not know Lisette Divac. I'd never seen her before. She was a fill-in for Chet, the regular custodian. I told you all of this before, and I don't see what this has to do with—"

"Do you own a gun?"

"No. I don't." Her eyes bore into his.

The chief took off his glasses and rubbed them meticulously with the handkerchief he carried in his suit pocket before he slipped them back on. "The powder burns on her skin indicate—"

"What exactly are you insinuating?"

"You seem defensive."

"Chief Carmichael, I don't think—" Finn started but it was like the fury radiating from Carmichael stopped him in his tracks.

Carmichael buried his attention in his notebook, jotted a few notes as if writing a grocery list. When he finished, he tapped his pen against the pad. It took all Bianca had not to reach over and snatch the damn thing away. "It appears there was a struggle, perhaps you argued and—"

"This is ludicrous. I tried to save her."

"The crime scene shows there was a lot of thrashing around. What exactly went on isn't certain. Unfortunately, it's difficult to learn anything from a compromised scene."

Bianca bristled, but his admonition that she'd done more harm than good locked any response in her throat.

He flicked through his notebook and scanned a page. "The ME's report puts time of death right around the time you found her. Anyone else in the building besides you and Lisette Divac?"

"As I told you, Ralph, the security guard, was somewhere in, or around, the building. As for anyone else, I really don't know. People are in and out. Students, other teachers, but I don't pay attention."

"Isn't the building locked in the evening?"

"Ralph locks it by ten . . . well, most nights."

"I've verified with Mr. Monroe. His procedure is to lock the building between ten and ten-thirty," Finn interjected.

"When did Ms. Divac arrive?" Carmichael asked as if Finn hadn't spoken.

"I have no idea. I didn't see her until I found her in the storage room."

"Isn't the studio cleaned at approximately the same time every night?"

"I guess."

"You guess?"

"Again, when I'm working I don't watch the clock."

Carmichael reached down for the canvas bag and plunked it on the table. He extracted an evidence pouch, pulled out a light bulb and placed it on the table with an exaggerated swish of his hand. The bulb twisted a quarter turn and stopped.

"I don't understand."

Poking around in the mysterious bag again, Carmichael produced a yellow form Bianca recognized. "Is this your signature, Ms. James?"

"A work requisition?" She glanced at Finn, who looked as bewildered as she felt.

"It was in Ms. Divac's pocket, and the light bulb was with her cleaning supplies. She'd gone into the storage room—at your request—the storage room where she was brutally murdered."

His intentions hit her with a gale force wind. He'd stop at nothing to pin this on her.

"She didn't wander in by mistake as you suggested. You made the request. You knew she'd be there. In a dark interior room. Where no one could hear her scream."

"I had no way of knowing Lisette would be there. I requested that Chet change out the bulb weeks ago, but—"

"This requisition is dated the day before the murder, Ms. James."

Bianca had to think a minute. "He had me fill out a new one because he misplaced the first one. You're certainly welcome to verify this with him."

"I spoke with Mr. Troutman. You asked him to move something heavy the day before the murder. Is that correct, Ms. James?"

"Yes, but—"

"Something heavy enough to injure his back."

"You can't be serious."

"And you're aware he has a history of back problems, aren't you Ms. James?"

Bianca straightened. The truth couldn't hurt her, could it? "Yes, I did. I even recommended a massage therapist."

Carmichael ignored her and shoved his hand into that damn bag again. "We just got these back from the lab. The blood on them matches the victim's. Are they yours, Ms. James?"

The shoes. "Yes." A siren went off in her head, but she lifted her chin.

"Would you care to explain?"

"Explain what?" Bianca watched the color drain from Finn's face before she continued. "They were an old pair. I didn't want them after—"

"After the job was done?"

"No! I accidentally stepped . . . well, I thought it was paint and started to clean it up, but then I—"

"What about the clothes you wore that night? Did they go in the trash, too?"

"Well, yes, they were covered in blood, from when I tried to help her."

The chief scratched another notation. "So, you purposely, with intent, threw out shoes and clothes covered with the victim's blood."

"Chief Carmichael," Finn said. "Ms. James has no history of violence, no priors, no record."

"Fingerprints near the victim match the ones in Ms. James' employment file. In fact, they're the predominate prints at the crime scene." Carmichael spoke slowly and methodically, in contrast to the way he clicked the top of his retractable pen. "And the fact that she got rid of her shoes and clothing demonstrates a consciousness of guilt."

Of course my fingerprints are at the scene. It's my classroom. It would be a bigger feat to find something she hadn't touched. She clamped her eyes shut in frustration and saw herself moving through the studio, hands alighting on each item. One frame showed her finding the necklace under the cabinet. But every minute with Carmichael convinced her he wasn't the one to handle Lisette's personal effects. It felt right to try to save the victim's family any further heartache. Still, a cold fear rippled through her. The necklace might bring Carmichael one step closer to locking her up.

"With all due respect, sir, are her fingerprints really an issue here? Wouldn't they be all over her workplace anyway?" Finn came to her defense, precise and steady.

Carmichael smacked a palm on the table. "Are you advising *me* about fingerprints?"

"No, sir, but—" Finn stopped, folded his arms.

Carmichael scanned Bianca before he maneuvered the chair around the table, closing the gap between them. "You were at the scene. That gives you opportunity, and it's just a matter of time before we uncover the murder weapon."

Digging deep, she found strength, snapped to her feet, and fastened her eyes on Carmichael. "Someone else killed that woman."

Finn rounded the table and picked up his jacket which had fallen to the floor, hovering beside her for a moment.

Carmichael forged ahead. "As for a motive, I'm sure we'll find one that fits. Ms. Divac was a pretty woman. Perhaps she got too close to someone you care about, Ms. James?"

Finn stayed beside Bianca.

The chief sipped his coffee and adjusted his glasses. "Tell me again. Why were you at the school so late?"

Bianca broke from Carmichael's visual vise grip, and her eyes fell to the table where the bloody-soled shoes took up too much space. The evidence slipped around her neck like a noose—and cinched tight. "I'm not saying another word without a lawyer."

"Time to lawyer up then?" Carmichael said.

"If you're going to treat me like a suspect."

He smirked.

"But understand something, Chief Carmichael. I don't need an attorney. I want one. There's a difference. I did nothing wrong, and frankly, I don't know why you're wasting your time, and mine, with these questions. Someone's been harassing *me*. Probably the same person who killed Lisette Divac."

"Ms. James, it's certainly within the realm of possibility that you've been fabricating the harassment, as you call it, to appear innocent, to shift the blame."

"Chief, I've known Bianca for years. I can vouch for her."

Bianca slung her purse over her shoulder. "If you're not going to arrest me, I'm leaving."

The chief's eyes swept from Bianca to Finn. "Are you a little too close to this case, son?"

Bianca sent him a silent plea. *Don't risk it.* She needed him on this case, needed someone to believe in her.

Finn appeared to be considering his options. "No, sir."

Chief Carmichael wheeled back around the table. "You're free to go, but this investigation is ongoing. Make sure you're available."

"I'm not skipping town, but you need to focus your attention elsewhere. The killer is still out there."

Finn was waiting, holding the door open for her. He ushered her up the stairway, out of the station, and back to his car. They didn't speak until they were inside.

He let out a growl of frustration as he grabbed her hand.

Heat rushed through her body at his touch, desire searching for more contact as her insides ricocheted with mixed signals. "Thanks for having my back in there."

What *was* it about Finn? Every time he was near, he pierced the skin of her emotions and stirred untapped feelings.

"Carmichael has already made up his mind. He's not interested in developing any other theories. He has his own agenda."

"He still hates me for sticking up for Dylan, but trying to pin a murder on me takes hate to a whole new level."

"I suspect there's more to it."

"Like what?"

"I overheard him on the phone the other day, all nice and accommodating. Carmichael is never nice and accommodating. I assumed he was talking to his wife, but turns out, he was sweet-talking the mayor. Tuck says the mayor is vying for a senate seat, so the only thing I can figure is that Carmichael wants his job."

"And wrapping up this case fast puts him in the mayor's chair that much sooner."

"The light bulb, the fingerprints, it's all just to trip you up. Like one of those personality tests where a question is asked multiple ways to see if you're lying. But don't assume he won't eventually find something that sticks."

Clearly Carmichael was her biggest foe. And even though she'd gone over that night until her head ached, she wondered if she could dredge up something, anything, that could save her.

"Bianca, if I'm going to help you, I need to know every single detail about that night. Everything."

"Trust me, I've been going over and over what happened."

He brushed a strand of hair from her face and gently tucked it behind her ear, letting his hand linger before dropping it to his side. "There's something else."

Bianca steeled herself.

"You and Lisette, well, you have similar features. Blue eyes, blond . . . beautiful—"

Beautiful? It was difficult to assign that word to the woman she'd found; harder still to reconcile it with how she was feeling right now.

He locked eyes on hers. "I think Lisette was murdered by mistake."

A burning sensation traveled from her head to her toes.

"You were the real target."

✎ TEN ✎

JUST as Finn was getting the hang of working nights, sleeping days, Carmichael slapped him with the crack-of-dawn shift. Jacking him around like a real rook. Even in his first weeks in Pittsburgh, where recruits pulled the crappiest hours, his old boss at least treated him like a human being, even managed to dole out a "how ya doin'?" along with a clap on the back once in a while.

The Peak was small—ten men, four squad cars, two motorcycles, and tactical boots for all—but Carmichael acted like he was commanding a hundred-man force. No time for a courteous hello. When the chief from the neighboring town retired, Carmichael had seized the opportunity to take over, and strutted around for weeks, all puffed up like a kid who'd just snatched Boardwalk and Park Place in a single turn.

A call crackled over Finn's radio. "Meet me out here on Highway 51. Exit 36."

"Everything all right?"

"Just get here, okay?"

Finn hit the strobes and pulled a U. Why couldn't Tucker just tell him what was wrong? He passed a slow moving white utility van with a dinged bumper, a decal featuring a boy pissing on terrorists, and no plates. Possibly stolen.

Let it go. Damn, he couldn't. He radioed dispatch with the van's description and location.

He hoped Tucker's call had nothing to do with Bianca, but what would she be doing way out here? And why were his thoughts constantly turning to her, anyway? He was traveling a dangerous highway, and he needed to find the off-ramp. Pronto.

After dropping Bianca off at her home yesterday, Finn had returned to the station to find a red-faced, steely-eyed Carmichael. Irate barely described him. In a barrage of spit, the chief threatened him with everything from being thrown off the case to losing his badge. If tarring and feathering were still in style, Finn had no doubt it would have come into play. Carmichael made sure Finn understood he had no business speaking up during the interrogation, and if he spoke out of turn again, he'd find his ass in the unemployment line.

What else could Finn do but apologize and promise to be more professional in the future?

Tucker's squad car was pulled off the road in front of a stand of pines. And twenty yards ahead of that, Mack's Lincoln—smashed into the exit sign. Finn parked behind the cruiser.

Mack, still behind the wheel, shot Finn an obstinate look. A good sign.

"Did you call for a bus?" Finn asked Tucker.

Tucker pivoted, scraped a hand over his mouth, and said, "Hell no. Made it pretty clear he didn't want no ambulance."

There was a gash above his dad's left eyebrow the size and shape of a paper clip. "Dad, you're hurt."

Mack's face screwed to a tight, unwavering grimace. "Nothin' to cry about."

"Get him home," Tucker said. "Bandage that wound. I'll wait here for a wrecker. We'll keep this off the books."

"Wrecker?" Mack bellowed.

"We'll get the Town Car towed and fixed up." Finn almost wished Tucker would write a ticket, slap his dad with a fine to reinforce what he and Dylan had been telling him: he shouldn't be driving. But there was an unwritten rule, especially for retired uniforms—they were untouchable on the roads.

Mack swung his legs around with premeditated effort. Finn reached for his arm, but he shrugged it away. After several false starts, Mack found his bearings and wobbled to his feet.

With his father belted into the passenger seat, Finn eased onto the highway, pointed for home. He scanned the horizon, that stable line dividing sky from earth. A lone cow standing against the familiar backdrop of Krechner's Dairy called up the childhood memory of Dylan and his friends duping Finn into trying to tip a cow, saying he couldn't hang out with them until he did. He learned the hard way that cows don't sleep on their feet, and they don't take kindly to being pushed.

"Where were you going?" Finn asked.

A rigid, nonverbal response from Mack, pursed lips, arms laced.

Finn knew his dad had been stealing away to the cabin more and more lately. What else would he be doing out this way? "What happened?"

Mack took his time answering. "Must've blacked out."

"Dad, you shouldn't be driving—"

"Don't tell me what I should and shouldn't do."

Finn tried to keep the frustration from his voice. "You're going to hurt somebody. Or yourself."

"Nobody got hurt. *Except* me." He pointed to his forehead.

"I should be taking you to the hospital."

Mack batted him away. "It's a scratch. They'd get me in there and want to run tests. I'm tired of being their damn guinea pig."

In the past few months, his dad had worn a path to the hospital. What must it feel like to surrender your body to test after test only to find out there is nothing left to be done?

They rode in silence the rest of the way.

Once home, Mack fell into the chair next to the kitchen door. He was visibly shaken. Out of sorts. Finn found the first-aid kit and swabbed the gash with antiseptic.

"Jeez, Bird. Enough with that crap. It stings!"

The silly childhood nickname surfaced without warning. "An infection will hurt a lot worse." Finn opened a butterfly closure and stretched it over the wound. "This will do. I don't think you have a concussion, but—"

The kitchen door opened, and Dylan sauntered in. "Tuck stopped by the construction site. Told me what happened."

"Let me guess, your phone's MIA again?"

"Whatever."

"You have to wear those muddy boots in here?" Mack barked instead of a greeting.

Dylan, dressed in filthy Carhartts, had wasted no time on personal hygiene today. His hair sprouted haphazardly, and a patchy beard stubbled his face. He ignored his father's comment and gave him the once-over. "Hate to see the other guy."

"There is no other guy!" Mack pushed the first-aid kit across the table, and a spool of gauze bandage rolled out.

Dylan dropped into a chair across from him. "It's what we've been telling you, Dad. No more driving." His eyes darted around the kitchen. "You shouldn't even be alone anymore."

"That's right. Treat me like some kind of invalid." Mack tucked his fists between his knees and slumped forward. "Go ahead, take away my ind—" His face crunched as his tongue searched from one side of his mouth to the other, eventually finding what it needed. "—indy . . . independence. It's all I've got left."

"We just don't want you to get hurt," Finn said. "Or hurt someone else."

Mack cradled his head in his hands.

"Did you take your meds today?" Finn asked.

Mack appraised each of his sons, settling on Dylan. "I'll give up driving when you give up the bottle." He draped himself across the table, stabbed a finger in the air. "Think I never had a bad day? Of course I did. It's part of the job. You soldier on. You don't drown your sorrows in a handle of gin."

Dylan slammed his chair into the table. "I gotta get back."

"You think your kid brother can do what you couldn't? You were the one I counted on." Mack jerked a thumb at Finn. "This one was always too much like his mother. Head in the clouds, nose in the flowers."

Another sharp-toothed reminder, as if Finn needed one. His dad didn't think he could hack it.

Mack pushed himself up from the table and waved Dylan away. "That's it. Go ahead and leave. You're nothing but a quitter."

He shuffled down the hallway to his room. The door slammed.

Dylan snapped the buttons on his jacket with exaggerated force.

"The tumor—" Finn started.

The reminder quelled Dylan's flaring temper. "He's getting worse."

"It comes and goes."

"The old man is stubborn."

"And dangerous. That Lincoln is more of a lethal weapon than those guns sprawled across his dresser. At least they're not loaded."

"You hope."

"I know." Finn opened a corner cabinet and reached to the back for a copper tin that Rose had once kept flour in. "I emptied all his ammo the last time he went to play poker."

Things were bleak enough, but guns, ammo, and a brain tumor amounted to a death-wish cocktail.

"What's going to happen when he wants to go for target practice?"

"I'll think of something." Finn tucked the container back into the cabinet and glanced out the kitchen window. "Can't believe you're still driving that thing."

"Nothing wrong with my ride."

"You mean as long as you can use my Toyota when yours is stalled out somewhere."

The truck was as weathered as the old drinking buddy who'd given it to Dylan in exchange for some tile work. Durwood, a square-faced, hog farmer with fleshy bags under his eyes. He'd never met an engine he couldn't fix and had a yard full of junkers in various states of repair to prove it.

"But you have to stop to refuel every fifteen miles in that thing."

"Naw, I can go about thirty now. Old Durwood hammered the dent out so it would hold more gas."

"He's lucky he didn't start a fire."

"He's not that dumb."

"We're talking about the same guy who landed in the hospital after the fireworks he was mixing in a coffee grinder blew up in his face."

Dylan chuckled. "You know, he never made it past the sixth grade."

Finn didn't mention the reason Dylan ended up with the truck in the first place, the night he totaled his car driving home against an inconsiderate fog. He never saw the tractor parked at the side of the road.

"You know, we may not have to worry," Finn said. "About Dad driving."

"Enlighten me."

"Durwood's hogs keep him more than busy this time of year."

Dylan flashed understanding. "Yeah, he's up to his waders in slop."

As they schemed, a mental finger tamped down and smoothed the tension that had been brewing between them. "Who knows how long it'll take for him to get to Dad's car," Finn pointed out.

"Maybe forever."

"How do we manage without him driving?"

Dylan pointed at the calendar posted on the refrigerator. "He's got an appointment tomorrow."

"I can't."

"You've got to. Foreman threatens to can me if I ask for a lunch break."

Finn made a fist and popped it into his open palm. "I can't take off either. Carmichael likes to keep his punching bag close by. He's already up my ass for defending Bianca during questioning."

Dylan's face collapsed. "He questioned Bee again? What's he after?"

"Not sure, but if he had his way, she'd already be behind bars."

"That bad?" Dylan asked.

"Relentless. Picture Tucker with a hoagie."

Dylan stared in open-mouthed amazement. "Son of a bitch. He's still torqued over her going ballistic to save my job."

"But that was, what, two years ago?"

"Doesn't matter. That man holds a grudge like no other."

"Here's what I'm thinking. He just wants to wrap up this case any way he can. Feather in his cap. Look at all this man does for Riley's Peak."

Dylan slammed a hand into the wall. "How does that jagoff get away with this shit?"

"You know better than I do."

"Too well." Dylan picked up an apple from the fruit bowl in the center of the table. "Watch yourself. You're just another Tierny for him to push around." He carved out a wedge with the Swiss blade from his pocket, and popped it in his mouth.

"Those aren't washed," Finn said. There was a moment of silence before Finn brought the subject back to the problem at hand, getting Mack to his appointment. "We could horsengoggle."

"We haven't horsengoggled since Camp Twin Pines."

"Horsengoggled who would pull the sliver out of Tuck's thigh that time in the woods."

"That thing was nasty," Dylan said with a crooked grimace, one eye screwed shut.

"The sliver or the leg?"

"Both."

Finn agreed, settling into the easy banter. "On the count of three?"

"Wasn't it in German?"

"So call it in German."

"Why couldn't Dad have sent us to a camp where they used rock, paper, scissors?" Dylan rolled his eyes. "Eins, zwei, drei."

Finn raised one finger. His brother showed four. Dylan started with Finn and counted. "Eins, zwei, drei, vier, fünf. Horsengoggle."

Finn wagged his head from side to side. "You always did win. I'll take him and hope Carmichael forgot where he left his thumbscrews."

Dylan had his hand on the doorknob, but turned back to Finn. "Tucker says you got a thing for Bee."

"What?"

"You know."

"He doesn't know what he's talking about. I told you, I've been working on the case. That's all." Finn felt Dylan's eyes pass over him. "Carmichael sure likes her for the murder. Saves us the time and trouble of finding the real killer."

"Bee couldn't hurt a thing. Seriously. Doesn't even own a fly swatter." Dylan cupped his hands and mimicked holding a fly. "She puts them outside when she finds a slow moving one so it can die of natural causes."

"I'm busting my hump to find the right perp, but the downright painful truth is, I think whoever did this really wanted Bianca."

A muscle pulsed in Dylan's jaw. "Mistaken ID?" Flat tone, flat affect.

Finn raked his eyes over his brother. It was impossible to gauge his reaction. "Yeah."

"Well, keep a professional distance, bro. Once I clean up my act, we'll get back together."

"You said that before. What do you think I am?" A dagger of guilt slid between his ribs, twisted.

Dylan tossed the apple core in the sink, wiped and folded his blade, and shoved it into his pocket. "I think you're a man, and she's a woman. But she's off limits, hear me?"

"You don't have to draw me a diagram."

Dylan opened the door without looking back at him. "We understand each other." A statement, not a question.

After he left, Finn returned the first-aid kit, slamming the cabinet so hard it sprung open again.

His dad's door creaked open.

"How 'bout bringing me a Coke, son?"

Finn grabbed one from the fridge, poured it over ice, and brought it to his dad, who sat in his room, watching a talk show. Mack hated talk shows.

"Don't you want one of your game shows, Dad?"

Mack took a sip of Coke and wiped the back of his hand across his mouth. "Naw, what these people are saying is real interesting."

The host of the show held a fistful of note cards. A woman sat to her right, legs crossed at the ankles. "Tell me, Paul, when did you first know that you wanted to change gender."

Paul wore too much makeup and a smooth shoulder-length hairstyle; a skirt ruffled around muscular, bowed legs. "Call me Paula," she said in a baritone-laced falsetto.

"Dad, you sure this is what you want?"

"It's all right." Mack looked up at Finn with moist eyes. "Passes the time."

Finn studied his dad for a long moment. He had become his own version of Dr. Jekyll and Mr. Hyde. Whatever was happening in his brain was truly a mystery.

"I need to go. You okay?"

Mack raised his Coke in a toast. "Dandy. Don't you worry now."

Finn curled his fingers into a mock gun and pointed it at his dad. It was their thing, something they'd been doing since he was a kid.

"Later, Bird." Mack returned the gesture and went back to his show. On the TV screen, Paul/Paula raised a tissue and dabbed at tears. Finn shook his head as he walked down the hallway and out of the house. It *was* kind of interesting. The world was full of people hiding their true identities. Finding what lurked behind their masks took perseverance, a certain skill set—a good detective.

If only he knew where the hell to find one.

Sadly, he might be the closest thing Bianca had to one now. He should check on her.

She's off limits.

Finn called up her face and allowed himself a smile, but it fell away when he thought about Carmichael's badgering. During the whole interrogation there had been a little wrinkle between her eyebrows that he kept wanting to rub away. Afterwards, when he told her his theory about mistaken identity, her reaction twisted his gut even more. He hoped she was tougher than Dylan said. She may need to squash a fly or two before this was over. He rested his head in one hand, elbow against the car window, and punched in her number on his cell with the other.

"Hello, Finn."

At the sound of her voice, relief sluiced over him. "I just want . . . I'm just checking in."

When she didn't respond right away, he felt like a fool.

"I keep thinking, replaying everything," she finally said. "I can't remember anything else from that night." Another deafening silence. "It was supposed to be me, Finn."

He wanted to run to her, wrap his arms around her, hold her, console her.

"I've been wondering," she went on, "shouldn't Riley's Peak be getting outside help? The state police or something?"

Finn had entertained the thought, but the suggestion from her lips was the equivalent of a reprimand. "Bianca, we're doing everything we can."

A coolness settled between them.

"But Carmichael—"

"We've got this." Yet even as he spoke, he wondered, were they doing enough? Was *he* doing enough? Possibilities eddied, and he fished one out. "It's potentially someone close to you, Bianca. Think about the people who know your habits. Your neighbor, friends, Maris—"

A blast of laughter from Bianca. "Maris?"

Damn. He had to latch onto the one thing ludicrous enough to make her laugh.

"Maris is my best friend. I'm not going to listen to you throw her name around like Carmichael does mine."

An unspoken "dumb ass" dangled from her tongue lashing. And he was beginning to feel like one. Responses in short supply, he half whispered her name. "Bianca."

She hung up before he could say more.

❧ ELEVEN ❧

THE Balfour, situated in the northwest corner of town center, was small and dimly lit, but Bianca loved the owner's sense of adventure. Only someone with pride in their eclectic taste would pair a life-sized, stuffed bear with art-deco wall sconces. She and Maris had been meeting at the restaurant on Thursdays for "Over the Hump Day" for years. Free wings, discounted house wine, and a passable jazz musician on the keyboard. It kept Bianca sane.

And despite Finn's warnings, she needed her routine. Besides, wasn't she safe in a public place?

True to form, Maris was late. A virtual savant with numbers, but when it came to clocks, she couldn't tell the big hand from the little one. Bianca usually made good use of the time, sketching on a pad she kept in her purse. Just about everyone filtered through the town's best restaurant at one point or another—elderly couples celebrating milestones, frazzled parents corralling active children, young lovers snuggled into booths—providing enough inspiration to fill a portfolio.

Bianca reached in her bag for a colored pencil, and her hand came out with a stray dollar bill. A bright yellow smear highlighted the eye at the top of the pyramid. It was a curious marking. Who did it and why? She appreciated these peeks into strangers' lives, phone numbers, the occasional declaration of love, and she wondered for a beat what this one meant. She returned it to her purse and stared at a blank page in her sketchpad.

"May I join you?" A man flanked her table, his confidence bordering on arrogance. The broad cut of his shoulders and strong jaw pulled her attention momentarily, but these attributes only funneled to thoughts of Finn. She pinched a bit of flesh above her knee between her thumb and forefinger. She'd recently watched a documentary about negative reinforcement and had been trying the technique over the last forty-eight hours. The pinch was supposed to extinguish thoughts of him, but all she ended up with was a row of black and blue marks. Finn's smile could pierce anything B. F. Skinner devised.

"Actually, I'm waiting for someone," she said.

"So am I. How about we wait together?" Even in the faint light, the snug shirt did little to conceal the grooves defining his chest. She'd never seen him before. He seemed normal enough, and she liked the smudge of facial hair, a soul patch, that held up his full lower lip. Probably passing through on his way to somewhere bigger and better. Bianca was accustomed to people alighting in her small town, offering a brief hello, and moving on before the breeze changed directions. She, however, loved Riley's Peak and couldn't envision living anywhere else. Though she had pockets of happy memories growing up in Wisconsin, Pennsylvania had given her a fresh start.

"Well . . ." Her thoughts trailed off as she watched him shove up his sweater sleeves. Dashes of black ink on his forearm chiseled to a point. Shaped and buffed nails. Tattooed *and* manicured? She imagined this stranger sitting across from her, reaching for a breadstick and running his fingers along her hand. Bianca tapped her pencil on the blank pad in front of her. "Thank you, but my friend will be here any minute."

He leaned in close. "Are you an artist?" he asked. "I know a little about the subject."

She fastened her eyes on the sketchpad. Hadn't she been clear? Was communication between the sexes really so complicated? Or was it her? Pushing fast forward, she caught a fleeting glimpse of herself, gray and weathered, sitting in her art studio, surrounded by dried-out paint tins and dying plants.

Some day she'd be ready to share her life . . . but this guy?

As she opened her mouth to tell him more plainly she didn't want company, Maris' cackle floated from across the room. She had the kind of laugh that could be heard from across the state. Bianca waved at her and eyed the man who remained steadfast despite her coolness. "My friend's here. Have a nice night."

"Can't blame me for trying. Just talking with you made my trip worthwhile. I love taking in Pennsylvania's natural beauty." His eyes scanned her with a final appraisal before he moved to the bar.

Dylan had often complimented her in a similar vein. "You're more beautiful than her" or "that sunset has nothing on you." It wasn't that she didn't appreciate his comments, but at times she wondered if he saw beyond her looks.

Maris suddenly filled the spot the handsome stranger vacated. Her dark outfit blended with her hair so perfectly it was as if they were one seamless thing—hair, jacket, pants, shoes. "Who's GQ?"

"Just some guy who was all, 'here I am, now what were your other two wishes?'"

"Fernando tried to grow one of those chin things, but I told him it looked like Hitler's misplaced mustache and made him shave it off."

As Maris sat down, Bianca took a deep draw of wine and glimpsed a flash of red in her periphery. "Oh, great."

"What?"

"Jewel."

So much for a relaxing night out.

"I can handle a tiny dose of her as long as Dylan's not in tow." Maris glanced over her shoulder. "We had an alpaca in Peru who looked the same way right before he spit at you."

"Can you blame her? Who wants to find their boyfriend at his ex's house?"

Jewel snaked her way toward them, and Bianca resigned herself to another uncomfortable conversation. Even though they worked at the same college, she and Jewel had an unspoken pact to avoid each other at all costs, and yet here they were.

When she reached their table, Jewel untied the belt on her long suede jacket, revealing a white button-down that accentuated her top-heavy figure. She wasn't planning to join them, was she?

"Hello, Bianca. Hello, Maris," Jewel said. Bianca couldn't help but think of the old singsong Camp Granada bit, Hello, Muddah. Hello, Faddah. The thought dissipated as fingers touched her arm, fingers that felt like they'd been groping through an ice cube tray. "I've been thinking about you. I'd be more than happy to schedule an appointment, if you need to talk. Maybe at my office off campus."

Suspicion pricked; Jewel had always been about as friendly as her fingertips felt now. "I appreciate that," Bianca said. "I'll keep it in mind."

Jewel adjusted the chunky headband holding her spiky red hair in place. Not many women could pull off her look. She was one of the few who could twirl the dial of a time machine and somehow land in the eighties and the future simultaneously—and with style. It was clear what Dylan saw in her, at least physically.

Icy fingers tightened on Bianca's arm again, this time with a tiny twist of desperation. "Memories fade and you can't work through what you don't remember. Don't risk forfeiting closure." She withdrew her hand, lifted her shoulders in a that's-all-I've-got shrug, and walked away.

"That was awkward," Maris said. "But in a way, I feel kind of sorry for her. She's been here almost a year but doesn't seem to have any friends besides Dylan."

"Not even Charity."

"I know, right?" Maris chuckled.

"Did I ever tell you how Charity showed up at my doorstep a few days after I moved here? We had lunch a couple times, and she was nice enough, but so obsessed with my age it was creepy. Like, 'what are thirty-somethings listening to now?' As if she was pushing eighty, not fifty."

"I went shopping with her once. She made me pick out a bunch of clothes for her. Said I would know 'youthful.' I never saw her wear any of it. She's a strange one for sure."

Bianca grabbed a handful of popcorn from the middle of the table. "A shame they don't associate because she and Jewel seem like kindred spirits. But then, the two of them together would be pretty scary." She thought for a moment. "I wonder if Jewel would be different if she wasn't so hung up on Dylan and consequently hating me."

"I'd wager Jewel's issues go way back, pre-Dylan."

"I think we could have a few things in common though." Bianca felt that old familiar loneliness, that longing for family, blossom across her chest.

Maris laid her hands on the table and leaned in as if anesthetized, brows knitted fiercely.

"Ah, the Venn diagram thing again. Zero family is where Jewel and I overlap."

Maris shrugged. "Does it help to know I'd write sane on your circle and cray-cray on hers?"

"Thanks. But maybe it just takes Jewel longer to warm up."

Maris motioned across the room. "There must be a warming trend."

Bianca turned to see Jewel cozying up to GQ at the bar.

"Wait, let me see if I can hear her drink order." Maris cupped her ear. "Yup, a Slow Comfortable Screw Up Against the Wall. He's toast."

"Makes Sex on the Beach sound like a Shirley Temple. And here I thought she was so into Dylan."

"Maybe she's keeping her options open. Or maybe the near lap dance for GQ is just a cover so she can spy on us. Who knows with that one," Maris said. "But enough about her. What happened at the police station yesterday?"

Maris remained uncharacteristically silent as Bianca filled her in and shared Finn's mistaken-identity theory.

"They should be protecting you, not questioning you," she finally said. "Clearly they're not doing everything they can to find the killer. Why don't they get some outside help?"

"I tried that route with Finn." Bianca searched for the server, found her, and lifted her glass for a refill, raising two fingers to indicate a second for Maris as well. "I'm afraid I insulted him."

"¡Y que! If they're bent on badgering you, then they should be insulted."

Bianca shook her head and ran teeth over her bottom lip. "I did something stupid. Well, in hindsight anyway."

"You bought another stuffed peacock? I still have nightmares about that thing."

"My students love Humphrey. A couple of guys even asked him to pledge Sigma Chi." Bianca drew a tornado of swirls on her pad. "Everything from that night was covered in blood, so I threw it all away. The police found my shoes in the trash."

Maris relaxed against her seat. "That's a logical reaction, not one that makes you a murderer."

"Obviously not to Carmichael. He thinks I have something to hide."

Maris wrinkled her nose as if something rancid had passed under it. "That's ludicrous. That man just wants to see his name in seventy-two-point font. What a publicity hound. Don't you see? The sooner he gets this wrapped up, the sooner he's on the front page."

Bianca was certain a hunger for power played into it, but where would it lead? From his demeanor in the interrogation room, it was clear he wanted to get even.

And why wouldn't he? Bianca massaged her temples with the pads of her thumbs as the past came stalking back. She saw herself storming into Carmichael's office, indignation leading the way. Every atom of her being begging, pleading for Dylan to be reinstated. Without the badge, he'd never recover. If Carmichael would only let him work the desk while he fought off his demons, Dylan may have had a chance. But Carmichael seemed determined to squash his last hope, and though she wasn't proud of it, she lost it. Panic muddied the waters of control and she lashed out, pointing to every broken thing about the man sitting in front of her. And everyone in earshot gathered to hear the gospel she was preaching. Carmichael's astonished blink evolved into a stare that settled on her and silently vowed he'd get even. Then he had Tucker escort her off the premises.

"I told Carmichael I was getting a lawyer," Bianca said.

Maris regarded her with a mixture of sympathy and caution. "I've heard that can be as bad as an admission of guilt."

"But if he's trying to pin this on me, I should at least have someone in mind."

"Brett does corporate law, but I'm sure he can recommend a criminal attorney. I'll get you a name. Just in case."

Bianca took a sip of her wine, then another, as it all spun around her. Interrogation. Consciousness of guilt. Criminal attorney.

"What a waste of time. And money," Maris said. "¡Eso es una locura! But I'm worried about the mistaken ID thing and the cops off in lala land trying to nail this on the most convenient person."

Maris slid Bianca's pad of paper toward her and grabbed the pencil sitting next to it. She flipped to a clean sheet and wrote in precise block letters:

DYLAN TIERNY

Bianca stared at the name until it vibrated. A chill spiraled through her, sliced through her stomach. "Let's be serious, Mare."

"Maybe Dylan is a stretch, but you can't just leave this to RPPD. If your life is in danger, you have to be proactive. Who knows your life better than you?"

No one. That was the sad truth. No one knew her life better than she did.

Bianca toyed with her sleeve, scratched at a spot of dried fuchsia paint. "You're right."

"So, start thinking about anyone, anyone at all who may be angry with you."

"Charity still hates me for that fiasco with the fake Miró."

"She should be thanking you for saving her from wasting more money. Besides, she's not smart enough to balance her own check book much less plan and execute a murder."

"If Finn's theory holds water, it wasn't exactly executed as planned. More like botched."

Maris winced. "True, but I'm still not seeing Charity go that far. And what about the guy who sold her the fake?"

"I heard he gave her money back and had to file for bankruptcy."

"Remind me how much again?" Maris asked.

"A million."

"Cha-ching. And you could tell it was a fake from the color?"

"Yup."

Maris raised her wine glass, clinked it against Bianca's. "To my brilliant best friend."

"Compliment accepted, but the certificate of authenticity claimed the sculpture was made in the fifties. Miró didn't use color until the sixties. Google could have told her that."

"I still think you're smarter than Google." Maris picked up the pencil, drummed it on the table. "Jewel."

"The new girlfriend has to hate the ex. It's a requirement, I think."

"He'd totally dump her if you agreed to get back together," Maris said. "It would ruin her plan to make little Tiernys with Dylan."

"Then why'd she just offer to help me?"

"You know the saying. 'Keep your friends close . . .'"

"And your enemies closer." Bianca sagged back in the chair. It was all so surreal, thumbing through a list of suspects, trying to find one who wanted to kill her. "I may not be the first person people think of when they're sending out wedding invitations, but do the math, Mare, does that equate to someone wanting me dead?"

"Even nice people have their limits. Ever hear about crimes of passion?"

"Ms. Statistic talking about emotions."

A server appeared with a bottle of champagne and two glasses and set them in front of Bianca. He cocked his thumb behind him. "He must really be into you. This is the best we've got."

Bianca's attention snapped to the end of the bar, and there he was, the guy whose picture you'd see if you looked up trust-fund baby.

Emerson Wade. The only person she could think of who might just hate her enough to want her dead.

And only in a town no bigger than a postage stamp would she run into the wrong person at precisely the wrong time.

He raised an empty glass as if to say you're welcome and strode over to their table. "Bianca," he said, touching her shoulder, lingering too long. She moved his hand away.

It wasn't that he called her by her first name, plenty of students did, but it was the way he said it, with a tinge of ownership. Emerson had crossed the line from day one, leaning in closer than he should, grazing her hand with his when he passed. He continued to dirty-dance around the rules, thinking he could rely on his sun-washed good looks and leading-man charm.

Pulling a chair from a nearby table, he joined them.

"Professor Romero and I are in the middle of something."

He picked up the champagne, filled their glasses. "You look great," he said, his back to Maris.

"As I said. Not a good time." Like there was or ever would be with Emerson.

He shot to his feet, leaving the chair between tables. Tendons flexed in his neck, exposing the same flammable temper he'd exhibited when she'd explained the boundaries of their relationship. Teacher and student, nothing more.

Hot tempered, cocky, but a murderer?

"Sure, yeah, whatever. I've got somewhere else to be anyway." It was then that she noticed something new. A look she hadn't seen before. Maybe a hint of defeat. "I've got a date." He upended his glass, drained it, ground it firmly into the tablecloth, turned, and strutted away.

"Nice talking to you, Emerson," Maris called after him with the sincerity of a lawyer hot on the trail of an ambulance. "This is getting easier."

Bianca grabbed the pencil and added a second name to the list: EMERSON WADE

She circled it in thick, dark rings. "It's possible. He's persistent and unbelievably arrogant, but—"

"Anyone is capable of anything under the right circumstances. I will say he has fabulous taste in champagne." Maris raised her glass.

Bianca clicked her friend's glass and rewound to the first time she'd seen Emerson at Brookefield, surrounded by girls flipping their hair and pouting their lips. He was a star with a gaggle of planets orbiting wherever he went.

When he was getting his way, he could charm the last chocolate nugget from a trick-or-treater. But the side she'd seen tonight, and once before, reminded her that like gold leaf over tin, charm could cover something altogether different.

Ted Bundy was charming.

Last year Emerson had painted a portrait of Bianca. It wasn't well rendered, but a primitiveness in the work had intrigued her. She told him she couldn't keep it. He'd slammed the painting on her desk, stormed off, and dropped her class. He'd surfaced a couple more times, once to deliver tickets to the symphony at Christmastime, which she promptly gave back, and another time to leave roses on Valentine's Day, which she dropped off at a retirement center on her way home from work. After that, she'd catch glimpses of him on campus, but she knew he'd never retreat. She'd been due for another encounter, and of course he picked tonight.

She should have put the portrait in the dumpster. Instead, she'd tucked it out of sight in the back of her storage room, unable to throw away even "bad" art. But she'd never forget the intensity of his anger.

Bianca flipped on her blinker and eased toward Surry Lane. Cat food. Picasso would keep her up all night if he didn't have his favorite, salmon and mackerel. The cat ate better than she did.

Partway into the turn, she remembered buying food last week. She adjusted and stayed straight, hoping the driver behind her wouldn't hold it against her. The other car corrected and stayed straight as well.

She hung a left on Broadwell, right on Dover.

She had two choices: ignore the spiky sensation climbing the back of her neck or check the rearview again.

The car was still there.

She cranked left at the next street, so sharp her tires squealed. The other vehicle did the same. Bianca squinted in the mirror, trying to see the driver, but it was too dark.

She slowed. The car drew closer, close enough for her to make out the hood emblem. A quartered circle, blue, white, framed in black. A BMW. Where had she seen . . . ?

Emerson drove a silver BMW.

✥ TWELVE ✥

FINN hadn't been in Brookefield's coffee shop since he was a student. Nothing had changed. Blond chairs circled glass tables; framed prints of steaming coffee in nondescript mugs decorated the walls. The place felt almost medicinal. And the name—Brew. Surely someone at a liberal arts college could have come up with something more creative.

The patrons were equally clichéd: a brooding guy at the counter running a highlighter across pages in a textbook, students worrying over wrinkled notes, and a middle-aged prof pondering the muffin of the day. Finn blanched at today's feature scrawled on the whiteboard: carob zucchini cardamom. What ever happened to plain old chocolate chip?

He spotted Bianca at a corner table, the little worry crease working between her eyebrows and the set of her mouth accentuating a tiny scar that crossed the right side of her upper lip, not much of a flaw, more like an arrow, a marquis pointing to an attraction you shouldn't miss.

She glanced up, shifted to look out the window. A subtext was growing between them—unspoken words full of if onlys and contingencies.

He dropped into the seat across from her. *Keep it professional.*

"This place must bring back some memories for you," she said.

"The food is better here than at the library. At least it used to be." Finn searched her eyes. "You said someone was following you?"

"It's probably nothing." Bianca crumpled her napkin, unfurled it, and started to fringe the edges.

He tried for a casual pose, arm cocked on the back of the chair. "This car that was following you, did you see who was driving?"

Bianca rolled her lips inward. "It was a silver BMW. A student of mine—former student—drives one. The car eventually went around me, but I couldn't see who it was."

"Why would this guy follow you?"

Bianca put her hand to the back of her neck, tilted her chin upward. "Emerson kind of had a thing for me. He was persistent, but I let him know it was inappropriate."

"How persistent?"

"He made advances."

"What kind of advances?"

She trailed her fingers along the side of her mug. "He was always brushing up against me. Sexual innuendos. Things like that. I told him he needed to stop or I'd throw him out of the class."

Finn picked up the glass salt shaker from the middle of the table and squeezed until he thought it might break. "The problem is, until he actually does something we can't nail him."

"I almost didn't call you." She pushed aside the neatly fringed napkin. "But I thought you should know—in case it might somehow be related."

Slashes of sunlight streamed from the window, giving her face an angelic glow. She wore her hair down today, and golden strands lay in soft wisps across her shoulders. What would it be like to hold her, to lose his fingers in that hair? His pulse surged.

"Finn?" Bianca broke through his distraction.

"I'll track the guy down, and we'll go from there."

Bianca toyed with a silk flower in a small arrangement at the center of the table. A petal fell off, and she reached for it, grazing his hand, sending a shiver through him.

He studied her delicate fingers so close to his own, and his heart beat triple time.

"I've had some calls too." She ferreted through her oversized purse. "Heavy breathing. Can't tell if it's a man or a woman. There's a lot of background noise and a sort of crying." She placed a cassette tape on the table. "I thought maybe you'd want to listen."

Finn reached for it. "What the hell is this?"

"From my answering machine."

"Analog? I thought those were extinct."

"It never stopped working, so I kept it."

He stared at her for a long moment, shook his head, and rolled the tape in his hand. "Are all the calls on here?"

"All but the first two."

"Tell me about the first two. The ones you deleted."

"Like I told you before."

Her clipped responses made him wonder if she was irritated with him. "Any on your cell?"

"My inbox is full. I'm bad about clearing it . . . So no, no new messages there."

Finn's jaw tightened, and he realized he was gritting his teeth. "Bianca, this guy following you, the calls, maybe they're not related to the murder, but in case they are, hell, even if they're not, you really need to be careful. What if you go stay with a friend until this is resolved?"

"And what if it never gets resolved? What then, Finn? Hide out for the rest of my life?"

Her stubborn resistance aggravated him, but even so, he wanted to lean across the table and feel his lips press against hers. He straightened, waved the tape in the air, and said, "Okay then. Pittsburgh has equipment that will amplify the track. I'll let you know."

The anxiety pleating Bianca's brow made it torturous to leave. He tucked the tape into his pocket and patted it. "Call if anything comes up. But I really recommend—"

"Thank you, Finn."

He might as well save his breath. She wasn't going to upset her routine, even in the face of danger. And as far as the other stuff went, he needed to leave before his desire found words.

During the hour drive to Pittsburgh, he luxuriated in thoughts of Bianca, the sound of her voice, the sweetness and texture of honey, how she made him feel, but he agonized, too. What if he couldn't protect her? He slammed his hand against the steering wheel inadvertently blasting the horn. *Damn it.* Despite Dylan's admonitions to back off, he couldn't. Not when she needed him.

In the department lot, he snagged a space, and hopped from the car. And there he was, right in his line of sight—Walters. The man who seemed to have a never-ending supply of kerosene to douse the flaming hell he'd created for Finn. Walters was circling a squad car, doing a vehicle check. Finn motored toward the front door.

"Tierny."

Finn stopped, pivoted. "Walters."

"Some balls showing your face around here." Hurled like hand grenades.

"Seems as good a place as any."

Walters' close-set eyes jittered in place, badgering Finn for a moment. Finn turned and kept walking.

"Then why'd ya run away?" Walters said to his back.

Finn turned again. "You know what your problem is, Walters?"

"I'm sure you'll tell me."

"No instinct."

"Instinct?"

"You know, like animals. They automatically know things. Like if they need to hide, they find a dark place." Finn waved a hand at the sky. "Bright sunny day we're having, eh?"

"You're calling yourself an animal?"

"I wouldn't expect you to get it, Walters." Finn hitched a thumb at the cruiser. "Hope the last guy left a little gas in the tank there for ya." He hoofed it to the station, determined not to look back.

Walters would stand there awhile trying to decipher the dig, but where he was short on wit he made up for in sheer meanness.

Finn stalled on the bottom step of the wide staircase leading to the old brick station house and bent to retie a bootlace that didn't need tying. He shouldn't be here, but he worked his way up the stairs, through the front door and the labyrinth of his doubts.

With a nod to Sabrina, the front desk clerk, he held up the

answering machine tape. "Chief Almeida said I could run this." A stretch, his exact parting words were "come back anytime," not "help yourself to our high-tech equipment." He had no beef with Almeida. A couple officers, thankfully new hires, glanced up from their paperwork and grunted greetings.

Sabrina ran talon-like fingernails along the row of empty buttonholes on her navy polo shirt. "At last, my prayers have been answered. It's been pretty boring around here since you left."

He offered a brief hello and kept going. Sabrina had always wanted to get her hooks into him, even back when she knew he was in a relationship. He was in no mood for her flirtations today.

Donning headphones in a back room, he popped the tape into place and played it several times, but the ancillary noise made it difficult to identify the keening and heavy breathing. Voices, clattering, laughter, and general commotion jumbled together. Toward the end, during the last track, he heard a distinctive voice he recognized with certainty.

"Lost," Finn said out loud. The seediest of the three bars in the Peak, Lost Treasure Tavern. Simply known as Lost since "Treasure" and "Tavern" on the sign had burned out and the owner, Gus Shook, was too cheap to replace them.

Finn played the tape again. Sure enough, the gruff voice that could only belong to the bar's proprietor came through loud and clear. "Get off the phone, jackass."

Lost was Dylan's bar of choice. No one hassled him there, and gin was cheap. But if these were Dylan's lovesick, drunken calls to Bianca surely they had nothing to do with the murder case. Finn snatched the tape and headed for the exit.

"Come back when you can stay longer," Sabrina called after him.

He did an about-face, wondering exactly when he'd become so rude. He hadn't been raised to be dismissive. "It was good to see you again, Sabrina. You're looking great, as usual."

Her face lit like a handful of fireflies. Just because his world was going dark, didn't mean he couldn't brighten someone else's.

❧

Gus hadn't opened yet for the day. Finn pounded on the door and peered through the scratched oval window like it was a speakeasy.

"Keep your socks on, jackass," came a bulldog croak from inside. The door swung open and Gus blinked like he hadn't seen daylight in months. Without a word, the stooped-over little man shuffled back to one of the high tables where he was set up with a newspaper, a cup of coffee, and a cigarette. He hoisted himself onto the barstool with considerable effort.

Finn took the stool across from him.

Gus had contracted the bends in a diving mishap several years ago and walked hunched over ever since. A settlement from Coral Diving Expeditions in Cayman Brac was enough to pay for a liquor license and the small bar. He took a drag on his cigarette and measured Finn with beady eyes.

A salty sea breeze almost cut through the stale nicotine haze from Gus' preopening smokes, and the place was cluttered with seashells, nets, coral, old bottles, and even a worn-out black boot. Things Gus had gathered from dive trips in his younger days created a certain rugged, yet inviting, atmosphere. The most unusual item on display was an old revolver with a long muzzle, like a pirate's.

"You don't get in here as much as your jackass brother."

"No—"

"What'ya want?"

"To ask a few questions."

The old man sucked his cigarette some more, then pressed his lips into an irritated line as he exhaled through his nostrils.

Finn pointed a thumb to the rotary phone sitting on the end of the bar. "Always wondered about that phone."

Gus smiled, revealing teeth the size and color of baked beans. "It works."

"Anyone ever use it?"

"Anyone who slaps a dollar down."

"Don't most people use cell phones?"

"Not in here." He pointed to a sign on the wall. NO CELL

PHONES, scrawled in black letters, leaning to the left, as if pounded by a steady, tropical zephyr. "All those damn little boxes on their ears. They need to talk on the phone, this is it. Or they can get the hell out."

"It costs a dollar to make a local call?"

"Naw, but these jackasses would be on it all the time if I didn't charge nothin'."

"Anybody in particular who uses that phone a lot?"

Gus sipped his coffee, puffed his cigarette, then bared his baked bean teeth in a snarl. "Lots of 'em."

"But no one in particular?"

The old man wagged his head, uncooperative.

"I could ask you for a list."

"I'd give you a list of all the jackasses that come in here. Or none of 'em. What you want with my customers, anyway?"

"We're questioning a lot of people."

"These jackasses are mostly drunks, lonely saps, not murderers."

Finn had trouble forming his next question. "What about my brother, Dylan? Does he make calls?"

"You suspect your own brother?" A shame-on-you edged his voice.

It was pointless to stay. If pressed, Gus would provide a long list, names copied straight from the phone book. Small town mentality at its best—every good ol' boy covering the next one's ass.

Finn got to his feet. "It's been a little slice of heaven."

Gus ground his cigarette in a shell ashtray. "I'd tell ya to go to hell, but you'd probably cuff me."

Finn lifted his eyes to the ceiling before returning them to Gus. "We're all going to hell, man, and I'm driving the bus."

As Finn left the building, he heard Gus say, "Next time buy something, jackass."

He was starting to feel like one. He dialed Dylan's cell. It rang so many times he almost gave up, but then the phone clicked, he heard some rustling, Dylan grunted, "Sleeping," and the call ended.

Had he lost another job?

Hanging a left at Highland Avenue, Finn coasted down the familiar slope known for its speed-trap potential. He clicked on his blinker at Family Dollar, turned, and passed Dylan's apartment building, a monstrosity that had seen better days, ironically named Paradise Hills. Parking was an ongoing issue. There weren't enough spaces for residents, and fights were common. "Trouble in Paradise" was code around the station that there was another dispute over two vehicles arriving simultaneously at the same eight-by-sixteen-foot spot.

Finn parked in front of a Mexican bakery, the baked cinnamon and sugar aroma an instant reminder he hadn't eaten. He pushed away the thought and hoofed it uphill two blocks to Dylan's. This felt too much like a police call, parking down the street to catch the perp by surprise. But he needed to get to the bottom of those calls from Lost.

After a couple rounds of knocking, Dylan emerged in cupid boxers. "Told you, I'm sleeping," he said, wiping a clump of sleep from his eye.

"Nice drawers."

Dylan looked down as if he'd forgotten what he was wearing. "Dad okay?"

"Yeah. Thought you might want to know about his appointment. Doc gave him something to help him sleep. I read through the three pages of side effects, some scary shit."

"It's damn early if there's no emergency."

"It's almost noon."

Dylan swung the door wide in a half-hearted invitation. Before Finn could get out a single question, Jewel came from the bedroom, moving toward them like smoke. She wore an old T-shirt of Dylan's, stretched to the side, exposing a knobby shoulder. One glimpse told Finn there was nothing underneath.

"Hey, Jewel." He'd always been uncomfortable around her, even fully clothed, and never understood how Dylan could go there after being with Bianca. Maybe the news about her tryst with the bartender would knock some sense into his brother.

"Hello, Finn." Jewel's lips pouted in annoyance. She scratched at her scalp with long fingernails and forced a chunk of spiky hair around her finger. This interruption wasn't what she had in mind.

He turned to Dylan. "When you gonna get some furniture in this place?"

"I've got a bed."

Jewel's lusty glance toward the back of the apartment sent Finn scrambling for a different subject. "No work today?"

"Late night, I took the day off." Dylan twisted away, headed for a coffee canister. "You my boss now?"

"Hardly." His brother needed a helluva lot more than a boss. "Stopped by to chat, but it can wait." He should have known Jewel would be here, gumming up his opportunity to ask a few questions.

She whirled and narrowed mascara-smudged eyes at Finn. "About the case? Too bad about Bianca botching the scene the way she did. Makes your job even harder."

"What do you know about that?" Finn asked.

She shrugged. "I'm the one wading through the damage to put a profile on the shooter."

Dylan's eyes widened, now fully awake. "You're doing what?"

"I told you, I'm working with Chief Carmichael on a behavioral sequence of the crime."

"No, I would have remembered that." Dylan turned to Finn. "Talk to me."

"Someone's been calling Bianca from Lost."

Hesitation, a vacant stare, flicked across Jewel's face. Finn was fairly certain she had a reserved barstool right next to Dylan's. If she didn't have an alibi . . . An alibi Finn didn't have the guts to tell his brother about . . .

Making about as much progress as a toothless beaver, he stepped out into the hallway, and Dylan followed.

"Still with her?" Finn asked. "I thought—"

"I've been trying to clear my head. She's a good listener."

"Mmm-hmm."

A woman in plaid rain boots and matching hat trudged down the corridor with a sack of groceries, put her key into the door across the hall, and eyed them suspiciously over her shoulder.

"He's my brother," Dylan said by way of explanation.

She scowled and hustled into her apartment.

"I think she was looking at your uniform, not mine," Finn said.

Dylan snapped his waistband. "Whatever. Now tell me what's going on."

"Someone is harassing Bee. Can't say if it's our guy, but I don't like it either way."

Dylan's nostrils flared.

A crackle of contention passed between them. Finn shouldn't have called her Bee.

"What do you mean?"

"Phone calls. Weird shit." Finn felt his face go warm under his brother's scrutiny.

"Well, good luck with that, hotshot." Dylan stepped back inside. "You're the only cop in the family now."

⚜ THIRTEEN ⚜

AFTER watching Finn leave the coffee shop, Bianca returned to her half-eaten sandwich. Tomato had soaked through the croissant, staining it an unappetizing pink. She pushed the plate away.

Rummaging through her bag, she pulled out her sketchpad and a handful of colored pencils. At her last visit to the dentist, she'd covertly drawn a little girl clinging to her mother in the waiting room. She'd captured the girl's hesitant smile, but the eyes weren't right. They didn't reflect trepidation but loss. An emptiness replicating her own after her mother died. Only eight years old, she'd carried the weight of her own sorrow as she watched her dad so bent by despair that he disappeared into his grief, staring at her as if she were a miniature of the woman he'd loved and lost.

Now, Bianca selected yellow ochre and added caramel highlights to the girl's hair. Another image surfaced, this time Lisette's daughter. Bianca dropped the pencil, and it rolled across the table, landing at her water glass with a clunk.

She grabbed her phone and speed-dialed Maris. "I can't stop thinking about her."

"Thinking about who?" Maris rasped.

"Are you okay? You sound funny."

"Scratchy thwoat."

"We can talk later then."

"I'm fine, and besides, I need a distraction from grading midterms."

Bianca thought about her students. They meant everything to her. The sooner she got through this, the sooner she could get back to giving them her all. "What Lisette's family's going through, I—"

"I know. I keep thinking about that sweet little girl too."

Bianca reached in her purse again and found Lisette's necklace tucked in a side pocket. She moved it around her palm. If it had belonged to one of her students, she'd know by now.

She needed to bring it to Lisette's family, but hadn't anticipated the crippling fear that kept her from doing so. How could she face a mother who'd lost her daughter? How could she face a daughter who'd lost her mother?

The drawing of the girl lifted off the page and hovered in front of her, a flesh and bone hologram.

"There's something else." Bianca told Maris about the necklace and why she needed to be the one to return it.

"It could be evidence. Shouldn't you give it to the police?"

"Did you miss the part about my dead mother?"

A filament of electricity sizzled between them followed by an extended hush.

"I'm sorry," they said in unison.

"Losing a mother is devastating enough," Bianca said. "But then to have cops process her things like . . . I just don't want that little girl to have to go through that."

"Call me after you go."

Bianca stowed the necklace back in her purse. "I will. Get better. Big date with Charity's brother coming up, right?"

"Yes, tomorrow. And, you can say his name. I'm wise to your not-so-subtle reminder that he's related to the Wicked Witch of the Peak."

"Brett. Brett. Brett. Happy?"

"Deliciously."

"Good, now go put your feet up. I'll bring you some homemade chicken soup later."

"You don't cook."

"I didn't say I was making it."

The joke was lost on Maris, who was consumed in a coughing fit.

Bianca gathered her things. "Marisela, have I told you how lucky I am—"

"To have a friend like me?" Maris said, her voice recovered. "Not often enough."

❧

Bianca plugged in Lisette's address on her phone. As she turned off the highway, doubt slinked through her. Was she doing the right thing?

She pulled into a Handee Mart where she stalked the aisles, not hungry, but wanting something, needing something. She grabbed a handful of Almond Joys, paid for them, and stalled at the newspaper stand to glance over the headlines. But all she saw was a pointillist arrangement of black and white.

Outside the convenience store, a woman was rooting through a trash can, putting each stained coffee cup and bottle to her lips. Bianca's thoughts turned to Prince Caspian. When she had shown up at Weaver without a sack lunch in hand, his expression had scrolled from confusion to anger to hurt. It was the hurt, the utter disappointment in his rheumy eyes that lingered now in her memory. Bianca raced back into the store, bought a bottle of water and a banana, and returned, offering them to the woman.

"You can shove those where the sun don't shine," the woman snarled. Steel wool hair hugged her head, and sheer hatred emanated from her like a blast of napalm.

"I thought—"

"I'm recycling. Ever heard of it? You must be one of them rich bitches who don't care about nothin' but yourself. Ain't you late for a massage or something?"

Bianca pushed the items into her bag, and returned to her car. She cranked the engine and drove to Lisette's as the caustic exchange gnawed at her.

Was she really trying to help or only assuage her own guilt?

As she turned into Willow Glen, a mobile home community on the south side of town, her moist hands nearly slipped from the steering wheel. Doubt weighted her pockets like stones.

A squirrel darted in front of her, and she screeched to a stop. It scurried into the woods, and a part of her wanted to yell, "Wait up" and then disappear with it into the dense wall of evergreens.

She stopped in front of 422 Willow Springs. Lisette's house matched the others, lined up like metal dominoes along a gravel road. The only difference was her door, not the typical dirty white or black, but a vibrant fuchsia. Window boxes overflowed with chrysanthemums, pansies, and potato vines, mostly brown with the occasional green spot, as if trying desperately to weather the cold. A child's bike was propped against a sign that read, "Santa Please Stop Here!"

Lisette's daughter still believed in Santa. Undoubtedly the Tooth Fairy and the Easter Bunny too. Who would be there when the time came to let her know they were only make-believe?

A new package of white tissue paper lay in the passenger seat. Bianca had agonized over how to present the necklace. She'd put it in a baggie, but the final *pop* of the Ziploc, closing air out, trapping the necklace in, made her cringe. She couldn't return a dead woman's jewelry in a sandwich bag. A silver-foiled box from Maris, tied with a silk ribbon, was no better. Too frivolous. Respect. Compassion. What type of packaging conveyed those sentiments? In the end, she'd decided on simple white tissue paper. She carefully tore away the cellophane and unraveled a large square, folded it in half, and then in thirds. Finding the center of the pristine wrapping, she positioned the necklace almost ritualistically.

Bianca moved toward the door with leaden steps. She counted the concrete pavers, noticing the mish-mash of sizes and shapes, as if someone had gathered whatever they could find. While she was summoning her nerve, the door opened and a woman startled, fingers pressed to her mouth. She was as wide as she was tall, and blotches of rosacea colored her cheeks.

"Oh," she said. "You scare me."

"I'm so sorry, I was about to knock."

"I am going for mail. How I help you?"

Bianca couldn't place the accent. Russian? Polish? She offered her hand. The woman took it, engulfing it in her own.

"I'm Bianca James. I teach at Brookefield."

The woman's eyes went wide, and she tightened her grip. "You try to help her."

A band of anxiety wrapped around and around Bianca, suffocating her.

"I have coffee. Come in? Please." *Please.* Stretched, pleading.

She must be so lonely now.

In the galley kitchen, wildflowers danced on beige wallpaper and a collection of red and white bowls marched across the counter in a ceramic parade. The scent of molasses infused the air, reminding Bianca of Gemma's gingerbread cookies.

"Cream? Sugar?"

"No, no thank you. I don't drink coffee." Afraid she'd insulted her, Bianca plundered on. "And, I'm sorry, I don't know your name."

"Nadya. Lisette was my daughter."

Was. The weight of it made Bianca's knees buckle. She lowered herself onto a chair next to a cork board plastered with pictures and coupons held in place with brightly colored thumbtacks. A business card loomed in the upper left corner. Jewel Glasser, PhD. Bianca wanted to hate her, but if she was trying to help . . . She zeroed in on a calendar, specifically today's date, and the notation in purple ink. "Kate and Lisette—Mommy & Me class." She bit her lip and looked away.

"Tea?" Nadya asked.

"Yes, thank you."

After lighting the stove, Nadya stretched on tip-toes to pull a box from the cupboard. "Lisette and I drink coffee, but we keep tea."

Bianca imagined Nadya and Lisette sitting here, sipping from colorful mugs, talking about what kind of chicken they'd make for dinner or what to get Kate for her birthday.

"Something bothers you," Nadya said.

"Well, I—"

"Who's here, Babcia?" The question came first, followed by a little girl. "I'm Kate, and I'm five," she said, shooting four fingers and a thumb into the air. "Who are you?" Donut in hand. Powdered sugar dappled her tiny mouth. A knot swelled in

Bianca's throat. Lisette's daughter. Her corn-silk hair fell uncombed down her back, and she had her mother's chin, shaped like the bottom of a valentine heart.

"Zaichik, bunny, this Miss Bianca." Nadya ran her hand down the tangles of wispy hair. "No sweets in front room, but today I think . . ."

Bianca remembered the concessions made after her mother died. As if a later bedtime or an extra dessert could ease her grief.

She pulled the square of tissue from her purse, unwrapped the necklace. "This was Lisette's. I didn't want it to get tied up in red tape and wanted to make sure it was handled with care, and . . . well . . . I wanted to bring it to you."

Nadya stared at Bianca's outstretched hand. She locked arms over her waist, tapping an index finger at her elbow. "Is not Lisette's."

"I found it in my studio. It's an L, and I assumed . . ."

"I would know." Confusion and then realization swept across Nadya's face. "Is this trick? You think she steal."

Before Bianca could respond, Kate, who'd been quietly licking the last of the powdered sugar from her fingertips said, "You look like my mommy," adding, "she died." Spoken like she had no idea what that meant.

Bianca's eyes burned. She turned to Nadya, whose round face pinched tight.

"I'm sorry," Bianca said. "This is a difficult time." She hastily rewrapped the necklace.

Nadya squashed the little girl to her bosom, released her. "Zaichik, go watch TV. Babcia with you soon."

Kate, lower lip pushed out, marched from the room.

Nadya fisted her hands on her ample waist and clamped her lips, "Did Beacham woman send you?"

Bianca froze, dumbfounded.

"You say my daughter steal. She's died." Nadya's hand flew over her shirt in two swipes, making the sign of the cross.

"It's not like that at all."

"Go, please."

"If I could explain—"

"Go, please," Nadya repeated.

"I'm so sorry," Bianca said in a strangled whisper.

Backing out of the driveway, she bumped into the mailbox. Could she make this day any worse? The mailbox was fine, but she wasn't. Barreling toward home, her thoughts twisted and spiraled as she navigated the corkscrew turns of Route 9. A stolen necklace? Charity? All the questions sharpened to a single point, a chiseled, black dot of reality.

Nothing could bring that little girl's mother back. Nothing.

Blue lights pulsing in her rearview mirror lassoed her attention. Tires squealed as the Pathfinder lurched to a stop, the police car behind her just inches from her bumper.

Tucker appeared at her window. "Practicing for the Indy?"

She dropped her head against the headrest. "I'm not having the best day, Tucker."

"Figured something was up. You were going twenty over. Did you know that?"

She didn't, but nodded anyway.

"And braking like that, when you're going that fast, makes me want to send you back to driver's ed." Tucker hooked his thumbs in his belt and dropped his shoulders, a casual stance, wrinkled shirt, conservatively buzzed and precisely spiked hair. A study in contrasts.

"You can give me a warning, right?"

He scratched at his cheek. "You're lucky I'm feeling generous today. And listen, I'm glad I bumped into you." He draped his forearms across the door, drawing so close she could smell salami and hot mustard on his breath. "Not a secret Dylan and I are best buds. Nothing will ever change that."

Tucker had taken Dylan's dismissal from the police force hard. He blamed himself for not stepping in, for not doing more. Bianca shivered, cinched her coat. Dylan's anguished eyes, the day it happened and each day after, burned in her memory, so clear it still broke her heart. A high-speed chase. A boy on his way home from football practice, in the wrong place at the wrong time. A ruined life.

Two ruined lives.

The boy wound up in a wheelchair, and each time Dylan saw him around town, the sight shredded his already tattered psyche.

No one blamed Dylan, but he couldn't stop blaming himself. Drinking numbed his pain. After showing up for work reeking of alcohol, they had no choice but to let him go.

Tucker rapped on the door. "I'd do anything for him, Bianca. He's like a brother to me."

Bianca fixed on a row of wind turbines in the distance, imagined them cartwheeling off their bases. "I care about him, too. It's over between us, but I only want what's best for him."

Tucker removed his sunglasses, and his eyes drilled through her. "You need to be careful about Finn. There's no such thing as a plutonic relationship between a man and a woman."

Platonic. She turned her lips inward to contain her smile.

"He's falling for you, Bianca. If you two get together, Dylan'll . . . well, I don't know what he'll do. Seeing you with anyone would kill him, but with his own brother . . ." Tucker shook his head. "He still loves you, that's all."

A car behind them drew their attention.

"Speak of the devil," Tucker said as they turned to see Finn striding up to Bianca's car.

"Everything all right?" Finn asked.

"Just havin' a chat." Tucker's focus bounced from Finn to Bianca and back. "What're you doing here, anyway?"

"Took a fun call over on Pineview. Neighbors got into a pissing match over the property line. Literally."

"Better you than me." Tucker backed away from Bianca's car and guided his sunglasses into place with his index finger. "Watch your speed. You need to make it home safe."

Finn struggled to avoid her eyes, and her face heated.

As they left, Bianca flicked the switch to close her window. She had her hand on the gear shift when her cell rang.

"Don't leave." Finn's plea rolled over her.

Tucker waved and motored away. Finn was adjusting his mirrors.

"All right," she said.

When Tucker had driven out of sight, Finn climbed from the squad car and into Bianca's passenger seat. "The calls have been coming from Lost."

She felt her face fold.

"You okay?" he asked.

Not even close. She turned to him, twisted her hands. "Just when I thought things couldn't get any worse."

He gave her a considering look.

She pulled the square of tissue paper from her purse and unfolded it. Lifting the necklace, she let it dangle from her thumb and forefinger, flickers of light refracting off the rearview mirror. "I found it in my classroom. Since none of my students claimed it, I assumed it had to be Lisette's and—"

Finn settled his hand on her shoulder. "Wait. When?"

"Sunday. After the murder. I tried to return it to Lisette's mother today. I know I waited too long—"

"What the hell were you thinking? Of all the impulsive . . . Tampering with evidence is a felony, Bianca. The shoes and clothes were bad enough, but you could argue lack of intent, now this . . . removing something that could have direct bearing on the case, knowingly hiding it from the authorities . . ."

Hands fisted in his hair, he tore at it until it was completely disheveled. She swallowed a burst of laughter, an ill-timed snort.

"You're laughing?"

"I'm sorry. It's just your hair and—"

"My hair? You're laughing at my hair?"

"Trust me, I know how serious this is. I messed up. But I laugh when I'm nervous."

"I thought you cleaned when you're nervous," he snapped, but there was a note of humor, and his face crinkled like an actor trying to deliver a line without cracking up.

Trapping her bottom lip between her teeth, she let the necklace drop. It nestled back onto the tissue, and she ran a finger over the L. "I thought it was hers."

"This just gives Carmichael more ammo."

After a band of silence, Bianca said, "When I was eight, my mother died in a car crash."

The frustration on Finn's face dissipated as confusion took its place.

"She was going to the store for medicine," Bianca continued steadily. "For me. That was the last time we saw her."

Finn reached for her hand. Holding tight, he grazed his thumb across her knuckles.

The simple touch, his touch, gave her the strength to continue. "After my mother's accident, the police were less than compassionate—it was all very routine—and the way they treated her personal effects . . . my dad snapped."

Now Finn offered his other hand and cocooned hers.

"Lisette's mother, Nadya, told me this isn't Lisette's."

His concern became more pronounced, turned her inside out. She rubbed at her temples, the beginnings of a headache.

"I'll take it into the station, give it to Carmichael." Finn reached for the necklace.

She blew out a puff of air, placed the bundle in his palm. "There's more."

He fell back against the seat.

"Nadya thought I was accusing Lisette of stealing the necklace. She asked if Charity sent me. What could that mean?"

"I have no idea."

"Charity does hate—"

"Let's not jump to conclusions. It's possible Lisette had jewelry her mother didn't know about. Maybe other secrets too." He deposited the necklace in his shirt pocket and patted it. "I'll take care of this."

Despite his assurances, Bianca's stomach churned. She'd really blown it this time, and felt stupid in about fifty different ways.

"I'd feel better if you were staying with Helen or Maris," Finn said. "Or . . ."

He wasn't going to suggest his place, was he?

The faintest of smiles played on his full, serious mouth. "Can't blame me for trying." He stepped from the car and returned to his cruiser.

Bianca had only driven a short distance when her cell rang again.

"How'd it go?" Maris asked.

"It didn't. I'm not sure what I was expecting, but Lisette's mom—"

"You did the right thing."

"Maris, can we discuss this later? I shouldn't be on my cell. I just sweet-talked Tucker out of giving me a speeding ticket."

"Okay. But . . ."

"What?"

"Have you seen a newspaper today?"

Bianca's thoughts traveled back to the convenience store. "Why?"

"That reporter finally got his story."

Maris paused and Bianca was in no rush to fill the void. She knew what was coming, and it wasn't going to be good.

"From Jewel Glasser," Maris continued.

And there it was.

"Pulling into a gas station now. Call you back."

Bianca stashed her cell in her purse, whipped into a parking spot, and hustled inside. She found a fresh stack of papers and scanned the front page. How had she missed it before?

From Elusive to Exclusive: Faculty Member Finally Speaks Out

By Jerry Kincaid

In an exclusive interview, Jewel Glasser, PhD, Director of Counseling at Brookefield College, shared her thoughts about the recent shooting in Weaver Hall. "A child has been left motherless, and I think it's vital that we pull together as a community." Dr. Glasser has volunteered her services and is working closely with Chief Carmichael, RPPD, to create a profile for the person responsible for Lisette Divac's untimely death.

Dr. Glasser's methodology advocates vigorous dialogue defined as, "healing at its core." Through intense counseling, she has already helped students, faculty, and family members of the deceased with their grief. "This is a highly unusual crime for our quiet town, but the silence surrounding it is even more unusual."

The doctor refused to comment on details of the investigation, stating it could compromise progress. She is hopeful the first person at the scene, art professor Bianca James, will recall something significant. "Bianca James may be key in this investigation."

Attempts were made to speak with Ms. James, but she refused to comment on the events surrounding November 13.

First Carmichael wanted to pin the murder on her, and now Jewel was implying to the entire town that she had something to hide. Bianca stuffed the paper in the rack, doing her best not to hyperventilate, but Jewel's accusation beat inside her, insistent as a heartbeat.

⚘ FOURTEEN ⚘

THE television wasn't even on, but Mack clutched the remote, eyes glued to the screen in anticipation. He'd been wearing the same getup for three days, camouflage shirt over plaid pajama pants.

"Good thing camo never goes out of style," Finn said, trying for a light way to tell his dad he needed a shower and a change of clothes. "Maybe tomorrow swap it for the sweater Aunt Sara made."

Mack stretched in his easy chair. "Not going."

"We always go to Aunt Sara's for Thanksgiving."

"Go if you want."

"I'm not leaving you here alone. Have you told her you're not coming? You haven't missed since . . ." Finn stopped short of mentioning his mom's departure, of how his aunt had tried for years to smooth over her absence on holidays.

Mack shrugged, punched a button, and the TV roared to life. "Give her a call for me, will ya?"

"Everyone will miss you."

Curling further into the chair, Mack seemed shrunken, pathetic. Two words Finn would have never imagined associating with his dad. Marked sadness, loss of interest, trouble sleeping and eating— signs the doctor had warned about.

Suicidal tendencies.

"All those kids running around, raising a ruckus." Mack clasped his hands and kneaded them before he went on. "Who knows how they'll turn out?"

The thought loomed—a future without Mack Tierny. Finn gave his dad's shoulder a squeeze. "We'll have Thanksgiving here then. Just us."

"Who's gonna cook it?"

"I will."

Mack let out a belch of laughter. "TV dinners?"

"No, a real turkey with all the trimmings."

A curious look of doubt from Mack. "If you say so."

"You'll see." Finn trigger-fingered his dad, and Mack responded with a half-hearted, matched gesture. "I'll go get groceries now before there's nothing left."

"Hold up," Mack said, struggling to pull his wallet from his pocket. He extracted a handful of crinkled singles, held them out. "Get some cranberry sauce, that . . . j—the one that holds the shape of the can."

"Sure, Dad, anything you want, but I have money."

A startled look crossed Mack's face as if realizing for the first time Finn wasn't a kid anymore. "Remember when we had Thanksgiving dinner at the cabin? Your mom and I fought all week about hauling everything up there. But it was the best. Remember that, Bird?"

"I'll make this one memorable too, Dad. Promise."

Once in the car, Finn reached for his phone. He scrolled through his contacts looking for Aunt Sara and locked on Carmichael. Wouldn't it be better to tell him about the necklace in person? But why ruin everyone's holiday? One more day surely wouldn't make that much difference, would it? He called Aunt Sara. Disappointed, she told him to make it a good Thanksgiving for her brother. "Unless there's a miracle, it'll be his last." Her words echoed after the call ended.

Finn made a mental list as he drove. *Turkey, sweet potatoes, corn . . .* The necklace. He'd never pull Thanksgiving together with it dangling over him.

The day Bianca gave it to him he'd taken it to the only jewelry store in town, a boutique on Main, and a hair salon that sold accessories. No one recognized it. One woman said she'd seen something similar on eBay, only in silver. "Gold is making a comeback, but this looks like something my mom would have worn." An online search yielded nada; this thing could have been drop shipped from China.

He cranked the wheel, turned toward Carmichael's house, and prepared for the fallout. A sinking sensation spread through his limbs. Was he delivering more than the necklace? Bianca's head on a platter?

Pulling up to 26 Granger Street, he did a double take. A modest house in stark contrast to the fancy pens and silk ties Carmichael flaunted. He checked the address again. This was the right place all right, but how many dictators ruled from humble, ranch-style homes behind a mailbox shaped like a birdhouse?

Carmichael answered the door, and Finn almost didn't recognize him in sweatpants and T-shirt. "Tierny?"

"Do you have a minute, sir?"

Carmichael opened the door wider, a puzzled look on his face.

Finn removed his hat, stamped his boots on the outside mat, and stepped onto the entryway rug. The house smelled of garlic and spices, and classical music drifted from the kitchen. A large dog lounged on his oversized bed in the living room. Shep.

"I'll get right to it." He reached in his pocket and unfolded the tissue paper, crumpled and worn from repeated wrapping and unwrapping. "Bianca James found this the Sunday after the shooting and assumed it was the victim's. She thought she'd do the family a favor and return it. She was trying to do a good thing . . ."

Finn stopped when he realized Carmichael wasn't reacting. Instead of exploding like a Roman candle, he froze, a hollow, catatonic look claiming his eyes. Finn was tempted to snap his fingers and yank him from that thousand-yard stare, but Carmichael coughed, cleared his throat, and closed his hand around the necklace.

"I'll take care of it. You have a nice Thanksgiving now, Tierny."

Nothing about Bianca.

As Finn turned to leave, Carmichael's wife appeared, wiping her hands on an apron.

"This is Officer Tierny," Carmichael said. "The transfer from Pittsburgh I told you about."

Her feigned smile conveyed suspicion, which made him wonder exactly what Carmichael had told her. Finn extended his hand, and she skimmed it with her fingertips.

"Pleased to meet you," he said.

She nodded, more in dismissal than anything.

"Just some police business," Carmichael said, the necklace hidden somewhere inside his tight fist.

A teenage boy strolled up behind his parents, but soon his curiosity melted into a vacant stare.

Just what the world needed, Carmichael 2.0.

"Have a happy Thanksgiving, Mrs. Carmichael, Chief Carmichael."

Finn hurried down the steps and into his car, wanting to make his getaway before the chief realized he had forgotten to throttle him. His reaction, or lack of reaction, to Bianca tampering with potential evidence had been downright weird. Like Tucker said, Carmichael was a damn chameleon, changing colors from one situation to the next. Finn didn't even want to think about what color the necklace would bring out once he emerged from his trance.

At Friendly Family Market, there were only five turkeys left in the deep freeze and a sparse inventory of canned pumpkin and cranberry sauce on the end caps. Customers roamed the store with frantic looks, at odds with the piped music suggesting a manufactured calm.

Finn dropped a bag of Idaho potatoes in his buggy. *How do you make gravy?* His visions of cooking Thanksgiving dinner morphed to a scene where he and Dylan piled Mack into the car and drove to McDonald's.

He picked up a sweet potato, turned it over in his hand, and muttered, "Bake or boil?"

A voice came from behind him. "It's a yam."

Finn swung around to find Bianca, hair tucked under a knit cap, half falling out. Painted-on jeans accentuated every glorious curve. No makeup. No evidence of any effort to enhance her looks. None needed. "Ah." He examined the vegetable. "That explains why it didn't answer me."

"They're the least talkative spud." A smile swept her face. "You're cooking?"

"Strict orders from Aunt Sara to make all Dad's favorites—like these." He tossed the potato and caught it.

"You know how?"

"No idea. Do you?"

Bianca raised a hand, surrender-style. She shifted, transferred her shopping basket from the crook of one elbow to the other. "I wanted to tell you . . . I didn't think it through, and you shouldn't have to—"

"It's done. I just gave the necklace to Carmichael."

"And?"

"And nothing. He didn't say anything."

Bianca winced. "The calm before the storm?"

Suddenly drawn to the strap of her handbag, Finn noticed the way it pulled against her coat, slipping down, revealing the beginning of a shoulder, a soft supple shoulder. A powerful wave surged through him. She moved him in an unexpected way, a way that grew stronger each time he saw her, a way that threatened his loyalty to his brother.

"Try to put Carmichael out of your mind." Damn, he wanted to put *her* out of his mind, but her eyes, the turn of her lips chipped away at his limited resolve. "You probably already have plans tomorrow."

"Helen's anti-turkey day. She'll be at a potlatch down at the Indian reservation, and Maris is on her way to the airport . . ."

No one should be alone on Thanksgiving.

"But Picasso and I make our own fun. We usually curl up on the couch watching *Finding Nemo* and pig out on all our favorites."

Finn peered at the lettuce and celery in Bianca's basket. "Invite a rabbit or two, and you've got a party."

A pimply stock boy rushed by with a case of Stove Top stuffing and was ambushed by a woman in a turquoise, polyester pantsuit.

"Where are those little red apples in the jar?" she pleaded. The boy gave efficient directions, complete with left and right hand turns and aisle numbers.

"Have dinner with us," Finn said.

"That's a nice offer, but—"

"Did I make it sound like a question?"

Bianca chewed at her lip. "It might be awkward. Dylan . . . and that means Jewel." She shook her head. "You saw the article, right?"

"I don't think Dylan will bring her after that. He was pissed."

"Like I actually know something I'm not telling."

"Journalists are . . . and Jewel . . ." *Show some support.* He reached out but stopped short of touching her arm, and ended up squeezing his fist like he was trying to remember something important. The thought of touching her, even through her coat, capsized the idea of friendship and steered him in a different direction. *Focus.* "Help me pick out a turkey."

"You're serious."

Finn locked eyes with Bianca. "I never joke about poultry."

She entered a number on her phone. "Maris is a gourmet cook," she explained as she waited. "Hey, Mare. Need your expertise on turkey selection. No, I'm not . . . I'm helping Finn." There was a brief pause, and then Bianca said to him, "She says we should have the food poisoning hotline number handy."

"And a fire extinguisher."

"Ask the butcher for fresh, not frozen. There's no time to thaw it properly," Bianca relayed. "How many people?"

It was good to see her like this. Happy. Certainly more lighthearted, temporarily shelving the horror of the last two weeks. He wanted to bottle this moment, the carefree banter. That way, they could share it again, together, take a swig of this sweet elixir that blotted out the rest of the world.

But that wasn't going to happen. He'd eventually catch another case. Bianca would go back to her life. Possibly back to Dylan.

❧

On Thanksgiving morning, Bianca arrived, celery in one hand, a bag of mini marshmallows in the other.

"Always a winning combination," Finn said. He imagined kissing her cheek, his lips lingering as if held there by magnetic force. Instead, he shoved his hands in his pockets.

Bianca presented the celery. "For the stuffing." Then the marshmallows. "For the sweet potatoes."

"I see you've thought of everything." Finn caressed her with his eyes. But his dad, Dylan. This was a mistake.

A beautiful mistake.

She moved to the kitchen window and stuck a finger into one of the potted plants on the sill. A nearby coffee mug became a watering can, and it struck Finn how she negotiated her way by feel, by texture, brushing her fingers across things as she went.

Mack came into the kitchen, and when he saw her, his face registered a blip of delight. She turned, and it sagged in disappointment. "Oh."

"Good morning, Mack. Happy Thanksgiving."

He grunted and left.

"Don't worry about him," Finn whispered as they watched him shuffle to his easy chair and settle in. Finn rubbed his hands together. "Time to cook this sucker." He hefted the turkey from the refrigerator, slapped it into the roaster, and snipped the wrapper away with a pair of scissors. "Can you turn the oven on? Let's see, it says 350."

"¡Hola!" A voice drifted in the back door.

"I hope you don't mind. Maris' plans changed."

"A few necessities." Maris stumbled to the counter under the weight of a bulging grocery bag. "Sorry to crash like this."

"It's not considered crashing if you're the chef," Finn said, relieved to have someone there who actually knew what they were doing but disappointed to have to share Bianca.

Maris' gaze flickered between them. "My mom called as I was boarding the plane to tell me they all had the flu. I don't do the flu." She brushed past them and examined the turkey. "You're kidding, right?"

"What?"

"For starters"—Maris reached into the cavity and pulled out a waxy bag—"you might want to remove these giblets before you put this guy into the oven." She glanced at the tag from the discarded wrapping. "Twenty-five pounds? Did you invite the whole neighborhood?"

"It was all they had," Finn said, adding, "We like leftovers."

In the living room, Mack punched through channels then turned the TV off. "Nothing but parades," he growled. "I hate parades."

"It's Thanksgiving, Dad."

Mack grunted and jerked his chin to the CD player. "Put some of that . . . Sss . . . music on that I like, Bird."

Finn picked up a CD and showed him the cover.

"That's the one." Mack pushed the lever to recline his chair. In a moment, Santana's distinctive guitar licks filled the room.

Maris and Bianca started dancing and twirling, weaving their way through the kitchen. Finn leaned against the counter, absorbing the scene, before tapping Maris on the shoulder.

She stepped away, and Finn took Bianca into his arms as "The Game of Love" started. She settled into him for a brief moment, then adjusted to a pose more fitting a middle school dance. But as the song played on, she moved closer, cinching her arms around his waist, filling him with a mixture of fire and ice. He closed his eyes and let the lyrics filter through him, wishing he could sing them into her ear.

Finn dipped Bianca, and as the song rolled through the second chorus, it dawned on him . . . there was no turning back.

"These potatoes aren't going to peel themselves," Maris said from what seemed like another world.

Bianca broke away, grabbed the potato peeler.

It took a few moments for his brain to grope beyond having Bianca in his arms. Her head on his shoulder, arms around his waist. Damn. He needed to peel potatoes or he'd be running down the hall for a cold shower.

Over the next few hours, they followed Maris' every instruction. "Baste. Measure. Stir."

"This has to be easier than cooking for your nine brothers and sisters back in Peru," Bianca said.

Maris pointed a wooden spoon at her. "¡Tu no tienes ni idea! Don't forget the truckload of relatives who came every Sunday. I was cooking for thirty by the time I was twelve!"

Finn was letting out an astonished low whistle when Dylan came through the door, alone. If he was surprised to see Bianca there, he didn't let on. Typical stoic mug, studied nonchalance. Maybe this would be all right.

Dylan approached Bianca as if she was there for him and kissed her cheek. "Good to see you." He moved to Maris, but she turned away and lanced the ends off a bundle of asparagus with a Ginsu knife.

Maybe it wouldn't be all right.

"Hello, Maris," he said to her back on a long exhale.

Dylan opened the refrigerator, grabbed a Bud from the bottom shelf, and popped the lid. After a long draw, he wiped the back of his hand across his mouth. "Football game on yet?" He started for the living room, pivoted. "Unless you need help." A lame afterthought.

Before Finn could respond, the back door swung open again. Jewel, toting two bottles of wine, her hair a shade darker than usual, almost matching the Cabernet in her right hand. Her attention snapped to Bianca.

The possibility of a drama-free day took a nose dive. In a glance, Finn sent Bianca an implicit apology.

"Thought we were on a break," Dylan said through clenched teeth.

Jewel responded by brushing her lips across his cheek and whispering something in his ear. Dylan shrugged, took another swill of beer, and followed her into the living room.

"Mack Tierny, you old sweetheart," she said in a pitch usually reserved for babies and puppies. As she threw her arms around him, the lever on his recliner gave way, sending him into an upright position. She rocked him from side to side and leaned close, saying something no one else could hear.

The scene set off a flare in Finn, and he started for his dad until

Maris interrupted with a question about seating. He kept a watchful eye on Jewel as he wedged two extra folding chairs around the small dining room table. Her fawning over Mack was a thinly veiled attempt to get closer to Dylan.

When Jewel released Mack, he said, "Who are you?"

A wave of chuckles wafted from the kitchen.

She sank to her knees, grabbed his hands, and bounced them on his lap. "Of course you know who I am."

Finn cringed. If she had her way, she might someday add, "your daughter-in-law."

Bianca strolled into the living room. "Jewel, maybe you could set the table," she said in a tone reaching toward civility.

Jewel took her time getting to her feet. "Sure. Sure, I'll set the table."

"Join me," Mack said to Bianca, brightening. "That is, if you're not busy."

She eased onto the couch. "I like Santana, too."

"Of course you do. Remember that night . . ."

"Mack, I don't think—"

"You don't, do you? And never did." Something was brewing behind Mack's eyes. "You wouldn't have done what you did, leave because it suited you, if you did think."

Finn was making his way toward them when fury stampeded in the form of a remote flung against the wall with all the efficiency of a looter with a brick. A coffee mug sailed next, before he upended the TV tray, sending tissues, pens, and nail clippers flying. Dylan and Maris were en route to him, but Jewel got there first.

"Let's give him some space," she said, laying her hands on Mack's, easing him back to his chair, her voice morphing to soothing tones. "Good. Breathe with me . . . listen to the water fall . . . the sun is warming your face . . . smell the fresh air . . . you're with someone you love . . ."

Finn watched in awe as she went on that way, reclaiming his good humor. Soon he removed a black comb from his pocket and started raking it through his hair as if nothing had happened.

After they put things back into place, Finn said, "Think we're ready to eat," eager to change the day's trajectory before the next disaster hit.

As they shuttled plates to the table, the door burst open. "Dibs on a drumstick."

"Tucker!" Finn slapped him on the back. "I didn't think you'd come."

"Melanie won't eat until she's seen the last float in the Macy's parade and made a couple of floats of her own. This guy's got a different idea." He patted his ample belly.

"Two Thanksgiving dinners?" Dylan asked.

Tucker grinned. "Been training all my life." He hooked a thumb in his sweatpants and pulled.

"So much for leftovers," Finn said.

After a round of greetings, Maris whisked past, balancing the turkey on a large platter. "Get it while it's hot."

The array of food resembled a Norman Rockwell painting. As everyone took their seats, Finn dragged his eyes over players in the scene, a very skewed version of the perfect all-American family.

Mack sat at the head with Bianca to his right, Maris next to her. Around the table: Dylan, Jewel, Tucker, and Finn.

Mack raised his glass. "We've got a lot to be thankful for." He scanned the group, stalling on Bianca.

A stifling quiet descended.

"Ouch." Red splotches bloomed on Bianca's napkin where she dabbed at her finger.

"What happened?" Finn asked.

"I thought I saw a chip on the rim of my wine glass and when I ran my finger over it . . ."

Finn moved to her side. "Let me see."

"Don't be silly. It's a little nick."

After a slug of wine, Jewel said, "I didn't see any chip."

"Are you okay?" Maris asked.

"Please, everyone, I'm fine. Let's eat."

"Let me get you something for that." Before Finn could take a step, Dylan was in the kitchen rummaging through the cabinet for a Band-Aid.

Maris carved the turkey, and side dishes rounded the table. The clank of forks against plates filled the room.

"Honestly, I didn't notice it," Jewel repeated.

Bianca locked eyes with her. "It's not your fault, Jewel. I should be more careful around sharp objects."

Though Jewel didn't respond, her expression said, "Damn right."

"It's Rose's fault if anybody's," Dylan said. "Just more of the damaged goods she left behind."

Mack pitched forward. "Leave your mother out of this."

And there it was, the past stealing into the present, ready to demolish the future.

Tucker tapped his fork on his plate and eyed Maris with admiration. "Attention please. This is the best stuffing I've ever had. The best everything."

Maris bowed her head in a deep nod. "Gracias." She hopped to her feet, curtseyed, and blew kisses to a ribbon of chuckles.

Dylan returned with a Band-Aid and carefully wrapped Bianca's finger.

A sense of panic spread through Finn. *What if they get back together?* A glance at Jewel's stricken face told him she was thinking the same.

Dylan plunked back in his seat, drained his wine in two gulps, and refilled his glass. "How 'bout another toast?"

All eyes turned to him.

He opened his mouth to speak, paused before he said, "No, can't say that." After a few beats. "Okay. Here it is. We're all on the same ride."

"That's it? That's your toast?" Tucker asked.

"Yeah, that's it. Got something better?" Dylan challenged.

"It's so—"

"Cryptic." Maris supplied.

"Yeah, that." Tucker's fork hovered over his plate. "What does it mean?"

Now Mack spoke. "Life. Means we're all stuck on this damn merry-go-round, and it keeps spinning and spinning and spinning." He leaned back in his chair. "And then you're dead."

A real Norman Rockwell Thanksgiving.

"It's true." Jewel jumped in. "It's like Lisette Divac. It's sad, but reality. Death is not the enemy here, fear of death is."

"And thank you, Jewel, for pointing out my part in her reality," Bianca said. "For suggesting that I'm withholding information."

Jewel canted her head, a deliberate tilt in Bianca's direction.

"Why'd you feel the need to throw Bianca under the bus?" The question exploded from Maris, each syllable a detonation.

"Let's not . . ." Finn was thinking Plan B, the Golden Arches, sounded like a five-star restaurant right about now.

"It's good therapy to talk about it," Jewel said. "In fact I suggested a town hall meeting to Chief Carmichael so people can air their concerns."

"Speaking of Carmichael." Tucker waited until he had complete attention once again. "You all know he doesn't work the day before holidays, right?"

"Yeah, yeah." All except Jewel seemed eager to move away from the murder. She let out a huff of opposition and adjusted everything in reach, her napkin, wine glass, silverware.

"Yesterday he came in out of the blue, and Charity Beacham, you know, the mattress heiress, came in too." Tucker scooted closer to the table, nearly dousing his shirt in the gravy pooled in his mountain of mashed potatoes. "They're always meeting about community stuff, but the night before Thanksgiving at five o'clock?"

After Finn delivered the necklace, Carmichael must have taken it straight to the station, but how did Charity Beacham figure in? Was it possible Lisette did steal it from her? And why was Carmichael suddenly willing to let Bianca off the hook for tampering with a crime scene?

"Charity's dad invented the twirling mattress." Tucker stirred the air with one finger.

Finn tried in vain to imagine a twirling bed.

"Wait, I remember those," Maris said. "I saw the commercials when I was visiting my sister in San Diego. Dr. Beacham conducted studies and found that people rested better at different points of the night depending on the direction of their head. The mattress slowly revolves, and after eight hours your head is back where it started."

Dylan scratched at his temple. "How do you know it went around if you were asleep?"

"Good question," Bianca said.

"Back to the story." Tucker stuffed a forkful of food in his mouth and pushed it to the side so he could speak. "So Charity and Carmichael are in his office for a long time—"

"I don't know anybody with a twirling mattress," Dylan said.

Tucker chewed his food, swallowed. "Never caught on around here. They're bookoo bucks."

Jewel rolled her eyes. "They're popular on the West Coast. Beacham made a fortune."

"Anyway . . ." Tucker brought attention back to himself. "Do you want to hear this or not?"

"Tell the story," Finn said, keeping tabs on his dad, whose eyelids thickened with boredom.

"Had something I wanted to ask Carmichael, so before I left I knocked on the door." Tucker straightened in his chair.

"And?"

"He opened it and, well . . . he looked all . . . ruffled." Tucker wiggled fingers over his head.

"Ruffled?" Finn asked.

"Yeah, not his usual perfect self." Tucker raised an eyebrow, lowered his chin, and flashed a cheeky smile. "Ruffled."

"Ruffled," Dylan repeated, as if enjoying the sound of the word.

Tucker nodded furiously as everyone around the table caught on.

"Was Charity ruffled too?" Maris asked.

"Both of them. Pretty darn ruffled."

"Carmichael and Charity Beacham?" Finn thought about the family photo in Carmichael's office, the way he'd taken such care dusting it off.

"What I don't get, well, she usually likes her men . . ." Tucker directed his comment to Dylan. "You want to explain it?"

"I don't know anything about what she likes." Dylan looked like the cat who'd swallowed the canary and a pet mouse to boot.

Jewel stood, tossed her napkin down, and reached for a bowl. "We need more gravy." She headed for the kitchen.

"Nice light little story there, Tuck." Finn was ready to change the subject, but curious just the same.

Tucker shrugged. "I tried."

From the corner of his eye, Finn noticed Bianca had turned to Mack, who was trying unsuccessfully to cut his meat. "Can I . . . is it all right?" she asked him.

Mack nodded and her mouth made a stiff little line while she sawed his turkey into bite-sized pieces. It was the maternal thing to do, and this must be the prescribed determination to go with it.

When she finished, Mack placed a hand on hers. "You always know what I need." He motioned across the table. "Now, will you pass me some of those sweet potatoes, Rose?"

∽ FIFTEEN ∾

BIANCA rolled two blue pills around in her hand before swallowing them with her morning tea. She rubbed her temples, hoping the ibuprofen would kick in soon. Thanksgiving had been tiring and confusing. And wonderful. She'd spent the rest of the weekend holed up in her studio, trying to work, but her thoughts kept tiptoeing back.

Making nice with Jewel, watching her nuzzle up to Dylan had been a tightrope walk—without a net. One wrong word, one misstep, and splat. A wave of guilt crashed. Bianca had been the one to end it with Dylan, so how could she be anything but happy for him no matter who he chose? He needed to move on, and so did she.

And Mack's behavior, his outburst, his mistaking her for Rose. It was so unbelievable, this thing that had hijacked his brain. She couldn't imagine not recognizing the person next to you, the swimming in and out of lucidity. It had to be hard on him. And for Dylan and Finn.

Finn. She poked her thigh, but stopped short of pinching. B. F. Skinner's grand plan for negative reinforcement didn't come close to working. Try as she might, her growing feelings were becoming impossible to deny.

But needing or wanting someone hadn't worked so well for her in the past. Losing herself in her art and teaching was safer, far less complicated.

Bianca drew a breath as if preparing to dive into deep water before she stepped into the storage room. Though crammed with art supplies, the space felt empty, cold. A life had ended here. And the victim's child, Kate—was motherless at five. Bianca squeezed her eyes shut as she pulled the supply cart from the room and slammed off the lights.

Students began trickling in, and she wiped her palms on her smock. The seminar on drawing the human figure was small, an elective most shied away from. Few possessed the talent to make it to this level. Finn did. He had painted as if born with paintbrush in hand, bypassing obstacles that plagued others. If only he'd stuck with it.

As the class set up easels, the familiar scrape and scratch, hinges screeching open, piercing the hush in the room, Bianca busied herself with her lecture notes. A tap on her shoulder wheeled her around.

"Are you all right, Professor James?"

Amanda. The student who reminded her of that sensitive sister in *Little Women*—what was her name—Beth? Amy? The fragile, sickly one. Bianca feared if she said the wrong thing, if she even looked at her the wrong way, the poor girl would burst into tears.

Innocent, harmless Amanda. Who had Bianca been expecting?

She manufactured a relaxed posture. "I'm fine."

"You look nervous or something," Amanda said. "The whole campus is talking. You've got a stalker or something, right?" Her voice as fragile as blown glass.

Amanda's lip trembled, and Bianca laid a reassuring hand on her arm. With school shootings so prevalent now, no wonder these kids were on edge.

"I know it's unsettling, but everything will be okay. I promise." An empty promise, but she needed to calm Amanda's fears. "Let's get set up. Eager to see what you create today." Once everyone settled and turned expectantly toward her, Bianca cleared her throat. "First, I hope you all enjoyed your Thanksgiving."

The students murmured, and Lahn, a pencil-thin Vietnamese

boy who didn't look like he could finish a Happy Meal, much less a Thanksgiving feast, patted his stomach. "Oh yeah, ate half the bird myself and spent the rest of the weekend in a tryptophan coma."

Laughter rippled through the room, a welcome break from the tension. Bianca let her shoulders relax and leaned against a table. She hated to spoil the mood, but she wanted her students to feel comfortable whenever they were here, not merely after a spate of laughter. They needed to get past the idea that something dark lurked behind the stack of canvasses in the supply room.

"Before we begin today, let's talk. Someone's been"—she fumbled for the best explanation—"harassing me with phone calls. It's a juvenile scare tactic and—"

"Is it the same guy who murdered that woman? Didn't she have long blond hair like you?"

The girl closed a fist around her own long blond ponytail and slowly glided the length of it. Did she think she was next? Bianca realized with certainty that her teaching methods classes hadn't come close to preparing her for this. "We don't know anything for sure, but the police are on it. We just need to go on as usual, but if you see something, say something. And remember, Dr. Glasser has extended office hours, so please don't hesitate to make an appointment if you need to talk."

Despite Bianca's personal feelings about Jewel, she respected her work. Her techniques were non-traditional breath work and core energetics. Students kicked, punched, and practiced controlled breathing through sessions, leaving her office renewed. Last year, not long after she'd arrived, Jewel had been called in when a train plowed into a Garrett County school bus, killing eighteen students. She often spoke at seminars and recently led a task force for online bullying. And the way she stepped up on Thanksgiving and handled Mack's outburst . . .

As much as Bianca hated to admit it, she'd caught her own hand hovering over the phone more than once, fingers twitching to dial Jewel's number to take her up on her offer to talk. Anything to stop the persistent visions of Lisette.

But in the end, she couldn't separate Jewel "the healer" from Jewel "Dylan's girlfriend who wanted to scratch her eyes out."

"Any other questions?" Bianca searched her students, hoping her assurances had been enough. "As soon as Justin gets here we'll begin."

Connor, an introspective boy with a trio of silver hoops in his lower lip, opened his mouth to speak, but stopped and turned to a commotion at the door.

Bianca expected Ralph, who'd been checking periodically since the murder, but was shocked to see Emerson, wearing a robe with wide red stripes and an even wider smile. He picked up a stool, strode to the small, elevated stage in the middle of the classroom and planted it there. His robe dropped to the floor, and he sat and posed like Rodin's *The Thinker*, polished muscles bulging.

He swung his arms wide. "Here I am in my birthday suit, and it's not even my birthday."

Several girls giggled.

"What are you doing?" Bianca questioned through tight lips.

"I'm your model," he said, settling back into his pose.

"Where's Justin?"

"Couldn't make it. He's . . . got a nasty hangnail." Emerson winked. "I assure you, ladies and gentlemen, he'll be back as soon as he can find a decent manicurist. Until then, try sketching a real man."

Certain Justin was already spending the stack of cash Emerson likely gave him to skip the modeling gig, she bent, picked up the robe, and thrust it at him. "Get out."

Students buzzed as she stood her ground, glaring.

"Do what she says." All eyes turned again to the doorway where Finn stood, hand resting on the baton at his waist. The room fell silent, save for determined footfalls heading for the stage.

Amanda let out a gasp, and Bianca moved to her, bracing a hand on the girl's shoulder.

"Get dressed," Finn said through gritted teeth. "Now."

"Relax, Iron Mike." Emerson shrugged into the robe in slow motion and took his time tying it shut. He headed for the exit in a jaunty swagger with an intentional shoulder butt directed at Finn.

"Push it, asshole," Finn said in a low growl, "and I'll arrest you for assaulting an officer *and* indecent exposure."

"Dude, this is art class. Naked models welcome. Capisce?" His mocking laughter filled the room. "Oh, I get it, you're jealous. What's the matter, afraid they'd need a magnifying glass to draw your junk?"

The muscles in Finn's jaw tensed. Bianca wedged herself between them, two stallions, heads lowered for battle. "Both of you. Out. Now." She shuttled the men toward the door where Finn blocked Emerson, creating a rampart.

"Just supporting the arts," Emerson said, flashing a grin over Finn's shoulder as he sauntered away, Finn falling into step behind him.

Bianca closed the door, pressed her back against it. "Change of plans. Let's review our gesture drawings from last week."

"That was sick," Connor said.

One of the girls whispered to another, covertly flashed her phone screen. Had they been taking pictures? Emerson was Brookefield's version of a celebrity, but she hoped her students would look deeper and see an insecure man, trying desperately to compensate.

As she attempted to redirect the session, knowing she'd lost them for the rest of the afternoon, Bianca wandered to the window. Her eyes narrowed to the parking lot where she saw Finn pinning Emerson against his BMW.

Several students joined her, phones poised to record the event, no doubt ready to plaster it all over social media.

"Put those away," she said.

With what seemed like a glance in her direction, Finn smacked his hand against the car and stormed off. Emerson got in his car, and a black Mercedes pulled alongside him. Charity. They spoke for a moment before he followed her from the parking lot.

Did everyone in town have a starring role in her nightmare?

Bianca glanced at the clock on the back wall, knowing that she, too, would be lost for the rest of the day.

At her doorstep, Bianca searched her coat pocket for her house key. She'd made a copy for Helen after Finn changed the locks and kept forgetting to put the original back on her key ring. Instead of finding what she was looking for, she pulled out a dollar with highlights matching the one she'd found in her purse at the Balfour. But on this one, angry slashes of red pointed to the creepy eye.

She raced to Helen's, wrangling through a cluster of boxwoods between their houses, thankful for a neighbor who spouted myths, legends, and ancient history like it was her own brand of Tourette's.

The door swung open as if Helen had been anticipating her arrival, and Bianca burst in, waving the dollar. "Do you know what this is?"

"Hello to you, too."

Bianca was momentarily drawn to Helen's snug Juicy Couture hoodie with bedazzled moon and sun patches.

Helen tapped at rays shooting from one of the suns. She shrugged. "I stitched them on. Juicy knows texture and color, but falls short in the celestial design department."

"I've found two of these, highlighted." Bianca pressed the dollar into Helen's hand and hammered a finger at the spot. "And these red arrows. What do they mean?"

Helen placed her hands on Bianca's shoulders. "Deep cleansing breath." Modeling her intent, her chest rose and fell.

Bianca mimicked Helen, but she didn't feel relaxed or cleansed. Anxious, vulnerable, frazzled maybe. Either someone was trying to drive her mad or she already was.

"Where did you find them?" Helen asked.

"One in my purse, one in my pocket."

"Who has access to your things?"

"I don't know. I guess anyone could—"

"Our possessions are material extensions of ourselves, don't you think?" Helen rifled through a drawer in a small end table and extracted a magnifying glass with a zebra-striped Murano handle. She examined the dollar. "Looks like someone's fascinated with the Eye of Horus. It's the symbol of Wadjet, one of the earliest Egyptian goddesses." Her pitch elevated to an excited vibrato. "So many different theories about the all-seeing eye. Many feel it's a symbol of protection, to ward off evil, but others—"

"Others what?"

"In Egyptian mythology, the eye wasn't merely for seeing, but was an agent for action. Either for protection, as I said, or a symbol of fury."

Protection. Finn was trying to protect her, and she kept shoving him away. Was her stubbornness going to get her killed?

Fury. She spun toward the door. "I need to go."

"Don't you want this?"

Bianca took the dollar, crumpled it in her fist.

Helen canted her head thoughtfully. "Have you had a dream about a lizard?"

"I've had bad dreams but no lizards." She considered the lizards in the Dali print in her office and wondered if daydreams counted.

"A lizard dream is a sign that you have a secret enemy. If you haven't had one, I wouldn't worry too much about these dollars."

Dream lizards and all-seeing eyes? Cue The Twilight Zone *music.*

In the same drawer where she'd found the magnifying glass, Helen located a small, red box. She fished around for something and placed it in Bianca's hand. "This should help."

"An acorn?"

Helen looked resolute. "An acorn should be carried at all times to bring good luck and ensure a long life."

Bianca pocketed the acorn and pressed a kiss to Helen's cheek. "I can use all the help I can get."

The second she walked through her door, she punched in Finn's number.

"I have something." She cradled the phone against her shoulder and unzipped her boots. "I've found these . . . dollars."

"Dollars?"

Was she being ridiculous? Helen's explanations about myths and symbols were as out there as the magic carpet on her wall and the tarot cards she flipped for guidance. "The dollars are marked." She continued to share Helen's theory about the eye, hoping he wouldn't send the men in white coats.

"I'm glad you told me. I'll see what I can find out."

She hung up and moved through the house to double-check the locks. Through the window, she caught a glimpse of Helen next door, hands pressed together in front of her. Was she praying to the Egyptian goddess? Helen knew so much about the Eye of Horus. It was almost like she was waiting to enlighten Bianca. The old woman swung her arms in an arc three times as if warding off some evil spirit. Bianca closed the blinds, fell onto the couch, tucking her feet beneath her. Picking up a novel about a boy and the dog who saved him, she started reading, hoping to get lost in a story other than her own.

She couldn't get past the first page.

Grabbing the phone, she redialed Finn. "What was that today, with Emerson?"

"I could ask you the same."

"What does that mean?"

"He was in your class. Naked."

"I was as shocked as you were to see him there. Naked. You sound jealous." Emerson had said the same thing. She wanted to reel it back in. "What did you say to him?"

"That he'd find his balls in a vise if he didn't stay away from you."

"And?"

"That I'd be watching his every move. Wait a minute. How'd you know?"

"You were in the middle of the parking lot, right outside my window. The whole building saw you."

He let out an exasperated puff of air, and she pictured him, face pinched in anger as he paced. Bianca ran her fingers over the chenille couch, her nails tripping along the ridges.

After an extended silence, Finn said, "He's just a pretty boy hiding behind Daddy's money—"

"He wasn't hiding behind anything today."

They laughed briefly, tentatively. She unlatched the front door, stepped out onto the porch, and tilted her face to the endless swath of black sky, but a chilling nimbus of unease spun around her, oozed through her. She moved back inside and locked the door. Playing it safe; living in fear.

"Almost three weeks since the murder, and we're no closer to solving it," he said.

The base of Bianca's neck throbbed, and a sharp pain pinched between her eyebrows. She closed her eyes and saw Amanda, glued to her chair, taking in the bizarre scene. Emerson disrobing. Finn bursting in. "Did you follow him there?"

"Didn't you tell me you thought he might be stalking you?"

"I really don't need to be rescued, Finn. I could have handled—"

"And what if he's more than just an exhibitionist?" he snapped. "You think you can—"

This time she cut the sentence off by hanging up.

⊰ SIXTEEN ⊱

AS Finn stared down the gun's barrel and narrowed sights on his target, he was thirteen again. Deer hunting on a fall morning so cold his breath walled in front of him like a dense fog. An opportunity presented itself after a short time, a buck foraging for food, and Finn raised his gun, hesitated. A nod from his dad confirmed he had a clear shot. He pulled the trigger, watched that majestic creature fall. Heard it thump lifelessly to the earth.

Before his dad or Dylan could congratulate him, he had run back to the house, faster than any deer could, whipped his camo jacket onto the couch, and flopped next to it. The TV guide took the brunt of his anger as he started doodling in the margins. Jagged lines. Circles and squares filled with the turbulent black ink his dad used to do the crossword puzzle. Why did his dad feel the need to force him into things he didn't want to do? Finn pushed the pen through the page and hatched a large hole through the Thursday line-up before his scribbling turned to curlicues. His mother would have ignored the destructive bent of his scrawls and praised whatever came out of him. She never tried to pigeonhole him into being something he wasn't, but just encouraged him, built on what was already there.

But she left.

An hour passed before Mack and Dylan returned.

"What happened to you?" his dad said, his face crunched up with that look he got when he was pissed.

"I hated shooting that innocent animal," Finn cried. "I didn't even want to go in the first place."

"Son, those creatures are running rampant, spreading disease, starving every winter," Mack said. "We're just thinning the herd, that's all."

"Lucky-ass shot." Dylan plopped beside Finn and threw his legs on the coffee table with a thud. "Thanks for sticking around to do the hard part by the way. But I guess that takes a real man."

Like it took a real man to gut a dead animal. Finn yanked his coat out from under his brother. He really hated him sometimes. He could be such a prick. "No feet on the table."

"Mom's rule, and she's *long* gone." Dylan recrossed his ankles, brought them down hard on the table again.

"And she's not coming back." Mack pawed through the refrigerator for a beer and banged the door closed with a force that rattled the hinges. "Might as well try to find her on the idiot box."

"Mom's on TV?" Finn asked.

"Jeesh, stupid. It's called exaggeration." Dylan gave him a look that made him recede. "It means there's about as much chance of seeing her walk through that door as seeing her on *The X-Files*."

Finn's eyes began to burn. But he wasn't going to cry, not in front of his brother. He sprang up to go to his room, and his dad clapped a hand on his shoulder. "Just the three of us now. And we're doing all right."

Dylan rummaged around his backpack and tossed Finn his MP3 player. He'd gotten it for his birthday but had never let Finn use it since his fingers were too "sticky" for the touch wheel. "Yeah, bro," Dylan said, waving his hand around. "Think of this place like a men's restroom. There's a man on the door." He thumped his chest. "The one with the dress on it is somewhere else."

Now a shot rang out next to Finn, pulling him back to this glassy November day. Target practice had been his idea. He had to think of something to get Mack away from a *Friends* marathon where he seemed more interested in the commercials than the show. He'd snuck into Mack's room and put the magazine back into his favorite Glock 32, and prayed he was making the right decision.

He fired his gun, and Mack came up beside him. "Forgot what I taught you, huh?"

In the academy, he'd been the best, even won the Top Shot Award. Only five years ago, but it seemed to stretch behind him exponentially. Was he living his life in dog years?

Finn had come home for the right reasons—his dad had always been there for him—so why did it feel like the old two steps forward, one step back? The case was unsolvable, Bianca was unreadable, and Dylan was plain unpredictable. If it weren't for his dad's illness, he'd . . .

"Sometimes you're a shooting star—" Dylan started.

"And sometimes you're Polaris," Mack finished, throwing his full attention, onus attached, on Dylan. "You stay put—a star to count on."

"Off my game today," Finn jumped in. "Better watch out, my finger could slip, and you'd be out a few toes. Or worse."

Dylan took an exaggerated step back and covered his crotch.

Mack elbowed Finn aside. "Let an ol' coot show you how it's done." He reached for the gun and stumbled into Finn.

If he was this unsteady on his feet, should they really put a loaded revolver in his hand? "But, Dad—"

"But Dad nothing. I'm not dead yet."

Dylan only lifted his shoulders in a shrug. Finn hated treating Mack like a kid. He handed him the gun. "Let's see what ya got."

Mack arranged his safety goggles, took his time aiming, and fired, nailing the target dead center.

A cloud of blackbirds scattered from a coppice of trees, their startled and strangled cries piercing the sky.

"Bull's-eye!" Finn and Dylan cheered in unison, slapping palms high in the air. A man walking by offered an enthusiastic whistle. "Impressive."

Mack beamed. It was a rare light moment. But then, why shouldn't his last days be filled with what made him happy? Maybe that was the secret of all secrets, finding the *what* and channeling energy there. Finn's sketch on Bianca's wall. Art mattered to him.

At least it had. He remembered her class, remembered her stopping by his desk, leaning in to offer a suggestion. He'd felt something then, deeper than his racing pulse when she was near, but he couldn't name it. Like the sculptures of Degas and Bernini, something other-worldly.

"One of your good days, Dad," Dylan said. "Hell, great."

Mack's shoulders sagged. He handed the gun to Finn.

Did they need to remind Mack that his good days were ebbing? Couldn't they forget about the damn tumor for an hour or two?

Dylan squeezed Mack's shoulders, possibly trying to smooth things over. "How about a bite to eat, Dad? I'm starving."

"Count me in," Finn said. Maybe a juicy burger could salvage the day.

After turning in their gear, they walked across the street to J & R's Jeet Jet. Once they'd settled in and started telling jokes, Mack's mood improved. He stabbed a French fry in the air. "So there's a nun, a stripper, and an aardvark—"

Finn's buzzing cell interrupted. "What's up?" He turned away and cupped the phone, but Dylan and Mack seemed lost in the jokes and double-bacon cheeseburgers.

"Be right there." Finn ended the call. Damn. He hated to cut this short. "Sorry, gotta go. Tucker just snagged a perp, and we need to grill the little bastard."

Mack laced his arms over his chest, eyeing him.

"We've been tracking this guy, hoping for a reason to nail him, and we finally got one. More than one." Finn hadn't told Mack or Dylan about what Emerson pulled in Bianca's classroom.

"And what did *this guy* do?" Mack asked.

"He's been . . . harassing Bianca . . ." Finn prepped for the fallout.

"Go get 'em, hotshot," Dylan said around a mouthful of burger. He scraped a napkin across his face and white-knuckled the table. His body language spoke with a bullhorn. Dylan wore his jealousy about Bianca and his resentment about not being on the force like a pair of prickly wool socks.

Finn tossed down a twenty. "Will do." He kissed his father on the top of his head. "I enjoyed this, Dad."

"Me too, son." Mack stared at his plate and then pinned him with moist eyes. "Me too."

৵

Tucker stood at the bottom of the steps leading to the interrogation room, a shit-eating grin on his face. "Pretty boy's in the box."

"Thanks for waiting," Finn said.

Tucker opened the door and allowed Finn to enter first. "He's all yours."

Finn sat down in the rolling chair facing Emerson. "I see you found your clothes."

Emerson glowered before his lips slid into a cavalier, downturned smirk.

This guy oozed arrogance. Only twenty-two but cockier than most twice his age. Maybe Daddy's money bought that entitlement along with the TAG watch on his wrist.

Finn had done his research. Pappa Wade owned a BMW dealership in the 'Burgh. Emerson would surely take over Wade Fine Auto one day, but in the meantime, he was playing college boy. Flinging Daddy's money like birdseed, hooking up with a different girl every night. Hell, their cougar moms, too.

He was accustomed to getting his way. And Bianca had rejected him.

"I know my rights. You can't keep me here." Contrary to his schoolyard bully tone, Emerson bounced his knee to a phantom beat like a kid sitting in the principal's office.

"If everything's cool, then you won't mind a little chat." Finn unbuttoned his shirtsleeves and took his time rolling them up.

Emerson glanced at Tucker, who lounged against the cinderblock wall, giving Finn full dominion.

"Love to hang and shoot the shit, but I've got a lady waiting. You know how it is." Emerson picked at a cuticle on his thumb, looked up. "Or maybe you don't?"

"Is that where you were rushing when the sergeant pulled you over?"

"Sergeant Bar-nasty hauled me in for no apparent reason."

Tucker stepped forward, slapped the police report on the table. "Here's a whole list of 'no apparent reasons.' And it's Baranski."

Finn read the report, enunciating each syllable. "Speeding, expired tag, no seatbelt, use of handheld device."

"Come on, 5-O, hardly federal crimes." Emerson snapped to his feet, pawed through his wallet, and flipped a business card on the table. "You can send the bill here."

"Sit down," Finn said evenly.

After a stalemate, Emerson fell back into the chair.

"Where were you Friday, November 13th?"

Emerson snickered. "Chasing my black cat under a ladder."

Finn's patience stretched to its breaking point, but he checked himself, held back from crawling across the table to rip the information he needed from Emerson's vocal cords.

"Let me consult my roster." Emerson pulled out his phone and swiped the screen with his index finger. "Her name's Maddie. Maddie spelled with a double D, if you catch my drift." He skimmed his tongue over his lips.

It took some doing, but Finn swallowed his anger. With any luck, someday this scuzzball would find himself sharing a cell with a 300-pound lifer named Shank. Wheeling his chair around the table, he planted himself across from Emerson. "So you were with her all night?"

"Yep, *all night long*." Emerson stretched the phrase like taffy.

"And she'll corroborate?" Finn scooted another inch forward in his chair.

"Yeah, corroborating is one of her many talents. I'll give you her number. Take a turn, man. Maybe you'd both like a turn. She might be into public servants." Emerson pocketed his phone. "Are we done here? Gotta drain the dragon."

Finn stood, sending his chair sailing to the wall, and strolled toward the door. "Sergeant Baranski, a moment?"

Emerson wiped a hand across his face. "You can't leave me here."

"You'll be fine."

"Asshole," Emerson muttered.

"That's Officer Asshole to you," Finn said as he closed the door.

"You know we don't have PC," Tucker said when they reached the top of the stairs.

"Some time alone in the box with a full bladder might bring probable cause right to the surface. And did you see the way he kept jiggling and touching his face? I know this is bullshit"—he waved the list of offenses—"but he's guilty."

"Guilty of being Miley Cyrus in a jock strap."

"You don't think he did it?"

"I know you want to find the scumbag who did this, little bud, we all do. But—"

"But what?" Finn snapped, wondering how he was ever going to be a respected cop when Tucker still talked to him like he was a snot-nosed kid.

Tucker reached for his shoulder. "Listen, I already talked to Bianca. You two need to cool it. Dylan—"

Finn wrenched away. "What's Dylan got to do with anything?"

"He's still in love with her, man."

Keep it professional. His brother's warning came back with blunt force, along with the crisp realization: Tucker was probably right. Finn was too quick to put Emerson in an orange jumpsuit.

A shrill voice rang through the station house. "Where is he?"

At the front desk, a woman stood on her tip-toes, jabbing a finger in Ford's face. She reminded Finn of his third-grade teacher, face pinched in a perpetual scowl. She wheeled around. "You can't keep my son here. Do you know how much money we donate to the police foundation?" Her eyes ran over Finn as if inspecting a garment for moth damage. "Does your boss know about this?"

He back-burnered his frustration. "You must be Mrs. Wade. I'm Officer Tierny. This is Sergeant Baranski. I have one question, and then you can take your son. Do you know where he was on the evening of November 13th?"

She stared at him for a moment. "At home with me. We were supposed to fly to a Broadway show in New York, but he had the flu."

"And Mr. Wade?"

"He's never really enjoyed musicals." Bands snaking above her upper lip emphasized her pack-a-day pout before her mouth bent into a frown. "Is this about that cleaning girl? You don't seriously think—"

"We ask everyone, ma'am," Finn said. "Standard procedure."

"I'll be sure to have a conversation with Chief Carmichael about your *standard procedure*. Now, bring Emmy to me."

Emmy? Finn could have used that little gem earlier.

"On my way," Tucker said.

Moments later, Emerson trailed after Tucker, head hung like a mutt who'd just encountered a rolled-up newspaper, but mouth twisted to a triumphant sneer.

Apparently, Emmy was mostly silver-spoon bark. He'd lied about being with a girl because he was too embarrassed to admit he was home with Mama. Either that or she lied to cover for him. Finn suspected the former, but had no intention of counting the little shit out just yet.

In the parking lot, Finn found Dylan leaning against the Toyota. His hands were jammed in his pockets, and he was searching the sky, a meteorologist anticipating a record-busting storm.

As Finn drew closer, he could tell by Dylan's slouch and the red veining his eyes that he was drunk. "You need a ride—"

Dylan's right hook landed on his chin with enough force to send him stumbling.

Finn scrambled to his feet. "What the hell?"

"Stay away from her."

Bianca. He should have known this was about Bianca.

Finn rubbed his jaw, felt his back realign bone by bone. "I'm trying to do my job."

"Tucker can do it."

"We're a team, we all work the case. Or don't you remember what it's like to be on a team?" A cheap shot, Finn knew it, but he couldn't stop himself. "You were a damn good cop, one of the best, but you chose to piss it all away."

Finn's palms throbbed. The loose asphalt that broke his fall had left sharp fragments. He brushed his hands together and reaped a new crop of pain.

"I didn't *choose* anything." Dylan's look of loss and heartbreak slayed Finn more than the punch. "You'll learn that someday. Life doesn't always give you a choice."

❧ SEVENTEEN ❧

BIANCA ran her fingertips over Courtney's mosaic. An ambitious design—ethereal mermaid suspended between land and sea. Her tile and color choices certainly showcased her talent, but there was something lacking. The mortar oozed thick in some places and was too sparse in others, as if finishing touches had been rushed.

Courtney was having problems with a boyfriend and was likely distracted. Bianca would pull her aside after class to see if she needed a sounding board.

A scream from the hallway nearly launched her through the ceiling. She dropped the mosaic, and the pieces shattered as she rushed to the sound. She found Ralph, doubled over, blood dotting his pant leg.

"Oh my God, Ralph. Are you okay?"

"Slashed it, but good." Wincing, he held up his hand, exposing a red line along his palm. "Pretty sure I'll live to tell the grands about it though."

Bianca noticed the boxes behind him, one splotched with blood. "What happened?"

"Embarrassed to say, I don't rightly know. Not like it's my first go 'round with a box cutter." Ralph gestured to the corner where a utility knife lay on the floor.

Bianca guided him to a chair in her studio and handed him a clean towel. "Keep pressure on it. I'll call the nurse."

"No need. Hurt myself worse one time playing backgammon, if you can believe it. Old Eugene and I was in his garage trying to ditch Agnes—that's his wife, and—"

"Hold that thought. Let's get you patched up." As she was heading for the first-aid kit, a voice stopped her in her tracks.

"I'd like to hear about Old Eugene."

Bianca pivoted to find Jewel bent over Ralph, inspecting his wound, her sweater hiked up, revealing a tattoo on her lower back: Tinker Bell, sitting cross-legged, head tilted in a coquettish pose. *Tinker Bell?* Bianca would never have pegged Jewel for a Disney fan.

When she turned to face Bianca, her red sweater made Bianca think of the letter T, a deep line of cleavage crossed with a bold collarbone. Anyone passing by might mistake her for a student, not a UC Berkeley PhD.

"I'll wrap it and get you to the nurse," Bianca said.

"I'm headed that way," Jewel said. "I'll walk him over."

"Weaver's kind of a detour for you, isn't it?" Bianca eased Ralph's hand from Jewel and stretched gauze around the wound.

Jewel shot her an incredulous look. "Not that I owe you an explanation, but Bill Saunders asked me to sit in on his orchestra rehearsal."

"I can take care of Ralph while you do that then."

"Already done. I'll be sure he gets what he needs."

"Never had two women fight over me." Ralph whistled, a dry, dusty sound. "And two such pretty fillies."

"Fillies?" Jewel repeated, then, as if realizing this was Ralph-speak, the taut lines in her face softened and she patted his shoulder.

Ralph's gaze bounced between them. "Maybe two felines, hackles up and all. I'm thinkin' I've got a front row seat to a gen-u-ine cat fight."

Bianca couldn't help but laugh at his perceptive comment. "Sorry, Ralph. No cat fights today." But she had to admit, it was fun to imagine—sharp fangs, flying fur, and the red-haired feline limping away.

"Sure gonna miss this place. Guess I'm a little glad they're dragging their heels finding my replacement." He pushed to a standing position, and offered Jewel his arm. "Shall we, little fil—I mean miss."

"Certainly, kind sir." She looped her arm through his.

"We'll hop on my white stallion." Ralph winked. "My golf cart."

Bianca watched them disappear and started moving the boxes into her classroom. Was it possible there was a thread of decency woven into Jewel's tapestry? Maybe the tension between them wasn't necessary. Bianca didn't see value in fighting over a man, especially one who was no longer in her life. The questions vanished when Bianca glimpsed mosaic pieces—strewn across the floor. There was no way to piece it back together.

Bianca went to the storage room for a broom. Reaching past a stack of old canvasses, a familiar dread tingled her scalp as she pulled out the painting she'd stashed last year. Chet had finally gotten around to replacing the bulb in the overhead light, and it shined a spotlight on Emerson's twisted attempt to capture her in a sultry pose. She shoved the canvas back into place with a brief thought about how Finn might react if he saw it.

As she swept up the mess, her mind looped from one thing to the next. She wanted her old life back, the one that revolved around her students and her art.

Without Finn filling every thought.

The way he'd bulldozed into her class had embarrassed and frustrated her, but at the same time, she was relieved he'd been there to deal with Emerson. Finn Tierny had her in knots. But what was she thinking? She'd been threatening herself, B. F. Skinner-style, to steer clear, and here she was falling for Dylan's brother.

Falling hard.

"Stop thinking about Finn," she mumbled, hating the way she'd turned into one of those people who talked to themselves when they were alone. Before she knew it, she'd be swatting at imaginary bugs crawling up and down her arms.

She started to unpack the boxes, and her thoughts rolled to Ralph. Since the night of the murder, he no longer disappeared for long stretches. Planting himself outside her studio after the students left, he refused to leave until he knew she was safely in her car. His grandfatherly care touched her, and for a moment, she pictured her own grandpa—bent over his cigar band collection, categorizing them by color and rarity. When Gemma died, organizing them became his priority, the one thing he could control.

Bianca began ordering the new brushes by size and bristle type. Not kolinsky sable, but she'd procured a good assortment of natural bristle brushes for her students.

"Hi."

The brushes clattered to the floor as she spun around. The way she was dropping everything in sight made her wonder briefly if stress could affect dexterity.

Oh God, please tell me he didn't hear me talking to myself. "How long have you been there?"

"Just walked in." Finn was strolling toward her.

She scanned his face for any hint of duplicity. Emerson's antics had humiliated her enough; she didn't need Finn to know he was the topic of her soliloquy. "Did you find out anything about the dollars?"

"Carmichael said getting them analyzed wouldn't buy us anything, excuse the pun, and for once I agree. Not a snowball's chance we'd extract a clean print from a dollar bill."

"Which means we're still nowhere."

"Basically."

"Well then, that's that. I'm wrapping up here, so you can go. I don't need a bodyguard." Direct. Maybe harsh, but she needed to fortify the wall she had tried to erect between them. She was frankly tired of caring about people . . . and losing them.

Images sheathed in an ebony haze. First the mother she'd lost in a car accident, then her father to an aneurism, followed by her grandparents, who'd died within six months of each other. The final image: a cold October morning, rain pelting her like stones as she stood numb to everything but the hearse carrying her grandfather—her last family member—away.

She'd let Dylan in, only to revisit the agony of saying goodbye.

Not again.

167

Finn stared at her, his face hardened. "I'm not trying to smother you."

He turned to leave.

"Wait."

Finn rotated slowly, his jaw still set. A Rembrandt, the epitome of chiaroscuro—a perfect balance of dark and light. She tapped her fist against her thigh.

"I don't mean to be ungrateful," Bianca said. "It's just—"

"It's weird for me, too. You were with my brother. You were my teacher, and now I ... " He shook his head. "And Carmichael—"

"He thinks I did it."

"Bianca." He closed the space between them. "I know it wasn't you. Everyone but Carmichael knows that. Hell, he probably knows it too. But my point is, it's my job to protect you and find Lisette's murderer. I need to stay close."

He turned his attention to the paintbrushes scattered on the floor, squatted, and started to pick them up. As Bianca knelt beside him, their knees collided, and the simple contact sent her heart racing.

Seeing the brush in his hand, Bianca remembered his paintings, the strong emotions they evoked. He'd painted a watercolor in her Traditional Techniques class, a father and son walking toward the horizon through a field of golden wheat. It had brought tears to her eyes. "You were so good with those."

"I haven't painted since I left here." His voice, infused with pathos, came from somewhere deep inside, as if longing for that better place, that field of golden wheat.

She looked past him, and her eyes stalled on the color wheel. Every Basics class started with a lesson on color. Primary. Secondary. Analogous. Complementary colors: red and green, yellow and purple, orange and blue. As she always told her students: placing them side by side in a composition creates visual excitement. She and Finn were complementary colors, sizzling with each interaction.

He touched her hand, brought her back.

"It's been a very strange few weeks."

"Strange" didn't come close to describing what had transpired since she'd walked into her storage room that Friday evening. She'd only realized later it was Friday the 13th. A day kids told ghost stories and thrill seekers flocked to theaters to see slashers. But even if she'd been lonely more days than she could count, Riley's Peak had been a haven, a shelter from the rest of the world. Murderers didn't run loose in her town, only in the movies.

Finn stood, pulling her with him. His hand found her waist, sending another warm vibration through her. She slipped from his touch and started shuffling through a tub of acrylics.

"I want to get to know you better. Would that be so bad?"

Bianca locked her shoulders, steeled herself. "It's so complicated."

"Because of Dylan?"

"Dylan, our age difference, your job."

"We're only talking about four years, and my job is just a job. For now."

Bianca rolled an uncapped tube of burnt umber in her hands, and her eyes held on a plug of brown that had oozed from the top and dried.

"Bee, if you're . . ."

Other than Gemma, Dylan was the only one who called her that. Hearing it from Finn's lips was both familiar and strange.

"Bianca," Finn said. "If you're still in love with my brother, tell me. I'll back off. But if not—"

"I'm not. I'm not in love with him."

She drifted for a moment, swaddled in his soul-caressing gaze before pulling away. "Every emotion has a color." Back to the color wheel again, babbling.

Finn slid behind her. So close his breath heated her cheek. *So close, too close.* Her pulse escalated as she rattled on, as if she could stave off the inevitable.

"Red is rage. Blue is calm. Green jealousy. Black fear."

Finn turned her to him. "What color are you feeling now?"

The wall she'd so carefully constructed dissolved brick by brick. She tilted her face to his; whispered in his ear. "All of the above."

He looked deep into her eyes, his hands cupped her face, and he brought his lips to hers.

Two words beamed, in giant brush strokes. Safe. Loved.

And it terrified her.

Finn's arms enveloped her as she rested her head against his chest and listened to the rhythm of his heartbeat, a rhythm matching her own.

"Bianca," he said. "One day this will be behind us, and we can . . ." He sampled her lips again.

Their tongues entwined in a delicious tango. She murmured, giving into a consuming kiss that transported her beyond the stratosphere. Unanchored, she drifted, until inevitable gravity, maybe common sense, brought her floating back. She wedged her hand between them, pushed away. "This can't happen."

Finn framed her face again and smoothed his thumbs across her cheeks. His eyes traveled to the color wheel and fixed there as if choosing colors for a painting. "We're two colors on that wheel, Bianca, and when we cross over to be together, we're a masterpiece."

⊱ EIGHTEEN ⊰

THOUGHTS of Bianca preoccupied—at times paralyzed—Finn. The kiss. Amazing, not just in a physical way, but like a balm applied to everything painful in his life.

"I want my damn car!" Mack's words. Finn's reality.

Mack shifted in his chair and worked a toothpick between his teeth. A slice of charred toast on the table, beyond that, a scatter of jigsaw puzzle pieces. "What's the holdup? I've called every day. That guy keeps putting me off."

"That guy?"

"The one with my car, dammit, that . . . you know the one."

"You mean Woody." His dad had known Durwood for thirty years. Finn took their plates, leaving Mack's untouched orange juice, and headed for the sink. He wondered briefly if he'd owe Durwood another bottle of whiskey for having to lie to Mack. "He's been busy," he said over his shoulder. He didn't want to look his dad in the eye. He didn't want him to know that the Lincoln wasn't even at Durwood's but stashed in Tucker's pole barn.

Lying was a new necessity. The truth would only needle the old man and send him into a rage. Mack Tierny's driving days were over.

Mack picked up the puzzle box and squinted through his bifocals. "What's this supposed to be, anyway?"

"An owl."

"It's all grays and browns."

Finn had spent an hour shopping for a puzzle that wouldn't frustrate Mack and yet wouldn't insult him. Nothing could have prepared him for this role reversal—taking care of his dad, worrying over every little thing.

Mack held the box at arm's length then pulled it close, trombone-style. "Oh, there. I found the eyes. What's that color? Looks like puke."

Finn studied the box. "Chartreuse."

Mack snorted, picked up a puzzle piece, and guided it over the table, searching for a spot to land.

"Here, Dad. It goes here." Finn pointed, and Mack clamped the piece into place.

Finn seized the opportunity to move away from the car discussion and sat down. They'd always worked puzzles together, scrambling to see who could find the next match. But in the end, Mack would inevitably nudge the last piece toward Finn, allowing him the satisfaction of filling in the final gap. Finn had grown to depend on his dad to pave the way, to set him up for success. Even when he moved to Pittsburgh, he always knew his dad had his back. But everything was changing now.

Everything had already changed.

Like this kitchen. Once filled with Mack's clanging pots and pans, his sardonic wit, and the smattering of greenery reaching for sunlight, it was now cloaked in a lifeless haze. The plants crowding the windowsill were withering. Shriveled, barely hanging on. Mack had insisted on keeping them after Rose left. When one would die, he plugged another into the pot. But plants had a lot longer life expectancy when she was around. Finn recalled how his mom would coax them into the afternoon light. "Look how well you're doing—growing and blossoming the way you were meant to. Look how you're thriving."

He should have seen the longing in her eyes, heard the envy in her words.

Mack stopped watering the plants after his diagnosis.

Staring at the jigsaw piece, Finn's vision fogged to the summer before fourth grade. He and his dad were closing in on a fifteen-hundred-piece Titanic when his mom entered the room. She laid a hand on his shoulder and whispered a hint about the right spot. Mack chided her, but only in jest, and she kissed Finn's cheek, wrapping her arms around his neck, the almond-cherry scent of her lotion filling his senses.

How could someone that nurturing just up and leave?

The plant shelf was a vigil, a shrine, and Finn wouldn't be surprised if Mack still expected his wife to waltz back in, pinch off the dead leaves, and grab a watering can as if she'd never left. Finn crossed the room and filled a large measuring cup. As he watered each plant, he thought about how Bianca had tended them on Thanksgiving.

Mack lifted his glass, and the juice sloshed in his unsteady hand. His bull's-eye at the shooting range a distant memory. Finn studied him. Sparse hair raked haphazardly, leaving uneven comb tracks, and a few rogue hairs. A generous dousing of Old Spice on a freshly shaven face. Patches of toilet paper stuck to blooms of blood along his jawline.

Was he getting ready to go out? Planning to sneak to the cabin again?

"Why don't you give him a call?" Mack asked.

"Who?"

"Woody. I need my *car*. And why can't we get a real mechanic? There's a good body shop in town, you know."

Finn rinsed the dishes and put them in the dishwasher, avoiding Mack's glower as long as he could.

"Where do you need to go? I'll drive you to poker. Dylan and I get your groceries and take you to appointments." He tried for tender, but it came out sounding patronizing. Like he was negotiating with a toddler.

"Played my last game of poker." Mack swished his hands in the air. "Numbers are all mixed up." He dropped his head to the table as if in sudden pain.

"Is it bad today?"

Mack didn't move or speak for a long moment before he jerked back to an upright position. "I have places I *need* to go. You think an old man's life is only about groceries and appointments?"

The sad truth? Yes. He'd watched his dad's slow decline, the way he was reduced to those exact mundane things, his slide from being a decorated cop who didn't take shit from anyone to an easy chair in front of game shows and hospital rooms where he was poked and prodded.

Finn read the desperation on his father's face. "I'll call."

He strolled away from the table and backed against the kitchen counter. He didn't want to bother Durwood again. He'd done that enough already. Tucker was on duty. It had to be Dylan. But the last time he saw his brother, Dylan had laid him flat. Would he even remember knocking him to the ground?

It didn't matter. The name of the game now was keep Dad calm. Another outburst could kill him, the doctors had as much as told them so. But giving him his car was too much of a risk.

"Durwood?" Finn said into the phone, shifting his eyes to Mack.

"Do I sound like some slack-jawed pig farmer?" Dylan slurred in response. Drunk. Again. Or still. At nine in the morning.

"This is Finn. I'm calling to check on Mack's Town Car. Have any idea when you'll get to it?"

"I know who this is, RP's finest. Shiiit." Dylan was mocking and indignant. "You got some nerve."

"Do you know when the part will come in?" *C'mon, Dylan. Play along.*

"What the hell're you talking about?"

"Help me out here, man. My dad needs his car."

"He needs more than his damn car. He needs a new brain," Dylan said. After a stretched silence, "I didn't mean that."

"It's okay."

"It's not okay," Mack snapped. "I need my car."

"Guess I'm fucking up every which way. I'm sorry for clobbering you too." Dylan, in his other ear.

Finn pivoted away from his dad and swept dead leaves off the sill and into the sink. "Dyl—" He caught himself. "Do the best you can. I'll check back next week." He ended the call. He hadn't expected the apology.

"Well?" Mack's single word pinned him for an answer.

"Next week." Finn trailed his fingers down his neck. Dylan seemed too remorseful over one lousy blow.

"Shoulda been last week."

Dylan was self-destructing, and there wasn't a damn thing he could do about it. There was something mulishly radioactive about him now, like he'd given up on everything except whatever brought harm to himself. He hadn't always been this way. Finn missed the brother he'd known. Sure, they'd fought, but when they were kids it was over who got the last Popsicle or who could get the last shower before the hot water ran out.

A vision of a trip to their cabin flashed, and Finn picked at the scab of memory.

The cabin, though only thirty minutes away, might as well have been in another country. A hideaway surrounded by the pastoral countryside. A place their mom found for the four of them.

The year before she left, Finn had been searching for the perfect spot to build a fort and fell into an abandoned mine shaft. He landed on his arm, fracturing it in two places. He cried out for an hour, eventually losing his voice before his dad arrived. Mack lowered a rope, but in his panic to get him out, wrenched his back. As his dad twisted in agony, Dylan appeared. Finn looked up to see his brother, sun shining around his head like a halo.

Dylan had been the one to pull him to safety.

Now, Mack groaned and pushed himself up from the table. "I'm going to go lie down."

He stumbled, and Finn reached out to steady him. "You all right?"

"Why wouldn't I be?" Mack stopped, wiggled his fingers, cocked his thumb, trying for their gun pose, studying his hand with no clue what came next. He took a few moments to balance himself and shuffled toward his easy chair.

The incomplete gesture tore at Finn. He watched his father lean back, and then almost as an afterthought, struggle forward to the coffee table, reaching for the TV remote. But he closed his hand around his wedding album instead.

Eighteen years had eked by, and Mack was still unable, or unwilling, to traverse the abyss he should have crossed a long time ago to leave his marriage behind.

He still missed Rose.

Finn reached for Mack's juice glass and studied the puzzle, three pieces remained. He snapped them together, and the owl's eyes glowed bright from a mélange of grays.

If only the pieces of his life fit together so easily.

❧

Finn's cell buzzed. A number he didn't recognize. "Tierny."

"How's it hangin', Rook?" Walters. What the hell had he done to deserve a double dose of Walters in less than a week?

"Hangin' longer than yours."

"Heard you like Taz Blazek for that shooting down your way."

The man got right to stating his business. But Finn trusted him about as much as he trusted a pedophile in a daycare center. "I'm listening."

"Fact of the matter is, I gotta guy on the inside, and he's pickin' up a vibe that Blazek knows somethin'."

"Not what I hear," Finn said.

"You heard wrong."

"Why the sudden rush to help me with the collar?"

"I don't give a rat's ass about helping you," Walters replied with a snort. "You nailin' the prick gets him off my streets. In regards to da 'Burgh, I happen to care."

That was Walters. Such a caring individual. No matter. Finn couldn't ignore any lead when he had zilch at the moment.

Walters went on to supply Blazek's favorite haunts. He owned a repair shop, but noise on the street said customers were getting high on more than gas fumes in that garage. Finn had retired the GTO for the winter, but she may just have to make another appearance. Geeto would be the perfect ticket in.

Fifty minutes later, Finn exited the interstate onto Lombard and wove through streets that held too many bad memories. Most of the people who lived here were just trying to get by, keeping the old hamster wheel of their circumstances turning. Low-lifes like Taz would always be there to make sure they didn't step off, or to scavenge the leftovers if they did.

At Tripoli Street, doubt crept up like an old friend, slapping Finn on the back. What're you doing in the worst neighborhood in the 'Burgh, alone? But going solo on his own terms seemed a damn sight better than his last six months at PPD when they'd treated him like a leper with a nasty case of the clap. He'd survived that shit with Walters and his merry band of Yinzers, and he reminded himself, what hadn't killed him only made him stronger.

He pulled into the parking lot of T And Z Auto Repair, and a guy with a red bandana clamped over dreadlocks approached. "We're closed."

Funny, nobody had bothered to unplug the sign flashing OPEN.

"Shit," Finn said, "drove in from the North Side, and traffic was a bitch. Bein' as I'm here, any chance someone could take a quick look at my ride?"

Bandana-man moved a wad of chewing tobacco to the other side of his mouth, hurled a blob across the grass. He slowly walked into the garage, reappeared after a beat, and waved Finn in.

Finn eased into the garage, cut the engine, and stepped out.

A tank with log-crushing biceps sauntered over, wiping his hands on a grease-soaked rag. The infamous Taz.

"How can me and my fine establishment be of service?"

"I'm jonesin' to put in a high-performance cam, and word is you're the man for the job."

Taz looked over his shoulder and then back at Finn. Two goons dropped their tools with a clank and sidled up to him. Bandana-man palmed a button on the wall, and the garage door clamored down its track.

Finn's jaw began to twitch.

Taz strolled to a boom box and cranked up the volume. Judas Priest screaming through "Living After Midnight." Nothing like a little classic heavy metal to kick ass by.

"Got anything from *Painkiller*?" Finn asked.

Taz flexed his meaty arms. "You bein' here for a new cam don't cut no ice."

"What're you getting at, man?" The gun inside Finn's boot seemed miles away.

Beefy knuckles gave him a shove, sent him reeling, landing him on his ass. Closer to his boot anyway, and he had to go for it. The instant he found the gun the two thugs grabbed him from either side and hoisted him to his feet. Thug One, who had taken possession of his firearm, shot a metal ceiling beam before he drop-kicked the gun across the oil-stained floor. Thug Two favored Finn with a sideways gold-capped smirk. Gotcha.

Taz punched him in the gut. Pain exploded on impact.

Finn gritted his teeth. "Call your goons off. This . . . tool smells like shit." Forced past empty lungs.

Thug One wrenched Finn's arm behind his back. Something cracked as pinpricks of light flashed across his vision.

"Sorry, it's not open mic night," Taz said. "Wasn't dat last night, boys?"

Thug Two grinned in response.

"Give him one thing. Sonofabitch's got style." Taz ran a palm along the GTO. "Take care of your lady, don't ya?"

Finn tried to twist himself loose, and Thug Two drove a knee into his thigh. He sagged between the two men, but they hefted him back up.

The song switched to a guitar riff, the opening for "Breaking the Law." How appropriate.

"Stoney," Taz said to Bandana-man. "Toss me that iron."

Taz caught it in midair, raised it above his head. Finn pressed his eyes shut, preparing for the worst. They snapped open when he heard the iron clank to the cement floor.

"Can't do it. Ain't got no beef wit' da car."

Relief flooded Finn, but it was short lived. Taz picked up the gun. He made like he was dusting it off as he moved close. "Beef's with you. Hear you want to nail me for some crime in East Bumblefuck. And if I dint do the crime, I sure as hell ain't doin' the time."

Thug One's fist flew from hip level, an upper cut that struck just below Finn's ribs with paralyzing force.

Taz drew closer, tapped the gun against his beefy thigh. He raised it, and Finn felt a circle of cold metal on his forehead. What was left of his leg muscles tightened as he heard a distant ragged howling sound and realized after a moment it was his own breathing.

Pain bolted through his head, sharp at first and then swallowed by a gulf of black.

⚓ NINETEEN ☙

"I know that glow. Spill it." Maris was standing behind her desk, hands planted on her hips.

Bianca patted her cheeks. "New exfoliating cleanser?" Concealing the truth from Maris was—to put it in her friend's terms—a statistical improbability. Her skill at parsing truth from lie, particularly where Bianca was concerned, was unmatched. Would Bianca's relationship with her mother have been similar? A bond that rendered one person transparent, inner workings of heart and mind exposed?

"If exfoliation works this magic, then order me a truckload." Maris cast her a ciphering look. "Seriously, it's good to see you happy. It's been a while."

A while? Try forever. The last time Bianca was this decidedly happy about something other than art, she was sandwiched between her parents, strolling the canopied paths of Orchard Park, the sun floating above them like a ripe peach.

A bright memory from her eighth birthday coasted in, vivid and whole.

"One more," Bianca had begged. "Ple-ease." They were playing I Spy.

"Just one and then home. We need to change for the portrait studio," her mom said.

"Ugh . . . I don't wanna get my picture taken. I look funny."

"You're in luck. Funny is the new awesome," her dad said.

"Nobody says awesome anymore, Daddy."

"Daisy-Bee, you know Daddy's always right . . . and awesome." Her mom gave him a sly look, then scanned the park. "I spy something that rhymes with . . . fog."

"Easy peasy." Bianca pointed to a spaniel bounding after a Frisbee. "Dog."

"Nope, I was looking at that Mog over there. See it on that branch?"

"There's no such thing as a Mog," Bianca said, turning to her father. "Is there, Daddy?"

He wrapped her in his arms. "Oh yes, a Mog is a furry creature that feeds on catalpa leaves and little girls. But you're safe—Mogs always prefer redheads." He nuzzled her neck, his stubbly chin tickling her, and she collapsed in a fit of giggles.

That night, life as she knew it was devoured by the Mog who was only supposed to eat red-headed little girls.

Her mother was gone.

Maris rounded her desk, and they sat down. "I can only think of two things that make a girl glow like this: pregnancy or love."

"The first option would require a miracle, so—"

"I knew it!" Maris plucked a pencil from a ceramic mug on the table and tapped it on her leg.

The room was a shrine to the number two pencil. A mug full on the desk, another on the credenza. All sharpened and ready to record every calculation. Maris, prepared for anything, like a full-grown Girl Scout.

And like any good Girl Scout, Maris would want to add an interrogation badge to her sash. She'd question the age difference. She'd ask how Dylan would react. She'd be concerned that Bianca was making the same mistake, stepping in front of the same speeding bus, only to suffer the same fate.

"Please don't worry. For right now, be happy I'm even considering the possibility of love, and we'll cross the bridge of uncertainty when we get there, okay?"

Maris plunked the pencil into its container. "I'm just concerned.

This has 'London Bridge' written all over it. And if I remember my nursery rhymes correctly—"

"Build it up with iron bars, iron bars," Bianca sang.

"You forgot the falling down part."

"I know. Common sense tells me we shouldn't, but . . ." For the first time in ages, she was letting her heart lead, and it felt damn good. "Let me have this, okay?"

She desperately needed to feel normal, the giddiness of falling for someone and looking forward to their next moments together, not dodging whatever darkness was coming down the pike.

"Only if you dish every single morsel." Maris hiked her eyebrows in a suggestive dance.

"I won't deny I've had a fantasy or three involving whipped cream. But it's much more than that."

Maris scooted forward in her chair, rapt.

"He's different, not your typical alpha with something to prove, but the way he handled Emerson was like—"

"Rambo?" Maris broke in.

"Try someone from this millennium, Mare, like Channing Tatum."

Maris squeezed her eyes shut. "Hold on. Let me put him in a tight blue uniform." Her throaty laugh and mile-wide grin. "That works."

Broad shoulders, shirt skimming taut abs. Bianca felt Finn's hands glide over her body, and her face heated. "You're right, a tight uniform doesn't hurt. But . . ."

"Dylan."

A mouse of a woman appeared at the door. "Maris? Charity Beacham has been trying to reach you. She said you're not answering your phones."

"Thanks, Gloria. I'll call her back."

The woman skittered from the room.

"That reminds me," Bianca said. "I never really got a chance to tell you what Nadya told me." She filled Maris in, the recriminations swamping her once again.

"But if Lisette had stolen the necklace, and Charity turned her in, wouldn't there be a police report?"

"Not if someone's got something to hide."

"I'll buy that, but I can't see Charity touching a gun, much less shooting one. She might chip a nail."

"But it's worth exploring. She hates me, she could hate Lisette. Maybe it wasn't mistaken identity at all. Maybe she'd been following Lisette and . . ." Bianca dropped back into the seat, her theory losing steam, but she pressed forward anyway. "She could get back at both of us at the same time. Kill Lisette and frame me. And don't forget what Tucker said about Charity and Carmichael."

Maris looked past Bianca, calculating, determining the odds. "I'm pretty sure it's not Charity. Riley's Peak is small town, U.S.A. Even if Charity knew the Divacs and they had a falling out, it doesn't really mean anything."

"Wouldn't hurt to check."

"You're right, but I'm not even sure where to start. It's certainly not like we could ask her. Charity is uber private. The most benign question freaks her out. Like when I first moved here, I asked where she was born, and she spun the subject so fast I got a bad case of vertigo. That woman guards her past with a machete."

"I could always ask Carmichael."

Maris rolled her eyes. "Oh yeah, I forgot how tight you are."

"What do you think about what Tucker said? That Carmichael and Charity are working on more than a college security plan?"

"I don't doubt Tucker saw something, but maybe he's letting his imagination run a little wild. Think about it. Carmichael isn't her usual type. Her last boyfriend flew her to Paris on his private jet. For dinner."

Before him it was Mr. Universe. And a male model. Didn't she date them at the same time?

Maris picked up a pencil again, rolled it between her fingers. "So why Carmichael? He's not unattractive, but I'm still not getting it."

"Power?" Bianca suggested. "Chief of police of our little town may not seem like much, but Charity latches on to the biggest fish no matter how small the pond. And speaking of ponds, hard to believe she and Brett are from the same gene pool. He seems so . . . normal."

"He's Charity's polar opposite. Like two halves of a black and white cookie."

"And the chocolate half could use a lot more sugar," Bianca

said. "Maybe you could get some intel from him. You guys are going out soon, right?"

"Numero tres this weekend." Maris jumped up, threw her arms above her head, and wiggled her hips. "And you know what they say about the third date."

"Is that some sort of statistic?"

"It's probable. And you're right, it wouldn't hurt to pick his brain about Charity. Have you told Finn what Nadya said?"

"I did, and he's checking into it, but there's no harm in me doing some investigating. Besides, no one will suspect an art teacher posing as a detective."

Maris let out a bubble of laughter. "A detective who's never even fired a gun."

Bianca tried to smooth a wrinkle in her pants. They'd had this discussion before. Maris begged her to go with her to handgun safety class. But she'd never had a reason to. Until now.

"Then again, team up with Finn and you could go *under cover*." A gleam passed over Maris' face. "Sorry, I couldn't resist."

Nor could Bianca resist the image. Finn, a rose-petal-covered bed, limbs tangled in bunched sheets. She redirected her thoughts and hiked an eyebrow. "Sounds like that third date can't come soon enough for you. And don't blow things out of proportion about Finn. It was only a kiss."

"Girl, you might as well rent a billboard. You're falling in love with that man. But how is this different than Dylan?"

It just is. That's what she wanted to say. But the truth was, she'd bent it over and over in her mind since their break-up. Before he started drinking he'd treated her well, almost too well, like a china doll on a shelf. Was that love? "I realize now that I *wanted* it to work. But with Finn it's . . . beyond my control. If only he wasn't Dylan's brother. I hope, with time, Dylan will accept it. He's a decent guy despite what you think. There's no denying he's troubled, but I know things will turn around for him."

Maris crossed her arms.

"Can't we concentrate on the positive?"

"Deal. How about we go out tomorrow night and raise a glass to optimism? Tre Pecora. My treat."

"I'll drink to that." Bianca hugged Maris and glided out of her office on the incandescent anticipation of a fresh start.

A handful of students sat cross-legged and pinch-faced on the floor outside the Math Department—books open on their laps, papers scattered. As Bianca walked by, she caught snatches of conversations. "Can't believe they still don't know who did it." "Weaver's giving off a bad vibe now." "A friend of mine knew the girl who was killed."

Bianca pulled out her phone, called the main office, and was forwarded to Charity's desk.

"Mabel Banks, how may I help you?"

The president's admin was a middle-aged woman with a noticeable overbite who wrote erotic stories on her lunch breaks. It was difficult to reconcile the painfully shy recluse with lusty bodice rippers published under the pen name Scarlett Lace.

Mabel's office was nothing more than a closet space with her small desk crammed next to Charity's massive one. Charity was director of community liaison reporting directly to the president—a trumped-up position to give the school access to her unlimited contacts and, more importantly, her cash. Whether or not Charity realized she was a stilettoed pawn, she flaunted the title at every opportunity.

"Ms. Beacham had something to take care of at home. Care to leave a message?"

"No, thanks, Mabel. Have a nice day."

Bianca wasn't certain what she would say to Charity anyway. Planning wasn't her strong suit. Maris had pointed that out often enough. But she knew it would eat at her if she didn't try. She checked her watch. An hour and a half until her next class, plenty of time to pay Charity a visit. She'd tell her she changed her mind about seeing the Cassatt and go from there.

As the Pathfinder climbed to the pinnacle of Riley's Peak, the air took on the leathery aroma of money. Beacham Estates, named after Charity's great-grandfather, Riley Beacham, the town's founder. The wealthiest of the wealthy lived here under a dome, sequestering themselves and their children from the coal dust that blanketed the rest of the area. It wasn't envy Bianca felt for them, but a pinprick of sympathy, because beyond all the glitz and glamour, bad things still happened to rich people, and all the money in the world couldn't change that.

The Beachams' terracotta mansion was nearly concealed by an over-the-top security gate. *Damn.* She needed to see Charity face-to-face, not through a silver box embedded in brick and wrought iron. As she pulled up to announce herself, a white truck with an Apex Home Audio logo zipped around her. A hand poked out, punched buttons on the keypad, and the gates yawned open. She followed, kissing the truck's bumper.

A woman stood at the door in a uniform straight from the history books—starched black dress, white collar, and apron with matching ruffle. She ushered the Apex guy inside and almost closed the door before she spotted Bianca.

"Is Charity available?" Bianca took in the formally landscaped grounds adorned with massive topiaries, flagstone walls, and precisely trimmed hedges.

"Ms. Beacham isn't here."

"Charity and I work at the college together, and I'm planning . . ." Bianca almost crossed her fingers before she continued. "A surprise party to thank her for her hard work on the fundraising committee."

The woman wrinkled her nose. "I won't be much help."

No love lost here. "I drew the short straw."

"Good luck trying to please that one."

"She's difficult."

"And a tsunami is a big wave."

Bianca saw her opening. "Have you worked for her long?"

"I started about a year ago, after she fired Lisette. It broke my heart what happened to that girl." She shook her head. "Her poor baby."

Lisette worked for Charity? A siren sounded in Bianca's head. Charity's insensitive comments at Maris' were all the more vile then. Talking about Lisette, a woman she'd employed, as if she were as expendable as the designer heels Charity pranced around town in. Dressing her employees like bit players in some swank story. Bianca tamped down the anger rising in her throat. "Do you know how long Lisette worked here?"

"Not sure. She warned me about Ms. High Society, but I needed the job." She blinked hard. "Wait a minute, I know you. You're the art professor."

"Yes."

"Well, aren't you something? I saw you in the paper, with that sculpture, the one you did after they found out hers was a fake. Boy if that didn't make her pull her extensions out. About ground the veneers off her teeth too when that crook dealer took his sweet time giving her the money back. She didn't get it until this very week, if you can believe it."

"She's lucky she even got it back."

"More money than sense, that one." A piercing alarm sounded from her watch. "Listen, I'm behind schedule. She's got me stuffing envelopes. Don't know what that has to do with keeping house, but if I don't have them done when she gets home . . ."

"I understand," Bianca said. "And good luck riding that big wave."

A conspiratorial expression passed over the woman's face as she wiggled crossed fingers and closed the door.

Bianca returned to her car. As she wound her way through the circular drive, another car turned in. A black Mercedes. Charity was flagging her down, trying to get her to stop. Bianca waved pleasantly like it was the most natural thing in the world for her to be there, and drove off.

⤙ TWENTY ⤚

FINN forced his eyes open and lifted his head from the headrest. His entire body ached, but the space above his right ear felt like someone had crushed it with a steamroller. Again and again.

He opened the car door, leaned out, and puked. Where the hell was he? Last thing he remembered was looking into Taz's ugly mug; then a flash of metal before the lights went out. His eyes fell to the gun resting on the seat next to him. His gun. The same gun the bastard used to cold-cock him. He was surprised, even grateful, they had left it with him. His career would certainly be over if they'd stolen his piece.

Every muscle screamed as he poured himself from the GTO. He ventured a look. The assholes left it unscathed. He on the other hand was scathed, very scathed. Was that even a word?

He couldn't think straight; there was a walloping buzz where his thoughts should be.

A shower. He needed to hose off the stink those grease-monkeys left on him, down a handful of painkillers, and figure out his next move.

Not necessarily in that order.

When he got home, Mack was asleep. Good. His father's questions would only grind rock salt into open wounds.

Finn sat on the edge of the bed, head in palm, silently berating himself for walking straight into Walters' trap. The devil's minion must have loved hatching this plan with Taz.

Just to make sure his hindsight was twenty-twenty, Finn called around and got the number for the cop who had originally vouched for Taz. She repeated what she'd said before, the part he wished he hadn't ignored, "That guy is bad news, but he wasn't in the Peak last Friday." Next he checked a few other sources who all said she was on the up and up, a good cop. All signs pointed to what his gut had been telling him all along: Taz had nothing to do with Lisette's murder.

He examined the lump on his head. Taz had aimed generously high, above his hairline. Thank goodness for small favors. Seemed to be about all he could count on these days. On his way through the bathroom, he picked up the shirt Bianca had lent him the night of the murder, and the bittersweet montage surfaced. For a brief moment, he pictured her wearing the shirt, and only the shirt, a vision that made his Y chromosome throb. Bianca's face floated forward, a permanent fixture now, her mouth quirked in a smile, eyes penetrating and beseeching.

A welcome distraction.

He eased his arm into his uniform sleeve, and pain shot through his right shoulder, thanks to Thug One, who had mangled his rotator cuff.

Buckling his belt, he headed down the hallway. Mack was up now, settled in his recliner, a spiral-bound notebook open on his lap, pen moving across the page in slow, choppy script.

"What're you doing?" Finn asked.

"Can't a man write? Or am I too far-gone for that?"

An unsettled feeling stirred Finn's chest. Mack never wrote letters; he didn't journal.

"Did you eat?" Finn braced his foot on the coffee table to tie his laces and bit the inside of his cheek to keep from grimacing.

A mug of coffee sat on a TV tray in front of Mack. "Not hungry. How 'bout you?"

"I'll grab something on the way."

"As long as it's not a donut. Donuts give cops a bad rap."

"I thought it was the other way around."

"Good one." Mack tipped his head. "Whatcha got there?"

Finn bristled. "A shirt."

"Show me." Mack lifted his chin, his eyes flashing with intensity.

Finn unraveled the shirt, and his dad's face creased in disgust. "Fear no color?"

"I really need to get going."

"Swapping clothes with the art teacher now?" Mack pulled himself forward, and the chair squeaked and groaned under his weight. "Does it have something to do with the investigation?"

The *investigation* that had him trapped like a rat in a perpetual maze? The case that made him so desperate that he took a tip from Walters of all people. Finn noted the lucidity in his dad's eyes. He had advice to spare, but now wasn't the time. "It's a long story."

"You'll tell me sometime." It wasn't a question. Mack settled back in the recliner. "I'm stuck here with nothing but time since Woody can't seem to get to my car. I'm a good listener, you know."

The irony jabbed. Mack, worrying about having too much time on his hands. "I know, but right now I've got to run."

"That woman left when things got tough. It ruined your brother."

Finn inhaled a slow breath past the pain in his ribcage and thought about Dylan's warning to stay away from Bianca, a warning punctuated by a right hook. Finn was beginning to feel like a punching bag. Had someone tattooed Everlast on his forehead while he slept?

Mack surveyed him, head to toe. "You wear it well. The uniform. Like your old man."

Finn ran a finger along the inside of his collar. It suddenly seemed tight and stiff, tailor-made for someone else. The reel playing of a younger Mack in uniform was an added intrusion, stirring memories Finn didn't want to revisit. "There's tuna salad in the fridge."

He scooted out the door before his dad's interrogation skills kicked into full gear.

Outside, he glanced at the garage where Geeto rested under a tarp. He climbed into the Toyota, and the vision of Mack in uniform strong-armed past his thoughts, towing an argument that took place years ago between his parents. A heated discussion and a boy crouched in a kitchen nook. He didn't remember much from their conversation, only voices seething with anger and accusations. He'd always wondered about their last fight and made the mistake of questioning Mack about it once. Only once. It gnawed at him that he'd likely never know what they argued about. Never know why she left.

When Finn walked into the station an hour before his shift, the front desk was empty. Good. He'd get in and out before anybody spotted him. He wasn't in the mood.

Despite Carmichael's repeated admonitions, Ford, the long-time dispatcher had never been one to anchor himself to the front desk. Radio and headphones strapped in place, he cruised the building like it was his beat. One of these days, Finn was going to buy him a Back in Five Minutes sign.

He scanned last night's activity log. Two hitches. One DUI and a call about boy-girl trouble. No reason to think today would be any different. He was relieved that nothing stood in the way of his first order of business: Bianca.

Finn unlocked the top desk drawer and grabbed the keys to a squad car. "Later, Ford," he said to the air around him.

As he opened the door to leave, the dispatcher rounded the corner. "Hey, Tierny, how was your day off?"

"Interesting." *If interesting meant getting your ass handed to you.*

Ford stretched like he'd just emerged from a long nap. "A couch, a six pack, and ESPN. Don't know if it's interesting, but it works for me."

Finn headed for the parking lot, debating his next move. The chief had been quiet lately, which probably meant he was getting ready to snatch the rug, padding and all, out from under him.

And Walters. He must be giving himself the old thumbs-up right about now. Let him flap his trap with his pals at the garage. Did he think this was over?

Finn drove to his favorite diner, Breakfast at Tiffany's, a hole in the wall with good food and great service. The owner, Tiffany Lioni, could have starred in *The Sopranos* as a mob wife. Brightly painted face and fingernails, dark hair teased and smoothed into a helmet around her plump face, she marketed an extra-strength brand of femininity.

Framed scenes from the classic movie covered the walls. One of those old-timey cigarette holders, a lighter, some sort of crown thing, and a long pair of black gloves were in a display case where the donuts should be. People and their weird obsessions. Why couldn't a diner just be a diner?

As he waited for his order, he stared at a black and white print of Audrey Hepburn in the pelting rain, her face turned up to kiss George Peppard. His mom had been obsessed with old movies, and these two were household names. Dylan would perch right next to her, gobbling heavily buttered popcorn. Finn never understood the appeal of those old black and whites, especially when a full-color baseball game was just a click away.

Tiffany draped herself over the counter. "That's my favorite." She sighed audibly and turned to the task of dousing a tea bag in a cup of steaming water. "There's just something about the way they love each other without giving a flying fig about the rest of the world."

"What's that movie about again?"

"It's about the truest kind of love." Tiffany handed him a carrier holding two cups. "Did you know that Marilyn Monroe was originally cast as Holly Golightly? I just can't imagine anyone but Audrey. And Audrey just hated Danish pastries, can you believe it? Anyway, she falls in love with an older man, and it's incredibly romantic. And . . . well, I don't want to spoil it for you. You need to watch it again. You've seen it, right?"

It was his mom's favorite. "A lotta years ago. I'll have to catch it again on Netflix."

On his way out, he caught another glimpse of Audrey, lying on her stomach, wearing a ridiculous dream mask, long hair draping her shoulders, and a cat, who bore an uncanny resemblance to Picasso, lolling on her back. He'd never noticed the poster before. Why now? He examined the picture again. Rain—the relentless downpour—couldn't deter them from their passion.

Rain. Bianca in the rain, collecting rainwater.

Once on campus, he crossed the parking lot, drink carrier in one hand, Bianca's shirt in the other. He felt about as uninteresting as a manila folder, yet every eye seemed to bore a hole through him. The uniform put him on display. "Hot cop." A female voice, followed by a wave of laughter from a group of students, convinced him to step up his pace.

Weaver Fine Arts was an unremarkable gray stucco building with rows and rows of large windows. Finn searched them, eager for a glimpse of Bianca. The anticipation made his pulse quicken, and he took the stairs two at a time.

In her studio, Bianca was attacking a canvas, stabbing it with a paintbrush and twisting with what looked like more anger than paint. Finn observed from the doorway for a long moment. In action she was strong, capable, confident. She paused, assessing her work. He tapped on the door frame so he wouldn't startle her. When she didn't respond, he knocked again, louder. "Bianca?"

She wheeled around, and surprise registered on her face.

He held up the cup of tea. "I got this for you."

"You didn't have to . . ." She plunged her paintbrush into a jar and pushed a rogue hair behind her ear. "I sometimes paint before my students arrive so I'm not tempted to stop teaching and join them."

"I like it." Finn admired the blotches of color dancing across the canvas. Then Bianca. He soaked her in. "Oh, I brought your shirt, too." He dropped it on a table.

George Peppard would be kissing her by now.

Bianca spread out the shirt and ran her hand across the splash of colors. "I remember the conference where I picked this up." She shook her head. "What a huge—"

"Bunch of eccentrics?"

"I was going to say conference center, but, okay." A dazzling smile that faded too soon. "What is this going on between us?"

The direct approach. Finn sipped his coffee and placed the cup next to the shirt.

He wanted to take her in his arms, crush her to his chest George Peppard-style and declare his love. Edging closer, they stood face to face, and he traced his fingertips over her features.

Shards of pleasure spun through him as his world shifted. Black was white. Hot was cold. Up was down.

"Morning, Prof." They turned to see one of Bianca's students coming in, unhooking the satchel crossed over his chest.

Bianca cleared her throat. "Good morning, Lyle. It's good to see you back among the living."

"Yeah, mono knocked me on my . . . back." Lyle's eyes switched from Finn to Bianca as he plopped down at one of the tables and began arranging supplies. "Thought I'd get here a little early to catch up."

Bianca checked the clock. "We should finish our discussion later," she said to Finn.

He reluctantly made his way to the door. Behind Lyle, he mimed a phone, thumb to ear, pinkie to lips, and mouthed, "I'll call you."

The subtle arch of an eyebrow told Finn she'd be waiting. He watched from the doorway, tracing her every movement as she walked over to Lyle and studied the sketchpad in front of him.

"I'm having trouble with the eyes."

"You need to add a light reflex. They look dead otherwise." For a brief beat, her gaze traveled to the storage room.

Lyle hammered his pencil on the table next to his drawing. "Still feels like I'm missing something."

Bianca raised a flat hand, palm side up.

Lyle stood. "I know. I know. You think ten percent faster on your feet."

"Now the solution will come," Bianca said.

Finn remembered a similar exchange, her ordering him to his feet when he'd been her student. This woman could order him to do just about anything.

When he reached the squad car, his phone rang. He looked at the screen and said the name aloud as if trying out a foreign word. "Shae?"

"I need to see you."

"I don't think—"

"I can't talk over the phone. It's gotten worse since you left. I need . . ."

He couldn't believe this. The timing.

"Can you meet me somewhere? Tonight?" she asked. "Mom has the kids."

He couldn't ignore the desperation vibrating in her voice. "Okay, there's a place in Whistler right off the highway that's a little closer for you."

Through his windshield he saw Bianca move across the classroom to her desk at the same time that he dialed her cell. She didn't pick up, and he left a message. "Something came up . . . with my dad. I'll call as soon as I can." A press of his thumb, and he tossed the phone onto the seat next to him. Why hadn't he come up with a better excuse? Why did he feel like he needed one?

Just when he thought he was climbing out of the rabbit hole, his past ambushed him and sucked him right back in.

❧ TWENTY-ONE ❧

STALE air greeted Bianca at the station house. Carmichael had called, asking her to come in as soon as possible. She knew it was only a matter of time before the necklace came back to haunt her.

At the station house, Tucker sprang up from behind the front desk. "Hey, Bianca." He waved a set of keys. "Not much of a welcoming committee, am I? Woulda been caught with my provincial pants down if you were Carmichael or, worse yet, the mayor."

"I think you mean proverbial."

He pocketed the keys. "Yeah, that. What can I do ya for?"

Chatting with Tucker, for a minute or an hour, would create a nice diversion, but she needed to get this over with. "Chief Carmichael wants to see me."

"I'll buzz him."

"Ms. James." Carmichael emerged from the hallway, all smiles. "I'm glad you're here. Come with me."

As they walked to his office, he rested his arm on her back, and she side-stepped his touch. He brought a fist to his mouth, cleared his throat.

"I only have a short break between classes."

"Yes, of course."

His generous office dwarfed the reception area. No surprise there. Carmichael pointed to a large leather chair. "Please, sit."

Her knees started to bend, but advice she gave her students about the vertical advantage kept her on her feet. "I'm fine. What is this about?"

Carmichael drummed his fingers on a marble pen stand, opened a drawer, and pulled out the necklace. "Tierny said you found this after the murder."

Her stomach swayed before rolling completely over. "I did."

He placed it on the desk, positioned the L so it faced her. "I really wish you'd sit, Ms. James. I won't bite." Laughter laced his request, but the set of his brow reminded her of a card shark scouring the black jack table. His smirk said he was already counting his winnings.

She sat. A ten percent advantage wasn't going to help her now anyway.

"Where did you find it?" he asked.

"Under a cabinet."

"And you've never seen it before?"

"No."

He leaned forward. "There's nothing familiar about it?"

"Again, no."

He relaxed against the chair. "Well, you should have brought it directly to me."

The necklace wasn't even in an evidence bag. Just how important was this to the case? "I don't see what difference—"

"These Tiernys, you're fond of them, aren't you?"

There was no good, no easy, answer to the question. Fond didn't begin to describe the feelings she'd had for Dylan or how she felt about Finn now.

Carmichael twisted a gold cufflink at his wrist, clockwise, then counter-clockwise. "Young Tierny needs time to prove himself. It's not in your best interest to align yourself with him. If he's anything like his brother . . ."

And now the falling axe. She needed to play a card of her own, and fast. *Who was Carmichael aligned with?*

The mayor.

Her focus riveted to a framed print behind him. A Warhol, John Wayne in earth tones, gun raised. How long had he deliberated between that and Warhol's Superman? "I'll remember that. About the Tiernys." She raised her chin to the picture. "I admire your taste in art. Unless it's not your taste. Did Mayor Ingram choose that?"

"Ms. James, I make all decisions regarding what happens in this building." He scratched at the corner of his mustache. "But I'll take the compliment."

Every muscle in her body wanted to leave this question-asking, advice-offering, compliment-snatching jerk far behind, but she stayed put.

He ran a finger over the necklace chain on the desk as though his mind hummed with the various ways he could trap her. "You sat on this evidence for a while, didn't you? Help me understand why."

"I assumed it belonged to one of my students, so I emailed them right away. When none of them claimed it, I thought it must have been Lisette's."

"But you gave it to Tierny."

"Yes, I gave it to Tierny. Finn."

Carmichael swept the necklace off the table and dropped it into his suit pocket instead of putting it back in the drawer. He patted it in a way that seemed almost tender. "I'm afraid we got off on the wrong foot before. Maybe if we got to know each other better."

Although the thought of being friendly with Carmichael was revolting with a capital R, the ace of spades dangled in front of her, and she snatched it. "I'm good with that. You first. Tell me about your family." She motioned to the credenza behind him, covered in framed photos. Carmichael and the mayor, Carmichael with his dog, a mostly tan German shepherd with a white-frosted muzzle, Carmichael flanked by two boys clad in baseball uniforms, and slightly offset from the other pictures, a woman in a floppy hat.

He pointed to each in turn. "My wife and sons, my dog, Shep."

Bianca leaned forward to get a better look as the conversation at Thanksgiving bounced back to her. "Oh, at first I thought it was a friend of mine under that hat. Charity Beacham." She chuckled. "But that wouldn't make sense, would it?"

Charity Beacham. Aligned with and then some.

"No." He swallowed hard and licked his lips as if his mouth had gone dry.

"How long have you been married?"

"Thirty-two years next week." The arrogance in his voice evaporated.

Thirty-two years seemed like two lifetimes with a man like Carmichael. "Quite a milestone."

"Yes." He checked his watch. "I'm sorry. I forgot I have another appointment. We'll have to finish this conversation another time."

"I understand. We've made progress today though, getting to know each other." Bianca made for the door before turning back to him. "Don't you think?"

A man like Carmichael loved to call the shots and hated being sidetracked from his agenda. Simply discussing Charity and his wife in the same sentence had made him squirm like a bug under a magnifying glass. He was nothing more than a womanizing, power hungry baboon, and she wouldn't let him get the best of her.

She may have won this hand, but she was careful not to gloat. Carmichael was far from ready to fold.

Bianca couldn't stop imagining how things might have gone with Finn in her classroom the other day if they hadn't been interrupted. She let their conversation play out, heard the words she wanted to hear, said the words she wanted to say, took their kiss a step further. But her fantasy would have to wait. Tonight was about girl time with Maris.

She sifted through her closet. Brown suede skirt with cream sweater. Dull. Navy sheath screamed wedding guest. Red skirt that skimmed her mid-thigh. Short, but not trying-too-hard short. Possibly.

Her eyes lifted to the quote she'd stenciled above her closet: "Feet, what do I need you for when I have wings to fly?" ~ Frida Kahlo. She'd always admired the artist for the way she'd faced challenges—with brio.

Spreading her wings, Bianca spun around like a little girl. She noticed the shirt she'd lent Finn and held it to her face, hoping his scent would pop like the bold white letters. Even as a teenager, she'd never experienced feelings like this. Not only wanting to be with someone, but to be a part of him, to see what he sees, smell what he smells, feel what he feels.

A picture surfaced—the two of them falling together, unable to keep their hands off each other. She wanted to kiss every part of him, lose herself in his touch. The desire lingered, heated her skin, but the ringing phone punctured her meandering thoughts.

Maris.

"I know I'm *always* punctual, but . . ." her friend started.

"But this one and only time you're running late."

"Crashed in front of the TV after my last class and got caught up in a *Three Stooges* marathon."

Bianca switched the phone to her other ear. "*Three Stooges?*"

Maris never ceased to reveal new sides to an already multifaceted personality.

"Blame my genes. Dad watched them religiously. He'd grab a chilcano de pisco the second he got home from work and plop in front of our little black and white until dinner."

"Chilcano?"

"Pisco, ginger ale, and lime. Easier than a pisco sour. I prefer them, too. Can't escape genetics."

"How much time do you need?"

"Give me thirty minutes so I can shower and do something with this hair. I don't want to be mistaken for Larry Fine's equally hair-challenged sister."

"Who?" Bianca asked.

"Larry. Of Larry, Moe, and Curly."

"Wasn't Curly the one with the crazy hair?"

Maris' characteristic cackle. "No, Curly was bald."

The side of Bianca's mouth ticked up in a grin. She hung up, glanced at the clock, and returned her attention to getting ready. With the extra time, she'd do her nails—something she rarely did since her hands were constantly in and out of water. Where had she left that bottle of polish? As she rifled through bathroom drawers full of lotions, lip balms, hair clips, and a half-chewed cat toy, the phone rang again, and she picked it up without checking caller ID.

The line crackled. She stiffened, clutching the cat toy. More silence.

"Listen, I'm hanging up—"

"Bianca James?" A man's voice, awash in static.

"Who is this?"

"This is Oscar with *Art World Magazine*. Your subscription has expired and—"

Bianca let out a one-syllable laugh. After renewing the magazine, she melted onto the edge of the bathtub. Not a single threat in days. Was this over? She said a silent prayer that they'd find Lisette's killer and give that poor family some measure of closure.

She pulled a snug brown sweater dress from the back of her closet and wiggled into it. After swiping a coat of "Dare Me" red on her nails, she appraised herself in the mirror, pleased for the first time in ages at the image reflected back.

On the drive to Tre Pecora, an upscale Italian restaurant in the heart of Whistler, Bianca's thoughts drifted. So much had transpired. A mere moment ago, she was hanging off the side of a cliff with nothing to pull her to safety.

"Little tidbit. Did you know Whistler was named for coal miners?" Maris asked. "The foreman would blow a whistle to signal that the miners were all right."

"Let me guess, you got roped into another Hysterical Society meeting."

"The *Historical* Society serves Mint Milanos and Lorna Doones. Besides, it's interesting. But the idea of being in the ground, not knowing if you'll see daylight again, que miedo . . ." She pushed up her coat sleeve and ran a finger along her arm. "Goosebumps."

Bianca felt the familiar rush of heat and triple-time pulse. She could smell the wet dirt closing around her. "Let's talk about something else." They did until the sign for Tre Pecora came into view.

In the restaurant, a large mural of a sun-kissed Tuscan vineyard spanned the back wall. Floor-to-ceiling plants, subdued lighting, and a corner fireplace extended an invitation to linger. As a hostess guided them through the restaurant, the chef emerged from the kitchen. Scarcely five feet tall, but when he opened his mouth a booming tenor, rich and melodic, erupted. He sang several bars from an aria, took Bianca's hand, kissed it, kissed Maris' hand, and waltzed back to the kitchen.

"That must be the new chef. Please, oh please, let his food be as amazing as his voice," Maris said.

The hostess led them to a corner table past a server carrying a large bowl of seafood pasta, and Bianca's stomach trailed the garlic wafting from the bowl.

When the dish arrived at a table along the back wall, she froze. She grabbed Maris by the wrist. "Finn's here."

"I thought he was with Mack tonight?"

"So did I."

A woman emerged from the shadows of the booth and took Finn's hands in hers. They laughed, and everything around Bianca came to a grinding halt.

Something came up with my dad. Humiliation eclipsed her anger. How could she have been such an idiot?

The hostess eyed them, pointed to a table.

"I can't wait to hear his excuse." Maris started toward Finn.

Bianca held firm to her wrist. "We should just go." Blood swooshed in her ears, anger bubbled. "But on second thought . . ."

The next thing she knew, they were inches from Finn. As he vaulted from his seat, his knee struck the table, rattling the dishes, and he snatched his beer before it toppled.

"No need to get up," Bianca said. "I just wanted to see how your dad is doing."

"He's fine. I—"

"Glad to hear it. Enjoy your dinner." She favored Finn and his date with a smile so broad it hurt, did an about-face, and moved to her table.

She dropped into her seat, snatched up the menu.

"We don't have to stay," Maris said.

"Why not?"

"You're right. Let him hang with that Katy Perry look-alike. You're better off."

"It's not like we're engaged. It was only a kiss." A kiss she could still feel in every nerve ending, still taste on her lips.

A server appeared with a slender white plate and placed it in the middle of the table. "Compliments of the chef."

Maris rummaged through the bread basket. "I'm always up for free starters and warm ciabatta. If you're sure you want to stay."

"Positive. Now take one of these before I eat them all. I'm starved." Bianca stabbed a marinated asparagus spear and bit into it. But the perfect combination of tangy balsamic and fresh parmesan that would have left her mouth watering any other time was lost on her tonight.

Damn Finn for ruining her taste buds along with a rare night out.

"Good, huh?" Maris asked.

Before Bianca could respond, Finn was at her elbow, remorseful eyes pressing her in place. "Can we talk?"

"While your date's in the bathroom?" Maris snapped.

"She's not . . . Please, just let me—"

"Save it." Maris split the air with a warning finger. "We know how skilled you Tiernys are at lying."

"The locks are changed. The windows are all closed," Bianca said. "But I'll be sure to call 911, or, better yet, Carmichael, if I need anything."

The server reappeared, poised to take their order.

"Tell us about your specials," Maris said. "And leave out the beef selections. We've had enough bull for one night."

"I'll call you," Finn said. But Bianca focused on the server as he droned through the specials, enlisting every ounce of control not to watch Finn leave.

"Our most popular dish is the chicken scallopini, but I'm partial to the shrimp with arrabbiata sauce. Simple and delicious. And arrabbiata in Italian means angry." He raised an eyebrow, indicating he'd picked up on the drama.

Bianca didn't hesitate. "I'll have the shrimp . . . with extra arrabbiata."

"I'd join you in solidarity, but I skipped my Nexium today," Maris said, closing her menu. "Chicken for me."

As they waited for their meals, Maris asked, "Did I tell you that Louisa picked out her quinceañera dress?"

Bianca had to think for a moment. Louisa her baby sister or Louisa her cousin? She hated to ask because she should remember which one was turning fifteen. "What does it look like?"

"It reminds me of one of those My Little Pony figurines I used to get her when she was little, the one with the rainbow tail. I get cavities just looking at it, but you should see how she lights up when she puts it on."

"Nice."

"Aunt Valeria was too proud to let me pay for it, so I slipped some money in her wallet when she wasn't looking. She'll be thanking the saints for a miracle on that one."

So, Louisa the cousin.

Maris continued talking until their food arrived. She took a bite. "His food is as good as his voice. Maybe better."

Bianca cut her pasta into smaller pieces with her fork, moved it around the plate.

"So Brett and I . . ." Maris started, but Bianca didn't hear the rest. Her mind was on Finn and how stupid she'd been to even consider the possibility.

"That's good," she said when she noticed Maris had stopped talking.

"Really?" Maris said. "You're good with us eloping and moving to Borneo? Because I thought you might just miss me."

Bianca dropped her chin in her palm. "I'm terrible company, aren't I?"

"Between the abbreviated answers, the half-listening, and the zombie stare?" Maris set her fork down, took a sip of wine. "I get it. You have a ton on your mind."

Bianca muddled through the next hour, pulling comments from her hat, engaging in all the right places. After they paid the bill, she practically ran from the restaurant and through the parking lot.

"Slow down, girl," Maris said between huffs. "Short legs here."

Bianca threw herself into the car and started the engine, barely waiting for her friend to close her door before she punched the accelerator.

"Watch out!" Maris screamed.

Bianca swerved and maneuvered past a car full of teenagers more focused on each other than the road.

The night was sliding from bad to worse. Bianca made it to Maris' house in record time, shot over the curb, into the driveway, and sat motionless, trying to steady her breath.

"Come in," Maris said. "We'll talk. Or make a Finn voodoo doll. And a silicone-lipped Katy look-alike one to match."

"It's not even about her. But why did he feel the need to lie?" And to use Mack as his excuse? Had she completely misjudged him? "I just want to go home."

"And sit alone with your cat?"

Bianca clenched her teeth until a finger of pain attached to each molar. "I suppose you have it all figured out. How long were you married again? Six months? And what is it now with Brett, two dates?"

Maris stared at her. "Is that you or the angry pasta talking? Fernando and I shouldn't have married. We were too young. But at least I'm not afraid to give it another whirl with someone else. Two dates is better than closing yourself off to the world. At least I'm *trying.*"

Closed off was putting it mildly. Cease. Terminate. Status quo when it came to thoughts of loving someone again. "News flash. A woman can be perfectly happy without a man."

"I don't disagree—"

"Then stop acting like I'm so pathetic because I'm not prioritizing getting laid like you are."

Maris jumped from the car. "Why don't you call me when Bitchy Bianca goes back to wherever she came from?" She slammed the door and charged up her sidewalk.

Bianca's anger spiraled to a cold reality. The truth hurt, slashed with knife-like intensity. She'd been behaving like someone she didn't even recognize, and for a brief moment, she wondered if she'd find her way back to herself before everything she knew and loved was irreparably damaged.

↜ TWENTY-TWO ↝

FINN left messages on Bianca's home and cell phones. Leaving more would only smack of desperation. Would she even give him a chance to explain? A vision of her passionate attack on the canvas in her studio surfaced and mingled with the disaster at Tre Pecora. He couldn't separate the two. Her commanding way, her force of execution, her fervency beyond compare.

After the episode in the restaurant, he'd walked Shae to her car. "I care about you and the kids, I really do, but I can't get sucked back in. I just can't." There were a few good memories in the 'Burgh, but mostly Shae was a reminder of all that had gone wrong.

Now, Bianca demanded his undivided attention as he looped through her neighborhood, practicing what he would say. "Bianca, I . . ." He tried for a more serious tone. "Bianca, I . . ." Damn. He sounded like a news anchorman.

His heart quickened as he approached Waterton Avenue. He had to see her, had to tell her what happened. He pulled in behind her car and surrendered to trying her cell, one last time. When she didn't answer, he pocketed his phone. Doubt slowed his steps to her door. Should he let her cool off? Call her again in the morning?

He considered the scene, how it must have looked to her. He and Shae talking about the past, about how he painted the twins' room and then proceeded to back his car over paint cans in the driveway, splattering his cruiser with pink paint. Shae had laughed and squeezed his hand at the memory. That was, of course, when Bianca walked in.

On her porch, he sucked in a breath, knocked. When she didn't answer, he pounded harder. He pressed his forehead against the door, and the tangy scent of fresh wood stain traveled up his nose. He tried the knob. Locked. At least she'd listened about that.

But why wouldn't she answer her phone, even if it was only to tell him to get lost? What if . . . ? He drew his gun, started around the back.

"Why don't you go on home?" Helen, next door, a colorful scarf draping her shoulders, fastened at her neck by a tight fist. "She'd have answered by now if she wanted to see you." Helen straightened in a no-nonsense manner, cast him an admonishing stare, and motioned him over.

Holstering his piece, he turned to leave. He didn't have time for the old lady's nonsense, but concern for Bianca compelled him through the bushes to Helen's porch.

"I just want to make sure she's okay," Finn said. "Until this case is solved—"

"We were on the phone moments ago. She's absolutely fine." She eyed him disapprovingly. "And you and I both know it's about more than that. Let's talk."

She gave him wide berth to enter and followed him inside. Her quirky décor was almost familiar to him now, the shimmering magic carpet overpowering the room, the sensual lamp giving off an oval of golden light, even Helen's choice of coffee table books. The place reminded him of a museum. Everywhere you looked, there was something startling. A tribal mask. A pair of jagged candelabras. Who has candelabras? A framed picture on the wall, the only thing that seemed halfway normal, drew him in. An old photo of dancers in what looked like a chorus line.

"Helluva ride," Helen said.

"Excuse me?"

She moved to the picture, pointed to a lithe brunette in the center of the row. "With the Rockettes. Maxine, the one to my left, and I shared an apartment near Radio City. It was no bigger than a matchbox, but to us it was the Taj Mahal." She waited while Finn took a closer look. "See, I'm not merely the wacky lady next door," she continued, unfurling the scarf from her shoulders and swirling it around like a matador. "I've got *layers.*"

Finn shouldn't have been surprised. A woman her age had a lifetime of stories to share, but right now, he needed her help, and before he could stop himself, his own story spilled out in a handful of sentences, the call from Shae, the encounter with Bianca, to which Helen interjected, "Mmm-hmm" with rising frequency.

"Do you love her?" she asked.

"Shae?"

"No, Bianca."

Emotion swelled as she filled his mind. "I do."

Something hinting at pain crossed Helen's face. "When love is not madness, it is not love."

What the hell kind of crazy was this woman spouting?

"From Pedro Calderón de la Barca," she said with a flourish. "The seventeenth-century playwright who wrote *Life Is a Dream.* It's about free will and predestination."

"Like whether we choose our destiny or it chooses us?"

"Exactly. In the play, a Polish king imprisons his son because he's afraid the boy will steal his crown as foretold by the stars."

"That's extreme."

"Yes, locking someone away always is."

He sat on the couch, eager to know the outcome. "Did it work? Did he keep his son from becoming king?"

"No. His son was freed in a peasant uprising and eventually crowned. It was his destiny."

The word *destiny* settled in Finn's chest, heavy and urgent.

"There's madness, and there's pain. The former doesn't need to cause the latter. Not like your brother did." Helen braced her hands on her knees and scooted forward. "He hurt her."

Finn leaned in, hoping to convey his conviction. "I love her, I'd never hurt her."

"Give her time, but not too much. If that's how you feel, you must tell her soon."

Neither of them spoke for a full minute, and Finn's racing

thoughts distilled to one. "About my brother, in his defense, he was pretty wrecked when—"

"You don't know what happened, do you?"

"What are you talking about?"

She flipped a few cards on the coffee table and tapped a fingernail against one featuring three swords piercing a heart. "Back when Bianca and your brother were together, Picasso was caterwauling so loud from the window late one night, and I wondered why. When I went to her door, I heard a commotion, so I used my key. There was Dylan, outside the bathroom with a crowbar. That antique lockset, the previous owner had put it on backward. Bianca never got around to changing it."

"I don't understand."

"Your brother pushed Bianca to the brink. She'd gathered the strength to call it quits, but he wanted no part of it. He locked her in the bathroom, thinking if he held her in place she might hear him out."

Fire sizzled through Finn, settled in his ears and cheeks. He shot to his feet. "That son of a bitch."

"And to add a huge scoop of salt, Bianca doesn't do well in enclosed spaces. It might make you feel better to know he soon came to his senses, but the trouble was, he'd broken the lock and had to pry the door open. He was begging forgiveness by the time I arrived, after Bianca gave him a black eye. But apologies in some situations are just empty words."

How could Dylan have done that, knowing Bianca was claustrophobic? No wonder she decked him. Finn felt a rush of admiration and the desire to protect, in equal measure. "I'd never do anything like that to her. Ever." He mustered a thank-you and bolted for the door.

As he trudged back to his car, everything seemed off balance, teetering on the edge of ruin. Dylan's actions were inexcusable. No wonder Bianca didn't want to trust another Tierny. She was fading from him fast, disappearing like a gorgeous sunset giving way to the finality of darkness.

And it hit him hard, he was about to lose the only woman he'd ever loved.

Finn placed his hands on the cold Toyota and steadied himself, desperate to will this obsession, this confusion, to pass. But the universe he now inhabited narrowed only to Bianca. As he watched his breath diminish in the cold night air, he realized winter had moved in overnight, frigid and unyielding, bringing with it a vacant sensation of loneliness.

Desperation. The Polish king who didn't want to lose his crown to his own son.

Fear made people do drastic things.

Part of him wanted to drive straight over to see his brother, but if he didn't cool down first, he might rip Dylan's head off. He drove home instead. When he turned onto Orchard, there was that hunk of scrap metal on wheels in the driveway. Fine, maybe he *was* supposed to kick his ass. Destiny calling.

He stepped from the car, and froze.

"Dad?" he shouted as he burst into the house.

"Shhh." Dylan, sitting on the couch, brought a finger to his lips.

Mack snored in his chair, head lolled back, mouth open.

Finn squared off in front of his brother. "What're you doing here?"

"I came to talk to you."

"Outside."

"Hell no, it's freezing out there. Have a seat, bro."

"Outside," Finn ground out.

Dylan pressed his palms into the couch and jerked to his feet with exaggerated effort. "Why the badass?"

Finn blocked the narrow path to the doorway. He wanted his brother to bump into him. *Give me a reason.*

"What're you so ginned up about?"

Finn's eyes traveled to a mug on the coffee table with a tea bag dangling from its lip. "Tea? Am I supposed to believe that's yours?"

"Not that it's any of your damn business."

"If you're doing this for Bianca, do you really think she'd take you back?" Finn grabbed him by the shirt, pulled him close, ignoring the fire in his shoulder courtesy of Taz's goons. "You son of a bitch!"

Mack startled. "What the . . . ?"

Finn couldn't stop. "You locked her in the bathroom?"

"She told you that?"

"It doesn't matter how I found out." Finn shoved Dylan away from him in a motion that laid the tendons in his shoulder bare.

"Has nothing to do with you. I'm not gonna punch you again though. Is that what you want?"

"Nobody's punching anyone." Mack struggled to his feet, moving toward them, fighting an obvious bout of vertigo.

Finn reached out, but too late. Mack tripped, thudded to the floor.

They rushed to him and shouldered him to a sitting position.

"Is this about that woman?" Mack skewered Finn with a look. "You still chasing skirt?"

"I'm not chasing—"

"No woman's gonna come between Tiernys."

They'd been raised on the notion. Dylan's advice came back to him: *Think of this place like a men's restroom. There's a man on the door. The one with the dress on it is somewhere else.* Finn guided Mack back to his chair. "Of course not, Dad." He hated that the lie slipped out so easily.

"I'll be damned if . . ." Mack stared off as if collecting his thoughts, his eyes heavy and his breathing shallow. In a matter of seconds, he was asleep again.

Finn backed into a rocking chair, hoping for the calm of its rhythm, hoping for a chance to temper his rage. For his dad's sake.

Dylan resumed his place on the couch, lifted his mug from the coffee table, blew the surface, and gulped. "I came here to check on Dad, and to apologize."

Finn didn't want to talk about the punch in the parking lot. He preferred to accept it and move on. Dylan had apologized to Bianca, too. The guy was a regular walking apology. Helen's wisdom percolated. *Empty words.* Guilt about his own feelings for Bianca harangued him, and now his dad too, and he began to rock, but the chair failed in the calming department.

"Why'd you do it?" Finn asked.

"What?"

"It's that easy for you to forget?" He tamped his voice to a whisper and read the pain on Dylan's face, a pain that said he would never forget.

"I'll never forgive myself for what I did to Bee. What do you want me to say? I was drunk, whacked out, desperate—"

"Don't."

"I don't know why I hit you before. Well, I do know, but I aim to do better." He lifted the mug in a toast before he deposited it on the coffee table, flopped back in resignation, and put his feet up. A toe stuck through a hole in his black socks, and something about this tugged at Finn.

He studied his brother, the determined set of his jaw. The tea. He was sobering up for Bianca. He'd do anything for her. Twin feelings of resentment and jealousy rushed at Finn; he needed to think of something else and fast. He eyed his dad, who was back to snoring. "We can't keep leaving him here alone."

"Guess we need to look for help. I can ask the foreman for some extra shifts to pay for it."

Finn's eyes circled the room. There was far too much furniture closing in, adding to his cluttered, uneasy mood. Shelves had grown opaque with dust, and a few cobwebs dangled from the ceiling. He stopped rocking and unearthed the wedding album from beneath a pile of newspapers. "Dad looks at this all the time now."

A muscle in Dylan's jaw clenched as an unspoken family history settled between them.

Finn leafed through the pages. "Do you ever think about her? Mom?"

"Why don't you close that thing?" Dylan said through tight lips. "I was fifteen when she left. *Fifteen.* One week before I got my driver's license. That's a teenage boy's freaking rite of passage, man. And she wasn't there. Didn't even call to wish me a happy birthday, to say, 'hey, congrats on getting your license, there, *son.*' That woman is dead to me."

"She might be dead for all we know," Finn said.

"You were only ten. Who leaves a ten-year-old?"

"She didn't exactly leave me alone. I had Dad . . . and you."

"Why're you bringing this shit up now? Don't we have enough to deal with?"

Finn was trying to piece things together. Coming up short. "Just thinking how things might be different if she was still around. That's all."

"Even when she was around, she wasn't. Spending all her time at that damn community theater like she was on Broadway."

Finn almost debated his brother, reminded him about all the times she was there—the last-minute school projects she stayed up all night to help finish, baseball games she suffered through in the rain, camp outs where she roughed it in a pup tent with them while Mack slept inside. But Dylan had made up his mind. He'd never forgive her for leaving.

"And don't be getting any bright ideas about trying to find her to help take care of Dad. We've got this." Dylan wrapped his right fist in his left and let his forearms rest on faded jeans.

"I'm not."

When had everything gone completely and utterly to hell?

Winter. His mother had left on a night like tonight. He'd tried to suppress thoughts of her, but here they were, riding in on the icy chill.

When she left, so many years ago, a piece of him had packed up and gone with her. Even worse, her departure had crushed his dad. Mack, the man Finn had always admired for his strength, crumbled. With effort, he'd pulled it together for his boys and filled days, weeks, months, and even years with a deliberate defiance that said he could make it without her. But he was never the same. Watching him, Finn had vowed he'd never let a woman have that power over him. And he'd been successful.

Until now.

Then Dylan. Had Rose's departure turned him into a monster who would lock up his girlfriend for fear of losing her too?

Finn felt his brother's eyes on him. "About Bee," he heard Dylan say. "You're torqued off about what happened. I get it. I'm not an idiot . . ." He stared into his tea as if searching for a way to complete the sentence.

The creaking rocker sliced through the silence. Finn hated himself for not having the guts to tell his brother how he felt about Bianca. But then, he'd already given himself away. "What now?"

Dylan just stared past him.

It was the abandoned mine shaft all over again, and Finn was painfully at rock bottom, depending on his brother's mercy.

❦ TWENTY-THREE ❧

BIANCA curled into the sofa pillow, unfazed by the small buttons stabbing her cheek. How could she have been so foolish? If she'd only listened to the voice in her head. *Another Tierny? Mega mistake.*

Try as she might, she couldn't scrub away the image of Finn with that woman. The way her hand sat comfortably on his, the ease between them. It was clear they had a history.

But it didn't matter. He could have dinner with the Dallas Cowboys Cheerleaders for all she cared. This was about trust.

Picasso's rhythmic purr rumbled against her back, and her future self materialized pixel by pixel, gray hair framing pinwheel eyes. And there were cats, lots of cats.

"No way."

As if reading her mind, Picasso leaped down and sauntered away, tail flicking.

Her cell buzzed, and she glanced at the display, hoping it was Maris, a salesperson, anyone. Instinct wagered Finn, and won—his number vibrated against the black background. She punched IGNORE but noted the time. 1:15 p.m. Time to return to Brookefield. She never came home on breaks, but today in her studio every sound whispered his name, everything reminded her of him and how stupid she'd been. As she grabbed her coat from the floor, her cell rang again. She powered off.

Back at school, Bianca wove through the faculty lot in search of a space. She noticed a moped with no faculty tag parked in one close to the building. *Seriously?* As she scribbled a nasty note on a Wendy's napkin, a student rushed from the building, backpack slung over her shoulder, books under her arm.

Anger clawed. Bianca rolled down her window. "That's a faculty space."

"I'm so, so sorry. I just needed—"

"I don't care what you needed. Do *not* let it happen again."

The girl crammed her books in her backpack, hopped on the moped, and zipped away. Bianca pulled into the spot, the buzz of the moped grating in her ears.

As she jammed her keys in her purse, she glanced up to see Courtney, the student whose mosaic she had ruined, hand in hand with a new guy. Bianca contemplated the shift as she watched them stroll away. Maybe there was a lesson here from her student: Pick up the pieces and move on. But here Bianca was, this impatient person who snapped at parking space poachers, and retreated home on her breaks to sulk. A rap sounded on the window.

Maris, arms waving, hailing-a-cab-style. Bianca climbed out.

"I've been trying to get you," Maris said.

"I went home for a bit. I—"

"Well, answer your phone next time, okay? I've got the dirt on Charity."

No hint from Maris that she was at all troubled by their exchange the night before. Her best friend, like her student, had moved on. But Bianca couldn't. Not while she was still shackled by the black chains of their conversation, the apology straining against her ribs to break free. "I said terrible things to you, and I'm sorry."

"You did, but a dear friend once gave me very good advice about the importance of forgiveness."

"She must be brilliant."

A sly smile from Maris. "On her good days."

Bianca grabbed her hand. "Walk with me."

Weaver vibrated with students moving from class to class or loitering in the hall—chatting, laughing, cell phones to ears.

"Brett opened the vault, gabbed on and on about Charity and

his family like the sangria he was sipping was truth serum. As we suspected, she was born a diva. So how's this? For her eighth birthday, they had beluga shipped in from Maine. Caviar? She wasn't even double digits yet! There's a ton more too. Trips to California. She *had* to go there for the latest fashions when she was in high school. She even talked her parents into letting her finish her senior year out there. But Brett says she was like a mother to him. Charity? Maternal? I just don't see it."

A pulse hammered in Bianca's temple. "What about Lisette?"

"Nadya's comment makes sense now. Charity did accuse Lisette of stealing. That's why she fired her. She pressed charges, but dropped them. Just like that. Black-balled her from cleaning for all her rich friends. That's how Lisette ended up working for the agency."

"Why drop the charges?" Bianca asked as they entered her studio.

"Brett doesn't know, but he didn't seem surprised. I don't think anything about his sister surprises him."

Bianca tossed her purse on her lecture desk. "Not much would surprise me either. She can play nice when it suits her, but if you cross her—" Before she could finish, her students began filtering in.

Maris squeezed her arm. "Come by my office later."

Bianca turned her attention to her class. When they'd settled in, she dove into her lecture on aesthetics. As she reviewed the four steps of the Feldman method—describe, analyze, interpret, evaluate—she noticed several heads swivel to the door.

Finn, sketch book under his arm, contrition brimming in his eyes. His glorious mismatched eyes. He opened to the first page, held it out to her. "I think I got the turrets right this time."

A castle. Similar to the one hanging on her wall. But this one showing a proficiency in execution the other lacked. The turrets were definitely better.

Bianca bit her lip and pivoted back to her students. "Rainwater. Begin collecting it now for your watercolor assignments. It's vital for permanency. Otherwise, the colors just fade . . . like they were never there."

"What watercolor assignment?" a student asked from the back of the room.

"It's on your syllabus. There's nothing wrong with planning ahead."

As she spoke, Finn strode to the front of the room and placed the sketch on a table. The same table where he'd laid the shirt. The same day he kissed her. He glanced at the color wheel before he locked eyes on hers.

The room dipped in silence.

Bianca felt her face spin through all the colors on that wheel before landing on red.

"And I've been doing some reading after our discussion about the color wheel," Finn said. "I didn't realize complementary colors are used in healing therapy." He moved closer. "I especially like the part about magenta."

Bianca knew all about magenta and prayed he wasn't planning to go on. Not here.

Finn looked to the ceiling as if recalling what he'd read. "Magenta isn't actually part of the spectrum. But it seems pretty important to me, I mean, the way it helps people release the past and helps them move forward." He shook his head. "It's something to think about anyway."

For a long moment, they were the only two people in the room. Her breath caught in her throat as he advanced, his oaky scent coiling around her. "But, of course, you know this stuff better than me." Then, he turned and gave a slight nod as if thanking the students for indulging the interruption, and headed for the door.

From the doorway, he addressed the class before he left. "Oh, and she's right about the rainwater."

After watching him leave, Bianca stumbled through the rest of the session. When it finally ended, she gathered her things, eager to get home. She looked up to find Finn.

She shoved a box of charcoal pencils and a stack of exams in her bag. Her cell, a notebook, forced on top. "Don't ever interrupt my class again. Unlike you, I take my commitments seriously."

"Let me explain. She called—"

"It's not about her."

"Her husband is a friend of mine. My first partner. He's having a hard time, and she needs my help."

Bianca succumbed to the tidal pull of his drawing on the table. He'd worked hard on it. He really had nailed the crenellation on the turrets this time. "Why didn't you just tell me the truth?"

"You're right. I just . . . it just came out. I guess the whole story, who Shae is, the stuff about her husband, seemed too convoluted to try to explain. It was stupid."

A Tierny staple. Dylan favored the same sorry excuse. *It was stupid.* He'd said it repeatedly after locking her in the bathroom. *I'm sorry. It was stupid.* Like a parrot with a limited vocabulary. The memory blended with this fresh hurt. Fresh lies. But Dylan was an alcoholic; he had an illness. What was Finn's excuse?

She tapped her thigh. Last chance, B. F. Skinner. "It doesn't matter anyway. You have your life, I have mine. Let's leave it at that."

A call came over Finn's radio. "Be right there. Thirty-three out." He turned to her. "You're right, our situation is complicated. But hurting you was the last thing on my mind."

Bianca waited until he was out of sight, then headed for the parking lot. She needed to get home, crawl into bed, close her eyes, and wish the last twenty-four hours away. The last month away.

Steps from the faculty lot, she froze. Her car wasn't there. She could have sworn she parked in front of the trio of scarlet oaks. Or maybe the north side?

As she scanned the lot, Ralph approached, hobbling more than usual. His knees again. Maybe he was right. Maybe he should retire. She hated seeing him in such pain.

"Everything okay, Miss James?"

"I just seem to have forgotten where I parked my car."

"Happens to the best of us. Wife says I'd forget my dentures if she didn't set 'em out with my morning joe."

When had Bianca boarded the same boat Ralph was drifting in?

"You drive a Jeep, right?" Ralph asked.

"Yes, and I generally park in this section. Could it have been stolen?"

Ralph took her by the elbow, spun her toward the side lot. "Isn't that you way over there?"

It was. But not where she'd left it. She was certain.

Or was she?

Fifteen minutes later, she found herself outside Jewel's office. She debated another ten minutes whether or not to get out of the car. But if her mind was slipping to the point where she didn't remember where she'd parked that morning, she needed help.

She ran her teeth along her bottom lip, went in.

Jewel's door opened, and she emerged, arm draped around a girl who was mopping her eyes with a tissue. "Thanks so much, Dr. Glasser. My parents almost pulled me from school and—" She noticed Bianca, stuffed the tissue in her pocket. "Well, thanks for everything."

"Of course. I'm here whenever you need me," Jewel said in a tone so calming Bianca's grip on the chair loosened, and her shoulders dropped from their tight position up near her ears.

Jewel waved Bianca in. "I'm glad you came. Sit."

This was someplace she never expected to be. Across from her ex-boyfriend's current lover, asking for help. "I'm not even sure why I'm here," she said. "It's just been . . . tough."

"Understandable. Talk to me."

"I'm not sleeping . . . that night keeps crashing in whenever I close my eyes . . . and when I try to block it out . . . well, I'm forgetting things too."

"The mind–body connection is stronger than most people realize. Stress can be disastrous, for ourselves and others." Jewel spoke without modulation as she lifted the potted orchid on her desk, brushed away some dust, and returned it to the same spot.

"I just want to get a handle on this."

"Talking certainly helps." Jewel reached for a pad on her desk, scribbled on it. "I'll have my admin try to find a time for you. In the meantime, I'll prescribe a mild anti-anxiety."

Bianca accepted the prescription. "Thanks, Jewel."

"Things will get better."

On the drive from Brookefield, Bianca kept glancing at the slip of paper in the passenger seat. She shoved it in the glove compartment.

For now.

She could get this under control without drugs, couldn't she? She breathed deep. One, two, three times. That was better. As she crossed Sycamore, she took a moment to absorb the scenery. The setting sun glazed the sky pale orange, a perfect backdrop for a giant tree with weeping branches at the crest of the hill. The scene begged to be captured, tucked away as a reference for a future painting, so she pulled off the road to snap a few pictures with her cell. Panning left, a barn next to a majestic silo reached toward the Creamsicle sky. Creative juices were flowing once again, and it felt good.

She swiveled to get a better shot, bumping the car door closed with her hip. Shit! It locked. With the keys inside.

Had she really pissed off karma this much?

Pinning her face to the window, she slapped her palm against the glass. Tires crunched over the gravelly shoulder as a car slowed behind her and came to a stop. The driver stepped out, and walked toward her.

"Lucky me," he said.

In the fading light, his soul patch seemed almost sinister.

"You were at the Balfour the other night," she said, at a loss for something better to say.

"I was." GQ smoothed a hand down his black cashmere sweater. "Everything okay?"

"I've locked my keys inside."

"Let me help." He stepped closer, brushing against her, and she backed away.

"Thanks, but I'll just wait for my friend. She'll be here any minute."

"Funny, that's what you said at the restaurant, too." He leaned against the car, settling in. He was staying. "By the way, is she psychic?"

"Excuse me?"

"How does she know? You only used your phone for the camera. And that was before you realized you were locked out of your car."

A sticky fear enveloped her. He'd been watching.

"You don't have to wait," she said, doing her best to mask her anxiety. "I'm sure you have somewhere to be."

"As I told you the other night, I'm drawn to beautiful things. And you look even better than your Brookefield profile picture." He smiled, but his words seemed booby-trapped. His gaze roamed the length of her body at a leisurely pace, making her skin crawl. "And let me think. I used to have a lot of places to be. My condos in Aspen and Hawaii, my catamaran."

"I really don't know what you're talking about." She took another step, stretching the distance between them.

"You cost me my reputation, my business, my best client."

Best client?

"Would it have killed you to let Charity have her little fantasy? To let her believe she actually owned a Miró?"

The Miró fiasco.

"From my perspective," he continued, "you owe me something."

The way he said "owe me," with an underlying verbal caress, maybe a command, nauseated her. "You sold Charity a fake. Not my problem."

He certainly didn't have the right to be bitter when he was the one in the wrong, and he certainly didn't deserve another second of her time. She started to dial Maris, but GQ clenched his fingers around her phone, terminating the call.

The tip of his tattoo registered, a misshapen dagger-like triangle. Where else had she seen it?

The dollars.

Her body went numb.

The calls. The Eye of Horus. U R Next.

Silence droned. "You seem nervous," he said.

Not nervous. Scared shitless.

As she fought the mounting dread, contemplating options that required more presence of mind than she could muster at the moment, a vehicle rumbled toward them. A dirty white pick-up with a crown of fog lights across the top.

She'd never been so happy to see the toothless hog farmer.

"Heya, Miss Bianca," Durwood said, removing his cap and screwing it back on his head.

Relief radiated from Bianca's chest to all of her limbs. "I locked my keys in the car. This *gentleman* offered to help," she said with a glower in his direction, "but you're here now."

Durwood cocked a squint eye from her to the art dealer, whose sly, loaded grin dissolved. Durwood, angel in filthy bib overalls and backward Steelers cap, grabbed the hint as if he'd been handed a chaw of tobacco. "I do tinker some. A regular poor man's locksmith."

GQ reached into a pocket inside his jacket, and she held her breath.

A business card.

Lance Oliphant, Fine Art Broker. "We have unfinished business. Call me." He hesitated before climbing into his car, adding, "Or I'll be sure to follow up with you."

Bianca keyed the license plate number in the notes app on her phone. She turned to Durwood, who had already broken into her car, started it, and hopped out. After thanking him with a kiss that tinted his cheeks, she raced home.

Once inside, she slipped off her boots, tossed her jacket on the couch, and dialed the station as she moved to the kitchen, hoping the Pinot Grigio in her fridge was still crisp. Ford patched her through to Tucker, and she left a voice mail about Lance Oliphant. After hanging up, she almost dialed Maris to share her trifecta of bad luck, but maybe it was time to dismantle this armature of habit, running to her best friend like she had an owner's manual for Bianca's problems.

Where was that wine?

She pulled a wine glass off the drain board, noticed a grainy ring in the bottom, and set it aside. As she grabbed a second one from the cupboard, the doorbell rang. She peeked out her window. Dylan? He had a bottle of wine in one hand, a grocery bag in the other. She swung the door open.

"I know you, Bee." He lifted the grocery sack on his way in. "You haven't food shopped in days, and you're living on cafeteria lunches and takeout." Dylan flashed the gleaming smile that used to make her feet slip out from under her.

Surprise, a collection of mixed feelings, shot through her. She followed him to the kitchen.

He studied the two wine glasses on the counter.

"I was about to pour myself some wine. One was dirty, so I got another."

Dylan handed her a Joseph Mellot Sancerre, her favorite. "This is for you, and this"—he presented a six pack of Sprite—"is for me."

He emptied the rest of the bag and opened a jar of pesto. "Cutting some corners here, but definitely better than . . . wait, is it peanut butter or ramen noodle night?"

Bianca pointed to a jar of peanut butter on the counter. "It's a Skippy night. But check it out, I've upgraded from saltines to Wheat Thins." She picked up the box and swiped her fingers over the label.

"The day you've had calls for real food."

"What do you mean, 'the day I've had?'"

Dylan lightly touched the space between her brows.

"My stress dimple?" Bianca remembered the first time he'd called it that, the year she forgot to send in her tax return and was expecting the IRS to beat down her door.

He took a lock of hair between two fingers, twisted, and tugged it playfully. "Looks like you've got the beginning of a dreadlock here. Still beautiful though."

Heat climbed her face. She rooted around for a corkscrew, hesitated, and then slammed the drawer. "Let's crack open that Sprite."

"I promise to stop at two. Okay, maybe three." His voice was charming, on the way to sexy, and something was different about him. His eyes. The clarity in them spoke of better days.

As he made dinner, pesto pasta with a tomato mozzarella salad, she sipped Sprite and doused chunks of bread in olive oil before popping them in her mouth.

They chatted about this and that, warming up to one another again. "Seen any good films lately?" Dylan asked.

Films. Bianca loved his rarely seen erudite side, the one that lifted what most people took for entertainment to an art form. The question from anyone else would have been a filler, an attempt to avoid the opaque silences that plagued too many relationships. But this was Dylan. He was passionate about the subject and could rhapsodize about the classics for hours, quoting movie lines, entire scenes. Old movies had never really been her thing, but his excitement was contagious as they watched *Casablanca* for the hundredth time and pondered the theme of loneliness in *Chinatown*.

"Maris had to drag me to *The Hunger Games*—"

"I can think of only one place she'd drag me. Down a dark alley to work me over."

"Well—"

"Don't worry about it," he said. "That's step eight, a long way off."

Step eight. He was getting help. "I'm really happy for you, Dylan."

"It's time." He paused. "Seeing Dad like that on Thanksgiving . . . he's slipping fast and . . ." He swallowed hard, unable to continue.

Bianca stroked his arm. "I understand."

"Enough about me. How are you doing?"

"I just want everything to be over. All of it. That poor family . . . Hey, do you remember ever hearing something about Charity filing charges against Lisette Divac for stealing from her?"

"Doesn't ring a bell." Dylan poured bowtie pasta into a pot of bubbling water. "There might be something in the case files though."

Bianca's first thought was to call Finn to see if he'd checked, but she snapped off the notion.

"I don't think she'd need a reason," Dylan continued, shaking his head. "A real piece of work, that one. When I saw her at Lost—"

She placed her hand on his arm, left it there. "Charity was at Lost?"

"Didn't seem like she wanted to be, but yeah. About knocked Jewel off her barstool and took her aside to give her a good talking to."

"What did she say?"

"Charity pushed her into a corner. I couldn't make out what they were saying."

"What day was that?"

"The day after Thanksgiving. I went in to settle my tab with

Gus, and Jewel insisted on tagging along. Then in comes Charity, loaded for bear."

"They don't even communicate at school."

"Looked like they know each other pretty well to me."

"Interesting." Bianca rolled everything over and over in her mind. "Some of the calls to my house came from Lost." Maris' repeated warnings about Dylan rang in her ears. But he was here, making dinner.

Dylan didn't respond at first but continued to slice tomatoes, sweeping the remnants into the garbage. "Town's favorite watering hole. Anyone could have made those calls," he said without looking up, reaching over to turn the burner off.

"Charity *could* have made them."

"Sure, she *could* have. And maybe she did. But, like I said, I only saw her there once." He twisted the tip of the knife against the cutting board. "Even if Charity made those calls, it doesn't make her a murderer. She could just be harassing you because she's a bitch."

"The whole thing is just so convoluted. What's her connection with Jewel? Think about it, Finn, she'd never step foot in Lost . . . What? Why are you looking at me like that?"

Dylan had her locked in a visual stronghold. "You called me Finn."

Damn.

"What's going on with you and my brother?"

Bianca's throat tightened. She took a sip of Sprite and set her glass on the counter. *Nothing. Everything.*

He deserved the truth.

"As Finn and I spent time together we . . . But that's over." She went on, telling him how she told Finn to leave her alone.

"So there's no reason for us not to try again."

She thought about how he had brought her food, how he cared for her, and a ladle of tenderness poured over her. But a cottony emptiness persisted; the air around her pulsed with it. She couldn't think of anything to say that wouldn't hurt him. "Dylan . . ."

The light drained from his eyes, and yet they looked as if they could cut ice. "If you're really not interested in my brother, why wouldn't we at least try again? We had something good."

"It's not automatic. Ending things with your brother doesn't mean starting them up with you again."

"It just felt like things were getting back to the way they were. My mistake." Dylan drew himself up slowly, crossed the room, and slammed the door behind him.

A rush of good memories trickled through Bianca's mind, all of them Dylan. Moonlit nights, a chorus of crickets, his lips on hers, their bodies pressed together. The sex was good. Was she making the mistake of her life? She fell against the couch and cried until the tears would no longer come. She pushed herself up, put all the food away, and scrubbed every inch of the kitchen, laboring over light switches, stove and faucet knobs, until her hands were red and raw. How could she have called him Finn?

She was wiping down the counter for the third time when Dylan walked back through the front door, a serene look on his face. "I circled the block so many times I thought Helen might come out and put a hex on me."

Bianca tried for a laugh but couldn't get it past the lump in her throat.

Dylan pulled her into his arms, stroked her hair. He lifted her chin, his lips moved to hers, as a familiar current of warmth ran through her along with swirls of confusion and emotion as the pieces of her life splintered and scattered around her.

"You know I love you."

She wiped her nose with a napkin. "I know." She attempted to transmit a depth of affection, a fondness beyond physical attraction, but she couldn't return the words he wanted to hear.

Her head swam; her heart ached. "Dylan, I . . ."

He took her hands in his, rested them against his chest.

As far as beautiful moments went, this was a ten, and if ever there was a time to employ the Feldman method, it was now. Describe: warm tingly feelings from head to toe. Analyze: she and Dylan just knew each other so well. Interpret: maybe they were supposed to be together. Evaluate: it all made for a gorgeous aesthetic, except for their history, which continued to intrude, and new feelings for his brother weaseling their way in.

His lips brushed her forehead, stopping at her temple. His touch constricted her insides, squeezing and squeezing as the past rushed her like a landslide.

⊰ TWENTY-FOUR ⊱

FROM the minute Finn walked into the station, it had been clear—this was going to be a shitty day. His first tip: yesterday's coffee. He tried to make a fresh pot, but some jagoff used the last of it. He'd have to face a mountain of paperwork—without caffeine. Halfway through a tedious writer, a burglary with a cast of repeat offenders, his computer froze.

Now Carmichael wanted to see him.

The chief pointed to a chair. "Have a seat, son."

The word grated. One of these days, he was going to set him straight. Tell him that word was reserved for his father, not some blowhard despot, but he restrained himself. Semi-cordial Carmichael meant bad news.

"I received a call from the Wade's attorney last evening. They're claiming you're harassing their son."

So Mama Wade's precious Emmy had a bite with teeth after all. "That's bullshit."

Carmichael glared.

A scowl replaced the glare, prompting Finn to add, "Sir."

"Bullshit or not, I have to look into it. In the meantime, you need to take some R & R."

"Are you suspending me?"

"Let's not get ahead of ourselves. But if the Wades so much as see you driving a squad—"

"And you believe the little shit?"

Chief Carmichael sighed, opened his desk drawer, and tossed a photo down. "A student took this from Weaver. I have more."

There it was in full color, Finn pinning Emerson to the hood of his BMW.

"What about the murder investigation?"

"I'm sure we'll get along just fine. The guys over in Whistler would be more than happy to fill in until this gets resolved."

Now he calls in the reinforcements.

"Bianca James needs protection, and I—"

Carmichael spurted a sanctimonious laugh. "As I said earlier, you're too close to this case. This could be the best thing all around."

Turning him into a house mouse wasn't the answer, but no amount of arguing the point was going to change Carmichael's mind.

"I'll need your weapon and badge, son."

Finn slapped them on the desk. "You've got two sons at home. Save the term of endearment for them."

Carmichael's face was as expressionless as water. "Think of it as a little vacation."

And that's how you start a shitty day.

Finn exited the shower and stood in the center of the bathroom, dripping water onto a powder blue bathmat that was almost as old as he was. Another reminder of how little had changed around here. The same brass fixtures and flowered wallpaper, chosen by his mom with a swell of pride, now screamed "needs updating."

He'd been able to sneak past Mack when he got home from the station, but he couldn't keep his forced "vacation" from old Super Sleuth forever. And the last thing Mack needed right now was something else to worry about.

Finn was stepping into his boxers when his cell buzzed. He glanced at the screen and scrambled to answer. "Bianca."

"It was Emerson." Her voice was brittle, about to break. "He was here and—"

"Call 911. Lock your doors. I'll be right there." Finn powered into his jeans, grabbed his personal gun from his bottom dresser drawer, and flew from the room while shrugging into a shirt.

Mack roused from his chair as Finn yanked on his boots. "What's going on?"

"No time to explain."

"It's about the murder, isn't it?" Mack strained for purchase on the well-worn carpet. "I'm going with you."

"Dad, no. I've got this."

"Two cops are better than one." Mack started down the hallway toward his room, each step an eternity. "I'll get my piece."

Two cops. Right. More like one retired cop and one a hair away from being fired.

"I'll call for back-up," Finn hollered after him.

Mack pivoted, seething with pure fury, gray eyes pronounced in their sockets. "Wait!"

There was no time to reason with him. "I'm sorry, Dad." Finn slipped out, but before he reached the bottom step, he heard something crash against the door. He hesitated, wanting to go back in, but his need to get to Bianca propelled him forward. Through the window, he spied Mack, shuffling back to his recliner. He'd have Dylan check on him.

A bank of dark clouds crested the distant outline of pine trees, making it seem later in the day than four o'clock. Finn was about to jump into the Toyota when he noticed the back tire, flatter than flat. Searching the sky, he growled out a scream. A spare tire would solve the problem. But the spare was already pinch-hitting for the other rear tire after Dylan ran over a nail at the construction site. He'd also lent their air compressor to a neighbor and promptly forgotten which one. *Thanks, bro, for making every road I turn down a freakin' dead end.*

Finn shoved up the garage door, hating what he was about to do. Geeto lay under a tarp in undisturbed slumber. Those clouds overhead meant snow. And snow meant a shitload of slush and salt. He peeled off the cover, piled it on the workbench, and jumped behind the wheel. "Don't let me down." Geeto responded with a turn of the key.

He sped from the garage while a slow, rolling pressure of panic mounted inside him, building to a crescendo. All the way to Waterton, he tried to paste an explanation on all of this, each thought pushing past the other only to be rejected. More scenarios, and then more, but still not enough. After hurling the GTO into Bianca's driveway, Finn shot from the car.

Her door swung open. Uncertainty expanded inside him as he worked out how to act after their argument. Hesitation dissolved after a long moment, and they scrambled for each other, trying to get closer than physically possible, limbs knotted together, forehead pressed to forehead. Finn inhaled her scent, hoping his embrace would dispel her fear. She responded, squeezing, as if the tighter she held him, the safer she'd be. His muscles were still raw, but he pushed through the pain, teleported beyond the physical into something deeper, and he lost himself in her.

Then, over Bianca's shoulder, Finn saw it.

"It was on my back patio when I let Picasso in."

"Is that supposed to be you?"

The face was pasty and misshapen. The eyes were wrong, painted without light reflex, lifeless. The hair, a flat, sickly yellow, resembled straw. The lips thin worms instead of full perfection. A swath of fabric draped below knobs of shoulders and a jagged line of cleavage. But as bad as the portrait was, he wasn't prepared for the desecration of it. Red paint, thrown Jackson Pollock-style, dripped down the face like blood.

And in the middle of the forehead, a bullet hole.

Before Finn could say anything, Tucker walked through the front door. He took one look at the painting and scowled. "I don't know diddly about art, but this ain't you, Bianca."

"Especially with the latest addition." She shuddered with what looked like a thin grasp on her last nerve.

"We'll have pretty boy in no time," Tucker assured her. "Don't you worry."

Finn swapped a look with Tucker and headed for the door.

Tucker grabbed his arm. "Sorry, bud, Carmichael told us. I'll keep you posted." He grabbed the painting and disappeared.

"What's going on?" Bianca asked.

Finn paced the entryway until she blocked his path, demanding an answer. "Emerson's parents are claiming harassment. Chief took my badge."

Leaving his badge with Carmichael was like leaving a dog to watch your T-bone. And the irony? History was repeating itself. This was the same shit that threatened to ruin his life in the 'Burgh, with a slight twist. He was the one being accused.

Fragile lines etched Bianca's face. "That's insane."

"A student took pictures of my *conversation* with him in the parking lot after he pulled that stunt in your class."

"Ouch."

"Listen, about the other night . . . I should have told you."

"I wish you had."

"Shae was so upset. Her call was completely out of the blue. And all the PPD stuff came back like a bad dream."

Curiosity teemed in her eyes, eyes that pressed him for the truth.

He sighed. Keeping her in the dark about this had already caused him enough problems.

"One night these two cops brought in an arrest. When they took the cuffs off, the perp said something stupid, reached out, and swiped the cop's forehead. You don't touch cops. They started beating on him, bad. I was afraid they were gonna do serious damage, so I stopped it."

"That's a good thing."

"For the guy getting beat, but not for me. I broke the code."

"Cops stick together."

"Like they're doused with Krazy Glue," Finn said. "IA got involved, and I answered their questions. The guys got a brief suspension. Got off easy, if you ask me, but that's not how they saw it. After that, every day was a living hell. When I needed back-up, they didn't show. Nearly got me killed. I knew I had to make a change."

"I'm sorry for the reason, but I'm glad you came back to Riley's Peak."

"Shae's husband wasn't there that night, but he's getting the same crap now because he broke code in another situation. I thought I could just move on, but seeing her stirred up everything I've been trying to forget."

"It's not like . . . well, if you just told me you had to meet someone, none of this would have happened," Bianca said.

"Lesson learned."

Her lips slid into a smile. "You've always been a good student."

A two-tone bell sounded, a text alert, and her smile vanished as she checked the display.

"What is it?"

"From Dylan: 'Ending it.'"

"Ending what?"

"I don't know." Her phone announced another text. A storm of anxiety brewed behind her eyes as she read it aloud. "Need to see your beautiful face . . . one last time."

"This isn't funny." Finn pulled out his cell and dialed his brother's number. It went straight to voice mail.

"This is crazy. Even for Dylan."

The chime again, sounding more menacing with each text. "Meet me at the cabin. 6849 Pine Ridge. Please."

Bianca clicked an answering text. "What's going on?"

A long moment passed but no response.

Finn shot to his feet. "That's it. Tell him you're coming."

She did.

Bianca reached for her purse, and they raced outside where she threw a puzzled look at the GTO.

"Toyota has a flat tire."

"I'd offer the Pathfinder, but one of my students borrowed it to haul his paintings to an exhibit."

He patted the GTO's hood. "Looks like this is our only option."

As they threaded through Bianca's neighborhood, Finn gathered her with one arm. He punched the accelerator and felt Bianca slam into him. Instead of righting herself, she pressed her head onto his shoulder and stayed there.

After a while, he took his arm back, scrolled the contacts on his phone, held it to his ear. "Jewel? Finn. Where's Dylan?"

"I don't know," Jewel replied, her voice weary. "I'm just leaving a workshop. I can't get ahold of him."

"Let me know if you hear from him. And, hey, can you check on Dad?"

"I thought I'd drop by there later, but I can go now."

"I'd appreciate it." Finn ended the call. Though all signs pointed to Dylan taking a nose dive, he wanted to believe otherwise. "I'm not buying this. Suicidal? It's just a ploy to get you back. Text him again. See if he answers."

Bianca shook her head when there was no response. "This is all my fault."

"Your fault?"

"He came over last night."

Finn's heart plummeted. "And?"

"He wants to try again." She tucked a lock of hair behind her ear. "He kissed me."

The image pulverized him, and in his mind's eye, he was storming in, pulling Bianca and Dylan apart, and landing a punch on his brother's jaw.

"In a way I'm glad it happened," Bianca continued.

Finn faltered on the cusp of a new epoch, which would either be fantastic or devastating, depending on her next words.

"The kiss told me what I needed to know," Bianca said, locking eyes with him. "And I told him about us."

The chokehold on Finn's chest loosened. "But he's still in love with you."

"He was upset about us, you and me, but said he wanted to move past it. That's why this texting is so—"

"Helen told me what happened. About him locking you in the bathroom."

She balled and unballed the fringe on her scarf. "I've put that all behind me."

Large snowflakes floated from the sky. They might as well have been filling his throat. He focused on the road, afraid if he laid eyes on her she might vanish like the flakes melting on his windshield.

The wind was building to a steady roar. Despite the weatherman's half-assed prediction to the contrary, Finn's gut told him the snow would be worse by the time they reached the back roads, roads at the bottom of the county's plowing schedule. They hit a patch of ice, and he placed both hands back on the wheel to correct the spin.

Decision time. Ignore the texts, or fight their way to the cabin. God forbid he didn't go and something happened to his brother.

He tore through the snow. The last few miles were treacherous. As expected, not a plow in sight. Snowflakes grew and bound together, creating a white sheet. It was all he could do to stay on the road. To find the road. The GTO fishtailed again, and he steered into the swerve. Tension crawled from shoulder blade to shoulder blade.

Please, God, let us get there in time.

He skidded and swerved through blasts of whiteouts and ordered his priorities. Get Bianca there safe. Then deal with Dylan.

The cabin came into view, and Finn heaved a sigh. No signs of Dylan's truck. Probably still at home taking a long shower and slapping on aftershave, getting ready to saunter into the cabin with a dozen roses and a bottle of champagne. Won't he be surprised to find baby brother seated in the front row for his performance?

The Toyota. Could Dylan have let the air out of the tire to keep Finn from following Bianca to the cabin?

None of it made sense. Finn couldn't reconcile any of this with the brother he once thought of as a hero, super powers, cape, and all.

"He's not here," Bianca said.

"Yet." Parking near a bank of bushes, Finn rounded the car and opened the door. His eyes fell to her shoes: they looked like ballet slippers. He swept her up.

"I can walk."

"In those?"

Objection vanished as she tightened her arms around his neck, and her breath warmed through him.

On the porch, he brushed the excess snow away with the side of his boot and created a place for her to stand. As he poured her from his arms, she leaned in with a kiss.

It was more than he could handle. He ached to give in to what he'd fought for so long. *Think of something else, something very unsexy.* He called up Tucker devouring the hoagie, sauce dripping onto his shirt. He rammed his shoulder into the door. "It sticks."

"You don't have a key?"

"Don't worry. Rabbits, squirrels, and raccoons are our only visitors." He looked one way and then the other in slow motion. "And the occasional mountain lion."

Bianca brought her head around with a jerk. "Mountain lion?"

"It's all good. They prefer smaller mammals."

"Not funny."

They stepped inside. A musty smell hit first followed by the tang of pinewood.

Bianca shivered, rubbed her arms, and took in the space. "How did your family ever find this place? It's kind of off the grid."

"Mom found it. She loved to disappear and just drive. Got lost once and stumbled onto this cabin. The setting alone sucked her in. It must not look like much under all this snow." A tight curl of longing clenched his stomach as he thought about carefree days at the cabin. He shrugged off the bittersweet memories. In four long strides, he was across the room, fiddling with the fireplace damper.

"I can tell it's beautiful, even under the snow." Bianca's voice came from behind him. "If only the circumstances were different."

Finn would never forgive his brother for pulling this stunt. But here he was with this amazing woman. Desire crashed through his resistance. He pulled her into his arms, a replay of their embrace at her house, but this time with a kiss, tender at first then urgent, exploding with passion. His heart beat in a quick, almost painful, staccato. It was like they were trying to outdo each other in a ferocious competition of surrender.

He tunneled his hands under her jacket and found her warmth. Her fingers pressed into his back, drawing him closer. His mouth sank deeper against hers as heat and need built inside him. Suppressed spasms of yearning surfaced and spread to his elbows, his fingers, his toes. Her body rippled toward him in response. The room was spinning, and Finn, dangerously swept away, forgot everything else, his busted ribs, his wall to wall bruises, and thought only of Bianca, of being with her.

But reality soon barged in. This situation with his brother compounded by a murderer on the loose. Finn reluctantly interrupted their kiss with a final brush over her lips.

Glancing out the window, he noted the deepening drifts, shifting and changing at the command of a brutal wind. There would be no way out without the miracle of a thaw or at the very least a great set of snow tires. He rubbed his hands together. "I should start a fire."

He found a blanket on the back of the couch and drew it around her. She sat down, and he leaned in to kiss her forehead, cheeks, neck, and lips, as if he would be away for a very long time.

Crouching in front of the hearth, he stuffed kindling into place, followed by a criss-cross of logs. When the flames stretched long and clawed up the chimney, he sat on the braided rug, indicating the space beside him. "It's warmer over here."

Bianca moved to him, included him in her blanket, and found his lips. The hypnotic stroke of her fingertips, the steady rhythm of her heart against his, consumed him. He shuffled through a multitude of emotions and settled on one.

They stopped kissing and searched each other's eyes.

Finn's phone buzzed. "Good news, bud," Tucker said. "We have Emerson. The little twerp claims he was home alone."

"No shit?" Finn scrambled to a sitting position.

An extended pause. "So you took Bianca to the cabin?"

"It's a long story."

"Well, Dylan's gonna—"

"Dylan is the reason we're here. He texted Bianca and—"

"Couldn't have. He can't find his phone."

The situation was growing more convoluted by the minute, piling up like the snow outside. "Listen, Tuck, I gotta go. Just keep me in the loop about Emerson, okay?" He broke the connection with a jab of his thumb. "We've got Emerson on the ropes," he said to Bianca. "But Dylan didn't send those texts."

"Who did then?" She drew up her knees, and looped her arms around them. "What if Emerson stole his phone to lure me here? But how would he know about this cabin?"

Finn rubbed his jaw. "I don't know what the hell to think."

Bianca sighed. "How about . . . we don't think for a few minutes."

The fire winked cobalt, gold and orange, devouring the logs. He took her hand and skimmed it with a kiss. Glancing to the window, her head on his shoulder, they watched clouds pour across the gray sky. "It's getting worse out there," he whispered into her ear.

"We can't go back," she said.

He pushed the tousled hair from her face, took her in his arms and was immediately drawn into her aura. His body surged with desire as he considered the serendipity of it all. Bianca in his life was nothing he'd planned for or arranged. And yet, here she was in his arms. Their kiss lasted only a moment, but it burst with a promise that seemed to go on and on and on.

They sat in silence, only breaking their embrace long enough for him to add another log to the fire. A chill seized the room. The flames distilled to embers, and the stack of wood was gone.

"I need to chop firewood if we want to stay warm tonight." He trailed nibbles along her ear and cinched the blanket tighter around her. Rising to his feet, he removed his gun from its holster where he'd left it on the couch. Though it seemed the most unromantic thing to do, he laid the Glock in her hand.

Bianca's eyes trained on the gun.

"Quick lesson." He indicated the trigger. "There's no safety. Just point." Enfolding her hand in his, he guided her aim to the door. "And shoot. Make sure you give it a good squeeze to fully depress the trigger."

"But why?"

"Big cat's hungry."

"Finn!"

"Seriously, it's better if you have it."

"I'll go with you."

He shrugged on his jacket, pointed to her feet. "I'll work fast. Just be ready to warm me up when I get back." He kissed her and stepped from the cabin, the bitter cold attacked his cheeks, his ears.

They were so close to solving Lisette's murder. He wanted to revel in the moment, but a jagged line of doubt crackled through him as he trudged into the white expanse.

↜ TWENTY-FIVE ↝

AS the door closed, Bianca settled against the couch. She stared into the fireplace, mesmerized by the glowing embers and the hum and pop of dying flames, and her mind hopscotched. Emerson. The painting. Lisette. Finn. She rooted there. He'd promised to be upfront with her from now on.

They both promised.

Restless, she meandered through the small, three-room cabin, imagining Finn and Dylan tracking mud across the knotty pine floor despite their mother's scolding. A pang of envy, then sympathy. Bianca knew the heartbreak of losing a mother. Over time, the details of her mom's sweet face had diluted, and she wondered if Finn's memory had faded as well.

She ran her finger over a picture of Mack and the boys, posed next to a freshly planted sapling, dirt smudged on hands and faces. Was this the same oak at the side of the cabin? In the photo, Finn beamed up at his father while Dylan stood a full step away, exerting independence, but something about his eyes gave away his Tierny pride.

Had the frame once held a different picture, one of the four of them?

Life twirled on a paper-thin dime.

Bianca scanned the room and landed on a thin slab of wood

painted with "Explore" in primitive script next to a poster of three wandering bears. No doubt Rose's touches, coated in dust and cobwebs.

So this was Dylan's man cave. No place for his "delicate Bee." Why had she never questioned how he framed her so differently than she truly was?

She strolled to the window and observed how the snow clung to spindly trees and lush evergreens, weighing them down.

I love Finn.

She wanted to raise the window and scream it to the world. Instead, she did the next best thing. Unearthing her phone from the mess in her purse, she punched in Maris' number, pleased to have something good to share, not another problem in need of a solution.

Maris answered after five long rings. "Hola, chica."

"What's all that rattling?"

"Just dropped my blow torch."

"Excuse me?"

"Making crème brulee. Blackberry, your favorite. I'll save you one."

"Save me two," Bianca said.

Maris' signature laugh—the one that sounded like she was jumping off a cliff—popped and then muted to a sigh. "So what's up? Have to get my face on soon. Dinner with Brett."

"Good news and bad," Bianca said.

"Rip off that Band-Aid and hit me with the bad."

"First, I'm at Finn's cabin. I'm okay, but Emerson embellished the painting he did for me, and let's just say his form of expressionism isn't for the faint of heart."

After bringing Maris up to speed, Bianca shared the history between Finn and Shae.

"Guess I'll take the pins out of the voodoo doll," Maris said in a sheepish tone. "And thank him for taking you somewhere safe."

Bianca explained why they were at the cabin, about the text messages.

"Mind games."

"Dylan's not into mind games." She told Maris her suspicion

that Emerson was the one behind the text messages. "He knows my history with Dylan and figured I'd come running."

"That's one screwed-up guy," Maris said.

"A gross understatement."

Where was the reverse button, the squiggly lines on the screen that meant they could start over? Outside the window, the setting sun tinted the underside of swollen gray clouds with burnt orange. But no sign of Finn.

"Tell me the good part," Maris prodded.

Bianca shared everything.

"Some mountain man ya got there."

The moniker made Bianca giggle. When was the last time she actually giggled?

"You're beyond happy, Bianca, but if he lies to you again, he'll be wearing his badge in a very uncomfortable place."

Maris would have to pry Finn's badge from Carmichael's clutches first.

Bianca's phone beeped, and she checked caller ID. Tucker. "Let me get this. It may be about Emerson. Call you right back."

"Hey," Tucker said when she'd switched calls. "Finn's not answering. Everything okay out there?"

"We're fine." She thought about the door that didn't lock, and her nerves jangled. "He's out getting firewood."

"Well, he's good with an axe if I remember right. He'll be back soon." A long pause. "Emerson's got a solid alibi."

She clenched the phone tighter.

"Little shit lied like Pinocchio. Said he couldn't have planted the painting, he was at his apartment. Well, he couldn't have delivered the painting, but not because he was home at the time. He spent all day in a workshop at Brookefield monitored by Jewel. Sensitivity and divisions or diversions or something like that. Jewel confirmed it. Guess he didn't want to admit the school was making him do it. Anyway, tell Finn I need to talk to him, pronto."

The killer was still out there.

So if not Emerson, then who? Maybe it was someone they weren't even considering. Bianca chewed on her lip, as she mulled possibilities. Again, her thoughts traveled to the surrealist painters she loved, those unexpected juxtapositions. Magritte's pipe that wasn't a pipe, or the hallucinatory effect of Ernst's *Elephant Celebes.* Nothing was what it seemed, and yet—

Something scraped across the roof. She spun to the window and inched closer to see a fallen tree limb.

When would she no longer catapult at the slightest noise?

The lights flickered.

Ice trickled through her veins. The Glock. She moved to a side table where she'd stashed it. The drawer whined open, and she reached for the gun, held it in her palm. Cold. So why did it burn her hand?

Could I put a bullet in another human being?

The lights died.

Bianca hesitated, snatched the gun, and bounded into the kitchen. She rummaged through a drawer by the stove, found a small flashlight, and flicked it on. A weak ribbon of light, but it would have to do.

Her cell rang, and she picked it up, still clenching the gun in her other hand.

"What's going on?" Maris' voice rushed from the phone. "I almost called the police. But then I remembered, you're with the police, and—¡maldita sea! Bianca, soy un manojo de nervios!"

"Translation, please?"

"I'm a nervous wreck."

"Service is patchy out here."

"Next time send me a telepathic message. Didn't Helen teach you anything?"

Bianca assured her everything was fine, while considering the irony of that statement based on the gun in her hand. What would Maris say if she could see the way Bianca held on to it for dear life? She hung up and checked the time. *What was taking so long?*

While ferreting for candles and matches, a stifled scream outside made her jump. The door swung open, and Bianca trained the gun on the intruder. "Finn!" She lowered the Glock, and her eyes traveled from the considerable bundle in Finn's arms to the split log resting on his foot. She rushed to him and pushed it aside.

"Think I broke my toe."

"So much for steel-toed boots. Told you I should have gone with you."

Finn frowned. "Now my ego's broken, too."

She kissed him. "Both will mend."

After settling the logs in a basket and getting the fire going, they worked in tandem to spread candles, lighting them as they went. They circled the room, ending up face to face. Finn pulled Bianca down on the couch. "That kiss before helped, but if I'm going to fully heal . . ." He pointed to his cheek. She kissed it.

He indicated the other side.

She brushed her lips against his face and feathered it with kisses.

"Damn. You've got healing powers, Doctor James."

His fingers tiptoed along his jawline, and she followed with her lips.

"Mmm. Doc, I'm going to need a refill on that prescription."

Bianca put her hand on his thigh. "There's no expiration."

A grin spread across his face.

Things were moving in a delicious direction, but Bianca needed to tell him before they went a tasty molecule further. "Tucker wants you to call him," Bianca said. "They cleared Emerson."

Finn phoned Tucker. "Emerson didn't leave the painting at your house," he said after ending the call.

"But that doesn't mean he didn't have someone else do it."

"True," Finn said. "Tuck's on it. Damn, I hate being trapped here."

"You wouldn't be able to do anything there anyway. Carmichael has your hands tied."

"Good point. Of course, being tied up isn't always a bad thing."

He pulled her close again, which sent a quiver from her chin to her toes. Bianca loved this man, wanted him with every ounce of her being. Running her hands around him, she slid his shirt from his jeans and caressed his back. His heartbeat thumped against her chest.

As she worked her fingers deeper into the tight muscles, he tensed.

"What?"

"I'm . . . sore."

She softened her touch.

"So those dirty cops in the 'Burgh I told you about? One of them gave me some bogus lead on a guy who ran with Lisette's ex. Turned out good old Walters only wanted payback. His thugs roughed me up and dumped me on the South Side." He shook his head. "At least these guys respect classic cars. Not a scratch on the GTO."

"But you—"

"I didn't fare so well."

"Should you get checked out?"

He laced his hand in hers. "I'm under the best care."

"Walters, then Carmichael. What happened to the old luck of the Irish?"

"Let's just say, I don't exactly buy lottery tickets these days." He shook his head. "Walters and his crew are ruining too many good cops, like Shae's husband, and someone needs to stop them."

"I'm guessing that someone is you. For now, if you're too sore . . ."

"Believe me, it will be a lot more painful if you stop touching me."

She nibbled his face playfully followed by a kiss that dislodged an avalanche of feelings. "I love you."

"I love you too, Bianca James. I've loved you since the second I saw you."

They held each other, basking in the words, words both foreign and glorious at once. The air around them blew all their past hurt and pain away on the warm exhalation of this declaration. The mobile of their lives stopped twirling. No more spinning, no tangling.

"Don't move." Finn went into the bedroom and returned with a comforter and pillows. He made a place on the floor in front of the fire. "Not the Ritz, but—" He pulled Bianca down beside him. After gliding his finger back and forth along the bare space between her pants and top until she thought she might burst, he gently eased off her sweater, peeled away her jeans, and propped up on his elbow, admiring her. He tripped a light touch over her bra and stopped at her navel. Taking his time, soaking her in. She melted under his stroke, wanted all of him, but wanted to take it slow too.

She arched to meet his lips as they wandered her body sampling, slowly, softly. When desire became unbearable, she squirmed from beneath him. They flung the rest of their clothes across the room. Finn lay on his back, and she nestled against him, enjoying his quiet murmurs as she skimmed her hands over him, savoring his skin beneath her fingertips. Her heart beat to a rhythm she couldn't control, didn't want to control. She gasped when he rolled on top of her.

He knew exactly how to touch her, to hold her, to move with her, as if they'd been loving each other for a lifetime. Each caress built on another until the ultimate moment when their bodies exploded with the irrepressible passion of the first time.

When their breath returned, Finn shifted, and they rolled to face each other. He traced her cheeks, her chin, her breasts, trailed down her neck, finding every inch that wanted his touch. Needed his touch. "What are you thinking?" he said.

Bianca whispered in his ear. "About how happy I am that you rescued me."

❧

Bianca woke, arms, legs, and heart entwined with Finn's. He'd fallen asleep as well, equally exhausted. The soft candlelight dappled his skin amber, and she watched the rise and fall of his chest, listened to the subtle grumble in his breathing. She wasn't sure how long they'd made love or how long they'd slept, and it didn't matter.

She stamped a kiss on his shoulder and drifted off again, ensconced in a blanket of contentment.

❧ TWENTY-SIX ☙

FINN'S eyes snapped open. They'd actually dozed off. The fire had distilled to a bed of white embers, and he found himself wanting only to replay the last few hours that had left them both spent. Hardly breathing so as not to wake her, he stared in awe of this woman he once thought so out of reach, a figment of his imagination.

He reluctantly pulled himself away, added logs to the fire, and stoked it. Gazing at the flames, reality surfaced in slow increments, crept forward, amplifying the needling doubt he'd slipped over earlier. Emerson had an alibi, but so what? Hadn't Mack warned him that things weren't always as they seemed? And the text messages. Someone was determined to get Bianca to the cabin. But who?

Finn reached for his phone. Still no bars. He hated being so out of the loop.

Bianca stirred and sighed, left arm under a pillow, right arm stretched along the silky edge of the comforter, elegant fingers reaching, posing.

He couldn't take his eyes off her, wishing for a sketchpad or some way to carefully preserve the way she looked in the warm candlelight. Every nuance, every contour, every subtlety that defined Bianca James. On second thought, no need to capture her on paper. She was indelibly branded into his brain.

She rose up on one elbow. Cradling her head in her hand, she threw Finn her full attention, and it shivered through him.

"You slept," he whispered.

"Guess I was exhausted. What time is it?"

"Nine o'clock. We were out for about an hour."

Bianca caught her yawn. "Any news?"

"Still no signal." He reached for a lock of her hair and twined it around his finger.

No more words were exchanged, none necessary. Her nearness surrounded him, swallowed him, rattled him. He was a bundle of contradictions in her presence and keenly aware that he had anesthetized himself to emotion for far too long. Everything frozen inside him thawed as he reached for her.

She caressed his pounding chest, and he watched her hand trail over him, her face suffused with delight at his eager response. A delicious pressure built between them, tension, an aching, a longing. She retreated, rolled onto her back, arms nestled at her sides as if enjoying a day at the beach, soft-eyed and dreamy. He accepted the invitation. A wave of primitive sensation guided his fingers over her lightly and then with mounting pressure. She rocked gently under his touch, pacing herself, arms looped around his neck. He joined in her rhythm, and they came together in a cadence that was wholly unique to them.

Energized, out of breath, they held each other.

Neither of them spoke as Finn traced figure eights on her belly. It felt wrong to have a head full of strategies, to break the spell and short-circuit their connection, but he barreled ahead anyway. The sooner they solved this case and put it behind them, the sooner they could build a life together.

He sat up and draped his arms over his knees. "I'm not ready to rule out Emerson, but I can't stop thinking about Jewel. I didn't tell you this before, but she cheated on Dylan the night of the murder. With some bartender at the seminar in Pittsburgh. An alibi, but there's still something fishy about it. And if that's not enough, Carmichael has her liaising between the school and the department, working up a profile."

"You shift gears faster than the GTO."

Finn planted a quick kiss on her shoulder, shrugged into his jeans, and paced. "Emerson. A head case. Flashing for a cheap thrill, desecrating a painting when he can't have his way. But Jewel . . . well, she's scary smart."

A band of disappointment followed by a flicker of agreement crossed Bianca's face. She reached for her sweater and snaked into it before she curled a leg under her and sat on the couch. "There's Charity Beacham too."

"I'm listening."

"I went to talk to her, but—"

"To her office or her house?" Finn jabbed at the firewood with a poker, sending sparks flying.

"Her house. I had to do something. And as it turns out, Lisette worked for Charity. That is, until she fired her for stealing. Apparently, Charity filed a complaint but, then, for some reason, dropped the charges."

"Lisette worked for Charity? It's not in her employment record. And Lisette was clean. Not a mark against her anywhere. But if Charity was involved in Lisette's murder, going to see her could have been dangerous."

"I can take care of myself."

Finn's first instinct was to charge forward with a rebuttal, but he sidestepped. Carmichael's response to seeing the necklace was more than uncharacteristic; it was downright alien. "What if the necklace you found was stolen from Charity the way she said? And for some reason Carmichael got rid of the arrest report?"

"I didn't know Lisette, but everything I've heard doesn't paint her as a thief. Hard worker, good mother, putting herself through school." Bianca probed her palm with her thumb, and Finn grazed her cheek with the back of his hand. Her expression changed again as she seemed to be remembering something. "There is someone else. I've only seen him a couple times. Once at the Balfour and then he just happened to show up when I locked my keys in the car. I gave Tuck his license plate number just in case."

"When?"

"Yesterday . . . when we weren't talking."

A muscle bunched in Finn's jaw.

"He said he'd been watching me ever since he saw me at the bar. Gave me the creeps. If Durwood hadn't stopped—"

"Durwood?"

"My hero."

"You're talking about the same guy who mows his grass at midnight wearing a helmet with a floodlight attached?"

Bianca's mouth pulled to the side. "That's my man. Anyway, it turns out this guy's the art dealer who sold Charity a fake Miró. His name is Lance Oliphant."

"Oliphant? What the hell kind of name is that?"

"One he probably found on the internet. Not sure there's much about the guy that's not made up."

"What does this have to do with you?"

"I'm the one who recognized the sculpture was a fake. He paid her back even though he said he didn't know it was counterfeit. Sounds like he had to sell off assets to do it. He made it pretty clear he blames me."

"I'll run a record and warrant check."

"Carmichael should be happy for the lead. But I doubt it will get us off his shitlist."

Bianca crossed the room to her purse, pulled out a tube of lotion, and smoothed it over her hands as she returned to sit next to him. The sweet smell sent him back to his childhood, to a wrist grazing his forehead, to arms encompassing him when he'd skinned a knee.

He started and blinked.

"What is it?" Bianca asked.

A stab of emotion punctured his thoughts. His mother had intruded, reminding him how she had vanished from his life, taking her sweet scent with her. And it was just dawning on him why she was claiming his thoughts so much recently. He'd always imagined going to her when he fell in love, sharing the news, asking for advice.

"Nothing," he said, but Bianca's expression told him their relationship had soared to a higher plane that required a new level of trust and disclosure. He felt himself opening, slowly at first, then completely.

"I've been thinking about my mom lately." He shrugged. "I haven't seen her in years, but she's still somehow a part of me, you know?"

"You and Dylan were so young when she left."

"I never really dealt with her leaving. Thought I was supposed to be a man and get over it. Hell, I even wondered if it was my fault."

She exhaled an audible sigh. "As kids, we think we're capable of understanding things beyond our years, capable of controlling the outcome," she said with a faraway look. But, you know you couldn't save their marriage, right?"

He reached for her hand, stroked each finger, kissed her palm.

"I know something about that kind of guilt," she said. "I always blamed myself for my mom's death, still do. The day she died, we were supposed to have a family photo taken. My parents cancelled the appointment because I told them I had a stomach ache. That lie had consequences that I'll live with forever . . . but, I was only a kid who was too embarrassed to have her picture taken with crooked bangs."

Finn curved his fingers around her neck and pulled her to him, pressed his lips to her temple, amazed at how quickly he made her sorrow his own. How quickly his past melted as he held her close.

A loud growl from her stomach lightened the moment.

"Mama cat's not the only one who's hungry. There's usually an emergency can of chili here." Finn crossed the room and rooted around in the cupboard. "How do you feel about beef stew?"

"Any other specials today?"

He came up with baked beans and peaches, one can in each hand. "You pick."

"Both." A playful gleam filled her eyes. "I did work up an appetite."

A spasm of sexual energy leaped between them and heat seared his cheeks, his ears. He pawed through a drawer for an opener, cranked open the cans, and dropped spoons into them.

"As long as we're sharing, I've been meaning to ask you something," Finn said.

"Anything."

"Well, it's about your house. Some of it is so organized, practically alphabetized, but then—"

"My natural inclination is to kinda let things go. I'd rather spend time creating. But my grandma . . ." She hesitated, and he understood. Opening the past was like running face first into a sideways rain. Finn took her hand, and she continued. "Gemma and Grandpa moved in with us after my mom died. Gemma essentially raised me because Dad couldn't. But she was more than my grandma, she was like a life coach before that was even a thing. I called her advice, Gemmaisms. My favorite was 'you won't always be able to control things that happen, but you can always control your things.' So when I'm stressed, I hear Gemma encouraging me to tidy up." The light in her eyes said she was loosening the grip on what she'd held tight for so long, held dear. "And as you've seen, I don't often get very far in the clean-up routine before my right brain stages a coup. Does that solve the mystery?" Bianca took a spoonful of beans and closed a sly smile around it. "Bird?"

"You don't miss a trick, do you?"

"Why does your dad call you that?" She switched to peaches, taking one bite, then another.

"It's a long story."

"I like long stories. You want some of these?" She poked her spoon deeper into the can.

"Are there any left?"

A grin played on her lips. "Here."

He took a bite from the spoon she extended. "When I was born, my parents couldn't agree on a name. Mom wanted Avery, a family name. Dad said it sounded girly, he wanted Finneus. We couldn't leave the hospital before they put something on the birth certificate, so Mom gave in and agreed to Finneus, but Avery had to be my middle name."

"Still not getting the Bird part."

He noted her mouth, glistening now with peach juice, making her more beautiful than ever. "Dad made fun of my middle name every chance he got. Mispronounced it on purpose. Finneus Aviary. Mom kept reminding him an aviary was a place for birds. Then one day he dropped the shtick and just started calling me Bird."

"He usually gets his way, doesn't he?"

"Me being a cop was his idea."

Finn's phone buzzed. "A signal. It's about time." He was surprised to hear his brother's voice.

"Listen, I'm halfway to the cabin. I should be there in twenty," Dylan said. "I think—"

"Good, because—"

A crackle, then silence.

"Damn. Got cut off."

Dylan was on his way. The thought rooted Finn in place. Was he ready to hash this out with his brother? He didn't have a choice. His eyes fell to the comforter in front of the fireplace. He scooped it up and returned it to the bedroom.

Bianca was pacing next to the couch, maybe equally anxious about the ramifications of Dylan's arrival. Neither of them were eager to replay the scene at her house the night of the murder. A surly, sentimental drunk picking a fight with his brother.

Banging, like boots stomping, sounded on the porch. Too soon to be Dylan. Finn reached for his gun. He was about to direct Bianca to a safe place when a gust of cold wind rushed in along with a snow-covered and red-faced Mack Tierny.

"Dad?" Questions bombarded him. "How'd you get here?"

"Toyota's always been good in snow," Mack said. "Woody brought over a spare tire. Said he never had my car in the first place. So where the hell is it?"

"In Tucker's pole barn. I'm sorry. I should have told you."

Anger, blinding frustration. Finn waited for Mack's fury, expected it.

But he didn't expect the gun.

Mack swiveled with solemn intention and pointed it at Bianca.

"Dad?" Finn's gut clenched. "*Dad?*"

"Knew you'd be here. Step away, Bird." Mack motioned with the gun. "She's the one I want."

"You're not making sense. Put that down."

"And you did a lousy job trying to hide ammo from me," Mack said with a sneer.

Shit.

Mack's breaths came in heavy gasps. He eyed Finn and then Bianca. "You always loved this place, didn't you, Rose?" He peered around the cabin. "You said we'd make memories here. Well, we did. So many damn memories I can't get them outta my head. If I could just get . . ."

Mack gripped the Glock in one hand, rubbing furiously at his head with the other, as if he could scrub away his haunted past, but he only managed to churn his hair into tangles.

Finn held his gun to his thigh, incapable of raising it against his father. He took a step with his other hand outstretched. "Dad, give me the gun."

"Don't move," Mack snapped, keeping his eyes trained on Bianca. "You shouldn't have left. Those boys needed you. I needed you."

"Mack, I'm Bianca James," she said in a calm voice. "Not Rose."

Finn moved toward Mack in prey-stalking steps. "Dad, let's talk about this."

Mack hesitated. His expression said he was weighing options, deciding his next move. He lifted the gun and cocked one eye over the barrel. Finn froze. He'd seen that look on his dad's face countless times before, during target practice.

But this time, the gun was pointed directly at Bianca.

"Get down!" Finn dove for her. A single shot cracked, exploding in his ears.

The bullet caught him in the chest, hurled him against the hearth, and onto the floor.

Bianca shrieked and scrambled to his side.

For a moment, Finn felt nothing, and he watched Mack sag to the floor, heard his gun smack against hardwood. Then the pain, stabbing fast and fierce, clawing from the inside out. He ripped at his shirt to free the ricocheting missile inside him. His chest. The bullet had entered the left side of his chest.

Bianca's hands were on him, but he couldn't feel them. They could do nothing to ease the pain. He couldn't breathe. Gaps with no inhalation, no exhalation. Searing knives carving each attempt for air.

Through a haze, he could see Mack aim again, hesitate, and turn the gun to his own head.

"Dad, no!" Finn struggled to his feet, somehow stumbled across the room, clutching his chest, feeling the warmth of his own blood. He pushed himself along through sheer agony to get to his father. Bianca got there first, snatched the gun.

Mack's cheek pressed against the floor. He closed his eyes and moaned, "Rose, Rose."

Finn was vaguely aware of movement in his periphery, noise at the edges of his consciousness, and he fought through a desperate haze to try to make out his circumstances. A puzzle piece. Withering plants. A canister of ammunition. Images came to him in waves, lapped over him as Dylan burst in. "What the hell happened?" He dropped down beside Mack. "Dad?"

Mack blinked from Dylan to Finn before he gave himself over to piteous sobbing. "I only wanted . . . I'm sorry . . ."

Finn reached for his father's hand as a brutal reality hammered in his brain. This was it. For both of them. "Dad . . . it's all right. You . . ."

"You didn't mean to hurt anyone," Dylan finished.

Mack's eyes registered understanding, flooded with tears and the call of a faraway, peaceful place. Emotion throbbed between the three men. A small sound escaped Mack's throat, then a strangled, "Bird" and his body went slack in Dylan's arms.

There was a sound, a voice maybe. Like Bianca's, but muted, distant. Finn's vision blurred; color drained from the room, and everything faded. He could barely make out the contours of his brother frantically searching his father's wrist, his neck.

The last thing Finn heard was Dylan's hushed proclamation. "He's gone."

❧ TWENTY-SEVEN ❧

BIANCA snatched her cell, punched 911.

"You won't get a signal." Dylan grabbed keys off the table and tossed them to Bianca. He wrapped Finn in the blanket and heaved him from the floor.

"The GTO?"

"I coasted in on fumes, and Dad smashed the Toyota into a tree. We don't have a choice." He threw the last phrase over his shoulder as he raced out the door.

Bianca reached for Finn's jacket and stole a glance at Mack on the floor. Her heart wrenched, but her attention snapped back to Finn.

Do not die on me.

Flashing blue lights and a piercing siren announced a police cruiser.

Tucker jumped from the Crown Vic, boots trudging through snow. His eyes fell on Finn. "Holy shit."

Dylan instructed Bianca to open the back door of the cruiser. She yanked it open and climbed in. He laid Finn across the seat, resting his head on her lap.

He moved toward the driver's side, and Tucker blocked him, an impenetrable linebacker. "Not gonna happen."

"Move your ass!" Dylan's determination trumped Tucker's girth. He shoved past him into the driver's seat. "Dad's dead. I'll explain later."

"Dead?" Tucker's face folded.

Dylan tossed him the GTO keys and threw the cruiser in reverse.

Tucker kicked at a snow bank and slammed his hat down before dashing into the cabin.

The car rumbled over the uneven ground, and Bianca held Finn tight, trying to shield him from the bumps as his breath came in fits and gulps. She wadded his coat and nestled it under his head.

Dylan kept one hand on the wheel while he snaked from his jacket and threw it into the backseat. "Keep pressure on it."

She balled up the coat, held it to the wound, watching helplessly as blood painted the camel color a sickening shade of red. With both hands firmly on Finn's chest, Bianca brushed her lips next to his ear, cooing softly. "Finn, stay with me. Finn, please."

When they reached the highway, the first layer of snow had been removed, and salt had reduced the rest to slush.

Her eyes tilted to Dylan in the rearview mirror. His mouth moved as if in silent prayer as the car lurched forward, the speedometer needle creeping toward 100.

Dylan grabbed the radio. "Patch me to Memorial."

"Tucker?" the dispatcher asked.

"Just do it!" After an agonizing wait, "This is Detective Tierny, Riley's Peak. I'm bringing in a gunshot victim, a police officer. I want a gurney and your best surgeon waiting, copy?"

As the lights flashed and the siren wailed, Bianca realized Dylan hadn't been in a police car since he was fired. This was the Dylan she'd known before the accident. Confident. In control.

Time became a figment as trees and eventually buildings barreled past. Smudged, flannel clouds blanketed the sky. Images flashed. Mack bursting in. The glint of the gun. Blood. So much blood.

Bianca rooted for something that would tamp down the scream forming in her throat. Finn, wrapped in firelight, loving her with his eyes, his touch. She held on to that, hoped there would be more, and dared a vision of their future. Marriage, children, even grandchildren, growing old, hand in wrinkled hand.

Leaning close, she prayed for him to hear. "I love you, Finn."

His lips moved in response. Or maybe she just wished they did.

She needed him to know that what happened at the cabin was real, as real as the transition from night to day. Her love overwhelmed her, and the possibility of losing him paralyzed her.

Tears flowed down her cheeks, and as she wiped her face, she caught Dylan watching. She plunged her hand in her coat pocket for a tissue, and found something small and hard. The acorn Helen had given her. *For a long and happy life.* Bianca slid it from her pocket, and closed Finn's fingers around it.

After she'd recited every prayer she'd learned as a kid and bungled through a few she made up now on her own, the cruiser slammed to a halt in front of the hospital. Two orderlies shivered outside next to a gurney, blowing warm air into clasped hands.

A nurse paced behind the glass door, the harsh lines on her face illuminated by hot overhead lights. Bianca cupped Finn's head as Dylan scooped up his brother and rushed for the door.

Dylan nodded to the gurney. "Follow me with that thing."

While one orderly stared straight ahead, dumbfounded, the other wheeled the gurney back into the hospital. Dylan lowered his brother onto it. Bianca held tight to Finn. She couldn't let go.

The surgeon, surrounded by a team of nurses, nudged her out of the way.

"Is he gonna be all right?" Dylan raced alongside the gurney. "Doc?"

The team turned a corner. "Only patients beyond this point."

"Fix my brother," Dylan called after them as they whisked down another hallway. "You hear me?"

Numb, Bianca trailed Dylan to the waiting area. They dropped into plastic chairs, chairs teeming with expectation and sorrow. She cried on his shoulder. How could she lose Finn when she'd just found him?

"He *will* make it. He's a fighter." Then in a whisper, "They can't both die."

Bianca, already submerged in her own pain, rolled in and out of the wake of his. She finally managed, "Finn will be okay. We all will." Her breath caught. "And Mack, he—"

"What happened?"

She told him about the text messages that had sent them to the cabin.

"I'd never do that to you. I'd never do that to *me*."

"I know."

"And what about Dad?"

The enormity of what had happened blocked any answer Bianca might provide. She'd give anything for a rewrite on the ending of Mack's story. Some gesso to cover his canvas and start a new painting. She shared how Mack had burst in, wielding a gun, and Rose's name.

"Dad thought you were my mom?" Dylan's fingers circled her wrist. "She was tiny like this too. I could almost wrap my fingers twice around." He searched her face.

"He must have had a breakdown," Bianca managed. Thick spaces, obstacles, between each word like speed bumps.

Dylan clamped his eyes shut.

"Could he have used your phone to text me"—this was so hard for Bianca to accept, much less articulate—"knowing I'd go to the cabin?"

They sat in silence, trapped in a moment they couldn't move beyond, in a room that was spinning around them. An image crept forward, a body posed with arms outstretched as if awaiting a hug. Had Mack positioned Lisette that way on purpose? Possibly out of guilt? A shiver climbed Bianca's spine. "So, Lisette?" she finally said, her voice teetering on a fault line.

He dropped his head in his hands, unable to speak as he seemed to be wading through a crush of emotions.

"It was his illness, Dylan. He wasn't Mack once the tumor took over." She faced him, waited for his eyes to meet hers. She saw the same panic she'd seen two years ago after the accident.

"But he tried to kill you." Thrummed in monotone. Then, as if struck with a blast of energy, he bolted upright and pulled his phone from his pocket. He called Tucker and asked him about the ME. Dylan waited while Tucker talked, his expression modulating into rage. "Let him arrest me."

He ended the call and collapsed, legs outstretched.

"Carmichael is blowing a gasket. It's against the law for a

civilian to drive a police car." He spat out "civilian" like a piece of rancid meat.

"How can he put that above saving Finn's life?"

Doctors, nurses, patients, and hospital equipment drifted through the corridor in a blurred collage.

"You love him," Dylan said, without looking at her.

"Dylan, I . . ." The truth flashed in Technicolor. He'd heard her in the car, read it on her face. "I do love him."

He drummed his fingers on his thigh. "Never thought you'd end up with my brother." Said with a laugh, an unforced, airy sound.

"Neither did I." She would have bet her life on it, but here she was, in love with her ex's younger brother. The man who took a bullet for her, who might just die as a result. She swiped at a tear.

Dylan settled against the seat for a moment, bowed forward, fingers laced together, thumbs tapping one another. "I'll always love you, but seeing you and Finn together made me realize . . ." His eyes grabbed hers, held firm. "I want that kind of love, you know?"

She nodded.

"I'm getting my shit together. One step at a time, but damn, I already feel better." He took her hand. "You'll never know how sorry I am for how bad things got."

For a brief moment, Bianca was back in the locked bathroom, the walls closing in, cursing Dylan. But now she could feel the honesty in his fingertips, honesty so palpable, part of their history faded away. "I forgive you."

His response, a slight nod and a softening in the lines on his face. Those three words were all he needed to hear. He rubbed each wrist in turn, as if freed from the chains of his past.

"And I'm glad you're not drinking."

Dylan brushed an imaginary crumb from his jeans. "Scott."

She'd never heard him say the boy's name out loud, not since Chief Carmichael called to tell Dylan that the boy who'd run in front of his cruiser was paralyzed from the waist down.

"Scott was waiting outside my apartment last week. Said we needed to talk. So I heard him out."

He stalled, then in a voice that seemed to come from a place deep inside, "He wanted to make sure I knew he forgave me."

Bianca let out a breath she didn't realize she'd been holding.

"He told me some other shit, some stuff, about when he was in a coma right after the accident. Said it wasn't his time to die, that he was supposed to do something here first. I guess he'd been running with the wrong crowd, doing drugs. Told me things happen for a reason, and if the accident hadn't happened, he wouldn't be where he is now. He's mentoring underprivileged kids, can you believe it?"

"You saved his life, maybe others."

Dylan shrugged. "Helluva way to save somebody's life, but, okay. And he saved mine right back."

It wasn't about circumstances, Bianca was coming to realize, but how you played the cards you'd been dealt. She also knew that what you sometimes see in someone else is actually yourself, and it was as if some part of his situation was plucking a harmonious chord within her. Now they stood together on the precipice of impending change, and it might do them both some good to talk about what came next. "What now?"

"Believe it or not, I miss police work, the detective end mainly. Trouble is, I've burned bridges."

When they were together, she hadn't understood how much it meant to him. They hadn't loved each other that way. Their kind of love seemed almost limited to writing each other's names in the sand on a sunny day with a plus sign between them, without a thought about an inevitable tide coming along to erase the evidence.

They sat for another quiet moment. Then Bianca asked, "Is Jewel a part of your future?"

He let out a puff of air. "That is one complicated woman. Smart. And believe it or not, when she's not obsessing, she's got a wicked sense of humor. But like I said, complicated."

"The definition of complicated."

"I need to break it off once and for all. Focus on me, figure things out with my fam . . . with Finn." Dylan's eyes squinted against forming tears. "He will make it." He said it loud and strong, as if saying it with conviction would make the improbable probable.

Bianca repeated "he will make it"—over and over in her head like a mantra. Dylan pulled her close, and she reached for his hand, interlaced it with hers. Visions played in her mind as she dropped her head on his shoulder and succumbed to sleep. A prologue, the opening to a beautiful story.

She woke to someone tapping her arm.

A doctor sat across from them, an imposing mountain of hospital green, rust-colored stains splattered in an expressionist, diagonal spray across his chest. "He's out of surgery, in ICU. The bullet lodged close to his heart. We were able to remove it, but the odds are stacked against him. He's still sedated. Now we wait. The next twelve hours are critical."

The words "stacked against him" stood opaque against the rest.

"We're doing everything possible," the doctor continued. "Do you have questions?"

"Is there anything we can do?" Dylan asked.

"If you pray . . . pray. If you don't, you might want to start." He fished for something in his pocket. "The nurse pried this out of his hand." He gave it to Bianca and walked away.

The acorn. She shuddered with the effort to hold in a sob, but crumbled as the arrow of sorrow pierced the very lining of her soul.

Dylan squeezed her tightly balled fist, rose, and worried a path across the maroon carpet.

Bianca moved to a watercolor painting on the wall—two sailboats meeting in a vast sea.

"A basic flat wash," she said, barely above a whisper. "Each color has its own physical property that affects how it feels and flows." Art grounded her and had always kept fear at bay. She needed it now more than ever.

Dylan came and stood next to her, arm draped over her shoulder. "I don't see it the way you do," he said. "The way you and Finn do."

Bianca stared at the seascape, straining to see it through Finn's eyes. She grabbed the boats' mooring lines, tied them together in her mind, and held tight against the approaching storm.

✄ TWENTY-EIGHT ✄

A slant of sunlight streamed across the room and woke Finn. Pain surged as his eyes worked back and forth under sedated lids. After some effort, he pried them open.

Wavy shadows flanked his hospital bed. Gradually Bianca, then Dylan, came into view. They were holding his hands and clasping each other's across the bed. The three of them formed an awkward circle, linked together like . . . His mind went stubbornly blank.

A damaged, bruised, and worn-out feeling reigned. He hurt all over.

Bianca, her face framed in golden hair, touched his forehead, his cheek. His dad's gun pointed at her—the black pall of Mack's intentions—swam up and stole the image. But she was here.

After several attempts to speak, he managed, "Thirsty," in a raspy voice, weak and far from his own.

Bianca took the cup on a nearby tray and held the straw to his mouth. He tried to wrap his lips around it, but they wouldn't comply. She took the straw, plunged it into the water, held the top with a finger. Placing it in his mouth, she released the contents, and water trickled down his chin.

As if on cue, a nurse whisked in with a cup full of ice chips. "Try these, hon."

Bianca ran a chunk over his parched lips. The cool sensation spread to his limbs. She placed ice on his tongue, and he worked at the corners of his mouth, trying for a smile.

"Did you see that?" Bianca studied Finn with what seemed like renewed hope. Anticipation filled the air, as if something extraordinary and miraculous were about to happen.

Fighting through his haze, Finn tried to piece things together. "Dad's really . . ."

Dylan cupped his hand in both of his own.

Hot tears warmed Finn's face, pooled in his ears as the nightmarish scene played out before him.

Bianca laced her fingers in his, stroked his hand with her thumb.

A shudder rolled down Finn's spine, and shivered back up to tingle at his nape. "The text messages."

"I found my phone wedged in Dad's recliner cushion." Dylan's revelation reverberated around the room. "I must've left it at the house. But him sending you to the cabin like that . . ."

Finn tried to work this information through the sludge of unanswered questions. "How'd you know"—he sucked in a painful breath—"to come to the cabin?"

"I was taking Dad something to eat, and he wasn't there. I thought maybe you were together, but the GTO was gone. Both cars gone didn't add up. I went to use the house phone and heard my cell buzzing in the chair. It was Durwood. He told me Dad seemed in a hurry to get out of town. Woody told him he shouldn't be out in a blizzard, but he wouldn't listen." Dylan raked a hand through his hair. "If only—"

"Don't." Finn gathered enough strength to prop himself up on his elbows, and Bianca adjusted the pillow behind him.

"He's right, Dylan," she said. "Even if you'd been there to stop him, what about the next time? And no one could have known how far he'd go."

He'd loved her from the moment he met her, but as she tried to put his brother's mind at ease, Finn loved Bianca even more than he thought possible. She'd been through so much, and here she was giving him a way to come to terms with what had happened.

A nurse, who'd been busying herself about the room, now examined Finn's IV. "What's your pain on a scale from one to ten?"

He inhaled, snagging his bottom lip between his teeth. *Eleven.* "Inching up past the midpoint, but I'm all right."

"Here, this should help." She fumbled with something on the IV bag before she turned to Dylan and Bianca. "You'll have to leave soon. Officer Tierny needs his rest."

Their voices faded behind the swish and hum of machines. Finn floated above it all, finding a spot away from the pain. He slept, and when he woke Bianca was in a chair next to the bed, hand clutching his.

Dylan came in with a Styrofoam cup. "Need to break you outta here soon. Coffee's as thick as motor oil."

Finn's eyes volleyed between them, questioning. Thoughts were coming easier now. "How long was I out?"

"It's Thursday. You slept through Wednesday." Bianca's touch broadsided him, ignited a glow of affection from his core, yet a question burned. Was Dylan okay with Bianca fussing over him like this?

As if reading his brother's thoughts, Dylan spoke. "Bee and I had some time to talk." He crumpled the cup, tossed it in the trash, and shoved his hands into the hip pockets of his jeans. "It's all good, bro."

Finn looked past Dylan as a man materialized in the doorway, "Dr. Holcomb" stitched in black letters on his lab coat. He removed a pen and pad from his pocket and started jotting notes while he strolled toward the bed. "You've been through quite an ordeal," he said, stopping to dash another swirl across his paper without looking up.

Finn wondered for a brief moment if, like the doctor's mysterious arrival, he'd dreamt the entire thing. Logic told him otherwise, and his spidey sense warned this ordeal was far from over.

"Where's his surgeon?" Dylan asked.

Dr. Holcomb peered down his hooked nose, threw the blanket back to examine Finn's feet, and worked his way north. He lifted the dressing and examined the incision, a clinical expression clouding his face.

"Dr. Karlene is a phenomenal surgeon with hands guided by a higher power. He prays before each surgery. Without fail. But he's the first to admit, he's not God. Even Dr. Karlene takes a day off now and then. He'll make rounds tomorrow. For now"—he pulled the blanket back over Finn and gave it a pat—"barring any unforeseen complications, we'll have you out of here in a few days." Dr. Holcomb deposited his pen and notepad in his pocket and left the room as mysteriously as he'd entered.

"Mr. Personality," Dylan muttered.

"As long as Mr. Personality says I can go home soon." Finn attempted a deep inhale and winced.

"Don't rush it," Dylan said. "You gotta get back in the ring with Carmichael. Who knows, maybe you'll be the Tierny who finally knocks him out."

His brother hadn't exactly been generous with compliments lately, and even this hint of one smacked of better times.

"I'm on *vacation*, remember?"

"That, bro, is bullshit."

"Right, but you know Carmichael isn't going to let this go." Finn cut his eyes to Bianca.

Bianca stood, moved toward the door. "I'm going to find something to drink that doesn't need to be pushed through a strainer first."

They watched her leave. "I gotta know," Finn said. "Are you really okay with Bianca and I together?"

An arc of silence swept the room before Dylan spoke. "It'll take her about a week to figure out what a punk you are." He moved to the IV bag and flicked a finger at the tubing as if to speed the flow.

Translation: his brother needed time. Finn sank into the relief that he hadn't flat out blasted him.

When Bianca returned later with a bottled water, Finn said, "We'll horsengoggle. That's how we always decide important things."

"What's a horsengoggle?" Bianca asked.

Finn could see his own mischief in Dylan's grin.

"Neutral party calls it," Finn said to Bianca.

"Calls what?"

Dylan pointed a thumb at Bianca. "Won't be in German."

"Works in any language," Finn said. "Bianca, count back and forth between us."

"Okay. . . One, two, three—"

"Wait, you don't know how far to count." Finn raised two fingers and Dylan four.

Bianca started with Finn and counted between them until she reached six. "Dylan." She shot Finn a perplexed look.

He feigned disappointment.

"Best two outta three?" Dylan offered.

"No, no, you won. We horsengoggled."

"What exactly *did* we horsengoggle, anyway?"

Finn lifted his chin and slanted eyes at Bianca. "Winner doesn't have to look out for this one." He grabbed her hand and squeezed. "You're off the hook, bro."

"I can live with that." Dylan's face grew serious. He studied Bianca. "But I have a feeling I'll keep an eye out, anyhow."

She turned to Finn. "You should get some rest."

His strength buoyed, he squeezed her hand again, harder, with conviction, with commitment. He couldn't deny the incredible fact that she was here by his side. Counting his blessings now confirmed there was so much to love about her. The way she went the extra mile for her students, her passion for art, and especially the independent streak that twined through her, seemingly attached to both a parachute lifting her above the fray and a boulder that grounded her in place.

"I'm gonna go." Dylan kissed his brother's forehead and Bianca's cheek.

He idled with his back to them for a long moment, then tapped the door frame in a gesture of finality.

"Is he okay?" Bianca asked once Dylan was gone.

"He will be. I'll make sure of it."

Bianca appraised him with a critical eye. "You know, you're a man of many talents, Finn Tierny." Leaning in, she trailed a row of kisses along his cheek. Her familiar scent overpowered the antiseptic tang in the room. Her presence transported him.

He brought her hand to his chest and held it there, wanting only to keep her in his grasp, in his sight forever.

"And this protecting thing you do." She nuzzled her face close to his. "There's definitely a certain art to it."

∼ TWENTY-NINE ∾

WHEN Bianca walked into St. Luke's Fellowship Hall, the first thing she noticed was the damp basement smell mingled with the heavy aroma of comfort food. A sparse group had gathered after Mack's burial, and questions hovered like dust particles, trapped in the canned light, light too bright for the occasion. No one mentioned that Mack was responsible for the sling Finn wore across his chest or the young woman, Lisette, in the cemetery not a stone's throw away—but it was there in their eyes, as they circled the room, hoping to land anywhere but on Mack's wounded son. Everyone seemed to be trying diligently, albeit awkwardly, to remember a great man, the way he was before he got sick.

Bianca stayed by Finn's side, girding him with her presence, hoping time would blur the hard edges. But in truth, they might never regain the balance lost. She linked her hand in his as they sat at a table along the back wall. Recent events had emboldened her, and it was gentle consolation that they could now hold hands in public without worrying about what people thought.

She scanned the near empty tables and repressed an urge to stand up and ask why more people hadn't come. She already knew the answer. These people had crossed minefields of doubt to get here; others couldn't, or wouldn't, traverse the uncertainty.

Aunt Sara sat surrounded by her grown children, worrying a

tight screw of tissue in her fist. Her shoulders heaved as a spurt of sobbing took over. She'd insisted on the church funeral and luncheon, complete with bagpipes playing "Danny Boy" and "The Dark Isle" even though Dylan and Finn would have been more comfortable with a private graveside ceremony.

Dylan sat several seats away, to Bianca's left with Jewel beside him, intermittently whispering in his ear and rubbing his shoulder. Despite her pawing, an obvious rift mushroomed between them.

A clanging sounded from the doorway. Maris, trying, with little success, to quiet the metal hangers she'd disturbed while hanging up her coat. The empty hangers another reminder of just how few people had bothered to come. Maris wove her way toward them, hugged Bianca, then Finn. Rounding the table, she tapped Dylan on the shoulder, and he got to his feet. She folded him into a serious embrace and expressed her condolences, earning a glare from Jewel.

Settling next to Finn, Maris reached for Bianca's hand. "I offered to bring Helen, but she doesn't do funerals. She said something about releasing butterflies on Mack's behalf today."

"It's December."

Maris shrugged, withdrew her hand, but her eyes held.

A large man stuffed in a faded police uniform approached the table. "Your daddy was one helluva cop," he said before spinning a folding chair around and straddling it. "I'm Able, Able Ames." He pumped Finn's hand and leaned over to shake Dylan's. "I wouldn't be here if it wasn't for him. He saved my life. He ever tell you boys that?"

"No." Finn spoke for both of them.

"Well, he wouldn't. All in a day's work for him." He rapped beefy knuckles on the table and recounted how they'd stopped a speeder late one night, how he'd asked for identification. "His ID turned out to be a .357, and my life flashed, just like they say. But your dad . . ." Able cleared his throat hard, and his eyes filmed before he continued. "Your dad was Johnny on the spot. Unloaded a round into the thug before I could reach for my piece. Not a second of hesitation."

Bianca rubbed three fingers across her forehead in an effort to squash the indelible picture of Mack's gun aimed at her as an argument took place in her mind, two sides quarreling about what had actually happened. But he had been a hero; it seemed everyone had a story. Hopefully these anecdotes would help frame him the way he should be remembered. Before the tumor took over. And maybe, clinging to thoughts of the former Mack, not the latter, her own recollection of that night at the cabin would eventually dissolve.

Able rearranged himself on the folding chair. White ovals of T-shirt peeked between gaps of uniform where his ample belly strained at the buttons.

"There was this one time." Able doubled over, slapped his knee. "Let's see, musta been 'bout twenty years ago now. Mack and Carmichael was investigating this report of arson. And while Mack was taking down the store owner's statement, there goes a guy running down the alley with a gas can, guilty as hell. Carmichael high-tailed it after him, tripped, and busted his ankle. Hollered to Mack from the ground, 'A guy ran down the alley with a gas can.' Your dad dropped his notepad and took off. Caught him too. Carmichael never lived that one down."

Dylan snorted. "Typical Carmichael," he said with too much volume. "Couldn't collar a perp if he walked right into the station house."

Bianca's eyes skipped over two tables where Chief Carmichael, seemingly on the fringes of cop camaraderie, sat with the priest and two bag pipers. Carmichael's expression said he hadn't missed a beat.

"Well," Able said, "your daddy didn't say nothing to nobody. It was the store owner who got in a snit. Wanted everyone to know how one of Riley's Peak's finest nearly botched the chase by tripping over his own feet. Didn't give your daddy props for nabbin' the guy though. Isn't that always the way?"

Dylan agreed.

Finn smiled, a smile that didn't reach his eyes, and he gripped his chest, puffing out a pained breath. Bianca stroked his forearm with her thumb.

Able pushed away from the chair, rotated it, and placed it back at the table. "Well, I suspect I've chawed on long enough. Didn't tell you nothin' you don't already know. Take care now."

"Mack certainly made a difference," Bianca said. "That's all anyone can hope for."

Finn looked drawn, skittish. So much had happened that Bianca found herself constantly taking inventory, assessing the situation, waffling between what she'd experienced and what she felt. A combination of blame and guilt and confusion whipped her emotions to a white froth. Finn searched her face, and in one look she knew he understood her internal battle. And she his.

Conversation from another table grabbed her attention. She couldn't make out what the hushed voices were saying, but when she turned to see who was talking, the women stopped chatting.

"You should eat," she said to Finn, motioning to the array of food on a long table at the focal point of the wide room.

"I'm not hungry."

"I sure am." Tucker's voice came from behind them. He placed a heaping plate of food next to Maris, gripped an arm around Finn. "Love ya, little bud." His gaze passed over each person at the table and came to rest on Dylan. "Couldn't ask for a better posse."

Tucker dropped into a chair, and the mood at the table lightened. How did he do that? Bring instant relief to any situation? All Bianca knew was that she loved him for it.

"These Catholic wives sure know how to spin a recipe. They should have a cookbook." Tucker sniffed his plate appreciatively and kissed his fingertips. "Bon aperitif." He tore into a chicken leg and washed it down with a full cup of lemonade.

Finn slapped him on the back.

Tucker stopped chewing a mouthful of crescent roll to speak. "What?"

"An aperitif is a before dinner drink—you know, to stimulate your appetite," Maris said.

Tucker's eyes widened. "Whoa! My appetite does just fine on its own thank you very much." As if to prove his point, he shoveled in a forkful of potato salad.

"I swear you have a tapeworm," Finn said.

"They do have a cookbook." Jewel's first contribution to the conversation. There was something unreadable about her, and the odd way she arranged her food, separating it into equal portions, measured rounds of salad, pasta, and fruit.

Bianca knew Jewel and Dylan had fought. Dylan argued that as a psychiatrist, she should have picked up on something when she checked on Mack. But Jewel had always been fond of Mack, doting on him like he was her own father. Perhaps she was taking this as hard as anyone, or was there another reason for the dark circles under her eyes and sallow skin?

"No food?" Dylan asked Finn.

"I'll get something later."

"The pain meds are messing with his appetite," Bianca said.

"Maybe he's holding out for . . ." Dylan winked. "What's your specialty again, Wheat Thins and spray cheese?"

"Guilty as charged," Bianca replied. "You know me too well." As soon as she spoke, she realized her error. Jewel's scorn radiated—an unnerving, unsmiling appraisal, which disintegrated to a vacant stare.

Finn did a double take.

Carmichael approached and pressed his hands on Finn's shoulders. "I need to leave, son."

"Thanks for coming," Finn said.

Bianca could see the tension pulse in his jaw as he tried to curb his annoyance. Was it Carmichael's touch, or the way he called him son, or both, that infuriated him?

"Your old man and I"—Carmichael smoothed a finger over the corner of his mustache—"didn't always see eye to eye. But he was a good man. It's a shame he went crazy is all."

Finn's back stiffened. Rage rippled across his face, tinting it red, but he composed himself and said, "Again, thanks for coming."

Dylan had already rounded the table. "Crazy? *You're* calling *him* crazy? You don't deserve to wear the same uniform!"

A thick hush descended as focus funneled to Dylan and Carmichael.

"Let it go," Finn said.

"Please." Anger gnawed at Bianca's already frayed edges. "Not here. Not now."

Jewel jerked from her seat and rallied to Dylan's side.

"I won't let it go," Dylan said. "He's outta line."

Carmichael's whole body heaved a sigh. "All right. Your old man wasn't crazy." He jabbed a finger in Dylan's face. "But you are. I didn't intend to bring this up here, but that was some asinine stunt you pulled."

"You mean saving a member of *your* police force?"

"You know exactly what I mean. You had no business behind the wheel of that cruiser. Baranski could have taken him."

"He's my brother. I make it my business to make sure he's all right."

"Rules and consequences be damned."

"That's right. When it comes to family I don't give a damn about rules, consequences, laws, procedures, protocol, or grudge-holding police chiefs."

An awkward beat. "Grudge-holding?"

"You've held a grudge against my dad ever since he tried to cover your ass so everybody wouldn't know you were a clumsy chicken shit. Well they found out anyway." Dylan held his arms out in front of him. "Now you've got a reason to lock a Tierny up. Go ahead. Cuff me."

Finn took his place beside his brother. "If you lock him up, you can lock me up too," he said.

Jewel wedged herself between the men. "Don't even think about it."

Carmichael ignored her. "It might be time for Tiernys to accept that they just aren't cut out for police work."

Jewel kneaded Dylan's bicep, holding him back, as Carmichael pivoted on his heel and made for the door. He was walking away. Good. Yet his departure didn't bring the relief Bianca had hoped for, but an undercurrent of urgency that dragged her downward, a sinking sensation permeating every molecule of her being.

᪗ THIRTY ᪗

FINN squeezed the bottle of Percocet on the counter before he swept it into a drawer. His chest ached, and pain shot down his arm, wrapping around his back, but he needed to be clear-headed. Almost everyone was happy to close this case with Mack as the shooter, but he didn't kill Lisette. Finn was dead certain. There was more to his breakdown than the mass growing in his brain.

Time to unpack the facts again. Emerson's alibi looked solid. Charity fired Lisette. Why? How did the art dealer factor in? And Jewel. She had an alibi, the hotel bartender, but . . .

Hell, anyone could have pulled that trigger. Badge or no, he'd be damned if he'd sit around working Sudoku puzzles while the killer still roamed the streets.

Finn slammed his fist on the bathroom door and winced. For a brief moment, he expected Mack to holler from the living room for him to pipe down. He rolled one shoulder, then the other.

His cell rang, and in a way, he was happy for the interruption. Happier still with the news. It was Chief Almeida. After a brief exchange, the corners of Finn's mouth twitched upward. Almeida was investigating everything Finn had passed on, and it looked like old Walters' round head was rolling like a bowling ball straight for the gutter.

There'd be repercussions. A guy like Walters didn't go down easy. But Finn would be ready.

Bianca was at school, working on her Wildlife Conservatory entry. He wanted to call her, to tell her the good news, and he would, but he wanted to respect her space too. She needed her routine. Besides, when she was painting, her focus was so intense, she'd be oblivious to an earthquake. A ringing phone wouldn't break the spell.

He made his way into the kitchen, picked up the African violet on the windowsill, and tapped the dirt like Bianca had. After splashing it with water from the faucet, he set it back on the sill with a clank.

A wave of sadness returned. Nothing could keep it from washing over him, not even justice catching up with Walters. Feeling like he'd been shoe-horned into shoes two sizes too small, Finn plunged into the living room and started to lower himself into the recliner, but the scent of charred toast and Old Spice rendered him immobile. The room seemed to spin with remnants of Mack's breakdown.

An old brass magazine rack sat beside the recliner, overflowing with books and papers. He sorted through them and found the notebook his dad had been scribbling in. He hesitated for a moment, flipped it open. Mack's early notes were lists of to-dos, groceries, reminders to take his pills, but then short, disjointed paragraphs, under the heading, "For the boys." A list of things that needed to be done after Mack was gone: Aunt Sara gets Mother's old Victrola, the rest goes to the boys, share and share alike. Finn's throat constricted as he read snippets from Mack's childhood. A pet ferret named Muckle that he'd trained to give high fives and roll over. A charm school that Grandma Tierny ran from their house when Mack was in grade school. Mack's role was to act out scenarios highlighting how not to behave. He hated that. But what he loved more than anything was jumping off a swing into the river with his sister, Sara, yelling Boom-Z-Bonzai! at the top of their lungs.

Finn sank against the chair as he read on about cases Mack had closed, criminals he'd put behind bars. One story, about a woman in an abusive relationship, resonated. Desperate, she'd obtained an unregistered .22, but Mack coaxed it away from her and gave her $500 to go back to her parents in Omaha. He kept up with her all these years. *The bastard finally gave her a divorce, and she eventually found another man. A nice one this time, a hard-working computer guy, and they have two kids. I call her at Christmastime. Guess I like stories with happy endings.* Finn pictured Mack paying the abusive husband a visit, setting him straight. He would never know the whole story, but he knew his dad would have put the woman's safety above all else, even if it meant sidestepping a few regs.

That's not the kind of man who murders an innocent woman. No matter what's going on in his brain. Still, Mack had pointed a gun at Bianca . . .

Finn flipped the page and read notes about his mom. How they met at a drive-in where Rose was a carhop and she spilled root beer all over him. How his dad proposed by showing up where she worked, blue lights flashing, professing his love over the cruiser's loud speaker. Rose's frequent butchering of a French accent, the way she swooned over Cary Grant, the time she and Mack drove to Niagara Falls each assuming the other had handled hotel arrangements. They ended up staying at a KOA, in a tiny cabin, with no heat. A list of specific ways they kept each other warm followed, and Finn felt heat shimmy up his neck as he skimmed to the end.

On the final page, her name filled every white space, written over and over and over. *Rose Tierny. Rose Tierny. Rose Tierny.* Stars in varying sizes guarding her name.

Finn went to the window, pressed his forehead against it, hoping his mind would find its way outside, but he could only think of one thing. *The unregistered .22.* He tore down the hall and into Mack's room. There was no .22 on the dresser among the other guns. Opening drawers, he pulled out the contents—clothes, books, and papers scattered onto the floor. Pain seared through his chest as he ransacked the closet, ripped the sheets from the bed, and upended the mattress. Nothing under the bed, under the chair cushion.

Did Mack get rid of the piece, or could he have imagined the whole story? In his fractured state, had Mack confused a cop show with reality? Or was this somehow related to the .22 they'd been searching for? The gun that killed Lisette?

As Finn returned items to the bedside drawer, his eyes latched on a baggie full of medicine bottles. Popping the top off the first one, he peered inside. He could still picture his dad taking a sip of water before lifting a square blue pill to his mouth, refusing a drink afterwards to wash it down, insisting once again on doing it his own way. Finn checked the bottle. The label showed a white oval pill. He balled his fist and pressed it against his mouth. His mind whirred before gaining traction.

He checked all the other bottles. None had a blue pill on the label. Someone must have switched the pills. Who had access? Dylan, the nurses . . .

She's always coming over, bringing something. Cookies, those little cupcakes. The tumor had toyed with Mack's brain in those final weeks, batting it around like a Nerf ball. But talking about the case on the heels of the murder, Mack had insisted Jewel was there with a lucidity that reminded Finn of Mack before his diagnosis, a far cry from the man who'd burst into the cabin.

Finn made his way to the computer and keyed +Pittsburgh +conference +psychology into the search box. Results filled the screen. Midway down the display, he found it. National Symposium on Psychology and Education; Pittsburgh Marriott. The itinerary for the conference was still available in PDF. *Choice Theory, Exploring Anger and Violence in Young Adults. Friday, November 13, 6– 10 pm. Presented by Dr. John Chilton.*

Another quick search led him to Chilton's number.

"Yeah, I remember that conference," Chilton's gatekeeper said. "Attendance was half what we expected. Had to lug fifty extra handouts to the car."

"It may be a long shot, but do you remember an attendee named Jewel Glasser?"

"There's a name you don't forget." A throat-clearing laugh. "Chilton teases her all the time. Says she's a shirttail relative of William Glasser. She plays along, but I can tell it pisses her off."

"William Glasser?"

"The mastermind behind 'choice theory' and 'reality therapy.' He's Chilton's idol. Maybe hers too."

"Did she participate in the session that evening?"

"Hmm, yeah, toward the end. Some people do that just to claim the continuing ed hours. Chilton called her out for it. She wasn't happy about that either."

Bingo! "Thank you for your time."

Thirty minutes later, he was showing his badge to the frazzled hotel manager again. "I need to see security tapes."

A disgruntled sigh and the manager led Finn to his office, pulled up the security footage. "I'm late for a meeting. Scroll through the list for the date," he said over his shoulder as he bolted from the room, heels slapping marble tile.

As Finn suspected, after looking at the Friday the 13th log for about ten minutes he spotted a woman in a baseball cap rushing through the parking lot. She climbed into an Acura and pulled away, tires screeching. The camera tightened on the time stamp—6:18 p.m. Plenty of time to get to Brookefield before the estimated time of death, return to make the end of the session, and work in alibi sex with Adam afterwards. Finn's heart hammered against his ribs.

He backed the tape up and zoomed in, his eyes snapping wide as he recognized the purposeful rhythm of her gait. And there, slamming against her chest as she hurried to her car . . . a glittering L.

Bianca wasn't safe.

❧ THIRTY-ONE ❧

BIANCA added her signature to the right corner of her Wildlife Conservatory entry and dropped her brush in cleaner. She'd struggled for months to get the composition right, to make the two ducks appear compatible. Stepping back, she examined the pair of cinnamon teals. Finally. Harmony where she'd seen only complacency, a true connection instead of two creatures merely standing side by side out of habit. Her father would have been proud.

She photographed her submission, taking several shots to capture the painting in the perfect light, uploaded it, and completed the entry form.

Her finger hovered over the keyboard reluctant to land.

Moving to the row of windows, she looked below at the nondescript asphalt slab sectioned into a yellow grid work of parking spots. Beyond that stretched the familiar outline of Riley's Peak peppered with trees and houses, church steeples, factory smokestacks, and neon signs flashing "Pizza N'at" and "Bowl!"

She loved this town.

"Enjoying the view?"

Bianca spun around to find Jewel creeping toward her, hatred burning in her gold-flecked, green eyes.

"I was just leaving." Bianca angled toward her computer, pushed send.

"Were you?" The sing-song quality in Jewel's voice did little to mask her hostility. Her gaze crawled from the tips of Bianca's boots, over her smock, and settled on her forehead.

Bianca's stomach heaved, and she prayed she wouldn't need what was in her pocket. "I have to go."

"I was hoping we could chat," Jewel said.

A slow, rolling pressure of panic built deep inside Bianca; a dull roaring whooshed in her ears.

Jewel wasn't here for girl talk. She sidestepped, filling the space that led to the exit, backed toward the door, and locked it. "They did a wonderful job turning this place into a fortress after the last school shooting, didn't they? You never know when some crazed, depressed, or drugged-out lunatic will storm the place on a killing spree."

"Jewel, I—"

"Shut up!"

Bianca's mouth went dry. The only escape route was through the storage room to the hallway. The storage room. She felt Lisette's presence, shuddered. This was Jewel's take two, and she intended to get it right this time. Bianca hustled for the door, was almost there, when she heard a click. She froze at the sound, pivoted as if in slow motion, and for the second time in the space of a week found herself looking down the black maw of a gun.

Jewel smirked. "You know I'll use it."

Bianca took in the chrome-plated weapon in Jewel's two-hand clasp.

"What do you want?"

A trace of a frown passed over Jewel's mouth. "What I want, you can't give. I want Dylan, but he's already wasted on you."

"That's ancient history, Jewel. I'm with Finn now."

"You like yourself some Tiernys, don't you? But Dylan will love you as long as you live, as long as you breathe."

Bianca's heart pounded in her ears. *Stall her.* "It's been over between us for a long time. Dylan wants you."

"Do us both a favor," Jewel spat. "Stop lying."

"Honestly, he—"

"He broke up with me," Jewel continued as if sitting in on her own therapy session, baring her soul to be picked apart and put back together again. "At first I thought he was just upset about Mack, but he won't take my calls. He won't even answer the door."

"I'm sure you two will get past this."

"It could have been so easy. I'd shoot you with Mack's gun and slip it right back into his collection. No one would think to look there, but if they did, they'd chalk it up to the tumor. And let's face it, Mack would never last through a trial. Case closed. But poor little Lisette took your bullet. Don't you feel guilty?"

Jewel jabbed the gun closer, her voice rising to a manic pitch. "I said. Do you feel guilty?"

"Yes, of course I feel terrible that she died, but—"

"Good. It was fun toying with you while I worked everything out. I had to dummy it all down of course so everyone would believe Mack did it. But I enjoyed watching you come unhinged. Slipping in and out of your house was way too easy. Do all your exes have your keys?"

Bianca steeled her jaw.

"Luring you and Boy Wonder to the cabin was easy too, a few texts. Tell me again how you don't care about Dylan?"

"So the calls, the dollars, the paintbrush, the messed-up painting—"

"What painting?" Jewel's face exhibited no fraudulence, only confusion.

"You didn't leave it at my house?"

Jewel snorted a laugh. "Nope. See how many people hate you?"

A shuffling noise snagged their attention as Ralph emerged from the storage room, bypassing the main entrance as he often did.

"Everything all right? . . . Oh." His eyes landed on the gun, and his hands flew up. "Now, Miss Glasser—"

"Stupid old man." There was a perceptible tremor of emotion in Jewel's voice that made her seem less like a cold, calculating killer. "Why'd you have to show up? Now I'll have to kill you too."

Ralph exuded nothing but calm, the kind of calm that comes from having led a long and full life. "How 'bout you drop the gun, and we'll have ourselves a nice talk like we did before?"

"Aren't you the cunning one, trying to out-shrink the shrink?" Jewel motioned with the gun to a stool. "Sit."

Ralph complied, but his eyes searched the room.

Jewel pivoted to Bianca. "And when you came to me for help I could barely keep a straight face. You should have followed through with an appointment for counseling. I'm quite good."

"I know you've helped a lot of people, Jewel—"

"They all denied the reality of the world around them." Jewel's eyes held a malicious glint before they faded to another place. She was gone for all of thirty seconds, and Bianca strategized while fear continued its snail crawl along her skin. "I helped them recognize the truth." Jewel started up again. "Trouble is, I can't face mine. My mother doesn't want me in her life. She won't even tell me who my father is. The man I love is in love with . . . well, you. I can diagnose myself, even map out a course of treatment, but I just can't get there, you know?" Her mouth quivered as she spoke. One tear rolled down her face followed by another. "I thought creating a new identity and moving here would fix things." She shook her head.

Jewel's unmet needs, her Inner Child piping up for attention, were undeniable. Now her tattoo made sense. She was Tinker Bell, flitting around frantically, searching for a safe space to land.

"Put the gun down, Jewel," Bianca said. "We can talk this out." A moment of empathy blipped, but reminders of Lisette, her daughter, Kate, and even Mack rushed in on a tidal wave of pain and loss.

Jewel's scowl deepened.

"I'll talk to Dylan," Bianca said. "You're much better suited for him than I ever was. I'll help him see that."

"But he—" Before Jewel could finish, Ralph lunged, wielding a box cutter. Jewel whirled, planted a bullet in his arm, without blinking, without flinching. Whatever modicum of compassion she'd felt for the old man earlier, gone. He collapsed to the floor, and the box cutter spun away. He touched his arm with two fingers, stared incredulously at the blood.

Bianca knelt beside him and shoved her hand deep into her pocket. "This has to stop!"

Jewel's face registered disappointment. "That first one never seems to go where you want it to." She started for the storage room door. "I should have locked this too."

Bianca made her move. She jumped up and smacked her hand against Jewel's forearm, the one holding the gun. The .22 fell to the floor, and Bianca kicked it toward the door. She held the pepper spray in Jewel's face. But before she could activate it, the door opened, knocking the gun back to Jewel, who seized the opportunity to grab it.

"Drop it." This from Finn, his own gun poised.

Jewel maintained her stance, arms locked in front of her, weapon ready. "As I was telling your lover here—"

"Put the gun down. Now, Jewel."

She lifted her chin defiantly, tightened her grip.

"This doesn't have to end this way," Finn said. "Ralph is going to be okay. We can sort the rest out."

Fire blazed in Jewel's eyes, eyes that belonged to one who kills for sport or vengeance . . . or plain insanity. "Sort it out?"

Bianca scooted so Ralph could rest his head on her lap, and pressed the hem of her smock to his wound as the memory of the night she cradled Finn on the way to the hospital flooded back. The night he took a bullet for her.

"Sort it out?" Jewel repeated with a hiss. "I've spent a lifetime sorting it out. Dylan understands. His mom didn't want him either. But at least she had the good sense to take off. Mine's here in town, but she'd rather pretend I don't exist."

"It sucks, having a mom desert you," Finn said.

Jewel's head folded forward as if she were considering his membership in her club for abandoned children.

Finn lunged, overpowered her, and pried the gun away. He pushed her to the floor, wedged his knee into her back, and clamped handcuffs into place. As the metal clicked around Jewel's wrists, Bianca quickly, yet delicately moved Ralph from her lap while she scrambled for her phone.

She was already dialing when Finn said, "Call an ambulance."

Jewel lay on the floor in a deflated heap, and Bianca realized how little she knew about her. She'd said her mom was right here in Riley's Peak. Bianca filtered through the possibilities and landed on one. The planes of her face, her sharp hewn features, the impossibly long legs. How had she missed it? A glance at Finn confirmed that he'd come to the same conclusion. For a moment, Bianca pondered the shared dialect between the three of them, the language of the motherless. Was it even worse for Jewel, having her mother so close yet so far beyond reach?

As Jewel sobbed in earnest, Bianca saw her lapse into her former self with heartbreaking clarity, a broken and battered red-headed child. Bianca knew that child well, was intimately familiar with the longing, the hungry ache for affection. But Jewel's hopes had somehow turned sideways and grown into unmitigated malice as if devoured by the Mog, the one who feasted on red-headed little girls.

⊸ THIRTY-TWO ⊸

HANDS cuffed behind her, Jewel trudged through the snow as Finn guided her to the police station. Heavy flakes fell and settled on her shoulders like a mantle of guilt. She moved, one foot in front of the other, with that strange, mercurial numbness still suffusing her. She'd been like this on Thanksgiving, her face, her voice, soaked in indifference. But after Bianca left, she'd brightened and let down her guard, even teased him with the wishbone. "Try your luck." Mack had snatched it from her, insisting he and Dylan do the honors.

Mack ended up with the short piece.

In many ways, they all had.

Tucker, Ford, Carmichael, and a handful of cops, stood in the lobby as Finn ushered Jewel through the front door. All wore startled expressions, with the exception of Carmichael, whose face contorted to a measured scowl. "What's this all about, Tierny?" he barked. "I thought we had an agreement."

"I was thinking bringing in a murder suspect would trump my *vacation,* but if you want me to go back to lounging in front of *Law & Order* reruns . . ."

A vein throbbed in Carmichael's temple, but he remained silent.

"I want my call," Jewel blurted.

Finn brought her to the phone, removed the cuffs. She stood

ramrod straight, jabbed at the buttons on the base receiver. "You need to come to the police station." Her face tightened as she listened for a few seconds. "Just come."

Finn hoped to God she wasn't calling Dylan. Carmichael's fangs were razor sharp and ready to strike as it was.

Jewel's gauzy silence returned as they fingerprinted and photographed her. She emptied her pockets, yanked a turquoise ring off her finger and silver hoops from her ears. Finn could practically feel Carmichael's hot breath on his neck through the whole process. When he started to put the cuffs back on, Carmichael stopped him.

"Those won't be necessary," he said. "You better have a damn good explanation for this one, Tierny."

Jewel blinked.

Finn wanted to lambast Carmichael right there in front of everyone, but he maintained the picture of cooperation. The chief was about to get the shock of his life, and besides, Finn wanted everything on tape. They were heading to the stairwell when the front door burst open and the scent of gardenia swooped in on a blast of frigid air.

All heads turned as surprise morphed to confusion.

Carmichael stepped forward. "What are you doing here, Charity?"

"Jewel called." Charity had one of those oversized, expensive bags looped over one shoulder. Her reputation preceded her, and Finn half-expected her to pull out a bank roll and start doling out C-notes. The woman obviously had never met a problem she couldn't solve with money.

"We don't need to turn this into a side-show." Carmichael waved his ancillary, gaping staff away. "Tierny, you Mirandized her?"

"I have the right to remain silent. Lucky me," Jewel broke in before Finn could answer. "I have the right to speak to an attorney thanks to Ernesto Arturo Miranda." She forced a mock pout as her mood kept swinging about precariously. "Poor Ernesto. Did you know he grew up in reform school? Discarded like *trash.*" She pierced Charity with a laser glare, which quickly faded to dry-eyed detachment.

The charged tension between the two women confirmed Finn's suspicion, but still left him stunned. In his wildest dreams, he would have never come up with this disastrous double whammy.

"Chief, we better head to the box, including Ms. Beacham."

Charity assaulted them all with one sweeping look that came to rest on Carmichael. "Benjamin?"

Benjamin? Wasn't the devil's first name Lucifer?

"It's no use, Charity," Carmichael said.

Carmichael, Charity, and Jewel. The odd trio, the reason they were all in this one place, crystallized.

"Bring the necklace, Chief," Finn ordered.

A pained sigh escaped Carmichael as he trekked toward his office. His posture, usually as steadfast as a flagpole, now twisted and bent.

Moments later, he angled past them and made his way down the stairs. Finn fell into step, guiding Jewel. Charity anchored the somber parade, her spiky black pumps pinging against the metal treads.

Once inside the box, Jewel threw herself into a chair. Charity sat, careful not to let her spine touch the metal seat back, and crossed her legs high.

Finn clenched his teeth as he remembered Bianca shivering in the same room . . . bombarded by ridiculous accusations.

Carmichael braced his hands on the table for a moment before he reached into his pocket and pulled out the necklace. All eyes shifted to the glittering L.

"My—" Jewel reached for it, but Charity intercepted her arm and pushed it back to her lap.

Another surge of adrenaline now mixed with a swell of anger. As much as Finn didn't want to believe it, all the lies, from all the participants, had grown into a boulder-sized deception. "Chief Carmichael, tell me what's been going on."

Carmichael released a breath that seemed to empty his lungs. "I gave this to Charity thirty years ago." He held out the necklace, tilting his hand toward her as if presenting it for the first time.

Charity drew back, the caricature of a woman scorned, sharp features hooded in disdain.

Jewel's chin snapped upward, like a hunted animal on high alert. But Carmichael barreled on, as if he and Charity were the only ones in the room.

"You were only seventeen." He rubbed his eyes under his glasses. "I couldn't leave Rachel."

Charity sputtered an incredulous laugh.

"I had my career to think of," he went on.

"Your career?" She waggled a finger at the necklace. "Were you thinking about your career when you bought that?"

Carmichael hung his head, but Charity pressed. "Tell them what the L stands for."

After a pained, interminable silence, he said, "Legs. It stands for legs. But if things had been different—"

"They weren't," Charity said, her words striated with bitterness. "You could have given me a heart, or how about *my* initial? But that's not how you thought of me, was it? You were never, ever going to leave her!"

"Charity—"

"Fuck this nonsense. I've held this secret long enough." She motioned to Jewel. "Meet your daughter."

The bomb dropped, and a mushroom cloud filled the room in slow motion.

Jewel's detached expression melted to realization. Eyes locked on Carmichael. She smacked her hands on the table.

Charity flared nostrils in her ex-lover's direction, her jaw clenching, hollowing out her cheeks. Or were they still lovers? "Why else do you think I left halfway through my senior year? Why would I give up being prom queen to sweat it out in California?"

"You said you were leaving to have an abortion," Carmichael shot at Charity. "If I'd known—"

"We'd have lived happily ever after?" she mocked. "One big, happy, screwed-up family."

Jewel bolted from her chair and stabbed an accusing finger at Charity. "I got nothing but lies from you my whole life. Did you think I was an idiot? You wanted me to believe that lesbian you pawned me off on had me by Immaculate Conception? And she had this beautiful best friend—you—who visited a couple times a year?"

Finn stood, ready to restrain Jewel, but he wanted this to play out, to let the twisted information spiral to the surface.

"Can you imagine how it felt to find the canceled check you wrote for my college tuition? I knew then something was off, and it wasn't so hard to get to the truth."

Jewel reached over and yanked the necklace from Carmichael. Dangling it from her fingers, she drew her face close to his. "She told me this was all she had left from you. She told me you were dead. That's how much she thinks of you."

Finn assimilated the train wreck. Anger, disbelief, and pity rolled to a fiery ball in his gut as he watched Carmichael fold forward as if buffeted by a heavy wind while Jewel barreled on, rocking, vibrating as she spoke in a ragged whisper. "She said I could move here, like I needed her permission. But our *relationship* had to be kept quiet, the shock would absolutely kill her mother. More like she'd lose her inheritance. Oh, and I wasn't supposed to ask anything about my father again. It was too painful for *her*!" Jewel hurled the necklace across the room, and it clattered against the cinderblock wall.

Carmichael sat immobile, head buried in his hands. Charity's veneer finally cracked, and she wept with a raw ferocity that seemed more like release than sorrow.

An unimaginable blow. Carmichael had just learned he had a daughter . . . and she was a cold-blooded murderer. But Finn wasn't about to feel sorry for the man; on the contrary, he wanted to throttle him. "You put Bianca in danger. And my father."

Two spots of pink rode high on Carmichael's cheeks. "At first I seriously considered Ms. James. She had opportunity. She bungled the scene. But when you brought me the necklace, I was sure it was Charity." Carmichael studied Charity before he went on. "I couldn't bear the thought of her in prison. I needed time to think."

"*Time* almost cost Bianca her life," Finn ground out. "*Time* cost my father his."

"Mack was a surprise to me. I swear."

Finn took a moment to rein in his rage. "What was my dad's part in this, Jewel?"

She stared at Carmichael, her father, a phantom finally come to life.

"Answer the question, Jewel," Carmichael said, his tone eerily paternal.

"He was easy to manipulate." Her voice monotone, emotionless. "I borrowed one of his guns. He had no idea."

The unregistered .22, the one Mack had mentioned in his note. If the weapon was somehow found, it could never be traced back to her. All fingers would point to Mack Tierny. Except, Jewel couldn't have known it was unregistered. The thought never crossed her mind that Mack would have such a thing. That would make her insurance policy null and void.

"I just wanted Bianca out of the way. Dylan would fall apart, but I'd be here to pick up the pieces. After Lisette, I thought maybe they'd nail her for it. They didn't. I needed a different plan," Jewel continued. "I persuaded Mack he was still in control. I told him that Rose was at the cabin, and if he killed her, and then himself, they could finally be together. He was always mistaking Bianca for Rose. I just had to nudge his obsession by manipulating his meds. It would have been the perfect murder-suicide."

"Jewel, I can't believe you'd go to these lengths over a man," Charity said.

"You're kidding, right? Take a look in the mirror. You've been waiting for thirty years, hoping he'd leave his wife. And you think you have the right to judge me? You lied and graced me with a visit twice a year, pretending to be a family friend." She flicked the end of Charity's silk scarf. "Those visits were more about you though, weren't they, *Mom*? Beverly Hills has the best shopping."

"What could I do? I never told him about you. I was still in high school. What kind of life would we have had? Everyone talking behind our backs." Her confession poured out like a scripted monologue, rehearsed for a tragedy's final scene.

"What kind of life do you think I had? Certainly not the fantasy parallel life I was supposed to be living. I hated being Jewel Jankowski. I should have been Jewel Beacham. But that was never offered. I chose Glasser. I felt closer to William Glasser—a dead man—than my own mother. Pathetic, huh?"

A thick silence droned before Finn stepped in. "The painting." He searched Jewel's face for an explanation and was surprised to hear Charity pipe up.

"She had nothing to do with that." Charity slumped forward. Shit had hit the fan, and she could do nothing to dodge it. "When Benjamin showed me the necklace, I realized what Jewel had done, but I couldn't tell him. I begged him to protect me." The color faded from her face as she continued. "It all started about a year ago when Jewel came to town, ready for a showdown. She confronted me about being her mother, and I told her the truth. She demanded to know who her father was. I told her he was dead. I thought that would be the end of it, but she found the necklace, and took it with her. I thought Lisette had stolen it, so I let her go and filed charges. I should have known better. I'd told Jewel the necklace was a gift from her father. L for love." She paused, shook her head at Carmichael, before continuing. "The next time I saw her, she was wearing it. I thought maybe that would appease her and that would be that."

Jewel swiveled to Charity. Her upper lip disappeared, her lower lip protruded, preparing a scathing rebuttal.

"The painting?" Finn urged.

"Jewel didn't even deny killing Lisette. I tracked her down at Lost and begged her to leave town, and I'd take care of things. Everyone knew Emerson was obsessed with Bianca and the story about the painting. I don't expect you to understand, Officer Tierny, but I carried around a lot of guilt for letting someone else raise my own child. The only child I'll ever have."

She blocked a tear at the corner of her eye with her thumb, and for the first time something approaching a soul emerged from this woman, who seemed nothing more than a hollowed-out mannequin.

Jewel shifted and fidgeted in her seat, her face glazed over in a languid stare. And there it was. That distinctive, empty look that linked father and daughter, the odd familial quirk.

Finn mentally crunched the numbers. A lie, one secret buried for thirty years had shattered three lives, ended two. Jewel had lost so much over the course of her life that she couldn't bear to lose Dylan, couldn't bear to end up with zero. The odd math somehow worked.

Not too long ago, Finn couldn't even fathom the kind of love that sent you in a forbidden direction, down a blind path.

But now, with Bianca in his life, he understood a love so consuming that two plus two doesn't always equal four.

✣ THIRTY-THREE ✣

Six months later.

WHEN Brookefield offered to let her teach a semester abroad in Italy and Spain, Bianca couldn't pass it up. Especially when she'd be teaching a class that included following Escher's footsteps, absorbing the Italian countryside, and ending up at the Alhambra in Granada. Inside the castle walls, she'd show students the intricate designs that had been such a powerful influence on his work. If she could somehow harness his mathematical approach to symmetry and pass it along to her students, now that would be an accomplishment. And wouldn't Maris have a laugh over Bianca's mastery of a subject that once made her brain go numb?

But twelve weeks away from Finn had seemed like forever. She'd secured an earlier return flight and planned to race home, shower the stale airplane smell away, and phone Finn. Jet lag or no, she needed to see him.

A rapid knock startled her as she dumped her suitcase and purse on the floor, and there was Finn in the sidelight, Irish mischief ratcheting up the wattage of his slanted grin.

The sight of him made her heart skitter.

"Welcome home," he said when she opened the door. She blasted into him. His arms encircled her, fingers fisted in her hair, and his lips devoured her. In a kiss that transcended time, they made up for the months apart. The room, the world, the universe tilted to one side, then righted itself again.

They were face to face, nose to nose, and he was peeling back her shirt, obsessing, orbiting over her camisole, about her neck, her shoulders, her face. And Bianca was sucked into a vacuum of desire. She wanted their reunion to be perfect, but there was that persistent eau de airplane. "I need a shower."

Finn breathed deep where her neck curved into her shoulder. "I've never smelled anything better"—he scooped her up and headed for the bathroom—"but if you insist."

She threw her head back and let out a yelp of laughter.

Steam filled the room as their clothes landed on the floor in a heap. Finn slowly lathered Bianca, trailed his fingers over every inch of her skin. The scent of grapefruit and lemongrass took over, and she knew she'd never be able to smell that combination again without experiencing a bit of arousal, without thinking of this moment.

"Damn, I missed you." His voice moved through her, turning her inside out. With newfound energy, her hands slid hungrily across solid shoulders, the cut of his chest and abs. No sculpture in all of Italy or Spain even came close. Pleasure spun into need, teetered on the edge of pain.

"Finn," she said on an inhale and shuddered an exhale. A request or maybe a command. Whether she wanted him to slow down or speed up, she wasn't sure. She wanted him, that's all she knew.

When he'd brought her to the brink, she was repeating his name over and over, pleading. His hands slipped around her, lifting her against him. She let out a squeal as he backed her against the tile. The water had gone from hot to warm, on its way to cold, but she didn't care. They continued, their lips and tongues live forces, and then as if beyond her control, shocks of pleasure were coursing through her. He responded to her cries with animal sounds of his own, and she knew at that moment that there was nothing on earth as consuming as their love.

Afterwards, they rolled together in a single bath sheet and stretched across the bed, still stroking, slower now, moving at a delicious pace. When Bianca caught her breath she asked, "How did you know I was back?"

"Just a little detective overtime," he said. "And a Peruvian informant doesn't hurt."

"I purposely told Maris not to tell you. I wanted to surprise you. Wait, did you say detective?"

Finn raised an eyebrow and favored her with a triumphant smile.

How she'd missed that smile. She squeezed him to her. "You made detective?"

"Let's go celebrate." Finn was strangely invigorated and already slipping into his clothes. Bianca reached for hers, and as she dressed, her eyes stayed on him, trying to parse out what was different, the same way she had that night outside Weaver. Then it dawned. Gone was the cop unsure of his career choice and in his place stood a man who knew who he was and what he wanted.

Who he wanted.

With a light pass, he grazed her arm, and an electric charge doubled her senses. His hands, his eyes, locked her in place with a ferocity that said he'd never let go.

"Detective, huh? I won't be able to keep any secrets from you now."

"No secrets. That goes for both of us." He framed her face in his hands, and his lips worked their magic once again.

A knock at the door. She hesitated, wanting to shut the world out. But a second rap, louder this time, forced her to respond. Not letting her out of his grasp, Finn spooned close as she headed for the door.

She nudged him away. "You really did miss me."

"Busted."

She opened the door to find Helen with Picasso under one arm. "We may have to share him now. He's grown quite fond of lounging in the Fiesta bowl on my coffee table." She looked past Bianca, at Finn, curling her fuchsia-painted lips. "There's nothing like the afterglow of a satisfying coupling."

Bianca laughed. "We were just catching up."

Helen waved her hand. "If that's what you're calling it these days. Want me to keep the cat a bit longer? Give you two some more catching up time?"

Bianca reached for Picasso and held him under her chin, his legs dangling while Finn encircled them both. "That won't be necessary."

Helen favored them with a knowing smirk. "Your mail is on the counter." She backed out the door and made her way down the sidewalk.

As soon as she left, Picasso squirmed away, headed for the kitchen, and started caterwauling.

"He's trying to convince me he hasn't been fed, but I know better."

Sure enough, Picasso was pacing next to his bowl like a junkie looking for his next fix. After she fed him, Bianca said, "I'm parched." She filled two large glasses with water, handed one to Finn. Her near euphoric state dropped a notch when she saw the mountain of mail Helen had left on the counter. It would take weeks to conquer. Thumbing through the pile, her heart stopped as she read the return address on one of the envelopes: Wildlife Conservatory. She tossed it aside. "I'll deal with mail later."

"Wait, isn't that the competition you entered? You should open it."

"I know how these things go: 'We'd like to thank you for your participation in the Wildlife Conservatory Competition, but after careful consideration blah, blah, blah.'"

He reached for the letter and pressed it into her hand.

Exasperated, she ripped it open and started to read. Halfway through the page, she smothered a grin. "I can't believe this."

"What?"

"I won. It says here, I won!"

Finn picked her up and started twirling. Laughter came in waves, tears streamed. When he put her down she said, "I've been trying for so long. This is . . . amazing." She closed her eyes. "I wanted this so much, to accomplish this for my dad, but maybe the timing wasn't right. Or . . ." She nuzzled up to Finn. "Maybe now I understand the special bond between two ducks."

"Quack?" Finn planted a quick kiss on her lips.

She read the letter again: "You Won." A gift for her dad. And her mom. "This is unreal."

"It's great to see you so happy."

Bianca broke away and rooted through her suitcase. "I got this for you."

Finn held the flat stone and ran his fingers along the grooves. "A castle."

"It reminds me of the one hanging in my kitchen. It seems like forever since we stood there that night. I may not have shown it, but you rattled me, big time."

"Tell me about that."

"The bazillion times I've told you already weren't enough?"

"Once more," he said, adding in a mock serious tone, "for the record."

"Of course, Detective Tierny. When you came back from Pittsburgh, you were different somehow. In class, your raw talent was so obvious, but I always thought of you as my student. Dylan's brother. Then we talked about your sketch in my kitchen, and something changed. Besides, when you took your shirt off that night . . . well, you had me at bare chest."

"Is that all I am to you? A boy toy?"

"I do like to play," Bianca said, trailing a finger down his chest.

His breath warmed her neck, and she melted as he stayed there, nibbling, tasting.

She squirmed away and rummaged through a desk drawer for a sheet of paper. "I really want to show you this." After placing it over the stone, she handed him a black Conté crayon.

"What's this?"

"You're going to make a rubbing."

He waggled his eyebrows seductively.

"Here." She positioned the crayon in his fingers, took his hand, and started moving it over the paper, back and forth with a motion as soft and subtle as a caress, until the castle came into view. A majestic, yet reticent building, spires reaching toward the sky.

Bianca kept her hand on Finn's, felt it tremor. The trip-hammer beat of his heart so close to hers reminded her of the first time they touched. She studied him, so entranced by the castle, but a hint of something else.

"Hell, I can't wait. I have to ask—" Finn eased his hand from hers and tugged her fingertips to his lips.

"No more interrogation, Detective."

"Just one more question, and I'll leave you alone."

The jet lag was hitting hard now, and a note of irritation entered her voice. "What is it, Finn?"

He lowered to one knee, reached in his pocket, and extended a small gray box.

Anticipation sped through Bianca.

"Will you marry me?"

She was powerless against the onslaught of tears. Through blurred vision, she viewed Finn's glistening eyes, that one brown star sparkling in blue as if shining just for her, pulling her in like a magnet, promising to never let go. She took the box, lowered herself onto Finn's knee, and flung her arms around his neck. "Yes!"

Finn squeezed her with such exuberance that he lost balance and they toppled to the floor, wrapped in each other's arms. A fit of laughter followed, along with an exchange of intermittent kisses. Bianca raised the box in the air. "I've still got it."

"Open it," he insisted.

As she eased the box open, her breath escaped in a rush.

"I couldn't wait to give it to you."

The diamond was an emerald cut, simple, yet elegant, an eye-catching gem floating in platinum. Bianca lifted it to the light, and it refracted into a thousand prisms, a myriad of colors dancing around the room. He slipped it onto her finger, then laced his hand in hers. She inhaled deep and reveled in the sudden rush of elation and expectation at the sight of Finn's hand entwined with her own, fingers woven together . . . in perfect symmetry.

A NOTE TO READERS

WHEN Nancy Smith and Cat Trizzino met in an online writers' group, their individual styles blended to a shared vision. Though they live in different states, Nancy in Michigan, Cat in Maryland, their passion for well-crafted stories makes the physical distance irrelevant. Tempeste Blake is the result of their combined voices, an author who writes grab-the-tissue-box, heart-in-your-throat romantic suspense and loves to throw her characters into the deep end to see if they sink or swim.

Chasing Symmetry is Tempeste's first novel.

Please stop by www.tempesteblake.com to chat about the story, characters, or whatever. And if you'd like to share your opinion with other readers in a review on Amazon or Goodreads, well, there's a double dose of good karma coming your way.

The second novel in the Riley's Peak series, *Chasing Gravity,* will be available September 2016. A sneak preview follows.

ACKNOWLEDGMENTS

WE wish to thank: Our TNBW friends for a nudge toward this genre. Michele Brant, Karlene MacKay, Linda Sandow, Susan Shafer and Pat Temple for inspiration, suggestions, and support. Chief Scott Silverii for letting us pick his brain about police procedure. Any errors in that area are ours, not his. Lauren Ruiz, who helped give this novel a final spit shine. Our friends who might just find little pieces of themselves throughout. Our families for enduring the non-traditional hours and spur-of-the-moment epiphanies that send us scrambling for a keyboard. And of course, our husbands, Randy Smith and John Trizzino, who are wise enough to get out of the way of this two-car runaway train we like to call writing.

❧ ONE ❧

DYLAN

Saturday morning. April 4th.

THIS was the last place Dylan expected to find himself on a Saturday morning. He should be parked in front of a bowl of Cocoa Pebbles, browsing through the sports section, feet up, Bugs Bunny chomping a carrot in the background. Instead, he was on a bogus mission, here to pacify a woman whose inner soundtrack might well have been Warner Brothers' inspiration for Looney Tunes.

The house reeked of curry, scratchy wool blankets, and forced heat. Sexy lamp on the table. Beads, bangles, and some sort of sparkling carpet spanning one wall. A regular hippie's hideaway. Helen was the definition of eccentric and certainly skirted the rules when it came to calendar ticks. Didn't look a day over sixty, but according to Dylan's calculations, she had to be at least eighty.

He walked the length of the living room and rearranged sheer curtains at a side window, his gaze landing on the bungalow beyond a thick hedge of bushes. A house both familiar and strange. His ex-girlfriend's house. Only now she was married. To his brother. Finn had stepped into his old life: watching movies in the living room, drinking tea on the back patio, sleeping in the same . . . he shook off the image.

"Did you call Finn?" he asked Helen, taking his time to turn back to her. "If your friend's really missing, a police report should be filed." Dylan had no idea why Helen had even contacted him in the first place. On her list of favorite people, he assumed he ranked somewhere between an IRS auditor and Kim Jong-un.

The old woman flashed a panicked glare. "The police won't give this *top priority*. I *need* a private investigator."

Private investigator. The ink on his license was barely dry. Dylan had worked a total of two cases. A woman trying to find out if her husband was cheating. He was. A man trying to figure out if his son was on drugs. He was. The job was almost too easy in Riley's Peak. A town where the Anonymous part of AA was anything but anonymous.

This he knew firsthand.

"Tell me again—" Dylan started.

"Elyse showed up here last night, a day early. Leticia, that's her daughter, is finally coming up to be with us for our annual Soul Cleansing Weekend. I haven't seen Leticia since she came home from Iraq. I couldn't be prouder. Anyway, she's on her way here from Savannah." Helen stopped, stared past him with a near-startled expression. "So much to look forward to. Now Elyse is gone."

"Maybe she just went out for a toothbrush or a gallon of milk or something." *Or maybe some extra soap for the "cleansing."*

Helen's lips pursed in a sour pucker. "We don't do dairy." She shook her head defiantly, tips of dangly, mismatched earrings brushing her shoulders. One feathery. One all beads and stars.

"But her car is gone, her purse," Dylan pointed out. "It seems like she left on her own. Whatever the reason."

Helen grabbed him by the hand, led him to the kitchen, and pointed to a half-empty glass of red wine on the counter.

"What?"

"Elyse would never do that. She'd drink it, or she'd wash out the glass. This simply isn't her style."

So this friend left without cleaning up after herself. Bad manners. Not a crime. Dylan was ready to tell Helen to call him if she had a real problem when her eyes lined with tears.

"The cards don't lie." Helen moved to the coffee table and spread five large tarot cards in a wide arc. "Someone wants to kill her."

He'd never put much stock in cards, tea leaves, or people reading the cream in their coffee. "Do the cards say who?"

Helen swiped at her wet cheeks, straightened. "Another skeptic. I'm not surprised, but Mr. Tierny, there are powers in this world you and I will never understand." She motioned to the table, her fingertips lightly touching a card featuring a scythe-swinging skeleton, and then tiptoeing to one with a star. "If you'll indulge me, this represents you. Hope and inspiration."

Hope and inspiration? He'd never been anybody's hope or inspiration. She needed a new deck of cards. "Where were you when she left?"

"I was out."

"Out?"

"I had plans. With Stanley. At his place this time. We alternate. I came back a little after six this morning. As I said, Elyse was a day early. She didn't want me to cancel my date even though I told her I could see Stanley anytime. She insisted she'd stay here while I went out." Her hands clasped together twisting, twisting. "She insisted."

He'd heard Helen was more "active" than most her age, maybe legendary. "Let me get this straight—"

A rap at the door interrupted him, and Helen ran to open it. A woman in a black leather bomber jacket and those pants that look like a second skin, gripped both sides of the doorjamb in a pose that was anything but casual. Freckles sprinkled her nose and marched in opposite directions toward perfect ears. No make-up. Dark hair scraped into a loose ponytail. A straight line of bangs nearly eclipsed what appeared to be her best feature. Her eyes. She certainly wasn't out to win any beauty pageants.

And yet she could.

Without waiting for an invitation, she stepped into the house, and Helen folded her into a hug.

"Aunt Helen, it's been too long!" The hint of a southern drawl worked its way through an attempt to downplay it.

Helen's niece?

"Leticia, I'm so glad you're here."

"It's Tish." Her tone instructive. You *will* call me Tish.

"I'll try, but Leticia is so ingrained."

"Mom's not here yet?" She unzipped her jacket. "I've been trying to call her since I got off the plane."

Dylan's first impression of Leticia, Tish, whatever, the pretty face with a figure to match, was swallowed by her military precision, the way she barked out questions in a caps-lock voice.

Tish spun toward him as though realizing for the first time he was in the room. "Who are you?"

At least she didn't ask for rank and serial number. Stepping forward he offered his hand, "Dylan Tierny," and let it drop after a few emasculating seconds. Okay, no handshake.

"As I said before, Tish." No last name required. Like Beyoncé or Kesha, he guessed. She stared at him a penetrating moment before she returned to Helen.

Helen's fingers crept to her mouth and dropped to her chin, rubbing, deliberating. "I don't want to worry you, but Elyse is gone. She was here last night, but now . . . something is radically wrong."

"Did you try RJ?" Tish asked.

"I've called cell and home a hundred times. No answer." Helen turned to Dylan. "RJ Corman is Elyse's common-law husband. She didn't want to marry again after Frank passed. Of course, it's been years, but—"

"Are you sure she didn't just run out?" Tish interjected. "Maybe to the store."

"I suspected the same," Dylan said.

Tish zeroed in on him now. "Excuse me, Dylan, is it? I don't mean to be blunt, but this is a family matter."

Most cases were. He didn't need to be told. His morning routine was calling, and maybe it made sense to leave and let Tish here help Helen break out her crystal ball. But the urge to stay and see how this turned out trumped his compulsion to walk away—this might be far more entertaining than the Saturday cartoon line-up.

"Why don't you start at the beginning, Helen," Dylan heard himself say. "Don't leave anything out."

Tish closed the space between the three of them and assumed an authoritative stance: legs shoulder width apart, hands on hips. Almost masculine. Almost. Who was she trying to kid? She oozed female from her haphazard ponytail to her shiny black boots. "Aunt Helen, that's not necessary." That drawl pulling at the edges of her words again. Then to Dylan, "Seriously, I've got this. We don't need you."

He felt the corner of his mouth involuntarily lift in a smirk. "At ease? Carry on?"

"Military cracks?"

"Just speaking your language. But I'm a *private* investigator not some *private* in the marines. I don't take orders from you."

"Army." Her gaze floated over him. "Listen, I'm not sure why Aunt Helen called you—"

"Please." Helen spread her arms in a referee's T, indicating unsportsmanlike conduct.

Dylan conceded. For Helen's sake. Plus, he might enjoy tooling on this one. He knew the type. Bitter. Felt like she had something to prove.

"A picture of your friend would be helpful, Helen." He watched as the muscle in Tish's jaw did a little hop skip. "Do you happen to have a recent one?"

"I do!" Helen clapped her hands together. "Elyse and I went to see the Spirit Gourds of Native America Exhibit in Allentown last fall. It's quite a drive, but we generally do something special on Anne's birthday. Elyse's mother. She was my dearest friend. I drove so Elyse could work. Don't know why she needs to switch from gadget to gadget like that, but it was still—"

"No need for a picture," Tish broke in. "I know what my mother looks like."

"I'd love to see it," Dylan said to Helen.

She moved to the bookcase, selected a framed photo, and handed it over. "Lovely, isn't she?"

A woman with her arm around Helen beside a fog-capped lake. Charcoal-smudged eyes, high cheekbones on mocha skin, her face had a beaming quality, like she'd just won a prize. Her arms, crossed in a prove-it pose, broadcast her confidence. Beautiful.

Like her daughter. "Helen, is anything of yours missing?"

"As I said—" Helen started.

"Now you're calling my mother a thief?" Tish made no attempt to mask her accent this time.

"That's not what I meant."

"Well the question sure sounds like an accusation."

"Yes!" Helen broke in. "Something very important is missing." She waited until she had their full attention. "Elyse."

TISH

TISH struggled to channel her inner warrior, not the worrier bombarding her with "what ifs." There had to be a logical explanation for Elyse being MIA.

Still, why would her mom tell Tish to meet her at Helen's this morning if she hadn't planned to stay? This visit had been on the calendar for weeks. Elyse had even surrendered a generous chunk of frequent flyer miles for a first-class seat for Tish from Savannah to Pittsburgh. Despite a delayed take-off, thanks to some dog-tired executive begging for the laptop he'd left at the gate, she'd made it to Helen's in record time. Now it was almost noon, her stomach was demanding food, a hammer pounded her temples, and she desperately needed to pee. But full bladder or not, Tish refused to leave until she knew what the hell was going on.

This Dylan chump was running his hand along the windowsill while Helen clung to him like lint. Private eye? Did he really think this charade was paycheck-worthy?

Real private investigators don't look like this. She tried not to notice how his goatee stippled the contours of his chin like a race track, and how his eyes shifted through a kaleidoscope of Caribbean greens and blues. She wouldn't be surprised if he'd ordered a license on the internet, bought a gun at Kmart, and advertised his services on Craigslist. Why had Helen called him, anyway? Was her sixth sense working overtime again?

As if eavesdropping on her thoughts, Dylan stopped what he was doing and shoved his hand in his jeans pocket. Jeans that gloved his body like he was a walking advertisement for Levi's.

Stop! The last thing she needed was to think about getting sweaty with this small-town, detective wannabe. Not that she wouldn't benefit from a little hot and heavy. It had been a while. Fraternizing with guys she worked with for the last eight years had been off limits. Anyone else she met on the outside turned tail and ran the minute they heard the word army. As if wearing camo and toting a gun cancelled out any chance of intimacy.

"I don't believe anything's wrong but—" Dylan parked himself uncomfortably close, so close his breath warmed her cheek.

A knock at the door, simultaneous with his words.

"Elyse." Helen swung the door wide. A man wiped his feet on the mat, stepped inside. "Saw your car," he said to Dylan. "Everything okay?"

"Helen thinks her friend is missing."

"I don't think, I know." Helen moved to the newcomer and admired him like a prized thoroughbred. This is Detective Finn Tierny. My neighbor."

He reached for Tish's hand, pumped it twice.

Tierny. Did all the good-looking men in town have the same last name?

"I didn't really want the cops," Helen said. "No offense of course." A flash of something flickered on her face, the drift of her warming thoughts apparent. "However, since you're here, maybe you can assist."

Tish nodded to Finn. "Nice to meet you, but you really don't need to get involved. My mom probably got an idea in the middle of the night and rushed home. It's hard for her to take a weekend off. I'll drive to Crestwood and find her up to her elbows in paperwork."

"No. I'm certain she didn't leave on her own," Helen said. "Certain as tomorrow's sunrise."

In Tish's mind, she was already on her way to Crestwood, but Helen's brow, knitted in her patented expression of concern, made her whip a U-turn. Eccentric or not, Helen was the spunky old lady version of Gorilla Glue, holding delicate family ties together, forcing connections where they might otherwise fall apart. If she felt reassured by the local cop, it was worth a few minutes delay.

But Helen's recounting of stories, the way she took the circuitous route describing every detail, was tantamount to verbal water torture. Drip . . . Drip . . . Drip.

"Helen, do you mind if I fill Detective Tierny in?"

"Please do. And don't leave anything out."

The slant of Dylan's eyebrow, which she was certain he intended to be inquisitive, was downright sexy. "Ms. . . . What's your last name?"

"Duchene."

"Ms. Duchene here is career military, so I'm sure her retelling will be spit-shined."

"If you think you're better equipped to explain," she said, "by all means . . ."

Utter frustration registered on Helen's face. "You two have been sniping at each other like horizontal mambo partners since you met."

Tish felt the sting of the verbal slap.

"I believe my mother got here last night at approximately 1900. Helen left soon after." She glanced at her for confirmation, and Helen nodded.

"You left?" Finn asked.

"Well, yes, Elyse didn't want me to change my plans just because she came early. There's still a good portion of juice left in this old lemon, you know." Her smile faded as her lips began to quiver. "I'd planned a nice brunch for us. For this morning, when Leticia, Tish, arrived. I intended to try a new recipe, quinoa salad with beets and kumquats." She scratched her forehead. "At least I'm fairly certain we discussed that."

Tish imagined the conversation. Elyse multi-tasking, phone to ear, jotting notes. Helen's finger twitching a zig-zag path over the recipe. It was like a grown-up version of the telephone game where the final message mangled the initial intent.

"When Helen arrived home just after 0600," Tish continued, "my mother was gone. There's no way to pinpoint what time she left."

"Wouldn't she have left a note?" Dylan asked. "Or called?"

Tish pictured her mother's face scrunched in an earnest grimace, eyes blinking slowly as she calculated the next wonder drug. Another image blipped, a dark highway, a car crashed into a viaduct. She elbowed the thought away.

"Where does Elyse work?" Finn asked.

"At Saycor with her boyfriend, RJ. They met there," Helen chimed in. "Oh, it took some time for them to get together, but it was in the cards all along."

"Saycor Pharmaceutical?" Dylan asked. "In Crestwood?"

"I was just reading how the CEO bought a villa in Tuscany," Finn said. "Not a bad gig."

Give the short answer. A tactic learned from her father to redirect a conversation. "The company does well."

"And your mom?" Dylan asked.

Tish felt her jaw tighten. "I'm not sure what you're asking."

"Just curious if she does well too."

"How is her income relevant?"

Helen pressed her fingertips to her cheeks. "Someone must be after her money."

"I know you're worried, Helen, but there's no evidence of forced entry," Dylan said. "No sign that anyone else was even here."

For the first time, Tish agreed with Dylan. They were flying blind, investigating a non-existent crime.

Finn wrapped an arm around Helen. "I'm sure everything's okay, but I can keep an eye out for her. What does she drive?"

"I'm not really a car person," Helen said. "But it's one of those fancy ones, named after a cat . . . Cheetah?"

Tish would have laughed if it weren't for the mind-numbing aggravation. "Jaguar. Which I'm sure is back at her house or in Saycor's parking garage." She extracted keys from her purse. "Helen, I'll call you as soon as I can." She jutted her chin to each of the men in turn. "It was nice meeting ya'll."

Dylan's mouth pulled to the side.

This yahoo could make fun of her stretched vowels like it was his job, but it was time to go.

"I feel it"—Helen grabbed Tish's elbow—"in my bones.

Someone is after Elyse."

Gripping Helen's hand, knowing nothing she did or said would be enough to convince her, Tish said, "Please don't worry."

Helen transferred her clutch to Dylan's arm. "Go with her. Don't let her out of your sight."

He opened his mouth to speak, but Tish lobbed him a look. *Humor her.*

They made for the door like two kids responding to the fire alarm, two unruly kids whose shoulders collided when they didn't exit single file.

"After you." Dylan splayed his hand in a magnanimous gesture.

This was no time to be noble. Tish charged out onto the porch.

"Wait!" Helen scurried toward the kitchen and yelled over her shoulder. "This will only take a minute."

Tish did as Helen asked even though her gut told her she didn't have a minute to spare. And not one split second to waste on this P.I. dude. Once they were on their way, she'd lose him like a bad habit.

Speaking of which: her hand traveled to her pocket, and she fingered her daily allotment. How she looked forward to the smooth effect of that lone cigarette, the nicotine sailing through her system, a brief recess. It was stupid. She'd quit before she enlisted.

But the army had a way of shining a floodlight on all your inadequacies and eventually brought her to her knees, then prostrate before her failure to do the most important thing.

She slid her finger along the last smoke. She needed to buy more. Needed the assurance of that one single slice of peace each day. Only a couple minutes of calm, but she'd take it.

Made in the USA
Middletown, DE
10 June 2018